KERRY POSTLE left King's Coll[...]
in her MA in French Literature. [...]
papers and magazines, and has wo[...]
German, Spanish, and English. Kerry's first novel, *The Artist's Muse*, about the relationship between Wally Neuzil and the artist Egon Schiele, came out in 2017.

She lives in Bristol with her husband. They have three grown-up sons.

Kerry is currently working on her third novel about the artist Raphael.

A Forbidden Love is her second novel.

Follow her on twitter @kerry_postle

A Forbidden Love

KERRY POSTLE

ONE PLACE. MANY STORIES

HQ
An imprint of HarperCollins*Publishers* Ltd
1 London Bridge Street
London SE1 9GF

This edition 2019

First published in Great Britain by
HQ, an imprint of HarperCollins*Publishers* Ltd 2019

ISBN: PB: 978-0-00-833079-8
EB: 978-0-00-831027-1

MIX
Paper from
responsible sources
FSC **FSC® C007454**

Typeset by Palimpsest Book Production Ltd, Falkirk, Stirlingshire
Printed and bound in Great Britain by
CPI Group (UK) Ltd, Melksham, SN12 6TR

To Paloma
and all the women who lost their lives during the
Spanish Civil War

'The poem, the song, the picture, is only water drawn from
    the well of the people,
and it should be given back to them in a cup of beauty so
    that they may drink –
and in drinking understand themselves.'

Lorca

PROLOGUE

March 1940, Malaga

Luis de los Rios ran out of the university building onto the Avenida de Cervantes, black jacket in one hand, tan leather folder in the other. The porter called after him, 'Running late today, Señor?' But the unlikely academic had already been swallowed up by the bushes on the other side of the road.

He was on the Paseo del Parque, a long pathway shaded by trees that ran between the harbour and Malaga's old town. Every Friday morning between ten and eleven Luis walked up and down it. Always on the same day, always at the same hour. He never taught then. He'd insisted it be written into his contract. No one knew why. And today he was running late.

At 9.50 a.m. a student had turned up at his door. Luis' instinct had been to brush him aside but the better part of him had won out. He'd sat back, listened to the boy. Or tried to. He'd looked at his watch – 9.52 – and rolled his eyes. Looked at his watch again: 9.57. He thrummed his fingers loudly on the desk. Why was he not able to focus on anything the boy was saying? By seven minutes past ten Luis had had enough. The wooden chair he'd been sitting on went crashing to the floor. 'I must go,' he'd said, running to the door, hurtling along the corridor and flying out of the building. And wishing he'd listened to his instinct in the first place.

It was ten minutes past ten by the time Luis set foot on the path in the park. Lined by tall plane and palm trees, it felt like a cool, dark, cavernous cathedral and it calmed him instantly. He blinked. His eyes adjusted to make out strips of light and shade on the path beneath his feet. He looked upwards. The sun shot through the green ceiling above. He blinked again. His eyes focused further. He saw people as they walked back and forth under the high, fringed canopies, an optical illusion of unbroken movements bathed in radiance.

Was she here?

He was later than usual – 'but not too late,' he said to himself.

He proceeded to walk along the path. Purpose pumped through his veins. His skin tingled, senses crackled, as parakeets flew through the air, their plumage igniting into a vivid green. Their fiery wings blazed a trail into his soul, lifting him on his way.

He went past the old men, acknowledging them as he passed, just as he did every week; nodded to the widows, and the young women who shared their grief. They were here, survivors all, leading a semblance of a normal life, just as he was, refusing to let the past destroy them. They milled around, sat on benches, talked about the weather. Luis winced, moved by the dignity of the everyday in the face of a memory of the horror they all shared: civil war. A nation could not recover from it easily.

Yet if innocence had gone forever, hope had not. That's why he was here, making his way to a clandestine meeting, the details of which he'd written in a note and handed to a girl over four years ago.

He didn't even know if she'd read it.

Meeting place: *the Antonio Muñoz Degrain monument, Parque de Malaga*

Time: *10–11 a.m.*

2

Day: *Friday*

I'll wait for you.

Luis sat on a bench and looked at his watch: 10.45. He thought back to the last time he'd seen her. He'd pushed her away. He'd had to. It was time for her to go. But he had given her the letter. She had it. He hoped she'd read it.

He leant back against a bench and cast another glance down at his watch. 10.55. Time to start making his way back to the university. He'd always been a good timekeeper. A smile broke out across his face as he remembered that the girl he loved had not. He ran his fingers through his hair, resigned to the fact he'd not found her. This time.

He went to pick up his jacket and folder when the screech of a parakeet overhead distracted him. Threat or warning, either way it was too late. The brilliantly coloured bird had already left its dull coloured deposit on the shoulder of his crisp, white shirt.

'Filthy beast!'

An old gypsy woman dressed in tattered clothes, a black shawl wrapped around her wiry grey hair, smiled at him through cataract-misted eyes. 'Supposed to be lucky,' she laughed at him. In the haze of her fading sight Luis had something of the angel about him. To Luis, she looked like a fat, old bird, too large and heavy for the tree above, sat as she was on a nest made of cloth, her skirts billowing up all around. He watched as she plunged her hand in amongst the many layers that surrounded her. She pulled out a dull-coloured patch with frayed edges and waved it at him.

For want of anything better to clean himself up with, Luis accepted her tattered offering. He rubbed away at his shirt as quickly as he could, his head nodding in the gypsy woman's direction, grateful that all that was left of the parakeet's slimy gift was a suspicious, damp stain on his left shoulder. She flashed her crucifix at him in response with a smile that made her eyes disap-

3

pear. But now he really had to go. He walked swiftly back along the dry, dusty path, shouting back his thanks.

He'd very nearly packed all the emotions he'd allowed to spill out over this last hour back into the neat compartments he'd allotted them in his mind when he lurched backwards, pulled back by a familiar voice. 'Don't run off now, Paloma!' A little girl, swift as a comet, hurtled past him, her flaming hair dragging his eyes along with her. When the speeding ball of fire screeched to a halt back along the path, not far from the Antonio Muñoz Degrain monument, Luis' heart missed a beat.

The child clung on to a young woman with long, dark hair.

It was her. It was Maria.

CHAPTER 1

'What are you going to do when you grow up?' It was a clear spring day in 1936 and Maria lay back under the gnarled, black branches of the olive tree and looked up at the Andalucian sky above: vivid blue, and as cloudless as the future she saw for herself. She and her friend Paloma often sought shade and solace in this grove, under this tree, far away from the dust and heat of the village. And here they would dream.

'When I grow up, I'm going to...' Paloma began. She flicked out her fingers in frustration, brushing Maria's own. 'Oh, I don't know!' she cried in answer to the older girl's question – but she did. She would grow up to do the same as her mother, and her mother's mother before her. A husband would be found for her, she would have children, and both she and her husband would work up on the landowner's estate. That was the way it was; that was the way it had always been. Paloma's fate was as set as if written in the stars. It was only Maria who saw a future full of possibilities for her friend as she gazed into the bright, limitless sky above. And Paloma loved her for it.

Instinctively she turned on her side to wrap her limbs around Maria's. Legs, arms, fingers interlaced, a tangle as fixed and as complex as the roots of the olive tree beneath.

The girls' skins squelched, mollusc-like, as Maria pulled herself away. Pushing herself up to sitting, she propped her back up against the solid trunk of the tree.

She looked at Paloma, cheek squashed against forearm. The skin, usually so plump and firm, gathered in folds and pushed her left eye closed. It struck Maria that in that moment her friend took after her mother Cecilia, whose skin cascaded in folds all over her body; ill-fitting, stretched and worn out, through overuse no doubt. Maria's father would often sing the woman's praises – how she fed her children well, repaired their clothes, kept a spotless home, worked hard – but the fact remained that Paloma's mother was irritable, illiterate and limited. There. Maria had thought it again. Guilt ran a feather over her skin, causing her to shiver. Perhaps she'd judged Paloma's mother too harshly – her father was always telling her so – but the fact remained: if she didn't show Paloma there was another way to live, a future other than the one she saw mapped out for herself, then her dear, sweet-natured friend would slowly but surely turn into a beast of burden, just like poor old Cecilia.

And Maria wouldn't be able to live with herself if she allowed that to happen.

'Sit up,' she snapped. 'So, what do you want to do when you grow up?' She would have a response.

Paloma rubbed her eyes and sighed.

'If you don't answer I'll have to ask somebody else.' Maria's voice was sharp and vaguely menacing. Her eyes scanned the olive grove for possible candidates. They alighted upon a herd of goats resting under a nearby tree. She recognised her own stupidity.

Thankfully Paloma did not.

'No, it's fine. I'll play,' the gentle soul said, her tone one of quiet resignation. Two years younger than Maria, she always felt grateful the older girl had chosen her and not her sister Lola to confide in. Lola was sixteen, the same age as Maria. It would have

6

made sense for the two older girls to be close. But they weren't. Never had been. They were fond enough of each other, and the fact that they were opposites in every single way was not, in itself, insurmountable. But that Paloma was so easy to be with, so innocent and good-natured, made her a perfect companion. Lola's little sister had become the little sister that Maria had always wanted. She could love and protect her, and teach her about all the great and good things in life. Lola, on the other hand, came fully formed with a tongue as sharp as a knife.

Paloma brought her chin to nestle in the curve between her knees, her black hair still curled up flat with perspiration around her face. A stray lock misbehaved and draped itself like a dark rope against the deep pink of a cheek that was soft and plump once more. If Cecilia had ever looked like this Maria could not imagine it. She leant over towards her friend and pushed the dark unruly coil back with tenderness and waited for an answer.

'Well,' Paloma began, unsure how to proceed. To get married was the pinnacle of her life, and the thought of a wedding with an abundance of flowers, food, finery, and all the froth that went with it, had started to fill many a quiet moment. But to admit this, Paloma knew, would displease her friend. She waited for guidance.

'Will you have children?' Maria asked.

'Y-yes,' Paloma answered. 'Once I'm married.'

'Why?' Maria asked.

'Why? Why what?'

'Why would you get married before having children?'

Paloma's dark brown eyes widened; Maria's creased with satisfaction. 'In fact,' Maria ventured, emboldened by the surprise in Paloma's eyes, 'why would you get married... *at all*?' Her young friend's already wide eyes turned into the fullest of moons.

The evening before, Señor Suarez, the village teacher who used to work in Madrid and still had family and friends in the capital, had come to eat with Maria and her father, Doctor Alvaro.

The winds of change were blowing and whistling their sinewy path around Spain and though they'd barely touched Fuentes de Andalucía in any significant way, the more travelled citizens, of which Señor Suarez was one, often brought back stories from the outside world whenever they returned to the sleepy little village. Suarez was teacher, philosopher, and general do-er of good deeds (mostly political), and a frequent dinner guest at Maria's home where the precarious state of the government and how to best help workers in the area were his topics of choice. But last night, as he had smiled over at Maria and realised for the first time that she was a young woman, his conversation had taken a new turn.

'You know, in Madrid, and I hear it's the same in Malaga, things are so very different for women now. They have more freedom. More choice.' He'd looked over at Doctor Alvaro who'd nodded for him to continue. Suarez had already told them that night about a growing vegetarian movement in the capital. Nothing his friend had to say, Alvaro thought to himself as he chewed on a particularly gristly bit of sausage, could be more challenging for both he and his daughter to swallow than that.

But then again.

'A woman no longer has to get married if she wants to live with a man.'

The doctor had choked on the wine he'd just poured into his mouth. He'd expected talk of work opportunities, education... not co-habitation. But he was open-minded, fair, forward-thinking; he knew his good friend to be so too. 'Please, carry on,' he'd spluttered, waving his hands around as he struggled to keep his eyebrows from arching.

'And it's true that some women no longer want to have children.'

This time it had been Maria who'd choked, though her father's eyebrows, try as he might to stop them, now leapt up to meet his fast receding hairline. This was a strange conversation indeed. Fascinating and embarrassing for Maria in equal measure. The

8

teacher's words had slapped her full in the face like a wave, waking her from her romantic dreams; as they receded, she'd taken in their meaning.

'To have or not to have children, women see it as their right, their right to choose. Times are changing.' And with that Señor Suarez had coughed most dramatically, prompting the doctor to slap him hastily and heartily on the back while pointing his daughter towards the door with his eyes.

Maria hovered around the old oak table, topping up wine glasses and clearing away dishes as if she hadn't noticed.

'How's the reading programme going up at El Cortijo del Bosque?' Doctor Alvaro asked his friend.

El Cortijo del Bosque was the name of the local estate owned by Don Felipe, principal employer in the area. Work on his estate was agricultural. His workers were paid a pittance. Don Felipe himself was fabulously wealthy. And that was how it had been for centuries.

But things weren't only changing in Madrid.

In February 1936 the left-wing coalition, known as *el Frente Popular*, had won the general election in Spain. This had allowed the good doctor and teacher to push through much needed reforms in Fuentes de Andalucía in general, and up at El Cortijo del Bosque in particular. In the early months of the year both had worked tirelessly to secure better pay and conditions for the estate's workers, Suarez at the negotiating table, Alvaro behind the scenes. Guido, the estate manager, represented his employer's interests, at times most savagely. But, snarl as he might, there was little he could do against what was legal; he had the will, but not the right, to resist.

Don Felipe, the landowner, was furious of course: with Guido and with the useless lumps of flesh who worked his land and whom he thought less of than his bulls and horses. As for Suarez and Alvaro, if Guido had ever mentioned them to him he certainly didn't care enough about them to waste his energy remembering

9

their names; they were men of no consequence. No, he was too busy shouting abuse at Manuel Azaña, the new prime minister, along with the motley collection of left-wing degenerates that made up the government, to take any notice of them. Don Felipe despaired. Even his beloved Falangist party, a party that believed in the true greatness of Spain, in the monarchy, the Catholic Church and centuries of tradition, was coming under attack.

Don Felipe's Spain, the Spain he knew and loved, was disappearing.

He had no choice but to whisk his family off to their second home in Biarritz.

And thus Suarez had no choice but to seize the moment and take education to the workers so that at the next round of negotiations they would be able to help themselves. That was what he was doing presently up at El Cortijo del Bosque. And Guido could do nothing to prevent it, no matter what orders his master barked at him from the south of France. But progress was slow.

'The truth is we need more teachers,' Suarez had confessed.

'The truth is very few people in the village can read,' Alvaro had replied. The sound of a creaking door disturbed him. His eyes had shot round like a searchlight at the top of a watch tower. There, standing in the kitchen doorway, a copy of *Don Quixote* clutched to her body, was his daughter.

'*You* can do it,' he'd said, knowing she'd been listening to them and confident that she would relish the chance. She'd nodded, pulling back her chair to re-join them. But before her skirt could touch the rush seat her father's voice had scooped her back up and pushed her out of the room and towards the staircase. 'Now bed, my girl!'

'But if I'm to help out surely I need to...'

'Bed!'

That night Maria hadn't minded that her attempts to stay up late had failed. She had gone to bed happy and excited. Happy that she would be helping Señor Suarez with the reading programme, excited at what he'd told her about women in Madrid. All night ideas of choice and freedom had stampeded around in her head looking for somewhere to live.

By morning they'd found a home. The teacher's words were now her own.

And so that was how Maria was here, under her favourite olive tree, about to take a familiar game in a new direction. Starting to feel sticky, she shook her hair, generating at most a slight, warm breeze. She cast a 'brace yourself' look in Paloma's direction: her friend was about to become the testing ground for her very own liberal education project.

She repeated, as word-perfectly as she could, what Señor Suarez had said about women, children and marriage the night before. She lingered on the phrase 'right to choose'.

Paloma said nothing. Maria continued.

'Señor Suarez—' Maria slipped in his name because Paloma liked him '—said that women in Madrid have more…' The older girl paused before opening her arms out wide and shouting out 'freedom.' She could not have drawn any more attention to the word if she'd underlined it and decorated it with a bright red ribbon.

Paloma fell back against the tree.

'Well, you could get married, if you want to,' Maria backtracked. 'But you don't have to. That's what I'm saying. Things are changing. Gone are the days when parents start planning a wedding the moment a boy looks at a girl.' Paloma breathed heavily out through her nose as if by the expulsion of air alone she could find room in her head for this shocking revelation. That she dropped her head to one side suggested that she'd failed. It was far too heavy a load for her fourteen-year-old brain to manage. She looked questioningly at Maria and rubbed the back of her head as if it were a magic lamp. A light flickered in her eyes.

11

'It's true,' Maria insisted. 'According to Señor Suarez, women are having babies and they aren't even married. In Madrid. Even Malaga!' Paloma screwed up her nose then let out a snort. Madrid and Malaga were both as alien to her as the moon and every bit as inaccessible. 'And some women in the city don't even want to have children. At all. Not ever,' Maria continued. 'That's what Señor Suarez says. They'd much rather have *a career*.'

The older girl looked up at the sky and hid herself there a while, a smile of satisfaction on her lips. She'd delivered what she told herself was her *coup de grâce* (a phrase she'd learnt quite recently after having found it in some book or other, and she congratulated herself on having found an opportunity to use it, even if it was inside her own head). She'd chased away all thoughts of husbands and playing children from this game of theirs.

Paloma scrunched up her eyes to scrutinise her friend more closely. Was she teasing? Admittedly, Paloma had trouble imagining a husband for herself. As she went over the list of local prospective suitors she could not deny that they were unappealing. She shuddered as she had them parade across the stage of her mind one by one. Maria liked to re-christen them, as pirates, or book characters, to make them more exciting for her friend, but even that didn't seem to be working for Paloma at this moment in time. Perhaps, if she were lucky, she might find a husband who came from another village. Or a nearby town. She pulled herself together. She would have a husband, one day, of that she was certain. But there was no point making herself distressed by going through all candidates just yet. As for children, of course, she sighed with relief, on safer and more comforting ground, she most certainly would have them.

Maria must want them too, surely, Paloma thought to herself. *'That girl has no sense of family!'* *'She's always been such a selfish girl!'* Her mother's unfair criticisms of her friend ricocheted around the confines of Paloma's own mind. Maria was an only child. She had no mother. Cecilia always used one or other fact as an accusation whenever Maria did anything she didn't agree with. Although she did not like the damning place that her mother's reasoning led her to, Paloma found her own thoughts heading in the same direction today. She knew better than to articulate them. Instead, she would enter into the spirit of the discussion.

'If you don't want to get married, or have children, then what does it mean to be a girl?' Paloma wriggled with what she told herself was justifiable indignation as she asked Maria the question. Maria gnawed on her thumbnail. She hadn't expected rebellion. 'What indeed!' she said, dodging the bullet. She sat back and looked up at the infinite blue of the sky yet again. 'All I know,' she replied at last, 'is that I don't want to tie myself to any man.' She stood up and brushed the earth from her clothes. And with that she drew the game to a close.

But Paloma hadn't finished.

'I don't believe you!' she retorted, still indignant. 'You're in love with Ricar.'

'Oh, don't be so silly!' said Maria. 'And if you're talking about Richard, it has a *ch* and a *d* in it. And it would help if you could learn how to pronounce his name. Properly. In English.' And with that she walked away and headed back to the village.

'What's love got to do with it anyway?' she called back over her shoulder.

CHAPTER 2

The villagers had never seen such a strange looking boy as Richard Johnson. They called him *el inglés* (among an interesting array of other, more colourful names – all of them unflattering). He was impossible to miss. His colouring was what had distinguished him most from everyone else when he'd first arrived; so white that small children would run to their parents, cries of *fantasma* trailing behind them. And now, six months on, the reaction he elicited was scarcely any better. Oh, what they called him was different. But their alarm was just the same. Once other-worldly white, now vibrant, throbbing pink; the ghost had been well and truly turned into the *gamba*, with dark orange freckles seared on burnt crustacean skin, cooking away as he was under the hot flames of the Spanish sun. Ghost or prawn, either way the English boy stood out.

But why had he come to their small village to live under a sun that seemed not to like him in the first place?

What he and his parents told people was that he was in Spain to immerse himself in the language and culture. The eighteen-year-old Richard Johnson had a place to study Modern Languages at Exeter College, Oxford, starting in October 1936, and it was true that he needed to prepare himself for the rigours of academic life, as well as to hear and speak the words he'd spent so many hours thus far only reading and writing in a cold classroom.

But the real reason, the reason that eclipsed all others in his mother Margaret's mind, was her son's health. That he was of a delicate constitution was plain to see and his doctor had thought it might do him some good to experience warmer climes. The poor boy suffered from two afflictions. The first was psoriasis for which there was no cure. Other than the sun. At home, where it was chilly, damp and grey, Richard struggled with the condition. It irritated him and distressed his mother. A constant reminder of the genetic legacy she had bequeathed to her only son, handed on down from her father and his father before him. A long illustrious line. The affliction had skipped a generation with her; a blessing which she would have gladly foregone if it had meant not affecting her precious child. Instead, she endured her son's absence, consoled by the knowledge that the sun would help him.

That his skin wasn't robust enough to withstand the raw rays of the Andalucian sun for long was a detail that no one had factored in.

As for the second 'affliction', it was in some ways more and in some ways less grave than the first. It was also another reason for Margaret to want her son as far away from England, and away from his father and his paternal grandparents, as possible. You see, Richard Johnson had been staring into space. And he'd been staring into space for years while sitting at the back of the classroom of his very expensive, fee-paying school where teachers were employed on the basis of personal academic achievement rather than any particular ability to teach, let alone care about the young faceless charges before them. Not one of them had noticed the red-headed boy with the vacant expression at the back of the class.

It was his grandfather who'd spotted it. One Christmas he'd asked Richard to pass the gravy. He loved gravy. Liked to drench Margaret's over-boiled sprouts in the stuff. When the damned fool of a boy didn't answer on the third time of asking, his grandfather knew: the boy was having a mild epileptic episode. 'Just like my old brother Vernon,' he'd said. He was promptly taken to see the family doctor who confirmed it. Poor Richard. Another genetic legacy, this time bequeathed (his mother was relieved to say) from his father's line.

His grandfather demanded that the boy be operated upon. From that day forward Margaret's mind was made up. Her son had to go to Spain. As far as she could see, if Richard's condition displayed itself as a little staring into the sunset every now and again, she was convinced that it could do him no harm. And it was infinitely better than submitting him to unnecessary surgery or endless discussions about its possibility.

And so, even with political changes afoot in Spain – news of it was beginning to make it into the nether regions of the press – both Margaret and Peter Johnson were convinced their son would be better off there until the family had stopped picking over the bones of Richard's epilepsy. And considering they hadn't noticed it for eighteen years there was a high probability that once out of sight, the vulture known as Family Concern would alight on the carcass of another victim soon enough.

And that was how, with a letter here and a telegram there, Richard Johnson had ended up in the care of a doctor in a village in Spain in the spring of 1936 where he would stay until the start of his first term at Oxford. And where he would become the most unlikely of heart throbs.

Maria hadn't realised she was restless before the strange vision that was Richard Johnson came to Fuentes.

She did now.

She longed for his visits to her home, reliving them as she went off to sleep. She knew that even Paloma laughed at the look of him when she was at home with her sister; but he, in all his otherness, showed Maria that a big, beautiful world existed out there. And this sign of otherness that leaked out of him she took for his soul, his appearance, like blotting paper, changed by it forever.

That her father should be the person who brought this exotic being to their quiet village did not surprise her. She only had memories of living in Fuentes. Her father had always been its doctor, stitching wounds, administering medicines, making up poultices, visiting the old, the sick and the injured, as well as disappearing on visits that he chose not to explain to her. It was his life. But every few months he would receive a letter that connected him to a time before, to a life spent far away. Then he would hide himself away in his study and look through the album he kept in a drawer in his desk. The people who inhabited the photographs would leave the page and he would let them dance round and round in his mind. And for a few moments he would lose himself.

Maria would too.

Whenever her father was out doing his rounds she would enter his study. Within seconds she would be stroking the flat images of the woman pictured next to him in the album, placing a finger on the delicate young woman's papery cheek and dreaming of the past. When both her parents were alive.

She would then shuffle through the post, looking at the postmarks on the envelopes of any letters her father had received; 'Madrid', 'Seville', 'Malaga', 'Granada', 'Cordoba'. Each place name had the power to erect exciting new worlds in her mind. She had no need to see what was written inside to be transported there. Not that she had any qualms about reading her father's letters. It was just that in the main their contents were always the same – disease and politics – and Maria was fed up with reading that people thought her father had the cure for both.

Shortly after Christmas 1935 the letters became more frequent, the postmarks more varied and far flung. An increasing number arrived from Madrid, followed by more still from Cadiz, and Barcelona. The words inside, when she chose to read them, were now feverish, about strikes and demonstrations. Yet they also brought with them a wild optimism for change that galloped off the sheets and into Maria's heart on the occasions she picked them up.

But for all their unbridled promise, nothing and no one had yet come to wake up their sleepy little village.

Then, one day in early January 1936, Maria noticed an English postmark. As usual the sight of it was sufficient to fire her imagination. Here was another bridge, this time to England. She closed her eyes and conjured up a country that was cold, green, wet, where people drank tea. Those bits did sound horrid to her. But it was also home to Shakespeare, and George Eliot, and well-loved by Voltaire for its religious tolerance and freedom of speech (she had listened well to Señor Suarez and her father over the years, though, strangely, never been tempted to follow up on their reading recommendations). When her imagination had no further details to draw on she read the letter. She wept with joy at its contents. Someone, an English someone called Richard Johnson, aged eighteen, from England, would soon be walking across that bridge to stay in Fuentes de Andalucía until October. Maria could not wait for his arrival.

She brushed up her English vocabulary, practised her English grammar, fell asleep reading Charles Dickens in translation one painful sentence at a time. Richard Johnson. She didn't care what he might look like. He would be in her life very soon, providing a window on the big, wide, wonderful world.

CHAPTER 3

The villagers of Fuentes thought the Alvaros an unusual family, and Fuentes was an unusual place for them to settle. People usually dreamt of moving to Madrid, and so when a finely dressed Madrileño holding a plump, well-fed baby in one arm held out his hand one Monday morning way back in 1921 to help a frail-looking woman out of a carriage, most of them couldn't believe their eyes. Sturdy trunks followed, full of books, bottles and medical instruments. By the end of the second day the finely dressed man had tended three babies with a fever, lanced twenty-seven boils, treated the infected wounds of seven farm labourers, and diagnosed nine cases of gout.

El doctor had arrived.

Within weeks he had become indispensable, caring for the infirm and curing the sick, usually with his robust-looking baby in tow.

'Poor doctor! Poor child! What sort of a wife must that woman be to let her husband do so much? She never leaves the house!' the women of Fuentes enjoyed muttering to each other, their eyes rolling in sisterly condemnation.

The answer came in the winter of 1923 when poor Señora

Alvaro left her home for good, in a coffin – thus putting an end to the muttering.

The response was rapid. All rallied round, some bringing him food, others looking after the poor motherless girl. It wasn't their fault the woman had died. They weren't doctors (they bit their tongues from running on to the inevitable conclusion their cruel thoughts had already jumped to). But they were mothers. And they would treat this Maria as one of their own. That she looked like she had sprung from the Andalucian soil made her easier to accept. She was strong and dark and not at all like the frail, colourless woman who had given birth to her (if, one or two of the more spiteful among them whispered, she really had).

And although many of the mothers in the village talked openly amongst themselves over the years that the doctor should show that daughter of his a firm hand, they too indulged the girl. Her growing spirit and fearlessness were a joy to behold. Most of the time.

As for the men, they acknowledged the doctor's loss at the funeral. They never gave it much thought after that. Pablo Alvaro was their doctor, first and foremost. They had no time to contemplate his suffering. Not when they had to endure so much of their own. The moment they stepped outside the church was the moment they put him back on his pedestal. Oh, they would have the odd drink with him, careful to be on their best behaviour when he was around, but they would never break bread with him. It wasn't because they didn't like him – they did. It was because they didn't understand him. He was good, well-meaning, but he came from a different world. They consoled themselves as the years went by that he had Señor Suarez, the teacher, and Father Anselmo, the priest, for company, thereby relinquishing themselves of all feelings of guilt and responsibility. To the villagers' ears these three pillars of Fuentes society may as well have spoken a different language for all the sense they made.

Occasionally people would pass through the village on their

way to or from the big cities. And, once or twice, an elderly couple had turned up asking, so the rumour mill had it, after the poor doctor and his girl. But, in truth, very little changed in Fuentes. And that included the people.

That was why, when Richard Johnson arrived in the spring of 1936, fifteen years after the last significant addition to the population, the entire village took a sharp intake of breath. Here was a true stranger, who really did speak an alien language. His presence had the power to clear streets. And so, for the first few weeks of his stay at least, the English boy found the usually pleasantly busy streets of Fuentes absolutely dead.

Yet what repelled the villagers about the English boy was precisely what attracted Maria.

He'd been in the village for less than a month when she told herself she loved him. It was ten o'clock in the morning, a sunny day in late spring 1936, and Richard Johnson had made his way along empty streets to discuss possible work with her father.

Doctor Alvaro had found him a room a few streets away with a family that could do with the extra pesetas. The kindly doctor had thought it would be good to throw the boy in at the deep end by housing him in the heart of the community. Unfortunately, the impact of the splash ensured that no villager would come within striking, spitting or speaking distance of him, not even the family with whom he was staying. It didn't matter. Alvaro took the boy under his wing: oversaw his progress; invited him round for food; discussed politics, history, family; monitored his health; checked on his happiness. If the rest of the village ebbed away from him, Richard was past noticing. The doctor's care and concern flowed towards him, warm and comforting, its gentle waves lapping all around. The boy's father could not have done more, and, in truth, had often done very much less.

That's why Richard Johnson was melting his way along the already hot streets, a book slipping from a sweaty palm, towards Doctor Alvaro's, determined to show his appreciation for everything the good man had done. He'd asked before. In fact, he'd asked quite a few times. But the doctor had always been too polite to take him up on his offer. Well, the boy was determined to ask again. He would offer his services to help out the doctor in any way he could (as long as – he made a note of adding as the perspiration dripped off the tip of his nose and sucked the shirt to his back – it was before ten in the morning and after five in the afternoon). Truly. In any way. Though how he could be of help to a medical practitioner when he had nothing more than a rudimentary knowledge of basic human biology (never mind the Spanish vocabulary to go with it), the eighteen-year-old wasn't really sure.

It was apparent that Pablo Alvaro's thoughts weren't any clearer.

'I'm here to help you, good sir. I am at your disposal. Completely.' The eager words tumbled out of his mouth the second the doctor opened the door in the boy's best formal Spanish.

'Wonderful to see you Richard. *Buenos dias*. Please, come in. Maria will be delighted you're here.' At the mention of her name, the boy gave a blush so intense you could light a cigarette with it. He glowed as he followed the doctor through the dark, cool interior of the house to the tiled courtyard at its heart. 'I just need to get something,' the doctor said, turning and bumbling his way back inside. He left his young guest standing in the open doorway.

Maria looked up from a pile of books and leaflets, her expression both amused and knowing. Richard must be here to discuss 'work plans' again. That always sent her father scurrying back inside, rummaging through notes and letters in search of a job, any job, for the English boy to do. It would have to be one that kept him out of the sun, Maria thought to herself as she caught sight of his bright red cheeks.

'Please, sit,' she said to him, instinctively pointing towards the chair in the shade.

They nodded at one another. Smiled. Waited.

Maria was the first to break the silence.

'What's that you're reading?' she asked. Then wished she hadn't.

'*La vida es sueño* by Calderón de la Barca. It's about free will and destiny. But then,' Richard said, sizzling up once more, 'you probably know that.'

Maria had heard of it. She smiled but did not reply. She hoped he would assume she'd read it.

'What are you going to do when you grow up?'

Before she knew where it had come from it was out. She was playing the game she played with Paloma. She put her hand up and shook her head with embarrassment, a gesture to say, 'What was I thinking of?' But she needn't have worried; this childish dreaming about the future provided safer, more fertile ground for the pair of them.

'I am going to see the world, after Oxford. Travel around the rest of Europe, go to North America, South America, possibly India…' Richard's blushes evaporated, his thoughts of Calderón disappeared, while Maria feared her eyes might pop out if he went on listing places much longer. This English boy's words were confident, his future assured. And that was the moment it happened. His answer, worlds apart from Paloma's, worlds apart from her own, defined him. He knew that he would do things that Maria, even in her most extravagant of dreams, had never imagined possible. Because he could, and she couldn't, not here, in Fuentes. It wasn't even a question of her father stopping her. The freedoms her father spoke of, he believed in. But within the village Maria knew such freedoms would be hard won.

'What about you? What would you like to do? When you grow up?'

'Writer!' Maria blurted out, throwing out the first thing that came to mind. Anyone could do that, she thought, even stuck in Fuentes. 'Yes! When I grow up I'm going to be a writer!'

She looked to gauge Richard's response but the sun was

blinding. She raised a hand to shield her eyes from the light that was starting to make her squint. 'Would you like to swap places with me?' he asked her from his sheltered corner. She declined – she'd already spotted a heat rash on his neck now that his blushes had subsided.

A gust of warm air rustled the sun-dry leaves above Richard's head. Maria lifted up her eyes, screwing them up tightly to see the precious movement, green against blue, and listen to the music of the rippling leaves. She went over the question in her head again: *Would I like to swap places with him?* Whether he'd intended it or not, Richard had opened up a world of possibilities to her. 'Thank you,' she said.

Richard went to get up. 'Oh, no,' Maria laughed, pushing him back down. He laughed in response without truly understanding why. 'What are you reading, if not Calderón?' he asked, fixing on something more tangible, with more than a hint of playful impertinence.

'Oh, these?' Maria cleared her throat, pointing to the heaps of pamphlets strewn across the table in front of her. 'Señor Suarez gave me these to look through. There are some pamphlets on workers' rights and organisations, as well as extracts from Karl Marx. It's part of a reading programme he started for the labourers in the area.'

'Karl Marx?'

'You must know of him. He's very popular in Spain.'

Infamous in England was how Richard would have put it, but he said nothing. *'Only eleven people turned up to his funeral… doesn't surprise me that he got turned down for a job as a railway clerk because of his atrocious handwriting. So he said religion was the opium of the people. Well, don't mind if I do…'* Peter Johnson's rants about Karl Marx danced their spiky rhythm across the revolving surface of the wheel of memory that spun round in his son's head. No, Karl Marx was not popular, not in his house.

'… Workers of the world, unite!' Maria read the rousing words.

'Isn't he a… communist?'

'It's not a dirty word.' Maria laughed. 'And yes, he is. Father is reading *Das Kapital*. In Spanish, of course. Promises he'll pass it on to me when he finishes. Says it makes a lot of sense. There's so much unfairness in this country. So many workers selling their labour at too low a price while rich, old families live lives of luxury on the backs of the profits. Um… capital is dead labour which, like a vampire, only exists by sucking the life out of living labour.' Her eyes flickered downwards as if reading from one of the leaflets in front of her.

'But aren't you causing trouble by reading Karl Marx to them?' Richard said, his father's tirades still resounding in his head.

'No. I wouldn't say so. Last time there was a problem Señor Suarez and my father had to help them out of it. It stands to reason that if we help them to read they will be able to help themselves next time. They'll be able to write letters, read contracts, represent themselves. Things like that. Things that *we* both take for granted.' She glanced at the slim volume he had in his hand, reminded of the fleeting ignominy she'd felt at not having read one of Spain's finest writers.

Richard Johnson thought for a moment. 'Can I take some of these leaflets? To look at them?'

'*Claro que sí.* You can take these,' Maria said, offering him a handful. 'As long as you get them back to me by next Thursday.'

'Next Thursday?'

'Yes. That's when he'll… I mean *we'll*,' she added, a look of bashful pride on her face, 'be needing them. That's when we'll be using them.'

It struck Richard Johnson that this was something he could do.

'If I read all of these and make sure I understand every word, could I help?' His heart beat with a sense of purpose.

'I've been thinking.' Doctor Alvaro appeared out of nowhere and was now standing behind his daughter, looking down at his visitor. 'I don't really know how I'm going to be able to use your talents. But don't worry,' he said reassuringly, relieved not to see disappointment on Richard's face. 'I'll ask around and see if I can find something else for you to do.'

'No need, father. I think I've found just the job. Isn't that so, comrade?' Maria gave the English boy a knowing wink. Then she turned round and planted a calming kiss on her grateful father's cheek.

CHAPTER 4

'No, she cannot. And you shouldn't be doing it either!' Cecilia shouted at Maria as the girl watched the large, hairy mole above her friend's mother's upper lip vibrate. Maria was on a mission to help Señor Suarez recruit volunteers to teach some of the labourers up on the estate to read. She'd successfully enlisted Richard Johnson, thereby making her father a very relieved man as he no longer had to invent jobs for the hapless boy to do. And so, emboldened, she thought she might try her luck with Cecilia in the (what she saw now as foolish) hope that she would allow Paloma to help out too. Paloma was a good reader: Maria had made sure of that. Therefore it seemed reasonable that her friend should be allowed to pass on the skills she'd learnt by teaching others. 'She'd make such a good teacher,' Maria insisted. Contrary to appearances Cecilia had a soft spot for Maria and the girl knew it. She'd got round her friend's mother many times before. Unfortunately, this was not going to be one of them. 'The answer's still no,' the older woman insisted, her arms crossed defensively across an ample bosom.

'And you can take this back,' Cecilia said. And with that her friend's mother thrust the pamphlet that she had given Paloma only hours before back into her hand. As clenched fist met unsuspecting palm, Maria felt Cecilia's entire body bristle with anger. The gratefully oppressed, that's how she regarded Cecilia, aggressively tenacious while holding onto the chains that enslaved her. She had no idea what the pamphlet said. But the older woman believed she didn't need to. If that communist Señor Suarez had anything to do with it (and he did) then it meant trouble. That was the point. Words, words and more words, probably written by that red troublemaker himself. They spelled out nothing but danger, Cecilia was sure of it. And she didn't want her daughter to have any part in it. No, Maria would not be getting round her today. She folded her arms one way, then the other, as if to prove it.

In Cecilia's small world, workers worked on the same estate – El Cortijo del Bosque. Her son Manuel had a labouring job there, her husband Fernando (God bless him) had died while working in its wheat fields, and she herself had gone from kitchen girl to housemaid to housekeeper, also cooking for the landowner and his family when the need arose: all on the same estate, all for the same family. Señor Suarez and his talk of workers' rights infuriated her. Divisive talk. She'd heard it all before. That teacher with all his false promises had given her Fernando hope – useless, backbreaking hope that one day he'd have his own plot of land to farm where he would at last enjoy the fruits of his own labours.

Something to do with government land reforms. Government land reforms: as insubstantial as dreams and as flammable as the paper they were written on. And it was that Señor Suarez who'd sold it to Cecilia's husband. But she knew, had always known, it was never going to happen. Don Felipe was a *latifundista* of the old school who believed in tradition, glory, church and the rightness of a social hierarchy where his boot had the God-given right to press down forcefully on the heads of men like her husband, keeping their noses well and truly snuffling in the soil. His soil. It was never going to be theirs. Don Felipe might pay them a few pesetas more, but give them his land? Never.

Fernando had been a fool. For listening to Suarez, for daring to raise his head and hope for something more. And the bitter memory stung like acid in Cecilia's soul.

He'd got above himself. And look where it had got him. Dead and buried under the very land he'd wanted.

Well, nobody could ever accuse Cecilia of not knowing her place – it was right up there on the estate doing exactly what she was told to do. And she would do her damnedest to make sure her children followed in her footsteps.

It was the only security she knew.

'There's no need for any of Don Felipe's workers to read,' she said, wagging her finger in Maria's face. 'That terrible teacher. Getting the farm workers to bite the hand that feeds them.' A guttural rattle vibrated at the back of the woman's throat.

'But Cecilia, because of him men can now provide for their families. Don't you remember? Children were going hungry before.'

That was it.

'Out! Out now!' Cecilia shouted, pointing Maria towards the door. Maria knew when she was beaten. She didn't mind that Cecilia had shouted at her. She wasn't afraid of her friend's mother, but she wouldn't convince her, that much was sure. Her eyes squirmed away from the fury in Cecilia's; she hoped she hadn't earned a beating for her friend. An unusually subdued Maria went to leave as a tired and taciturn Manuel entered.

'Maria.' Manuel greeted her. He had been working all day and his young body was wet with perspiration. His skin, Maria couldn't help but notice, was a deep, glistening, golden brown, and, his dark hair shone in its blackness, swept back as it was from his strong jawed face, with its dark brows and liquid brown eyes. His stomach was taut with hunger, his throat parched with thirst, while his heart, though she didn't know it, was heavy. He was perfect. All apart from a small scar on his left cheek. The sight of him reminded Maria why she'd thought him beautiful not so very long ago: because he was.

'Good evening Manuel.' Maria forced her eyes to meet his. Cecilia looked on suspiciously. A coil of hair fell about his eyes. He swept it back with a large, strong hand. For a moment his beauty threatened to break through and touch Maria's soul, but the moment passed quickly. She shook her head to stop it from catching on and commended herself on being made of more cerebral stuff. A smile of relief blew across her face.

Maria held out a pamphlet and offered it to him. 'Oh no you don't, my girl!' said Cecilia, flinging her arm out and intercepting it as though it were a poisoned arrow.

'It's tomorrow. Up at the estate—' But before she could say any more Maria found herself hastily turfed out onto the road.

She looked back at Cecilia, disappointed but not surprised, the faint smile on her lips that signalled superiority enough to push the poor woman into a rage.

'And if you don't want tongues to wag you'll heed my words and not have anything to do with it either,' the red-faced Cecilia called after her, loud enough to bring all the neighbours rushing to their windows. 'And,' she shouted, now to the back of the girl's head, furious that Maria appeared disproportionately collected in the face of Cecilia's own fast-burning fury, 'you'll ruin your chances of ever getting a husband if you carry on this way! I'll be having words with your father about this.'

'Oh, Cecilia!' Maria said calmly as she walked away.

*

The designated meeting place for the lesson was in the courtyard of the estate. The estate manager, Guido, didn't like it but the law was against him. Still, he'd done his best to warn the workers off. That was why, when Señor Suarez turned up, the teacher had only found three boys up for the reading challenge. They looked a little beaten around but the smiles on their faces as they came closer soon blinded him to their bruises. He recognised Manuel, as well as Pedro and Raul, the Espinoza brothers. 'We've come to read,' poor Fernando's son said, holding out Maria's scrunched up pamphlet as proof. Disappointed not to see the girl who had given it to him, Manuel's eyes searched all around. There, in the distance, he recognised the one known as '*el inglés*', his hair as golden as the crops all around him, next to whom, Manuel realised with a heavy heart, was Maria. The pair seemed to be in no particular hurry. 'Manuel? Manuel? Do you agree Manuel?' The teacher's words pierced the surface of the boy's consciousness. 'Manuel? Manuel? Did you hear me?' The Espinoza brothers laughed. 'A teacher each,' Señor Suarez repeated. He too had seen the English boy and Maria.

Cecilia was still in the kitchen. She was working later than usual and would be working well into the night. Guido had recently broken the news to her that the landowners, Don Felipe and his wife, Dona Sofía, were planning to return *soon. For good.* Guido had said they were back *to make Spain great again*, but Cecilia hadn't really been listening. All she knew was that Dona Sofía in particular would be expecting to find everything in order. The larder would need to be stocked, the rooms opened back up, and every floor, surface and ornament would need to be scrubbed, cleaned and polished. Then there were the menus to plan. Guido could not tell her how soon *soon* would be, as he walked across her newly mopped kitchen floor in his dusty boots, so Cecilia had no choice but to assume that her employers' return might be as early as the following week. She mopped the floor once more and went outside into the courtyard while she waited for it to dry.

That was when she saw Maria, walking past the farmhouse, her head, Cecilia noticed, held high like a haughty mare, laughing easily with the strange-looking foreigner by her side. 'Such an arrogant child!' Cecilia said to herself, the tinkling, confident sound of the girl's happiness ringing like an insult inside the older woman's head. Cecilia was still smarting from the youngster's cheek the day before. 'Look at her! With that boy! She'll get a name for herself and then she really will have trouble finding a husband!' But Cecilia knew that wasn't true. The rules that applied to Cecilia and the rest of Fuentes did not apply to Maria. They never had. As Guido crossed the courtyard the girl thrust a pamphlet into his hand. Cecilia almost smiled. But then pulled herself back. Only Maria Alvaro could do something like that and not get punished for it.

Rules. Cecilia wore them round her neck like a hangman's noose. And the very mention of her employers' return pulled the rope tight once more around the ageing, hardworking Cecilia's throat leaving her gasping for air and concerned for her children in a future that, if Guido was to be believed, her employers were intent on forging in the image of their once glorious past.

And so, as she stood in the kitchen doorway, Cecilia's heart sank when she saw her son chewing his finger, watching Maria. He couldn't take his eyes off her. Maria didn't even grace him with a glance. 'Heartless girl!' *Careful what you wish for Cecilia* – for no sooner were these words of judgement out of her mouth than the gods took pity on Cecilia's love-struck son.

Maria beamed at him.

His mother now winced to see her son's body burst into life at the light in the girl's eyes. He rushed up to Maria, ran round her, a puppy desperate to please. Cecilia heard the girl's laugh again. It cut across the courtyard and stabbed her in the heart. Manuel's mother had seen enough. She went back inside and closed the kitchen door, wounded.

*

Mother and son cadged a lift home on the back of a cart two hours later. Cecilia had scrubbed as many floors as she could face for one day, and Manuel could no longer pick out the words on the page.

'The great leveller. That's what education is,' Manuel said to his mother as he wiped his tired face with a rag, his hand shaking in time to the revolving of the cartwheels over bumpy ground. 'Great leveller, my arse,' she mumbled to herself, her voice rising and falling in time. 'There's no shame in it, you know, a good day's work,' his mother said, irritated to see her son had a book in his shaky hands and hope in his lilting voice. 'All this talk of education, it will only lead to trouble. The likes of Don Felipe don't like it, you know.'

'The likes of Maria Alvaro will break your heart,' was what she'd meant to say. But her beautiful boy glowed with happiness in the pink-purple twilight and she did not have the stomach to take it away from him. Maria would do that soon enough. Cecilia prayed that she would let her boy down gently, though, recalling how the girl had paraded round the courtyard like a queen earlier in the day, she doubted that she would.

Yet as Manuel talked about Don Felipe's unfairness, some strike that had happened in Asturias in 1934, and the Russian Revolution (a load of nonsense he must have got from that teacher), it occurred to Cecilia that it wasn't only Maria who had ignited a flame in his heart. As her eyes fixed on the book her son had clutched in his hands, she saw there were more dangerous fires still that her son had started to play with.

CHAPTER 5

No one saw it coming – not Paloma, not Manuel, not even the ever-vigilant Cecilia, and certainly not Maria. No one except Lola, and, of course, Richard, had any idea what was happening in full view of everyone.

Maria, Paloma and Richard were going on a picnic. It was Sunday morning and they were all setting off from their respective homes to meet up just outside the village when Cecilia followed Paloma to the door and took her youngest daughter brusquely by the arm. 'You're not going unless she can come too,' she bellowed, nodding in the direction of a well-groomed Lola, dressed up and ready for anything but a picnic in the country. She had her best shoes on and the dress she wore to village parties and her dark wavy hair was gleaming. Paloma stopped in her tracks. No one could accuse Lola of being a shrinking violet, and no one would say she was a girl that was easily overlooked, left behind at home by a callous, selfish sister to hide her light under a bushel. And yet, here she was, standing next to her mother, eyes on the verge of tears, saying, 'Don't worry mother. If Paloma doesn't want me to go with her, I understand.'

'Oh no, my girl. You're going. You both go or neither of you go. Those are my conditions. Now go and get whatever it is you

34

need.' Lola clattered up the stairs making a pretence of getting ready, thankful that her usually observant mother hadn't noticed that she already was.

That Cecilia should allow her girls to skip church was unprecedented, and that she should allow them to go off into the country with a foreigner as strange-looking as *el inglés* equally surprising to people who knew her. Ever since she'd got wind of her employers' return she'd been distracted, yet it was Guido's latest piece of information that had really set the poor woman off like a whirling dervish: he expected the fine owners of El Cortijo del Bosque any time after lunch on Sunday. That was it. Even the devout Cecilia wouldn't be attending church now, may the Lord God forgive her. She feared God, but she feared Don Felipe and Dona Sofía more. Especially Dona Sofía. There was still a mountain of work to do up at the house and Cecilia knew that if it didn't get done there would be hell to pay. God would forgive her for not attending church this once, whereas Dona Sofía on the other hand would not be so gracious if she didn't make sure all the rooms were aired, all the beds made up, all the silver polished, all the floors scrubbed and, heaven forbid, if the larder was not well stocked. And as for the ugly English boy, Cecilia believed he was as interested in Maria as much as she was interested in him. And they would both be out of sight of her beautiful Manuel. Let that girl do what she wanted. She usually did. It was up to Doctor Alvaro to stop her, not Cecilia. And so when Paloma asked if she could go on a picnic with Maria, her mother screamed 'A picnic?' put a hand to her chest, collapsed on a chair, then said in a breathy whisper, '*Perdoname, Dios mio*,' before saying emphatically, 'Yes.'

'I'm ready!' Lola ran down the stairs, kissed her mother, then charged out. She was on her bike and nearly at the end of the road when she shouted: 'Hurry up Paloma, you big lump, or we'll be late!'

Maria was waiting at the stone water trough in full sun. Richard was waiting close by in the shade. At the sight of the sisters Maria gave a whistle to the English boy and set off ahead of them all, leading the way to their chosen picnic spot which was a thirty-minute ride out of the village. The girls cycled there in silence, the only sound coming from Richard as he puffed along in the heat. He struggled to keep up on his bike. A thirty-minute cycle ride hadn't seemed so very testing when Maria had first suggested it to him. But then he hadn't reckoned on the ferocity of the sun. As he passed shepherds' huts he saw their walls perspire, while olive trees throbbed under pounding rays. As for Richard himself, he was starting to melt. Would there be anything left of him by the time he'd reached the destination? That the girls said nothing seemed perfectly reasonable to him. He had no idea that Paloma was sulking because Lola had hoodwinked their mother into letting her come. Nor that Maria was sulking because she thought Lola would spoil their day. The only one of the girls not to be sulking was Lola. She'd wanted to come along and here she was. She hadn't come to talk to either Maria or Paloma and so the silence suited her perfectly. That the other girls radiated every kind of animosity towards her didn't bother her in the slightest. They were going to have to try harder than direct bad thoughts at her if they wanted to put her off her stride. She'd come here for a reason and these two silly little girls weren't going to stop her with their sour looks and huffy puffy ways. The hot air slipped around their bodies. It kept the girls cool, made Richard sticky and red. They cycled along dusty tracks, past fields of corn, olive groves, vineyards, passing the occasional donkey moving slowly under the weight of a heavy load. Richard had never experienced such peace. Nor such heat. He stopped for a while, pulled a handkerchief from his pocket and wiped the sweat from his brow, his neck, and his palms. It was quickly sodden. 'How much further?' he called out, but the girls were too far ahead to hear. As he rubbed his already wet palms, getting ready to set off again, he heard a car.

Toot. Toot, toot, toot. Tooooooot. The horn sounded. Insistent. Furious. It roused the boy's flagging senses.

A deep voice, raised in anger, yelled out at him, sounding angrier the closer it got. The driver to whom the raging voice belonged was tooting the horn as if he were in heavy traffic in the middle of a city. He'd already encountered the girls and now he was furious. They'd made him slow down when he shouldn't have to, least of all when he was driving along his own lanes, leading to his own estate.

For a brief moment a cloud in an otherwise cloudless sky blocked out the sun. Richard experienced a strange feeling of menace. He wheeled his bike as quickly as he could into the adjacent field to make way. The car hurtled towards him, the driver's arms waving in wild accompaniment to the shouts that continued to whip him. The dusty vehicle sped by, its wheels throwing up a spray of small stones and grit in its wake that caught in the boy's eyes. The driver's foot pressed down hard on the accelerator. The furious tooting of the horn continued. Richard Johnson shuddered briefly. He rubbed his eyes and looked for the girls through the gravel haze. The car had gone one way, Richard and the girls another: the cloud above had passed. And there, through the settling dust, he saw a sunlit Lola, black hair glinting, white dress dazzling. She was standing next to her bike at the corner up ahead.

She was the only one who'd waited for him.

*

Maria was already at the picnic spot. She'd cycled away from the group. She'd beat Lola there if it killed her, she'd said to herself, Paloma too. Nothing would distract. Not even the car.

'I'm hot now!' Maria threw herself under the tree as she hurled her bike to the ground letting the back wheel spin round and round. She gasped as she leant against the trunk and looked on victorious as Paloma followed her, close behind.

Lola turned up ten minutes later.

Paloma watched her sister suspiciously. Lola had nothing more than a few delicate beads of perspiration across her forehead, though she pulled the straps of her dress down to expose her shoulders, fanning herself as if exhausted. She was about to say something to her big sister but bit her tongue, momentarily distracted by the shallow breathing of Richard following on close behind. All three girls looked at him. His face flushed brightly. He nodded, too hot and short of breath to say a word.

Paloma noticed her sister rub her bare shoulder in the way that she'd only ever seen her sister do, in a way that was somehow indecent though she couldn't explain how. But Richard's reaction, Paloma was relieved to see, wasn't the one Lola was expecting. English men with pale skin weren't made for cycling under an almost cloudless sky in the heat of the day. Richard Johnson let his bike drop to the ground. He let his body fall soon after, grateful that these sun-hardened Spanish girls had seen fit to set their picnic up under the shade of a tree.

'Who were the people in the car?' he asked when he'd eventually cooled down enough to speak. 'Are they from here?' Maria chose not to answer. The sisters shared a look of deep concern. 'Owners of the estate, Don Felipe and Dona Sofía.' Lola was the first to break the silence. She gave her shoulder another rub as she looked the still panting Richard in the eye. But it was no use. Her heart was no longer in it. The thought of her mother's employers had unsettled her. 'Mother said she was expecting them soon,' she said turning to Paloma and dragging Richard's attention with her. He sat back and listened.

'I couldn't see the son with them.'

Maria pounced on Lola. 'Disappointed? And anyway, I didn't know they had one.'

'You don't know everything.' The older girls' antipathy towards one another was showing through. 'And yes, it's a pity he's not with them. Mother says they're better when he is.'

'We've never seen him, but I know they sent him away,' Paloma whispered, waiting for her friend's questions. Not a single one came – Maria had no wish to expose her ignorance about the mysterious son any further in front of Richard Johnson. She imagined his eyes boring into her wondering what else she didn't know. She would leave the stage to the sisters while the hole closed up. 'Poor Cecilia!'

The sisters talked quickly, angrily, conjuring back up for him the image of the dusty black car, thundering its way furiously along the lanes to unleash the blackest of storms upon their mother...

'They drive her like a slave.' Lola pulled up her shoulder straps in a temper. Richard, touched by the intensity of feeling in her words, looked at her. She looked straight back and for a moment he was disarmed. The shock of her vulnerability passed through him. He looked away, afraid to relive the experience. Instead he fixed his gaze on the calm, self-assured face of Maria.

She was at the top of the pecking order once more. She smiled at him but in doing so she noticed the damp patches under the armpits of his shirt, observed how his breathing was still heavy, that his face looked like the skin of a blood orange. He didn't look like much of a catch. Still, his eyes were upon *her*, *not* Lola.

She looked at the girl who was not her rival. Lola. Cool, strong, almost regal. Though Maria found her difficult she could not deny that Lola was indeed beautiful. With her dark, long eyelashes framing deep brown, sparkling eyes, glossy dark hair that shone in the light, and her flawless olive skin, she reminded Maria of Manuel. She looked back at Richard Johnson. She crinkled her nose with displeasure at the unwelcome comparison. He really was a rather unimpressive physical specimen, she thought again.

Maria stood up. She walked out into the sunshine, away from Richard in all his weak, disappointing reality in order to better preserve the perfect dream of him. 'Coming?' she asked, knowing Richard could not. He'd had enough full sun for one day. Paloma got up. Lola and Richard remained. They sat in silence, watching the two girls walk away, their bodies breaking up in ever-growing ripples of heat.

Richard was the first to speak. 'I'm sorry about your mother,' he said to a subdued Lola. She said nothing. She had wanted to flirt with the English boy. That was why she'd put her best clothes on. But now concern for her mother had quashed all lighter thoughts. Confusion filled her mind forcing genuine tears to well up in her eyes. She wiped them away with the back of her hand and apologised. 'I don't know what's the matter with me!' she laughed. He offered his handkerchief and touched her tenderly on the shoulder.

'Oh, don't be kind to me,' Lola said, fighting back the tears.

'Let's play a game,' Richard said. 'Take your mind off it.'

Instinctively, he pushed Lola's cascading hair away from her eyes, and cupped her face in his hands. 'I'll look after you,' he said, not really knowing what he was saying nor why he was saying it. The words came of their own accord. Easier to utter for being in a language that wasn't his own, perhaps. Yet no sooner were they out than he let his hands drop down. His eyes plummeted to the ground.

A small brown hand with pretty pink-tipped nails squeezed his still pale hand gently in response. She didn't touch him for long but it was enough. The shock he'd felt earlier when he'd looked into her eyes surged through him once more.

Flustered, Richard looked around. What could he speak to her about? English. Yes, he could teach her some English. 'Say a word, any word. Ask me anything! What would you like to know?'

She looked at him, put her lips to his ear and whispered '*Qué pasa?*' He cupped his hand around her ear in response. 'What's happening?' he whispered, tickling her neck with his warm breath. An hour slipped past, lips getting ever closer, shoulders rubbing, heads getting thrown back by the strength of the laughter that grew more assured the more comfortable they felt in each other's company. Lola's fingers worked their way bit by bit over the back of his hand, along his arm, around his shoulder, until by the time they came to rest on the back of his neck they felt as if they'd always been there. She brushed the fine hair at the nape of his neck lightly. It made him tingle inside. '*Te quiero*.' Whispered words wove themselves magically around his heart, pulling his lips towards hers.

The sound of Maria's laughter as she finally decided to grace them with her presence once more shattered the spell. Richard stiffened. Both he and Lola moved as far away from each other as they could. They looked at the ground. A joint expression of guilt. Maria mistook it for boredom. She sat herself down between them as if filling the conversational void she assumed must have occurred in her absence.

'I'm hungry,' Maria said as she rummaged through the picnic basket she'd packed. She now knew as much as Paloma did about the landowners' son having pumped her friend full of questions on their walk: and it wasn't very much. She couldn't even tell Maria what he looked like, having seen him only a handful of occasions herself many years ago. All Paloma could remember was that Cecilia had said that he was a 'good boy'. Maria recalled that Cecilia had also said Dona Sofía and Don Felipe were 'good employers' and so that was no recommendation. She smiled at Richard. 'You must be hungry too,' she said, as she handed him some bread and ham. She sighed as she looked into the distance, satisfied that she'd restored him to his rightful place in her heart.

Paloma's eyes settled a little closer to home. The look on her big sister's face unsettled her. The more familiar expressions of defiance and self-satisfaction had been replaced by something more reflective and humble. She shot a glance at Richard. There was something different about him too, though she couldn't identify what it was. But it was clear to her, from the way he repeatedly ran his fingers around the back of his collar and the way he dropped his gaze to the ground each time she caught his eye, that he was feeling more than a little uncomfortable about something.

For the remainder of the picnic Paloma watched Lola and Richard's every move. She found it uneasy viewing.

'Oh, I would love to travel,' Maria chatted on happily, still transfixed by the infinite possibilities she read in the sky as she got up to have a better look. She was oblivious to the fact that Richard was moving, little by little, ever closer to Lola, while on the blank, blue canvas up ahead her imagination was delighting in the creation of a fiction of her life that drew little on reality. There she saw her future as it stretched itself out, on a path as unbroken as the familiar cloudless sky along which she would travel. She could envisage no impediment to her personal plans. Not even a summer shower.

She was of an age at which life is taken for granted and a happy-ever-after assumed.

As for love, she believed that it was something that she could choose. She had no idea that, when the time came, it would choose her, whether she wanted it or not.

And if she only had eyes to see she would have noticed that it had the English boy Richard Johnson in its grip.

'Excuse me while I break myself some bread.' 'Oh, would you pass the ham?' 'Oh, would you mind passing me the knife?' Richard was drawn to Lola like a magnet, her touch as she passed bread, ham, knife to him sending an electric current that brought an altogether different part of him to life. It was true that Lola was not as intellectual as Maria, her conversation not as witty or engaging, that the only English she spoke were the few words he'd given her that afternoon, but when she pushed herself against him it made his eyes gleam and his body melt in the most delicious of ways. He'd told himself only the day before that the warmth he felt for Maria was love. If that was so, then what was the name of the passion that had now taken him over body and soul?

By the time they cycled home together everything had changed for Richard Johnson. And even though Maria did not cycle away from him – she slowed down, kept pace – it made no difference. Lola had awoken something deep within him and he within her.

'Spain has been a Republic ever since the start of the 1930s, when King Alonso XIII was deposed. The Popular Front, in power since February of this year, is a coalition... left-wing. The right-wing tried to upset ballots with bullets in Madrid and Barcelona but failed. The labourers who work these fields went on strike just after the last election. Don Felipe the landowner had no choice but to pay them more. He wasn't happy. Oh look! I can see Guido in the field over there. He manages the estate...' Richard tried to follow what Maria was telling him – about politics, the running of the estate, how far Cordoba was with its beautiful mezquita, that the mezquita had once been a mosque before it was turned into a Cathedral after 1236, that the Moors had ruled southern Spain before that, about the Alhambra in Granada and the gardens of Seville. Did he know that Señor Suarez had family in Seville, as well as Madrid?... Maria. She was a mine of information if only he cared to listen. But he did not. Instead his mind, heart and eyes were pulled along by a laughing Lola, who, bored by the bombardment of information that was detonating within her head, decided to break away to let off some fireworks of her own.

He let out a complicit laugh as he watched Lola whizz by. Her skirt was pulled up high, exposing her thighs. As she cycled into the warm air, a gentle breeze blew through her hair. Maria was tempted to race her. She resisted the urge. She was ashamed of herself for cycling away from Richard earlier on, felt guilty that she'd recoiled at his inability to cope with the heat. He was cerebral. So was she. And she would prove it. The life she longed for was that of the mind. Bodies were an encumbrance. And so, she chatted on, skating over the history of Spain and around Spanish literature, skilfully encompassing *Don Quixote* with a figure of eight... And Richard nodded his head as if listening, though his eyes and thoughts were taken up with the vision of Lola, beautifully seductive, cycling into the deepening blue of the late afternoon sky.

The lane widened. Paloma, up until now stuck behind Maria and Richard, manoeuvred around the pair.

'I'm telling on you,' she hissed at her sister, when she'd caught up with her. 'I have no idea what you mean!' Lola answered, her laugh extending across the summer fields.

CHAPTER 6

It may have been true that Don Felipe and Dona Sofía had planned to return 'sometime next week' but times and dates, like everything else in life, were theirs to change.

'Sunday? Sunday? I thought they weren't coming back until next week. The house isn't ready. And I always go to church on a Sunday.' But it really didn't matter what Cecilia always did. Cecilia had been blindsided.

That was how she found herself allowing her daughters to go off for a picnic with a foreigner and why she was here in the kitchen on her hands and knees scrubbing away at the flagstone floor while perspiration dripped off the tip of her nose. She wondered if Luis, the landowners' son away at an English boarding school, would be joining them. She hoped so. He would be eighteen years old now. Same age as her Manuel. A broad smile broke out across her face at the thought of the boys.

*

Fifteen minutes away in a speeding car bumping over stones and re-acquainting themselves with their estate were her employers. Their son was not with them. Dona Sofía was holding on to the

45

door handle for grim death, concerned that her wrist might dislocate at any moment, while Don Felipe was driving as fast as the car would allow. He congratulated himself on the fact that he was master of all he surveyed: land, animals, and people. Dona Sofía held a handkerchief to her forehead with her free hand, taking care to close her eyes for fear that she might inadvertently poke one of them out as the wheels of the car jolted over small stones.

'See that Sofía? Our workers!' Her husband shouted at her in order to be heard over the sound of the engine. 'We'll whip this place back into shape.' He swerved past two girls causing the wheels of the car to momentarily spin out of control. 'Unbelievable!' His wife's eyelids sprang open, her eyeballs very nearly popping with surprise as she saw the feral creatures wobbling around on their bicycles. Her husband slammed his palm down on the dashboard. Who were these girls getting in his way? And why weren't they at church? Girls out on bikes on a Sunday morning. The thought of it made his blood boil. He stamped his foot down hard on the accelerator as he saw another one, dressed in white, standing by her bike at a turning. A furious cloud of dust and grit filled the air. The car roared and so did its driver. And he continued to do so as the first thing he saw when the dust cloud settled was Richard Johnson careering off the road and into one of his fields.

'What *was* that?' A fish out of water cooking under the strong sun, the sight of the English boy stunned Don Felipe, and Dona Sofía no less so.

'Must be a Bolshevik… or a Jew.' Inconvenienced by the jerkiness of her husband's driving, she sat forward and blinked repeatedly, perplexed by the ghostly apparition. She remembered the article she'd been reading only the day before calling for the need of 'a new Reconquista' to purge Spain of 'contamination'. It acknowledged there were few Jews left 'thanks to their expulsion the first time in 1492 by Catholic monarchs Ferdinand and Isabella', but now their friends, 'communists, socialists, freemasons, liberals and the like', were growing 'like noxious plants', destroying the very fabric of Spanish culture and tradition 'from within'. She'd felt it a little extreme at the time. But, seeing this boy, so alien, so near to her estate, it did make her wonder.

'Thank heavens we've come back,' she said, a loud tut of disapproval punctuating her words. Don Felipe growled.

He pulled up outside the farmhouse ten minutes later. He tooted on the horn six times. Cecilia looked up from the floor she was scrubbing in time to witness Guido the estate manager open the car doors for Don Felipe and his wife. Opening car doors – one of the many jobs her employers couldn't do for themselves, she caught herself thinking as she pulled herself up to standing. She smoothed out the folds of her apron and rushed into the hall. It was a surprise to her that Don Felipe hadn't used his chauffeur to drive them here.

As landowner and manager walked around to the back of the house, Dona Sofía wafted delicately into the house, a forced smile on her face as she greeted Cecilia and the three house staff all lined up at the bottom of the stairs to welcome her.

'Would you like refreshments Dona Sofía?'

'Cecilia! Girls! How lovely to see you all again. Pilar, isn't it? No? Julietta? Are you sure? Ah well. Never mind. Nothing for me, nothing at all. Just bring an orange juice up to my room, would you? But I can't answer for Don Felipe.' With a flick of her wrist, she gestured that her husband was somewhere outside and that Cecilia, or Pilar, or Julietta, or whatever her name was, should go and find him. 'And now I need to lie down,' she said abruptly. 'We've had an encounter of the most unpleasant kind. With some hideous cyclists. You wouldn't happen to know who they were?' And without waiting for a reply she floated up the staircase leaving Cecilia feeling as though someone had trampled over her grave.

The housekeeper made her way towards Don Felipe.

'… My workers have been doing *what*?' he said to his estate manager, his voice at once angry and incredulous. Aware of his housekeeper shuffling towards him like something brought back from the dead he broke off long enough to snap, 'Orange juice – verandah,' while shooing her back inside the house with his own inimitable wrist action.

'Reading, you tell me!' Don Felipe's words rang in her head as Cecilia scuttled away. 'But why, Guido? Why?' he bleated with all the emotion of a man betrayed.

In the kitchen Cecilia squeezed, pummelled and beat the oranges, extracting every drop of juice from them that she could. She placed two glasses on one tray, a single glass on another, filled them to the top, then, as she went out onto the verandah, she told one of the house girls to go up to Dona Sofía's bedroom. By the time Cecilia had placed the tray down outside her unsettled thoughts had travelled down to her wrists, palms, tips of her fingers, causing her usually steady hands to buckle and shake. The orange juice cascaded over the rim of the glasses, spilt out over the tray, spread across the table, until finally trickling, drop by hard-pressed drop down onto the ground beneath. She watched the scene unfurl before her, and though she willed it to stop, she was powerless to stem the flow now that it had started.

'Careful! Clumsy woman!' The clumsy woman dashed off to fetch a cloth.

'Names! Give me names!' She felt Guido's eyes burning into the back of her head as she retreated. They burned no less when she returned.

'Perhaps Cecilia can help you,' the sly fox said. 'Speak, woman!' Her employer's words, pushing her to give an answer, shocked her like the point of a sharp knife. She looked at Guido, searching for help. She found none. What was she to do? She had to name someone. Señor Suarez? No. That English boy? No. Then, before she knew what she'd done she blurted out 'Maria!' 'Maria?' Don Felipe echoed back at her. 'Yes,' Cecilia confirmed. 'Maria. Maria Alvaro. The doctor's daughter.' She felt no guilt. Rules, after all, did not apply to Maria Alvaro.

CHAPTER 7

It was the day after the landowners had returned to their estate and Don Felipe was having breakfast while scanning the paper looking for news. He put it down in frustration. 'Still nothing in the papers about any coup, dear?' Dona Sofía asked. Her husband gave a loud shush, followed by a hasty glance at the door to make sure none of the servants were listening. 'Oh, it's not the coup I'm looking for. Though in view of the strikes all over the country,' he said, jabbing his finger at some article, 'it had better come soon.'

Pools of unrest had been bubbling beneath the surface right across Spain since the start of the decade. Tension. Civil unrest. A struggle for the heart and soul of Spain. Made all the worse by an international politics of extremism. The growth of fascism in Germany and Italy whispered to the Spanish masses that the ruling class would never give up its power without a fight. The victory of communism in Russia murmured in the ears of the ruling class that the workers would rise up if not kept down. A tug of war was being played out where right and left struggled for supremacy. Up until now an equilibrium of sorts had been maintained. Up until now Don Felipe had had to allow his workers to form unions, had had no choice but to approve of liberal absurdities such as reading programmes. But all that was about to change. Bullets were about to overcome ballot boxes and the landowner couldn't wait. It was the reason for his return.

'You'll have to talk to her dear,' his wife said.

'I know,' Don Felipe replied, picking up the pamphlet that Guido had handed to him the previous evening. 'I don't care if she is the doctor's daughter!'

'Oh, I'm not talking about the girl, silly!' said Dona Sofía, who, contrary to her show of interest, had little time for some child who wanted to play teacher to the workers. 'No. I'm talking about Cecilia. It's her arms. Did you not see them yesterday? They're hideous. The lower classes have no sense of shame or modesty,' she said, breathing heavily. She put down her magazine full of beautifully dressed young women and put a hand to her well-coiffed curls checking they were still in place. One had dropped. She closed her eyes and asked for strength. The ceiling fans simply moved hot air around and she couldn't stand keeping the shutters closed. The heat combined with the sight of her housekeeper's indecent arms was making Dona Sofía irritable, as was her husband's inability to grasp what was truly important. And now her hair was losing its shape. It was really too, too much.

'Cecilia!' Don Felipe called. The housekeeper rushed in, her fleshy arms wrapped round a heavy pile of freshly ironed sheets. 'Why are you doing that?' Dona Sofía asked. 'Put them away, then come back,' she tutted.

When Cecilia came back in she rubbed her arms repeatedly with worry. She'd been worried about Manuel all night. What if Guido had given him away?

'Cecilia, dear,' Dona Sofía said, a fixed smile nailed to her face. 'We have something to say to you.'

'I'm sorry,' Cecilia said, waiting for judgement. If only Luis was here. He had always been able to curb the worst of his parents' excesses. 'I promise that I will work hard to make amends.' Cecilia wasn't past begging to keep her son in employment.

50

'Well, we do expect to be having some very important guests staying with us in the not too distant future,' Dona Sofía replied, frankly surprised at her housekeeper's eagerness to accept responsibility and expressing regret at having let herself go. 'And so your diligence and commitment will be much appreciated. Behind the scenes.'

Relief flooded Cecilia's body from head to toe that Manuel's name still hadn't been mentioned but Dona Sofía's lipstick-coloured lips still moved up and down with unstoppable purpose.

'I don't want you serving... Best we keep you in the kitchen.' She then nodded over to her husband. He coughed three times. 'Yes. Play to your strengths,' he said. 'Cooking, cleaning, stuff like that.' His wife pushed him on with her eyes and touched her upper arm, 'Yes,' he continued. 'And we'd like you to wear sleeves from now on, old girl. More decent on a woman of your age, don't you think?' And with that he turned round and went to look for Guido. It was time to get to the bottom of that unpleasant reading nonsense.

Dona Sofía gave the *old girl*, who was five years younger than herself, her most beneficent smile, full of pity. She lowered her eyelids in imitation of the Virgin Mary in her favourite painting by Filippo Lippi, *Madonna and Child with Two Angels* that she'd seen in Florence.

'How's Manuel?'

Dona Sofía clutched a letter to her chest not really caring to know about her housekeeper's son one way or the other but the question put the fear of God in poor Cecilia. She needn't have worried. Her employer's interest in Manuel was the same as it had ever been – a flimsy pretext for talking about her own sweet boy, Luis. And he was a sweet boy.

'He'll be back soon. He has a fine mind. Reads philosophy... and the finest novels – in English, of course.'

That her employer boasted, Cecilia found tedious, but she was grateful for the opportunity to remember the child she'd loved so well. When he'd been first sent away to school he'd been so young. Such a gentle child. His parents weren't the only people to miss him when he'd gone.

Luis and Manuel were the same age, possessed the same generous natures. Manuel was the only one of Cecilia's children that had ever been allowed on the estate. Dona Sofía had even allowed a friendship to blossom between the boys. They'd been inseparable.

Until they'd been forcibly torn apart.

Don Felipe's gift of a ball to Luis had seen to that. The boy had kicked it around the house, breaking a porcelain ornament. As it had fallen to the floor it had shattered into a thousand pieces, one of which had lodged in Manuel's left cheek. Luis had called for his mother, called for Cecilia. Both women had come running to find him cradling his injured friend in his arms.

There was to be no friendship after that. 'Luis knows better than to kick a ball around the house. He knows the value of things, whereas that half-wit of a boy Manuel has no more respect for civilised living than a wild animal,' Dona Sofía had cried.

'But Mama. It was me. It was my fault. All my fault,' her son had told her bravely. 'Can I see Manu? See if he's all right?'

But it was no use. No matter how many times he had reasoned with his mother there was to be no shifting Dona Sofía from her position. It was all Manuel's fault. She blamed him for everything. And when Luis had run to the village, determined to see how his dear friend was getting on, Dona Sofía had blamed Manuel some more. Dona Sofía had always managed to keep her son away from Fuentes de Andalucía and its inhabitants until then.

That Cecilia wasn't dismissed there and then was a miracle. A miracle brought about by Luis. He'd pleaded with his mother on Cecilia's behalf and she had given in. But she was determined not to do so again.

Four months after the ball incident Luis was sent away to school. Dona Sofía wouldn't have him going to the village again.

The child was ten.

Poor Dona Sofía. What had she done? She'd waited for a child for such a long time, had feared she might never be able to find one. And then she'd sent him away.

Of course, his mother missed him terribly when he'd gone. And she would pour out her heart to Cecilia whenever she could to shout about the fact. And Cecilia wouldn't – couldn't – condemn her for that. But Luis was homesick. And Dona Sofía's eyes were forever red and sore, her nose constantly streaming. 'What should I do?' the wealthy landowner's wife asked her penniless housekeeper. An observer would have thought Dona Sofía regarded Cecilia as a friend. Cecilia made the fatal mistake of thinking so too. As one mother to another. Cecilia dared to give Dona Sofía her most truthful counsel.

Oh, the insolence.

Cecilia had very nearly lost her job that day. 'How dare you Cecilia! We're providing that boy with a first-class education. But then, I wouldn't expect you to understand.' The housekeeper had put her fingers to her hot cheek, her employer's red hand print upon it. She had momentarily forgotten her place. She wouldn't do so again. It was clear that to Dona Sofía, Cecilia was no more sentient than a wooden sculpture that she'd had fashioned to her pleasing.

And so now, though happy to hear that Luis was coming home, Cecilia kept her excitement well and truly to herself.

CHAPTER 8

Maria looked at the page in front of her; apart from the title, *Cumbres Borrascosas*, the only marks on it were the rings left by the numerous cups of water she'd had and the ink that had splashed as she'd thrown down her pen. *Cumbres Borrascosas*. Even that wasn't original. She'd taken it from the English classic, *Wuthering Heights*. She looked through her window, exasperated. As she watched the heat vibrate over the expanse of countryside beyond the village, inspiration hit her with its golden arrow. She picked up her pen. Crossed out her first attempt. Replaced it with *Campos Sofocantes*. There. *Sweltering Fields*. Much better. Now she could start to write her epic story of love between wonderful strangers from different lands, where the heroine was from Spain and the hero from England. She put pen to paper once more and wrote '*based on a true story*'. She was on fire.

But something had changed, after the picnic. Maria, for all her knowledge of the secrets of the human heart, was the only one who didn't realise it. Blinded by her own importance she still believed that Richard loved her, and that she loved him, despite her body repeatedly telling her to the contrary – though it had been thankfully quieter of late. Perhaps due to the fact that he wasn't coming round as frequently as he once had. Not that she minded. In some ways she preferred it. His absence as ever gave her the space to preserve his image, perpetuate the myth that she loved him.

In truth, before the picnic his constant attention and desire to please her had been vaguely irritating. He'd once brushed her fingers with his which she'd found deeply disturbing. And not in a good way. She hadn't been able to look at him without feeling nauseous for days. She'd convinced herself then that this was because she was lovesick.

But one Tuesday morning, as she anticipated Richard's visit, she questioned the heavy feeling in her heart. Tuesday was the day when her father would check on the English boy's health as arranged, and this Tuesday Maria had started to feel anxious about his impending visit the moment her bare feet touched the wooden floor as she got out of bed. She busied herself in the kitchen, peeling the vegetables and getting everything ready for the evening meal. She'd not seen Richard since the Wednesday before; Señor Suarez had taken him to Seville. She told herself she was looking forward to seeing him, hearing all about his trip, what he'd seen, what he'd eaten, who he'd met. She played at being in love again. But as she set about getting everything ready in the kitchen and as the hour of his arrival approached she could not stop herself from shaking with fear.

This wasn't love.

She'd gone out to meet Paloma earlier in the day. They'd sat under their olive tree, played their game. But Paloma too had been preoccupied. The heavens were raining down upon her mother up on the estate, thanks to Don Felipe and Dona Sofía, and something had happened to Lola which she didn't want to talk about. The future, Maria could see, was not looking bright for Paloma. But her own had also lost its lustre. The thought that she might have to spend the rest of her life with Richard Johnson had turned her winged sandals to stone filled boots. The girls brooded, too ill at ease to let limbs interlace and hopes soar.

They said goodbye and went home, both deep in thought. Dark clouds of their own making were gathering on the horizon for both of them. Little did they realise that these would soon seem as refreshing as summer rain when the real storm broke out.

CHAPTER 9

On 17th July 1936 Spanish soldiers rose up against their own government in North Africa and mainland Spain. The pools of unrest that had been bubbling away under the surface of the country were starting to erupt. Ordinary working men and women gathered around radios in neighbours' houses and listened for news. Señor Suarez and Doctor Alvaro poured over newspapers and relayed their contents to the villagers. Father Anselmo prayed for peace. The mayor called an emergency meeting, then another one, followed by another one. Richard Johnson sent a telegram home. Uprisings were stopped in one part of Spain, re-started in another. These were the stutterings of war. The nation watched and waited, hearts in mouths.

By the 19th and 20th of July the rebellion had been defeated in Madrid and Barcelona. 'Stopped two days after it started. That means that there will be no war,' Doctor Alvaro assured his daughter, although the meetings that were being held in the village hall signified the opposite. The military uprising, no matter how many assurances Doctor Alvaro gave his daughter, had begun, and though held at bay in key cities, it was sweeping its bloody way up from the south.

For weeks, rumours seeped on ahead, wraith-like. They rustled

57

through the olive groves at first, too remote and far-fetched to be believed. But as the soldiers got closer so the rumours threw up dust on stony roads, stamped their way down streets and round corners, eventually making their way up the stairs and into the study of Doctor Alvaro.

Soldiers, Spanish soldiers, were on their way. They were marching into Spanish towns and Spanish villages, shooting Spanish men, Spanish women and Spanish children.

The stories were too preposterous to be believed.

The doctor was in shock. Reason told him this shouldn't be happening – *couldn't* be happening. Yet slowly, forced to dredge through the deepest, darkest recesses of his mind, he had to accept that what he was hearing was true. It was a madness, no doubt. He hoped his country would be cured of it soon.

Outside in their village nothing had changed. The sky was still blue. The sun still scorched the fields. The English boy's skin was still red. Maria still talked to her friend Paloma under the olive tree, for the moment. When the world looked the same today as it did yesterday it was hard to imagine it otherwise. But civil war was marching its way inexorably towards them. Doctor Alvaro knew that it would leave nothing, and no one, unscathed.

Though not everyone feared its arrival.

'At last! Thank heavens!'

The morning after the rebel forces rose up in Madrid the newspapers were full of it. This was what Don Felipe had been waiting for, ever since his return to the estate. The coup. At last the boil that to him was Republican Spain was about to be lanced. Left-leaning, liberal, lax, it had threatened to destroy everything he and his wife held dear, to rob them of their God-given power and wealth. Not any longer. An atmosphere of breezy excitement permeated every room of the house, even in the stultifying heat of the summer.

Don Felipe attended the emergency meetings in the village to calm proceedings and offer himself up as the voice of reason. The rebellion was coming. And it would save them. Spain would soon be great again. And his farm, no longer prey to the evils of land reform, nor held captive to the destructive demands of workers, would return to its former glory. In a world where everyone knew their place there would be work for everyone.

'We really must decide on the guests for *the dinner*,' Dona Sofía said to her husband when he returned from the latest village meeting. Don Felipe entered the living room, waving his hand dismissively.

'There's a change in the air already,' he started. He was in no mood for discussing social plans now. It might be guests his wife started with but then she would go on to the menu, the table, the dress… No. He'd felt a growing respect directed at him at the meeting today and he had no desire to dilute the pride this instilled within his breast with a discussion about chiffon or crêpe de chine, chicken or rabbit. He looked anywhere but at his wife so as to avoid the look of utter disappointment that he knew to be on her face.

'We're on the brink of greatness again. I feel it,' he said, determined not to give in to his wife by answering her. 'Order is returning, I can taste it. With each meeting at the town hall there are fewer dissenting voices. As for the ones that persist, they aren't as excitable as they used to be.'

'It's done. Luis has enlisted in the rebel army,' Dona Sofía said with quiet acceptance. 'Funny how our side is called *rebel*,' she sighed. 'I always think of those terrible communists in Russia with their frightful revolution whenever I hear the word. Can't we be called something else? I find it such a disturbing, ugly word.' And with that, having given up on getting her husband to engage in dinner party planning, she handed Luis' letter over to him to read.

She'd been expecting news of her son's entrance into the army for days, and although she told herself she was delighted about it, there was something in her that urged caution.

'I've also had word from my father's friend, Captain Garcia, that he will be in charge of the regiment – Luis' regiment – when they come to Fuentes.' Dona Sofía held out another letter. She attempted to squeeze out a broad smile but could manage only subdued pride.

'The... the... the... It will turn out well, won't it, Felipe?' she asked, unable to bring herself to say the word. War. She'd wanted it to come. Dreamt Luis would sign up for it. But now that he had... flames of truth licked around Dona Sofía's icy heart causing a stammer of doubt to creep into her voice.

'Luis. A soldier. Why, that's excellent news darling,' her husband boomed with confidence. He allowed his eyes to meet hers for the first time since entering the room. 'Of course everything with be all right,' he thundered with blind belief. 'Spain will be for the Spanish once more. The Russians have been pulling the government's strings for far too long. The Republic will be crushed at last. '

'Will it be so very dangerous?' his wife asked, still perturbed. 'The w-w-war?'

'No,' he roared. 'But it will be glorious. Glorious, I tell you Sofía. We will win the war and crush the rats, snakes and spineless creatures that have tried to ruin this great homeland of ours with their Marxist ways.'

Dona Sofía felt a fingernail drag itself lightly down her back. War. Its meaning exploded within her mind. 'Will it be dangerous?' she asked again, suddenly afraid what war might mean for her son.

'No, my love. It will be over before it's begun,' Don Felipe said. His brow furrowed, vaguely irritated by his wife's momentary lack of enthusiasm: not least because it threatened to cast a shadow over his own optimism. 'Now,' he said, 'I suggest you draw up a list of the people you want to come to dinner when Captain Garcia is here.'

'Oh, that reminds me,' she said as an afterthought. 'The Captain says that he wants you to draw up a list of troublemakers. Standard procedure. He wants to make sure that once secured, he leaves our village in good hands, disarms the bad. But, apparently, you know about this already.'

CHAPTER 10

Summer in southern Spain, always hot, usually calm, often sleepy, turned into a screaming hell as rebel soldiers scourged it with their fire and brimstone rain. The region was hit hard, leaving troughs of devastation so deep that rivers of agony trailed in their wake. This too was standard procedure. The earth and people were scorched to ensure that once regained by the rebels the country would never fall back into left-wing hands. For every rebel killed, ten from the opposing side would be destroyed. And that was a promise.

Yet before this hell was let loose upon Fuentes a strange calm descended upon the village and its inhabitants. Many found it unsettling, oppressive. While for the owners of Cortijo del Bosque it heralded a return to the proper order of things, their workers were quiet. Some called it cowed. Little matter the word used to describe it. The point was that this was how Don Felipe (and Dona Sofía, in spite of her occasional pangs of conscience) liked it. Troops – 'our troops' – were bringing with them a new future that, not just Felipe and Sofía, but landowners all over Spain believed would be the heroic restoration of a golden past. All talk of reading and rights would soon evaporate, becoming nothing more substantial than a quivering mirage in the heat of the day.

61

As for Dona Sofía's pain triggered by concerns for her son, that too would be rendered equally insubstantial once replaced by the excitement elicited by the planning and preparation required for their 'very special' dinner party.

'I really do believe that no guest will have been to a dinner as truly splendid as the one we're having, Felipe!' Dona Sofía beamed as she clapped her hands together and brought her index fingers to rest on her chin.

Her husband nodded as he read an article about Britain and France and their policy of non-intervention in the war. Now here was something to celebrate. 'Splendid! Truly splendid!' he mumbled in his wife's direction.

Dona Sofía paced the room with anticipation and beamed with delight, clapping her hands some more.

'There will be twelve at table. You, me, and – of course – darling Luis, then there will be the Captain, and…' She paused, unable to think of another soul, despite having drawn up a list the day before, and the day before that… 'You've been to all the planning meetings in the village Felipe, who else deserves an invitation? You decide,' she said to her husband.

Yet while the landowners were in a celebratory mood, back in his house in the heart of the village, Doctor Alvaro was entering a state of mourning. He'd not slept at all the night before.

Not long after the rebellion had broken out, a little-known rebel general had taken to broadcasting daily updates on the progress of the army and Doctor Alvaro had taken to listening to them. Every evening he would sit next to his radio and guffaw at the colourful language, ludicrous claims and comic timing of this bombastic fool.

Queipo de Llano was the name of this trumped up little man, prone to lavish exaggeration, who had entertained the doctor so well. Until reports started reaching him from neighbouring towns and villages confirming that the General's gruesome stories were true. It was true that working men were being killed for being part of a union, it was true that to have voted Republican was enough to make you a criminal, it was true that having an uncle who had a son who had a friend who had once spoken to a Republican was also a crime. The doctor shuddered at the loss of reason. The world, his world, hadn't always been like this. He scratched his head. Was it his age that was making him see things this way? Had life always been this absurd? He didn't believe so.

And last night he knew so when he tuned into the radio to listen to Queipo de Llano once more. Doctor Alvaro was not the one losing his moral sense. As he sat, crouched as if in pain, next to his transistor, he flinched. For one obsessed with purity the General surpassed himself in defining sin. The General's little tales of appropriate punishments meted out to women struck the noble doctor repeatedly in the heart. Women seen talking to the 'enemy', women related to the 'enemy', Queipo de Llano shared his methods for converting them all. Shaved heads. Castor oil. And worse. Oh, how his soldiers would teach them a lesson they would never forget.

De Llano. Alvaro had thought him a caricature of a tyrant in an old melodrama, had found his radio broadcasts hugely entertaining, full of bombast and boasting. Until the doctor found out that all that the General threatened he meant.

Which was why, that night, Doctor Alvaro could not sleep. Every time he closed his eyes nightmarish images of punished women appeared to him, and every time they turned to look at him they had his daughter's face.

The doctor got up, crept quietly to her room and looked at her in the darkness, fast asleep on her bed. She was curled up, her knees tight to her chest, her hands held together as in prayer. He moved closer to her, and the paternal feelings of love and protection became so strong as to cause a strain in his chest. Maria. His daughter. So perfect, so young. Life still hadn't furrowed her brow. He thought of a time when age would wither this most vibrant of flowers. But the idea didn't sadden him. He, more than most, knew how a body grows old. There were many trials worse than age, he said to himself. His only hope, as he looked at her at peace in an untroubled sleep, was that he would be able to help her navigate the troubles ahead.

She had health and youth on her side. He had experience.

He went back to his own bed and looked up at the ceiling, wide awake. Her affection for Señor Suarez, her involvement with the reading programme, that she was his daughter (if his politics came out) – these were things that would all go against her, he feared, if the rebels came into their village and continued to 'cleanse' southern Spain.

But she was a child. Surely only the most inhuman of judges would condemn her well-intentioned misdemeanours. And as village doctor, Alvaro hoped that the care he'd shown the inhabitants of Fuentes without exception would be taken into account and sway even the most ardent of rebel supporters in his family's favour. As he stared into the blackness he reminded himself that he would have to be more vigilant than ever to not ruffle any feathers from this moment on. And anything he did to help so-called enemies of the true Spain would have to be done in secret.

His heart hurt again as he thought of his daughter. Because she had no mother he'd allowed her to grow untethered. She was independent of spirit, unpredictable, outspoken. A wild bloom that knew no bounds. But now he needed her to curb her tongue, rein in her opinions. To persuade her to act with caution would prove difficult, he knew. And he blamed himself for this. He tossed and turned, thinking of ways to contain her.

By the time the sun crept under the shutters the poor man was exhausted. The doctor had wrestled with his conscience for hours over what to do for the best. He got up, pulled his clothes on and let out a sigh. The doctor had wanted to protect his daughter from the horrors of life. But it was no use – de Llano's little radio chats had told him in the most lurid of terms what was coming to the village. He pulled open the shutters to let the light flood in. He'd made a decision.

It was late afternoon by the time Doctor Alvaro told her that he wanted her to listen to something on the radio.

In truth Maria was excited about the war. Life in a village could be dull, uneventful. Richard Johnson had stirred things up for a while, made her think of love – but not for long. Besides, he would be leaving soon.

And so the idea that battles would be fought, wrongs righted, roused her. Workers of Spain would rise up, united, as they'd done in Russia. That was what she believed. War was coming and it would be good.

Richard Johnson, too, felt the blood pump passionately through his veins at the thought of armies marching towards Fuentes. He had spent a happy time here but that it might soon buzz and crackle into life of a different sort thrilled him. He'd come to Spain hoping to see the strikes and demonstrations he'd read about in the newspapers back in England. But these were happening in the big cities and his parents had had other plans for him. And so now he considered himself fortunate indeed to have war come to the quiet village they'd chosen for him. A war was on its way. He prayed it would arrive soon, before he'd left.

There was a knock on the door. The doctor had asked Richard round: he wanted the boy to hear the broadcast too.

'Come, children.' Maria winced and let out a tut while Richard pulled his shoulders back. He opened the heavy wooden door to his study, a grave smile on his face, and ushered them inside, aware of their displeasure and wishing that this could be the only unpleasant blow he was called upon to dish out to the pair.

'Please, sit,' he said, careful not to repeat the offence. His daughter smiled at her friend. Her shrug told him she had no idea what was going on. It struck her father how firm and strong the two young people were as they followed him in, whereas the certain knowledge of the disturbing nature of what they were about to hear aged Alvaro beyond his already advanced years. His back appeared rounded, head collapsed forward, legs buckled. 'It's nearly time,' he said.

Richard and Maria arranged themselves on the floor in front of a large wooden cabinet that was home to a transistor radio with shiny knobs. It was clear that some radio address was about to start. Maria's hand span out on the floor, her head giddy with the thrill of expectation at what she was about to listen to. Richard fidgeted as he tried to get comfortable.

Doctor Alvaro crouched over the cabinet and twiddled with the radio knobs, catching then losing tunes and foreign voices. 'The reception is not good,' Maria complained as she wound her arms in and placed her hands together in her lap. Eventually the voice her father was looking for crackled into life, freed from the soaring, discordant sounds either side of the wavelength. 'Russian interference,' he said jokingly. Maria and Richard laughed. Neither of them had any idea that it would be a long time before they laughed again.

Alvaro took a last fleeting look at them. There sat Richard, cross-legged in front of the radio, his hair sticking up from his head in tufts, his colour high, face eager. Alvaro noticed for the first time that the boy was attempting to cultivate some sort of beard on his chin but it only made him seem younger, so unnatural did it look. And there sat his daughter, legs folded to her left, hair braided to the side, her expression serious. Alvaro ached to protect them. But they had to know. He braced himself for the attack on their innocence they were about to receive. He smiled at Maria, gave her a knowing nod. She smiled back, behind her eyes a look that said *I'm ready* although she had no idea for what.

Maria's father waited, head in hands.

Maria and Richard glanced at each other. Their excitement tinged with the first signs of fear.

66

Then the great General began. He spoke of 'my triumph, my heroism'. He was not just a man, he was 'an emissary sent by God to save Seville… to save Spain… to save Western civilisation.'

Maria sniggered. Richard arched his eyebrows.

'Pacification' was coming their way, the shrill voice promised over the radio waves, and, he assured them it would be 'brutal.'

Maria's father pushed his fingers against his skull, a need to reach into his own mind and stop this madman with a microphone from sullying everything good within but the excited, angry little voice continued. It threw up fervour, passion, bloodlust. Talked of God and country. Threatened punishment. Promised annihilation.

The harsh voice blasted out of the radio and shrieked in their ears.

Maria shivered. Richard felt a chill. Alvaro got up, unable to bear it. He turned the radio off.

'Can't we hear the rest?' she asked, strangely drawn into the darkness of de Llano's vile world. Richard nodded to show that he too needed to listen. Alvaro turned the radio back on and walked out. He'd heard enough over the past days and no longer had the stomach for tales of squealing Red women with kicking legs. He didn't want his daughter to know about them either. But war was always evil, ugly. And she had a right to know how evil and ugly it was becoming.

The young pair sat and listened. When the broadcast had finished neither of them said a word, did not even exchange a glance because they could not bear to look at one another. Maria's body had lost its youthful, hopeful tingle of only minutes before; Richard felt sickened at the memory of his. De Llano had banished them from paradise.

The English boy got up and left the house. It was perfectly understandable that he should go out and get some air.

CHAPTER 11

Doctor Alvaro was apprehensive about the impending arrival of the army to their village, now more than ever. He knew a peaceful takeover had been agreed upon by the leading councillors, that there shouldn't be any trouble. God knew he'd attended enough meetings, made his voice heard. The mayor would surrender, there would be no violence. People who had done nothing wrong would have nothing to fear. But his contacts from elsewhere in the area thought otherwise. They'd heard the rumours. Of looting, rape, murder, even when villages had gone for peace. And then there were the broadcasts made by the Commander of the South, like the one his daughter and Richard Johnson had not long listened to, where there was more talk of the same.

But, he told himself, they were only rumours in some cases, dangerous boasts in others. These atrocities were surely only carried out in areas where the army had met with resistance. Reason told him this was so. He would not give in to the fever. And Fuentes would show no resistance. They couldn't. There were a few old hunting rifles to pass round, and an assortment of farming tools. That was all. The village was not equipped to defend itself in any meaningful way. The sooner the Rebels, Nationalists, or whatever they wanted to call themselves, took over, the sooner the war would come to an end. It was the will of the people. That imbecile de Llano had said as much.

But de Llano was a liar. The republican-turned-excellency of the southern territories did not have a reputation for trustworthiness. And so Alvaro – and the rest of the village along with him – watched and waited as the army drew ever closer. They could almost smell the sweat and boot polish, hear the sounds of crackling guns across rivers, on the other sides of mountains, over plains. And it was making everyone go slightly mad.

As for Maria, the shrill voice of de Llano still echoed around the dark recesses of her mind. Around the house she appeared dejected, fearful. Her father didn't like that he'd disturbed her so but it was timely, necessary. She needed to not draw attention to herself in these most sensitive of times and that the broadcast had subdued her could only be to the good.

Especially when she encountered citizens such as Señora Gonzalez.

Señora Gonzalez was married to a businessman of small stature but great wealth. And, as always with those in possession of a great amount of money but very little brain, she believed this gave her the right to make judgements and spread gossip. She had airs. Maria did not like her and made her feelings very apparent, as a rule. And the feelings were fully reciprocated. But where the young woman was mocking so the older woman was vindictive. She bore a grudge and everyone knew about her *little black book* where she recorded the names and offences of all the people who had ever crossed her. It was said that to be caught looking at Señora Gonzalez in a strange way was enough to warrant an entry. Before the uprising this would have been seen as a badge of honour by many. But given that her husband was a leading light in the local Falange party, it didn't do to cross her now. The Falangists were for hierarchy, authority and order; they backed Franco and his generals, the very men responsible for the war that was now eating its way through the country. The

Falangists fully supported the rebel invasion no matter the loss of lives. Communism, democracy and liberalism were the enemy.

Like Richard Johnson, Maria had needed some air. She was out in the street and she really couldn't care less if she upset Señora Gonzalez or not. She'd heard the radio broadcast only two hours before and her mind was still plagued by nightmarish images. She needed to see Paloma, if only to make sure her friend was all right.

'Maria!' The woman's cry was attacking, in anticipation of the confrontation to ensue. But no confrontation came. Before she could stop herself Maria had said 'Good morning, Señora Gonzalez,' her voice quiet, expression distant. The older woman, mistaking the girl's tone for deference and her glazed expression for respect, stopped and made a note of it. Quite literally. She took out her notebook and pencil from her bag and wrote down 'Maria', adding a tick next to the name. 'Good morning to you too Maria, my dear.' Her father would have been proud of her. Maria watched Señora Gonzalez scuttle away, beetle-like, away from view, then turned and carried on in the direction of Paloma's.

As she got closer to her friend's home, Maria crashed into a flustered Cecilia. The collision brought her to herself. Her friend's mother was pushing a pram piled high with crockery, glasses and necklaces Maria knew she'd never worn. Neighbours from either side ran after her, like ageing bridesmaids their arms full of beads and bowls. 'Good morning,' Maria shouted after them as the dimple-armed women ran, hobbled and limped out of sight heading out of the village, weighed down by all their worldly goods. If their intention had been to be discreet Maria didn't think they'd managed it.

'I saw your mother and her friends.' Maria was at Paloma's house. As she followed her into the kitchen, her young friend swept her arm up towards the empty shelf on the wall, a magician showing her latest trick. 'She's taken all the cups and although we didn't have many glasses she's taken those too. To hide. In a

70

field. Or somewhere. She's been acting odd, odder than usual, like a cat before an earthquake. But it was only after Richard left not long ago that she started piling everything into the pram.'

'Richard?' Maria asked, surprised. 'My Richard?'

Paloma reddened, realising what she had said. 'Unless you know another,' she answered, hoping directness would disarm Maria and that would be the end of it.

'What is it to do with him?' Maria asked. 'What was he doing at your house?'

'He was… He wasn't…' Paloma paused, momentarily flustered. 'He told Lola that when the soldiers came there would be looting.' Her eyes sought out the floor as she spoke her sister's name. 'And Lola went and told Mama.'

So Richard had come to warn Lola just as Maria herself was here to warn Paloma now.

'Mama almost took this too,' Paloma said, taking something from her pocket and showing it to her friend. 'Remember?' she asked her. As Maria looked at what her friend held in her hand, she smiled broadly. It was the enamel sunflower pendant she herself had given to Paloma for her birthday when she was four-teen back in November. 'But it's yours, Paloma. I gave it to you,' she said. 'I know,' her friend replied, 'and it's very precious to me. I rub it you know, and it brings me luck.' She smiled. 'But if you don't look after it for me she'll find it and bury it too. You know how fixed she can be.' It was true, Cecilia was as stubborn as the proverbial mule.

Maria held out her hand, slipped the pendant into her own pocket and leant over to kiss Paloma on the cheek. 'Who knows, it might bring me some luck too.'

'Oh! It's you!' The moment of peace was shattered by a disgrun-tled Lola. She made a striking entrance, walking elegantly into the kitchen, a hand running through her hair. She stopped, placed her hands on her hips and thrust out her chest, then walked back out again. The gesture was aggressive. There was no mistaking it.

'Hello Lola,' Maria called after her. 'Goodbye,' came the reply. It was spoken in English.

Maria shot Paloma a quizzical glance. Her friend shrugged shiftily, looked once more at the floor.

'Mother is looking after her valuables,' Lola shouted back down the stairs. 'You'd better take care and look after what's yours too, Maria Alvaro. Before it's not yours anymore.' And then she slammed a bedroom door.

CHAPTER 12

Doctor Alvaro listened. Rebel soldiers had reached Cordoba, then Baena. They were getting closer all the time. The business of healing the sick picked up apace. The doctor found himself so in demand, preparing a linctus here, applying an ointment there and generally soothing foreheads hot with the worry, that Maria rarely saw him. And when she did his mood was downcast. 'They're coming. They'll be here any day now, the Rebels,' he said to her, his voice a violin string pulled too tight.

And that night, as the doctor lay in his bed and Maria lay in hers, they, along with every other person in the village, went rigid, their eyes wide open, their hearts pounding, as they heard the rumble of war reverberating in the night sky. It was getting nearer and nearer. They lay awake, paralysed. Not one of them could do a thing to stop it.

At six o'clock the next morning on the 24th July 1936 Doctor Alvaro got up to answer two urgent knocks at the door. When he pulled it open he was presented with a choice.

'Xavi,' he said in sombre greeting as he looked the mayor's man in the eye. Xavi was big, broad and weather-beaten and his enormous girth filled the door frame. 'I've been expecting you. So it's time,' he said. 'Indeed it is Doctor,' Xavi replied.

73

Alvaro went to fetch his hat in readiness to join the other citizens chosen to welcome their military saviours not far now from the village boundaries. As he stepped back towards the door he heard a quiet sniffling sound. It was coming from the other side of the mayor's messenger. Xavi moved aside to reveal a little boy with sticky up hair, and a face and top lip that, if Doctor Alvaro didn't know any better, he would have sworn a snail had slid over. 'It's Papa,' the frightened child said, his voice small and tremulous. 'Something's happened to him in the night. He can't move.'

'Something's happened to us all,' said the doctor with a wave to Xavi to go on without him. He reached out to pick up his bag. He'd made his choice. He could always join the 'welcome party' (his eyes rolled involuntarily at the thought of it) afterwards. He went to check on Maria. She pulled her eyes from the ceiling to look at him.

'Do not leave this house,' he ordered. 'I will be back soon.' He squeezed her hand, pain in his eyes, then was off, running to keep up with the little boy with the mucus-covered face and tear-filled eyes. 'Be careful,' Maria whispered after him, putting a hand out to touch Paloma's pendant that she'd placed on her bedside table. She rubbed it for luck. 'Be careful,' she said again, her eyes now back on the ceiling.

The war, the war she'd longed for, was waiting at the gates, about to march into her life. A sudden feeling of nausea overwhelmed her. She ran to the washstand.

Two hours later, tyres – of cars, trucks and motorbikes - - threw up clouds of yellow, gritty dust as the military cavalcade the entire village had been anticipating all night drove into Fuentes.

Maria still hadn't made it out of bed preferring to read *Don Quixote* in the hope that she might be able to sleep through it all. But the friction sounds of heavy wheels braking on stony ground shook her wide awake, defeating even her most trusty soporific.

Her mind flooded with so many thoughts it felt as though she was drowning.

Where's Papa? They won't invade us. Where's Papa? They won't hurt us. Where's Papa? We're Spanish too. But the stories of what they'd done in other villages flooded her mind still further… *Don't worry, don't worry, don't worry. We will be all right. Even de Llano on the radio said we'd be all right.* Her mind fluttered around wildly, desperately searching for good news. *Richard. He's safe. Safe now. The mayor has a letter and a white flag. Father says he has several, ready.* Stay inside, her father had told her. *I must stay inside. I'll be safe. Where's Papa?*

Two streets away the doctor had managed to revive his patient paralysed by fear. That the man was called Lazaro made Alvaro chuckle. But not for long, as no sooner had his patient revived than the doctor himself had been struck down.

Fear. It started in the walls. Caused shelves to rattle. Crockery to shake. The sound of invasion, mechanical, relentless, that had run through the village like electricity all night had finally reached out and connected a wire to him.

His mind lit up like a lightbulb. What should he do? Run home to his daughter? Make his way to the 'welcome party'? His thoughts buzzed like red hot filaments, crackling in the air. They rooted him to the spot. But he had to fight the paralysis, heal himself.

He stumbled outside, made his way in the direction of home. Light and the noise and the sight of the men in uniform and cars still rolling in overwhelmed him. He lurched on. Soldiers were filling the street up ahead. He'd never seen such a throng of people.

Wait, wait. He made his way to a workshop. Hid inside. He peered through a closed wooden shutter at the military circus unfolding beyond. He and nearly every other citizen of Fuentes, in every house, shop and workshop, looked on with bated breath, waiting. Waiting for the moment when the mayor would hand over the letter of complete capitulation, wave the white flag.

More brakes screeched. More tyres spun up dust and stones. Doors opened. A slender man wearing a neat uniform with buttons that glinted in the sun, his boots polished to a black mirror, got out of a black car. Whether a captain, commandant or general, Alvaro could not tell.

The doctor watched, his breath shallow, as the mayor proffered a weathered, fleshy, sweaty hand, in it the letter that would save the village, to the man in the unnaturally shiny boots. Alvaro had helped to pen that letter. Long, pale fingers took it.

Houses sighed.

Doctor Alvaro fell back against the wall. His hand searched round desperately in his bag for something to hold on to, take the edge off the anxiety that he was feeling. Maria. She was alone. But she would be fine. He'd told her to stay inside. And the mayor had handed over the letter, waved the white flag. This moment of uncertainty would soon pass.

His hands stumbled on an old packet of cigarettes. It must have been at the bottom of his bag for years. He didn't care. He put one in his mouth and lit up. Its smoke curled round the edge of the shutter, disappeared into the already throbbing heat of the day. Nicotine-coated relief filled his lungs. It tasted good. For now.

He turned to look outside, fearful, fascinated, confused. Still more soldiers jumped down from trucks, kitbags slung over one shoulder, rifles over the other. They flooded the streets in waves. Some were laughing, others leaning against walls and smoking too. Men of all colours, shapes and sizes. The doctor's eyes flickered at the sight of three Moors. The lascivious tones of General Queipo de Llano sounded in his ear like an annoying fly, conjuring up scenes of brutality that played out in his head. Doctor Alvaro blinked them away. If the Moors were guilty of the crimes he'd heard of, he told himself as he looked at the huge number of Spanish in uniform all around them, they were not alone. The glint of a rifle blinded him momentarily. He rubbed his eyes. By the time he looked back up boys had appeared in his field of vision. Little boys. Very little boys.

There, leant up against the whitewashed wall on the other side of the street, watching the troops as they walked by in their heavy dusty boots, were the Redondo brothers. All three of them. Salva, Lolo and Ignacio. The oldest, Salva, couldn't be any older than ten.

Stories of slaughtered children entered Alvaro's mind. He had to get them off the street.

He threw open the shutters. 'Kids! Kids!' he shouted above the pounding of military boots on bone dry earth. 'Quick. Over here!' The children could not hear him. Passing soldiers could. Their eyes wandered towards him then moved on again. Alvaro would have to go and fetch the children.

He tried to step outside. Rifles were pointed, rough hands shoved him back in. It was impossible. He was not going to be able to swim across the tide of men blocking his path.

He scanned the windows on the other side of the street anxiously. He gesticulated to closed shutters, pointing to the children now crouching below, secure in the knowledge that peering eyes would be watching out.

But no one dared put a hand out to pull the annoying monkeys in off the street.

Alvaro thought he saw a shadowy face at an upstairs window but no sooner seen than it quickly withdrew from sight. The doctor looked back at the boys, his eyes casting a protective net around them.

But the boys were starting to look frightened. From the expression on his face it was clear that the youngest, Ignacio, was crying, although no one could hear him over the noise of boots and voices.

Alvaro had no choice but to go out again and drag them in.

His foot had not crossed the threshold before he was pushed back inside again with one forceful thrust to the chest. A soldier had spotted him. In less than a second another soldier, eager for action, lurched forwards, his face leering, mouth slobbering, his head on his countryman's shoulder, waiting for the word *attack*. But it didn't come. The same hand that had pushed Alvaro back inside shoved the bloodthirsty soldier back into the sea of men. He floated on by, his head bobbing up and down as waves of men carried him away into the distance.

Alvaro's heart pounded, the pulse in his temple thumped, his stomach clenched as the soldier who'd defended him now followed him in. Instinct told Alvaro this could be it. Reason assured him it wasn't.

'Lock the door when I leave. Open up when I knock,' the soldier commanded. Then he turned and left, slamming the door as he went. Alvaro's fingers fumbled at the lock with fear. Turning first one way, then, in response to the knock, turning the other.

Moments later the three boys were sprawled on the workroom floor yelping and climbing over each other like puppies. 'Keep the children safe, Señor', the soldier said, his voice deep, clear and young. 'You were brave boys,' he added, bending forwards to ruffle the hair of the youngest, Ignacio, still crying, 'but stay with your family, inside, while the army is here.' He growled at them. 'I don't want to catch you outside again!' Doctor Alvaro looked gratefully at their saviour, now silhouetted in the doorway, the sunlight radiating around him like a halo. There was something unusual about the young man's eyes though try as he might he couldn't make out what it was. And then he was gone, bobbing along with the rest of the men.

'Oh boys!' Alvaro the doctor scolded them. Alvaro the father comforted them. Poor, poor boys. 'You'll be safe at home soon,' he said. But for how long? he wondered.

CHAPTER 13

That people can adjust to change is testament to their will to survive – but embrace it too hastily and they can look like fools.

Within hours of arriving, a man with a black moustache and slicked back hair had stood up, flanked by the mayor (purple-faced with anxiety) on one side and Don Felipe (calm, confident and collected) on the other. He had proceeded to address the welcome party.

Life would carry on 'as normal', he decreed without a trace of irony. Labourers would still work the land, shops would be opened up as usual and he anticipated only a change for the better with the arrival of his troops. The true order of things would be restored and Spain would be great again. However, all guns and objects considered to be weapons would have to be handed in by the end of the day. He'd paused deliberately after this. Applause started half-heartedly. He cast his cold eyes over the assembled crowd. It ended rapturously. As he'd known it would.

He had then turned to the mayor standing to his left and given the now only pink-faced man a hearty slap on the back. He'd then turned to the right and held out his arms generously all the better to embrace a seigneurial Don Felipe.

A soldier had made his way from the back of the hall up to

a serene Dona Sofía, a large bouquet of flowers filling his arms. He'd bowed with the greatest of deference, presenting them to her as to a queen. She'd lowered her eyes in gratitude in front of the hand-picked crowd, the Lippi Madonna still in her mind. The restoration of the true order had begun.

News of the address spread quickly enough. It did not matter that the doctor had been unable to get there in time.

The day after the arrival of the troops, workers left their homes exhausted after talking late into the night. Most felt like condemned men and women. Ravaged by fatigue and fear, they leaked out, drip by drip, towards the farms and fields, shops and bars. Afraid of what would happen when they stepped outside. Afraid of what would happen when they didn't.

The soldiers kept on coming, flowing throughout Fuentes and filling every lonely corner, every empty road. 'Stay inside' was whispered behind doors less and less as people acclimatised to their new normal. The steady drip, drip of villagers out on the streets on day one, by day two had turned into a trickle of people eager to get on with their daily business. And after day three, by which time most of them had stopped jumping out of their skins at the sound of boots on gravel and soldiers' shouts, there was a constant flow.

Heads emerged at windows. The soldiers were still there. Heads were pulled back tortoise-like into their shell. Families throughout the village whispered, argued, agreed, disagreed. The workers had ventured out. Women at home were next to go forth. One by one, doors opened. A woman with a basket would open her door, assess the danger with a look to the right and the left, then launch herself outside. Her neighbour would see her and quickly do the same, rushing to join her so they could walk along together. And though a cloud of anxiety came down upon them that pulled taut their every sinew and weighed heavy on each of their hearts, they still went about their everyday business. This was their new way of life; they had no choice but to live it.

Yet while most of the adults of the village went about their business much as before (though now factoring in should they greet a soldier? Look him in the eye? Not look him in the eye? Intervene when a neighbour was being questioned? Pretend you hadn't noticed it?) most of the children were kept inside. And no matter how grown up Maria thought she was, she was still a child in Doctor Alvaro's eyes. His child. And although he knew that to keep his daughter inside was not a long-term solution he prayed it would give him time to come up with one.

Maria was sleeping better – Cervantes had made sure of that – and though her world had been knocked off its orbit she was in the mood to re-align it. Richard had gone. Her father had seen to that. She imagined he must be back in England by now. She'd not seen Paloma for days. And although she could hear and see soldiers outside, she found that the alarm she'd felt when they'd first entered the village could not be sustained. The arguments to stay inside were there but she was getting lonely. She'd even started to believe that perhaps she had loved Richard Johnson after all. She certainly missed him now.

She slumped over the iron railings at her bedroom window and looked with longing up and down the street. She could see and hear neighbours chatting in the coolness of the morning, catch the laughter of children rippling out from open windows. Even the sight of young men in uniform smoking and joking together as they walked underneath beckoned her down. It all seemed so normal. So familiar. As if it had always been this way.

She smiled as she watched a barrow boy struggle to wheel a cart weighed down by a precariously loaded mountain of oranges. The boy wobbled on as single oranges rolled away in his wake. A donkey followed slowly behind, baskets loaded with apricots on either side, his hooves squashing the barrow boy's escaped fruit and releasing the juice and fragrance. Maria breathed it in then ran down to the kitchen.

She looked at the empty fruit basket. She checked the box where her father kept the money.

The next moment Maria was out in the street.

She'd been incarcerated for days and now she was outside, free, she felt conspicuous. But, she reasoned, she only wanted to buy some oranges. There was no crime in that. But she still walked towards the fruit-seller, basket held close to her chest, as though everyone knew that she shouldn't be out. She pushed at her hair trying to brush the sun away and walked briskly, still clasping the basket tightly and looking to the ground.

And while she'd been unalarmed at the sight of so many soldiers when looking down on them from the relative safety of her bedroom window, now, on the same level as them, walking along the same roads, she felt their presence as a threat. She would not look up; she refused to allow them in her field of vision.

Her heart pounded furiously throwing itself against the cage of her ribs, demanding to be freed. She walked on, dared to raise her eyes a little. She could make out dark shapes to the left and right, identify uniformed figures up ahead. She kept walking, with each step becoming less fearful. She looked around, still cautious. She saw soldiers. Everywhere. Milling around stalls, wandering down shaded back streets, sitting against walls. Smoking, laughing, chatting. They did nothing to stop her going about her business. Her heart relaxed to a flutter as she unfurled herself open like a flower.

Her blooming presence in the street soon attracted whistles and shouts of 'guapa.' By the time she made it to the orange-seller the sense of menace had transformed into a strangely thrilling tingle. She raised her head high and shook the not altogether unwanted attention off with a flick of her dark hair before stooping down to weigh up the juiciest fruits. Admiring soldiers watched her, their appreciative glances following her as she strode back home. Maria swung her basket confidently by her side.

In the course of a short stroll the soldiers had become to Maria nothing more than boys in *gorillo* caps and uniforms, as keen to catch her eye as she was to catch theirs. Many of them had rifles but now that she'd seen how young and fresh-faced most of them were, she doubted they had ever used one, let alone knew how to.

She was nearly home, on the point of stepping over the threshold, when she realised that she didn't want to go back inside where she had only her imagination for company. It had shown itself to be darker than anything she'd seen outside. She was gripped by a desire to stay roaming the streets for as long as she could. Fuentes was alive, its people going about their business on its streets in the clear light of day. That was the reality. Not the nightmarish images conjured up by the memories of a lunatic's words and sounds that came to her in the lonely, shuttered rooms of her house.

She pulled back, let the sun bathe her in its light, then headed towards Paloma's.

As she made her way through the sea of soldiers, a group of them stood back to make space for her to pass. They whistled as she knew they would. She ignored them. Further on down the road, still more soldiers showered her with 'hola guapa's. She tutted in mock offence. Her pace quickened in time to her excitement. She couldn't wait to get to Paloma's to tell her all about it. It was true, strictly speaking nothing had actually happened. But Maria felt alive again. The life force within her was strong. So strong that when an attractive voice called out 'Buenos dias Señorita' as she skipped by Maria couldn't help but turn to the young soldier who'd said it and smile with a 'Buenos dias' in reply.

She stopped. His eyes. There was something about them that bewitched her. She stared into them. They were brown. No, blue. She pulled herself away, quickly, dragging her reluctant eyes over skin like alabaster and thick, wavy black hair, before dropping them to the stony ground. 'I would like to carry your basket for you, if you are in agreement,' he said, offering out his hand. The formality of his words reassured her. She trusted herself to look up at him.

And he looked magnificent, leaning back against the white-washed wall, rifle slung over his shoulder, cool in the shade, a broad smile on his handsome face, and a book held in the hand that was hanging down at his side. The soldiers nearby had cigarettes in theirs and they watched and whistled. But Maria was now deaf and blind to them.

She swung her basket excitedly with one arm, back and forth, back and forth, as rhythmic as a metronome. With her free hand she pushed back her long hair. She stole a look at him. Dared to let her eyes catch his. And there they were, waiting to be caught. Those eyes. They first dazzled then unnerved her, caused her breath to catch. She looked away. Didn't dare look up again. Instead she picked up time with the swinging of her basket. His hand was still stretched out waiting to carry it for her. 'Oh, thank you, no!' Maria said, flustered and suddenly aware that she'd been waving her basket around wildly. 'Goodbye, Señor,' she said, tripping in her hurry to get away.

'My name is Luis,' he called after her. 'What's yours?' His name rang a bell. But she rushed on, carried forward by the now considerable upswing of her basket. 'Maria,' she whispered. 'What's that?' he shouted out. 'Maria!' she said, more loudly. 'Maria! Maria! Maria!' he called her name out loud and watched her walk away, hair bouncing and looking for all the world as if she was about to take off so great was the arc of the upswing of her basket.

He watched her turn the corner. She was gone.

'Oh. It's you!' Lola had nothing to laugh about and so, when she opened the door to see a giggling Maria with dancing eyes, she was surprised and more irritated than usual at the sight of her sister's friend.

'Paloma. It's Maria for you,' she shouted into the darkness behind her. 'She can't come out,' she added with a lazy wave of her hand as she disappeared into the back of the house giving her sister a push as they passed each other by.

'But you've got to,' Maria said to her friend in frustration as she emerged into the light.

'I can't,' Paloma replied, her eyes scouring the floor in front of her.

'But I have something to tell you.'

'I really can't. Mother will beat me,' her young friend said, her voice starting to break under the pressure. Maria puffed her cheeks out. It was true, Cecilia was formidable by anyone's reckoning. It was no use hoping that Paloma would be able to talk her mother round.

Lola watched the two girls silhouetted in the doorway. Their whispers grew louder, their gestures more animated. Maria laughed. Lola couldn't stand it any longer.

'Paloma! Mother says you've got to come in now,' Lola shouted. 'And that *you*—' she wagged her finger at Maria '—should get yourself off home. Your father won't be happy when he knows you're out and when he does find out he'll be needing a doctor himself as he'll be worried sick, she says.'

Lola came closer and stood behind her sister, arms folded, one leg bent, leaning against the wall. The friends' time was up. There would be no further secrets discussed, not unless Maria wished to share them with Lola too. And she didn't.

Paloma gave her friend a disappointed wave goodbye. Lola, satisfied that her spoiling task was done, walked back into the house.

'Paloma!' An angry voice screeched down from upstairs. And with that Maria's faithful friend, and Cecilia's dutiful daughter, closed the door.

Maria crossed back over the square. There were tens of soldiers all there together and for a moment she thought her perfect book reading soldier with the alabaster skin had gone. Her eyes searched every wall, squinted under every tree, until they found him, this time sitting on the floor, his head stuck like glue in his book. She looked at him, hunched over its pages and willed him to put it down, to look up at her. But he didn't. Another soldier, shorter, with heavier brows, a more pronounced jaw and a thick neck caught her eye and flashed her a smile. Her eyes creased in grateful response. Then he turned, laughing, to his bookish friend, and, with hands like hams and fingers like sausages he pointed in Maria's direction. Her perfect soldier held his head down, listening as if in pain, his sausage-fingered friend's mouth close to his ear. When he eventually looked up, Maria felt a blush of pleasure explode through every pore of her face in expectation of the admiring look he would surely cast her way. Her eyes danced all the way to meet his.

But when he looked at her, the boy with the perfect features, his eyes delivered a message so alien to the one she was anticipating as to turn all her pleasure into shame.

With thrusting eyes, he shoo-ed her away – his look gave her a warning. Maria felt an iciness run through her veins. She felt silly. Judged.

His ham-handed companion leered at her with a smack of his lips. Poor Maria shuddered. Lowered her eyes. She didn't raise them again. If she had done, she would have seen her bookish soldier remonstrate with his squat friend over such despicable behaviour, then drag him away by the collar to talk to him about respect, honour, good conduct.

Maria held her now stilled basket tightly to her chest to press against the pounding of her confused heart. She walked quickly on, beads of cold sweat breaking out all over her body at her own naivety. She picked up her pace. Broke into a trot. Then a run. Luis looked on, until he was secure in the knowledge that she had made it safely home.

CHAPTER 14

Don Felipe had the most magnificent wine cellar, he produced the most delicious olive oil and his larder had the sweetest smelling hams and sausages, all strung up from the ceiling, probably anywhere in the world. Cecilia had worked at the farm house for nearly thirty years and had been cook and housekeeper there for the past sixteen. These had been some of the best years of her working life. Especially as Don Felipe and his wife had taken to spending more and more time at their preferred residence in Biarritz with the smart set while their son was away at boarding school somewhere in England.

But now they were back.

This had irked Cecilia nearly as much as it irked her employers. But the kitchen was still very much her domain and she felt blessed that this was so. She called the larder '*el catedral*' and each time she entered its hallowed space she stopped still, if only for a moment, to breath in '*el aroma del paraíso*', as she liked to call it. She could taste the salty sweetness at the back of her throat, touch its richness in the air. It made her feel that life was good.

And so, even though there were Rebel troops in the village, Manuel might lose his job, and Lola was behaving strangely,

Cecilia still had the dutiful Paloma to be thankful for, and she still had the kitchen and larder to spark joy.

Not that the landowners were good employers. They were not. But she'd grown accustomed to the pettiness. She had seen all too clearly how covetously they'd guarded what they considered theirs over the years. When their workers sought to educate themselves Don Felipe and Dona Sofía saw this as an affront not to be tolerated. And, of course, they were right. It would spell out the beginning of the end, it would help peasants break free of the chains of servitude that had kept them on their bellies and close to the earth for so many centuries. Workers: they had come from the earth and to the earth they would always return without ever really moving very far away from it. Birth, a life of toil, death. With a handful of pesetas thrown at them for their sacrifice. To teach them to read and write would be to equip them with the tools to see, understand, learn, question, and ultimately challenge. Reading, writing – they could spell out many words yet the one that Cecilia feared most was trouble. And Manu might bring it down on his mother's head. But, Dona Sofía knew a good thing when she saw it. Cecilia was worth her not inconsiderable weight in gold. She was the best cook the family had ever had and the envy of many a guest to the estate. Although it wouldn't do to tell her so.

The day of Dona Sofía's dinner party was nearly here. The dinner party she'd starting planning even before she'd left Biarritz. That for which so many royalists, landowners and clerics had been working towards was finally coming to pass. Republicanism was about to be smashed into a million bloody pieces. And that was cause for very serious celebration. And discussion of how to smash it still further.

Now that the army had arrived in Fuentes the date of the dinner could finally be set. And that date was 14th August 1936. Dona Sofía was thrilled beyond words to be holding a party for those she saw as saviours of the true Spain. And news that her own son was part of the regiment that had come to save them all sent her – eventually – into still greater paroxysms of delight. Could he be billeted at home? No? Well, the least she could expect was that he should be allowed to attend the dinner. Good. It was decided. Oh, how simply marvellous.

'He's coming home. Our brave son will be here. Luis. Can you believe it? Sitting with us. Soon. So soon.' Dona Sofía babbled on to Cecilia in between choosing the menu and finalising the guest list.

'Luis will be so pleased to see you,' she said to Cecilia, and in truth, he probably would. 'I remember how our boys used to play together,' she waxed, acknowledging their shared past with rare candour. 'You'll be so proud of him.'

Luis had been a rare and special gift. Cecilia still remembered when Don Felipe and Dona Sofía had come back with him from Madrid as a baby eighteen years ago. She looked into the eyes of the woman who called herself his mother and recognised no trace of him there. They looked so unalike.

Dona Sofía blinked, sensing the intrusion. She quickly changed the subject. 'But now back to the dinner!' Dona Sofía exclaimed with a clap of her small soft hands. 'It has to be marvellous, Cecilia! Quick, I'm having an idea for the main course, get me a scrap of paper, anything will do, so that I can write it down.'

Cecilia rummaged round in the pocket of her apron and pulled out a pamphlet that she'd taken from Manuel. She blanched at the sight of it but it was too late; Dona Sofía had already recognized what it was and her eyes registered irritation. Cecilia held her breath waiting for the accusations to fly.

Instead, her mistress said, 'Duck à l'orange.' She snatched the paper out of her housekeeper's fingers, irritated now at having to write it down herself. Nothing, it seemed, was as important as this.

Everyone involved in the planning of Dona Sofía's big dinner was either excited or fraught. That was because Dona Sofía was one moment excited, the next fraught, on occasion both. It had to be marvellous, wonderful, perfect. She had held important dinners in Biarritz and there, she told anyone who would listen, 'we had an excellent cook. French.' Cecilia was excellent too. But she wasn't French.

The guest list had been decided at last. 'What do you think of this, Cecilia? It's the final list. The invitations have to be dispatched today!' Dona Sofía put down her pen, picked up a sheet of paper and started to read out the names of the chosen. 'Captain Garcia, his aide – whatever his name is – Señor Gonzalez, you know who he is, don't you? He's the businessman, he's made a lot of money and made many generous donations to the Nationalist cause, then there's his wife Señora Gonzalez, I've not met her yet, have you? No? Well, we just *have* to invite the priest Father Anselmo though I'm not completely happy with some of the masses, but he is a man of God, and God is on our side, and then there's Doctor Alvaro. He's been to all the meetings at the town hall with the mayor and although he's a little too wishy-washy for Felipe's tastes, he is what you'd call a good man, but sadly he has no wife. Died. Though how a doctor can let such a thing happen is beyond me, makes me question what sort of doctor he is. What was I saying? Where was I? Ah, yes, Doctor Alvaro. No wife. What's the name I've got down here. Maria. His daughter. You must know who she is, Cecilia. Tiresome to have a child at the table, but what can you do? But isn't she the one involved in the reading? Can't be the same. Ah well. Never mind. It's decided now, her name's on this list. Funny if she turns up on the other one too. Oh, you don't know about that list, Cecilia? Pretend I never mentioned it. And we're allowed to have Luis with us too,' she cried. She stopped to draw breath and tot up how many guests she'd listed so far. 'That makes, how many? Ten? Oh, and I nearly forgot. We'll have to have the mayor and his wife. That brings the total to thirteen. Oh goodness me no. I mean twelve. Twelve, twelve, twelve. A much better number. We were going to have the teacher too – see, I've written *Señor Suarez: teacher* here but I've had to scribble it out. But then you of all people must know by now why we can't have him. He *is* on the other list,' Dona Sofía said obliquely.

Cecilia stood, waited and watched while Dona Sofía wrote the names of the fortunate few on envelopes in her finest handwriting. 'And there will be three cars and Luis will be on one of those military motorbikes. I don't suppose you've seen one Cecilia, but you might have heard of them. Powerful beasts by all accounts.' Cecilia was trapped. She asked herself what the mysterious other list was and felt concern that the teacher was on it. Señor Suarez was not a bad person, she thought to herself. Misguided. But not bad. Confusion careered around Cecilia's mind like one of those powerful beasts that Dona Sofía assumed she'd not heard of.

'Perfect!' Her mistress added the final flourish to the last envelope. 'Here!' And with that, she handed them to Cecilia and directed the woman out of the room with the tip of her index finger.

The door to Don Felipe's study was wide open and as Cecilia made her way along the corridor towards it she saw her master with a sheet of paper in his hand. 'The girl doesn't count,' she heard him say to someone she couldn't see. 'Everybody will laugh if we put the name of a child on the list. You've given me Suarez. Now who else was involved?' he demanded. Guido's voice started up from behind the door. 'There were two brothers, I've already dismissed them, called—' Before he could say any more Cecilia coughed loudly. Don Felipe looked up and dismissed his estate manager with a frown and a snappily muttered, 'Later. And close the door after you.'

When Guido stepped out of the study and into the unlit corridor Cecilia thrust the invitations into his face. 'The mistress needs you to deliver these.' She looked at him with an expression intended to look into his soul and make him do the same. He was a snake and he squirmed uncomfortably in her sight as he took the sealed envelopes and walked quickly away.

CHAPTER 15

The List was starting to give Don Felipe a headache. He envied his wife that she'd only had to compile a list of dinner guests. He'd e had to draw up a list of enemies of the new regime and it was proving to be more problematic than he'd anticipated. When General Queipo de Llano, Commander of the South, had issued his *banda de Guerra* – Edict of War – at the very start of the uprising, the landowner had nodded at the rightness of it. 'Anyone who opposes the uprising should be shot. Sound idea.' And prior to drawing up the list, Don Felipe had always believed himself to be as vindictive as the next man. But now he wasn't so sure. The problem was that he didn't really know many of the accused. And he certainly was not going to be adding the names of any women. Let alone girls. Perhaps he was getting soft in his old age. He wanted to punish subversives but death? A little final, wasn't it?

And now he was faced with a dilemma: Guido had just given him another name. As he sat in his study he weighed up the crimes of the suspect on his personal scales of justice.

He looked at the pamphlet on his desk that Guido had given to him as evidence. His eyes skimmed it and stopped on the word 'revolution.' He breathed in deeply then read on. 'You have nothing to lose but your chains. You have a world to win.' He'd read enough. With a batting of an eyelid the scales of justice crashed down heavily to 'crushed'. Anyone involved with this Marxist muck deserved a place on the list but could he trust Guido to have given him the right name?

He marched into the living room where his wife was flicking through another fashion magazine. He brandished his paltry list around in one hand and the incriminating pamphlet in the other. 'What's that in your hand?' she asked, pointing at the leaflet. 'I do believe I've seen it before.' She let her magazine drop as she rooted around in her box of ideas. She picked out a torn corner of a matching pamphlet upon which she herself had written 'Duck à l'orange', Cecilia had given it to her. 'Give me *your* list,' Dona Sofía said, delighted with her own finely tuned powers of deduction. Her husband did as he was told and his wife picked up her pen and in her own fair hand wrote down the name of their housekeeper's only son. 'Done,' she said, with a little laugh at her own cleverness. 'Now that didn't hurt.'

'He can't work here anymore,' she added, pointing to 'Manuel', relieved that her son's childhood friend would be departing before her beloved Luis came home. He would only try to revive an old friendship, and that was something he couldn't be allowed to do. Not now.

'We'll have to let Cecilia go too,' Don Felipe said, following his wife's deductive thread. 'Really? I don't see why,' she replied. Cecilia couldn't be dismissed. Not before the big dinner.

'Cecilia! Cecilia!' she called out. Don Felipe looked puzzled.

The poor woman rushed in looking worn. She hoped she would not be required to make any further *minor adjustments* to the menu or root out different serving platters.

'Haven't we always provided for you, Cecilia?' Dona Sofía asked, her tone one of long suffering.

'Yes, Dona Sofía.'

'Then why, Cecilia? Why? Answer me that?'

The poor woman didn't know how to. She'd seen many men and women braver than her dare to respond with an 'I might be able to give you an answer if you asked me a proper question,' or a 'Why what?' Even an 'I'm sorry but I don't know what you want me to say.' But Cecilia was infinitely respectful, the way her employers liked it. And so she waited. Silent. Subservient. Confused. After what seemed like an eternity Don Felipe let out an exasperated, 'Your son, damn it! After all we did for him.' He waited for her to nod.

'Didn't we give him honest employment on our land?' He waited for her to agree. 'And this is how he repays us.'

With that Don Felipe thrust the leaflet in Cecilia's face. She looked at him to see what she should do with it, not prepared to take one move without her employer's sanction. He nodded. She took it. She looked at it. She'd seen it before. She knew what it was. She scoured every shape and mark upon it trying to wrestle all meaning from it. But she couldn't.

'She can't read,' Dona Sofía said wearily, a languid derision seeping through. Don Felipe snatched the leaflet out of her hands. He shook it. 'She can't read!' he exclaimed in triumph.

'You see my point?' he asked Cecilia. 'You can't read,' he said, summoning a note of praise in his voice, though unable to suppress the smirk that travelled like lightning across his face.

'It's precisely because of this sort of thing,' he said, waving the leaflet up and down, 'that we've been dragged back here in the first place.' He paused. The poor woman's arms were now covered but her sleeves shook like leaves in the breeze. 'So why did your son need to read and write when he knew that he had a job here with us? Was it not good, honest work we offered him, Cecilia?'

'The list,' his wife mouthed at him. 'Remember. Names for the list.'

'I blame the teacher, of course. Should have known better. Señor Suarez, isn't it?' he asked.

Cecilia nodded.

'Ah yes. And those two boys. Friends of your son. Those two boys he was seeing the teacher with. The…' Don Felipe said, with cunning.

'The Espinoza brothers? Raul and Pedro?' Cecilia asked.

'Yes, They're the ones,' Don Felipe said, 'Espinoza. Raul and Pedro. That's what I thought.'

Cecilia watched as Don Felipe wrote what she could only assume were the names of the Espinozas on his list. She breathed deeply and waited for Don Felipe to bring up Maria. It was a bittersweet moment when he did not.

'Along you go now,' Dona Sofía said, dismissing her. 'You don't need to read, Cecilia dear. Now return to your chores. There's so much to do for tomorrow I don't know where I'm going to find the time to fit it all in.'

And with that Cecilia returned to the kitchen and Dona Sofía returned to her magazine.

CHAPTER 16

Cecilia had not lost her job. Manuel had. But it wasn't only losing his job that Cecilia now had to worry about. She felt sick with a vertiginous dread for his future shot through with a maternal anger that her precious fool of a son hadn't listened to his mother's words of caution in the first place. She might soon lose Manuel and it was all his fault. It was all her fault. Her mind vacillated wildly.

Her body yearned to run to him, protect him. But it didn't have that luxury, bonded as it was in servitude to employers upon whom she had come to depend her whole life.

As she busied herself with preparation for the dinner, she found herself pushed into thinking seditious thoughts. While she peeled, chopped, diced and sliced, salted, oiled, broiled and boiled she hatched a plan. For the first time in her life she was going to follow her own mind, put her head above the parapet. She was ready to be counted, ready to do the right thing. Her son's life depended on it and she summoned up every cliché, proverb and rallying cry to back herself up.

Cecilia knew everyone on the estate, everyone in the village. Knew what they did and didn't do, what they thought and who they sided with now that this madness called war had begun. She knew who she could trust and who she couldn't. She saw everything, the unfairness on the estate, the quiet resistance in the village. No one realised. Cecilia – the dutiful housekeeper, put upon, under-estimated. She said nothing about the things she knew. Kept away from action, be it positive or negative. She was the epitome of servitude, the essence of passivity.

But now Manuel's life was at risk. And the realisation that she had condemned the Espinoza boys just by naming them jolted her into action. She would call on those who could help them. It was her duty to give the boys a chance to escape.

It was dark by the time she got back to the village and although Cecilia was exhausted, she was relieved to see her son at the table, eating some dry bread, alive and well. She burst into tears. Then told him her plan.

Within seconds Manuel had set it in motion, making his way along dark lanes, slipping past patrolling soldiers and knocking on the door of the only man who could help.

'Doctor Alvaro,' Manuel said in hushed tones as he stepped inside.

The next day was the day of the dinner. Up at the farmhouse Cecilia had cleaned the monographed dinner service, ironed the table linen, wiped the crystal glasses with a cloth and was now polishing the cutlery and sharpening the carving knife on a stone. She'd already been working for hours in the kitchen by the time Dona Sofia made it downstairs. She fully expected that her mistress would find her additional jobs to do. And Dona Sofia, one never to disappoint, came down and sent her to cut some wild flowers to put on the table. And so, Cecilia wrapped her newly sharpened tool in a cloth, placed it in the voluminous pocket of her apron and went outside, past the stables and into the fields and woods beyond.

In Doctor Alvaro's house, there was also much excitement. Maria was delighted to be going to the dinner, although she was a little tired, after having been awoken by a knock on the door the night before. Her father had ushered her back to bed but the fact remained that her sleep had been disturbed, which was why she was now suppressing a yawn as she embroidered a sunflower onto her only lemon dress. It would go with the sunflower pendant Paloma had entrusted into her care and which she had decided to wear to her first grand dinner party.

She was also needed to accompany her father on a visit that morning, a fact that she'd found strange as he didn't usually allow her to go with him.

He had been called out to pay a visit on the Espinoza brothers and, to give his daughter a change of scene, he was taking Maria with him.

When daughter and doctor arrived, the pair were taken into a darkened room by Pedro Espinoza, the older of the two brothers. Raul, the younger, was lying on the floor. The doctor touched the boy gently on his shoulder. He opened his heavy lids to reveal bleary eyes.

He'd had an accident up at the farm over a week ago and injured his leg. The wound had become infected. He'd also lost his job – a fact the doctor already knew, told to him as it was by Señor Suarez before he'd left.

Señor Suarez. As Doctor Alvaro thought of his dear friend he breathed a sigh of relief and a smile touched his lips. The good man had had too much involvement helping the workers, had been too public in his hostility towards what he openly called 'right-wing forces', namely Don Felipe and his Falangist friends, to remain safe for long. The new regime was tightening its grip on the region and those against it were being punished in every village and every town. It would soon be the teacher's turn to feel the force of its wrath, which was why both doctor and priest had hatched a plan to help their friend escape – he'd stood up and been counted far too many times to be able to stay on in Fuentes without being shot at.

When the priest had told Alvaro he'd been called upon to administer the last rites to a dying man who lived a good hour's cart-ride away from the village the doctor saw it as the perfect opportunity to steal the good teacher away. 'Why Anselmo, your God truly does work in mysterious ways.'

Raul Espinoza was also at risk. Alvaro needed to help him escape but first he had to make sure he was fit enough. He thought of Suarez. He would be miles away.

The doctor laughed as he imagined his friend lying on the floor of a dusty, wooden cart, covered by hessian and inhaling the pungent aroma of Father Anselmo's feet. If anyone could smuggle a godless communist past Rebel troops it was a man in a cassock with a scapular, a bottle of holy oil and a flagon of sacramental wine.

Suarez hadn't wanted to go when his friends had first told him of their plan to smuggle him to safety. He had wished to stand his ground, stay on in solidarity with the villagers. But he knew that it was only a matter of time before that fateful knock on the door came in the early hours of the morning.

The doctor looked at Raul Espinoza and ran a finger around the neckline of his own shirt, undid a button. He would have to work fast. If Manuel's information was to be believed, then the knock on the door was fast approaching for his young patient too.

Maria laid out the scalpel, tweezers, scissors and bandages, and cut strips according to her father's instructions.

'You'll be ready,' Alvaro whispered in the lad's ear. 'Make a parcel up,' he instructed his daughter. He pointed to a small bottle of iodine and the cut dressing and went to talk with Pedro, the brother, in the adjacent room.

'We need to be quick,' the doctor said as he closed the door behind him. Then all Maria could make out was 'Manuel', 'Cecilia', 'tonight' and 'horses' but little else, despite straining her ears to hear. Raul opened one eye to watch her. 'Your father is a good man,' he said.

'Come, Maria,' her father said when back in the room. 'We need to make two more calls before we can go home,' and then he embraced both brothers as if he didn't expect to see them again for a very long time.

CHAPTER 17

'Two horses are missing!' Guido rushed into the house and started calling out for Don Felipe, alarm in his voice. The land-owner was upstairs, called on by his wife to help her pick out a dress to wear to the dinner. The big day was upon them and Dona Sofía had a mountain of decisions to make, none bigger than selecting an outfit to wear that evening, the enormity of which rendered her deaf to the protestations of the estate manager.

Don Felipe turned with the intention of going downstairs to find out what the matter was but the sudden sharpness of his wife's nails as she placed her fingers tightly around his wrist made him think again.

'But he's calling out about the horses,' Don Felipe reasoned. Dona Sofía pulled a face. 'He's the estate manager. What on earth are we paying him for if he can't deal with issues on the estate himself?'

'Don Felipe! Don Felipe!' Guido's shouts intruded into the dressing room once more.

'What, in heavens name, does he do when we're not here?' Dona Sofía snapped, becoming angrier as insistent cries about missing horses trampled in and disturbed her peace. 'He must have left them somewhere,' she said to her husband. 'Either way the man's an incompetent fool.' With that she pulled another dress to her and contemplated her reflection in the cheval mirror. 'Oh, go on then, if you must!' she said to her husband as she caught his look of concern hovering behind her shoulder, marring as it did the otherwise elegant vision she beheld of herself. 'Go see the man, if only to shut him up.'

All the while Cecilia rushed round and in and out of the house. Dona Sofía, when not deciding on which frock to wear, still had a few 'wonderful ideas' and 'tiny tweaks' to make to the evening's plans and Cecilia's head was full of them. *Shall we have fish? Too late? We'll need ten bottles of wine, no, twenty, no, fifteen. We'll sit her by him, or shall we place him by her? Do I have to invite that insufferable bore? Oh, I wish we'd gone for Duck à l'orange now! Didn't I say we should have gone for duck à l'orange? Try the flowers here. No, here.*

But there was nothing in the preparation of tonight's dinner that Cecilia couldn't handle. She had everything under control. The only thing that troubled her (well, the only thing that she could admit to) was the possibility that her beloved Luis would not come and seek her out in the kitchen. It had been such a long time since she'd last seen him. But he always did, on those rare occasions when he returned home. Why would tonight be any different? Her heart started to race and her head to pound. Though she believed she was on top of everything, her emotions were running high.

She pushed open the back door to let some air in. The sleeves of her dress were making her hot. The second she did so three flies flew in buzzing around the meat. Dona Sofía had given her strict instructions to keep all doors to the kitchen closed – she hated flies with a passion bordering on obsession. Cecilia then went to the larder and pushed the door open there too. Her mistress would fly into a fury if she came in and discovered that her cook had left open not one but two doors. But today not even that disturbed Cecilia. The arrow had left its bow and there was nothing she could do to stop it.

Clip, clip, clip. Cecilia made out the sound of expensive shoes tapping their heeled and pointed way down the staircase. It was Dona Sofia, followed by the familiar flat-footed stamping of her husband. Cecilia arched her neck towards the door that was still shut, the one leading onto the hall. She opened it enough to hear better but not so much as to draw attention to herself or to anything happening in the kitchen.

'I must speak to you about the horses.' It was Guido. She heard a snap – the familiar clicking of Don Felipe's fingers that indicated 'go'. The cacophonous footsteps of husband and wife disappeared into the air as they went one way, while the angry male footsteps of the estate manager pounded their way towards the kitchen. Cecilia moved back just as Guido swung open the door and stormed in.

She looked momentarily flustered. He didn't notice. 'Two horses have been stolen,' he said. 'Have you seen anything? Noticed anything?' The look on his face told her that he expected nothing worth hearing from her. It was a longshot, last chance. His expression told her that he thought her a brainless imbecile. She made sure she did not disappoint. 'What's that Guido? No!' she cried in mock horror. 'There's something strange going on around here, that's for sure,' she said, conscious that to say something while saying nothing at all was a rare and wondrous thing.

Cecilia picked up her knife and set about her next task, preparing the meat. 'Now Guido, there's more than one way to skin a rabbit,' she whispered to herself as he went outside.

CHAPTER 18

Manuel had been a very sweet baby, attached to his mother more than most. Cecilia would have to bring him up to the estate with her and he would sleep on the kitchen floor wrapped up in a blanket. He grew up loving it on the estate. For a short while he considered it his home. He grew up loving Luis. He considered him his brother, and the boys played together as equals. Dona Sofía allowed it because she would allow her only child no contact with anyone else in the area. He was never taken to the village. A doctor would be brought in from elsewhere for him rather than call on Doctor Alvaro. And Cecilia was even made to swear never to talk about him outside of the estate. Allowing her son to have a friend his own age was a concession Dona Sofía was willing to make.

Yet as the boys grew older so Manuel was made to feel owned while Luis was forced to adopt the attitude of owner. Not that Luis was comfortable with this. He showed signs of resistance and his mother would laugh indulgently – about her own son's generous spirit, his happy, kind heart, his goodness. But it irked her intensely. When the ornament smashed into a thousand pieces so did the boys' lives. Luis was ripped up from his native soil, sent to a boarding school far away in a cold land. Manuel was

103

banished, only allowed to return years later when he could be put to good use and worked like a beast of the field.

Luis was lonely, living in a strange country. Manuel was confused, abandoned like a toy. Cecilia was heartbroken, disappointed. As for Dona Sofía, it was as if she'd torn a limb from her own body such was the anguish that flooded every fibre, but she had done it to herself.

But now Luis was coming back. Both women would see him again. And Cecilia hoped that he would be the same kind-hearted boy he'd always been. Her future and the future of Manuel depended on it.

Cecilia couldn't afford to think it would be otherwise and she threw herself into her work completely, losing herself in its endless repetitions and reassuring smells, textures and tastes.

She began gathering together all the ingredients she needed for the dinner.

She stepped into the generously stocked larder, checking that no one was around. She looked up and reached out to press the meat of a ham appreciatively between her thumb and forefinger. She brought them to her nose. Inhaled deeply. She had never helped herself to anything extra in the larder – not once. The fact that she had known such riches existed had been enough to feed her soul. And she had been truly grateful. But the events of the past few days had changed all that.

She reached up and took down a huge well-hung ham from its hook, shifting the ones either side so as not to leave a space. She rolled up her sleeves and as she stretched up, she looked at her own fleshy forearms. They wobbled on the bone. As she slapped the ham on the counter at the side she held up her fingertips, shrivelled like prunes from immersing them in water, scrubbing worktops and floors endlessly. Her hands were dry, her skin scaly. She was an old woman. Illiterate. Stupid. She saw herself as others did and felt relief. No one would suspect her.

She looked along the row of hams above her, looked all around the larder as though looking for someone. 'Manu,' she whispered. His presence caused ripples in the air that washed up against her until she saw his face appear to her out of the gloom. He bowed his head. His mother kissed him tenderly then moved on along the suspended hams, stopping by the most majestic, placing them on the counter, then popping the tell-tale empty hook in her apron pocket. She took down five in all.

Next she put out cheeses, preserves. Manuel placed his hand on hers. The sack his mother was helping him to fill was bulging. It was time to stop. Manuel, the Espinoza brothers and whoever else her son was set to join tonight would not be going hungry. Cecilia went over all the things she'd stolen. And felt no guilt.

CHAPTER 19

On the menu for the dinner of the year was serrano-wrapped rabbit in Cecilia's wine sauce, which, Dona Sofía had to admit, was quite delicious, if a little heavy for her own refined tastes. The dessert was a fig concoction to which Don Felipe was particularly partial and the cheese was their own as was the wine. Dona Sofía had toyed with the idea of a French menu to share their sophistication with guests undoubtedly less well-travelled than themselves but then thought better of it. The dishes would most likely be a little too unfamiliar for some. Certainly for Señora Gonzalez who had airs that did nothing in Dona Sofía's eyes to hide the lack of taste crying out in everything the woman wore, said and, probably, ate. She worried that the menu might say 'peasant' but it was too late to change it now.

She walked down the staircase with her husband to inspect the dining room. They were briefly put off the task by their estate manager still bleating on about some horses but thankfully even her husband found the man's approach tactless and timing thoughtless.

Annoyed, and secretly grateful to have an excuse not to have to measure distances between place settings, Don Felipe went to take some air at the front of the house, while Dona Sofía pursued the matter in hand.

Cecilia had already set the table. Beams of sunlight played on the silver candelabra, reflecting out to the fastidiously polished cutlery, ricocheting as far as the cut glass, going on to shatter into a thousand scintillating parts that created brilliant patterns on the white linen table cloth all around. It really did make a most splendid impression. Dona Sofía gave a smile of self-congratulation. She'd planned everything, even thinking to keep Cecilia out of the way in the kitchen. Never mind the extra expense of having to employ one of the woman's daughters to help out. Surprisingly pretty girl, Dona Sofía thought to herself. And such lovely arms.

The hands of the clock spun round quickly. In the kitchen Cecilia chopped, basted, stirred and seasoned. In the dining room Lola lit the candles and positioned the napkins. In the bedroom Don Felipe tried out a cigar and tasted the wine. In the dressing room Dona Sofía changed her lipstick and made a few last-minute adjustments to her hair. And in the darkest corner of the larder Manuel crouched by his sack of food, and waited.

The wheels of a car pulled up in front of the house, its headlights illuminating the beautiful façade. Don Felipe looked down from the upstairs window. It was Señor Gonzalez and his wife, always first to arrive at any gathering. Don Felipe gave a heavy sigh as he saw them climb out of their car.

Señor Gonzalez was a short, dark haired man of about forty-five with a fast expanding middle. His wife, tall, slim and beautiful, all the things her husband was not, stopped to survey the grounds of the estate. Her eye line skimmed the top of her husband's head, careful not to let it fall lower as otherwise she would have to contemplate the pot-bellied gargoyle he was fast becoming. He was a good husband – well-connected and rich – and she allowed him the occasional public show of affection to show others that she was a loving wife. Catching Dona Sofía who had now joined her husband up at the window, she judged now might

107

be a good time for one such display. 'You look beautiful,' Señor Gonzalez whispered to his wife as he stretched his neck up to kiss her cheek. She smiled and whispered an exaggerated *thank you* for all to see.

'Welcome,' Dona Sofía said with gushing insincerity, slightly breathless having rushed down the stairs. The sound of heavy wheels on the long gravel drive saved her from having to say more. Two further cars made their way towards the house.

In the kitchen Cecilia shouted, 'Go, go, go! Lola, do the drinks!'

'But I've not finished adding the garnish to this...'

'I can do that,' Cecilia hissed. 'Now go, or she'll be furious.'

Doctor Alvaro and his daughter had arrived too but still hadn't joined the party. They'd arrived by cart and so had gone round to the back of the house where the stables were.

It had struck Maria on the way there that her father was preoccupied. But she didn't think a great deal about it as she was too. Yet whereas her mind was full of gaiety and laughter, and her face alight as she imagined the pleasurable sounds, smells, tastes and sights of the coming evening as she bumped up and down the stony lanes, her father's was focused on less intoxicating, more vital matters. He'd planned to tell his daughter that Señor Suarez was gone, and safe. The journey to the estate seemed a perfect opportunity. But he couldn't tear his mind away from what he had to do at the dinner tonight. It was serious. Lives depended upon it. He could not fail in his duty and it was all he could think about on the way there. And so the pair sat in silence, their minds distracted by the loud voices in their heads.

When the doctor and his daughter got down from the cart, Alvaro insisted on leading the horse to the stables himself. He'd made a note, as they'd passed the front of the house, that there was one guard posted there. He then made his way to the stables situated at the back, where he saw that another solitary guard was quite sensibly posted. His heart sank at the sight of them. His daughter's lifted. She turned her sunflower pendant round and round between her fingers, willing one of them to be the soldier she'd met in the village, the one with the book and the unusual eyes that she hadn't been able to fathom. 'Wait here,' her father had said, leaving Maria outside the kitchen, the door of which faced onto the courtyard at the back and was adjacent to the stables across the way. She stood there, hopeful, still turning her pendant around in the fingers of one hand while pulling down on her lemon dress with the other.

By the time she'd followed her father inside the house she felt flat. She'd raised her eyes to meet those of the young men on guard outside and now the dazzling beauty awaiting her inside the house could do nothing to make up for the fact that neither of them was the soldier she'd been looking for. She gave herself a stiff talking to. It wasn't as if she knew him. It wasn't working. She still felt empty. *Remember how silly – and wrong – you were about Richard. And you knew him.* But none of it made any difference.

She was surprised and cheered to see Lola serving drinks.

The guests were still milling round in the drawing room and as Maria milled around with them she couldn't help but be disappointed. The snippets of conversation she was party to were dull. A conversation about the power of someone's car here, the size of the hosts' estate there. Maria hadn't known what to expect coming here this evening, but it certainly wasn't this. A smile of shared acknowledgement that the social world of adults was boring passed between the two girls. Maria watched Lola disappear towards the kitchen with something akin to envy. At least she could get away.

Maria let her eyes wander around the room. They were drawn to the Captain's pistol glinting in the light, nestling in its holster, captivated by the diamond necklace around Dona Sofía's neck, dazzled by the glass drops of a chandelier sparkling overhead. That was it. Her eyes had been dazzled enough. She looked at the portraits and stifled a laugh. The artist was better at necklaces, she said to herself, than he was at people. She eventually let her eyes rest on a vase of simple, wild flowers, positioned in front of a wall covered with family photographs. She went up to them to take a better look and as she did so, her eyes strayed to look through the window to the side. A soldier turned up on a military motorbike and made his way round the back of the house unnoticed by everyone apart from Maria. He looked familiar. She looked at the photos. The boy in them looked remarkably like her soldier with the book. She squinted then opened her eyes up as wide as they would go to refocus. She looked again. He still looked exactly like him. She turned away to look outside and caught sight of the military motorcyclist as he walked in front of the window. He looked like her soldier too. Maria rubbed her eyes. She looked out again. He was gone.

Don Felipe joined Maria and picked up a photograph. He bent over and whispered conspiratorially, 'I do believe Luis intends to surprise his mother!' Maria stood silent. How did he know her soldier was called Luis? Before Maria could say a word Don Felipe was already whispering in his wife's ear. 'It's time to go through, darling.'

'But Luis is not here yet,' she sighed. 'Shall we go through?' she said to her guests, struggling to conceal her disappointment. 'After you, please,' she said, a fixed beam on her face, hand open and showing her guests where to go. 'The girl will guide you to your chair,' she said, waving a finger airily in Lola's direction. Her guests dutifully shuffled out, Señor and Señora Gonzalez at the front, Maria, Doctor Alvaro and Father Anselmo at the back with Dona Sofía.

Maria watched her hostess as she went back to the window and looked outside. Though making a pretence of waiting for the bottleneck of people in the doorway to subside, the doctor's daughter thought she saw an unexpected vulnerability in the woman's face as hope and despair flitted repeatedly across her features.

Her father pulled her to him to make way for a young soldier who had just entered the room. The boy crept past them, throwing his hands around Dona Sofía's carefully made-up eyes. Recognition and confusion erupted within Maria's breast causing her to gasp in time with the older woman's cries of joy.

It was Maria's soldier with the dark hair, skin like alabaster and eyes that once looked into had revealed his soul to her and hers to him. It was her Luis.

'Mother!'

'Luis! My boy!'

That he was also the landowners' son was a revelation Maria hadn't anticipated. She watched as father and son embraced. That her soldier should be theirs perturbed her. Could they really be the same person? The way he made her feel as he winked at her while he embraced Don Felipe gave her the answer.

Dona Sofía had arranged the seating so as to have her son close to her. Maria was sat at the other end of the table next to her father who smiled, delighted to see Lola. But as his eyes scanned the guests the life drained out of them as he observed the hosts' son exchanging meaningful glances with his daughter. Doctor Alvaro, usually so kindly and indulgent, tapped her on the arm. He gave her a withering glance. It disturbed her deeply. It was meant to. Flustered, Maria looked around for Lola, smiled at the priest, then settled for listening to Don Felipe as he had the deepest voice of all those assembled, anything other than risk having her father intercept the secret communication passing between her and her soldier.

'If we can be of service to you and your men in any way,' the host boomed to the Captain, 'you have only to ask. Any one of us, I am confident that I speak for everyone around this table, will do all in our power to help you in any way you think fit to help you secure the village and surrounding areas.' Maria's eyes inspected the Captain's face. His head nodded but it was clear from his satisfied expression, that he was elsewhere, and judging by where his gaze was fixed, he was elsewhere with Señora Gonzalez. That one could tell so much about a person simply by observing them made her self-conscious and more determined than ever that her father should not see her looking at Luis.

Maria looked at the woman that was Señora Gonzalez, seeing her through the Captain's eyes and conceded that she was a glittering vision to behold. But, Maria knew, this dazzling façade concealed a heart of the thickest, dullest, heaviest stone.

Her own eyes strayed back to Luis, flickering in the direction of her distracted father on the way, only to be distracted herself, seconds later, by the ringing, metallic sound as Lola dropped a knife onto the tiled floor. Instantly she noticed the look of sympathy on Luis' face as Lola struggled to pick it up while balancing a pile of dirty plates with one hand. He rushed to help her. Had Maria's father witnessed this instinctive act of kindness that had quelled the ire that would surely have erupted from Dona Sofía if it had not been her son who had acted with such gallantry? Maria hoped so.

But the doctor was too busy performing his own act of kindness to be impressed with that of his hosts' son. 'Please, have mine,' Doctor Alvaro said, offering Señor Gonzalez a napkin with which to wipe away the food that was currently dribbling down his chin.

'Who's on your list, doctor?' Señora Gonzalez piped up from the other side of the table, hoping to dilute the embarrassment that was her husband. Doctor Alvaro did not reply, though that he nodded at her with a polite smile made it clear that he'd heard her. He turned away and looked at the clock then the door. And waited.

Conversations broke out all around the table. Señora Gonzalez and her talk of lists had alarmed the doctor but she had clearly excited others. Maria could make out a few familiar names bandied about by some of the guests but she thought little of it. Her father had told her that tonight would be a chance for some to indulge their love of tittle-tattle and try to settle old scores. Not a pleasant thing, she agreed, but it didn't cross her mind for an instant that a person could be punished on hearsay.

The priest, Father Anselmo, had been quiet most of the evening but the wine was beginning to have its effect. He'd already spotted a comfy chair that he would soon be making his way towards, but first he had to put Señora Gonzalez right on very nearly everything she was saying. By the sour look on her face as she talked with him it was clear that she'd had quite enough moral instruction for one evening. But the alcohol had loosened the priest's tongue and he wasn't going to stop just yet. Though a delicious post-prandial nap was calling him he would carry on administering to the morally bankrupt and spiritually needy until his eyelids gave way. The time for talking niceties was fast drawing to an end for Señora Gonzalez and the priest.

Señora Gonzalez ('I'm a generous benefactress') gave a small amount of her husband's money, in regular instalments, to the church. All she asked for in return was a little absolution – as well as a little tacit agreement this evening. A slight nodding of Father Anselmo's head about who should be punished in this civil war of theirs – was that too much to ask?

She'd started with the Republicans. Depraved vermin. Unhappily, the holy recipient of her husband's largesse had seemed less than keen to agree, so she was now forced to move quickly on to the Communists – safer ground with a man of the cloth. 'We patriots should rid our country of them, shouldn't we? They are, after all, godless. And I see it says in the papers that they are damaging our churches, burning our statues.' The priest smiled benevolently at her as he drained his glass of red wine. Mistakenly taking the priest's actions for assent, Señora Gonzalez relaxed back into her chair and fluttered her eyelashes in the direction of the Captain on the other side of the table. She waited for the priest's response. Her ears opened themselves up, wide and trusting, as flowers to a bee.

113

She didn't expect it to sting her.

'A church can be repaired, a statue replaced, Señora Gonzalez. But if a husband or son is killed, communist or no, he cannot. In times such as these we need to remember that.'

If anyone could get away with being holier than thou it was a priest, and the fact annoyed Señora Gonzalez greatly. She wished she could add the priest's name to her list. Instead, she reached out to more attentive ears ready and waiting across the table. The person to whom they belonged was all too willing for an opportunity to rescue her and apply some soothing balm to her heaving bosom.

'Captain,' she cried out, 'communism?'

'A threat to our Christian values and social order. Damaging our churches, destroying our statues,' he boomed back. Señora Gonzalez beamed. 'Thank the Lord,' she said.

'A Satanic scourge that seeks to contaminate pure Spanish blood, isn't that so, Father?' he continued. But before Father Anselmo could mark himself out as the only priest the Captain had ever come across whose principles were dictated by his conscience and not the amount of gold bestowed upon him by the Don Felipes of this world, Lola rushed to save him from himself. She topped up the good man's glass, deliberately spilling a small amount of wine on his sleeve. The scene that ensued, worthy of a farce, put the Captain off the priest's scent. By the time the priest had allowed Lola to lead him to the comfy chair for a little rest, the tragedy had been well and truly averted.

The doctor, nervous at the altercation between priest and soldier, breathed a sigh of relief that it had come to an end. He smiled as he saw his holy friend's head nodding to the side, his eyes closing.

Señora Gonzalez was relieved to be rid of Anselmo, but her scales had been rubbed up most definitely the wrong way. She sat quietly for a while concentrating on maintaining a smile on her lips if not in her heart. Couldn't she reasonably add the now quietly snoring Father Anselmo to her list?

She thought not, for now. She looked around the table for a dog to whip.

'Didn't I see you visiting the Espinoza brothers this morning, Doctor Alvaro?' Her voice, freshly shrill, provoked a civil nod of the head. 'But they're not people like us, are they?' she said, a sly smile on her face. 'Why were you there?' she cried. Alvaro smiled back but did not reply. 'Well?' she repeated, so loud that the rest of the table fell silent. A challenge had been issued. It was Maria who took it up.

'Because my father is a doctor, Señora Gonzalez,' she said.

'Yes, we all know that, my dear girl. But the Espinoza brothers!' the older woman cried out with a snort of derision. 'They conspire against *you*,' she said to the Captain. 'That's why they're on my list,' she added as an aside, her laugh tinkling in the light and ricocheting from glass to glass as several of the more kind-hearted guests raised them to their lips to hide their discomfort.

Maria looked at her, then at the people gathered together at the dinner. Doctor Alvaro nudged his daughter's foot with his, but to no effect. 'My father has a duty of care to the community, a duty to heal everyone,' Maria said with fierce pride. Luis sat back in his chair to wonder at her spirit. He put his glass down. It was time to help this girl.

'Yes,' he said. 'Surely you've heard of the *juramento hipocratico* Señora Gonzalez?' But before she could answer Maria quipped, 'Not to be confused with the *juramento hipicritico*. Ow!' Her father kicked her hard under the table. Maria had said enough for now.

'Another drink?' Lola asked the Captain.

CHAPTER 20

Maria sat in silence, in semi-disgrace. But her audacious interjections had aroused similar expressions of dissent around the table. One that aroused the girl's particular interest was taking place at the far end of the table between Dona Sofía and her son.

'But mother,' she heard Luis roar. 'How can you say that?' She observed the look of guilt that passed across Dona Sofía's face. 'Nudists, vegetarians, philanthropists, enthusiasts of Esperanto, oh, of course, and Marxists, yes Marxists, are worse,' she added in a desperate bid to shake her son off her tail, trying to recall groups considered a threat to Spain by the newspaper ABC. She would have added Jews to the list but remembered that an English woman had taken her to task about this some months back in Biarritz. She'd taken exception to the inclusion of philanthropists too, if her memory served her well. It had probably been foolish to buy an English education for her son, she thought to herself, but it was too late now. Luis' face registered confusion. 'Since when has teaching someone to read been a crime? I read. I imagine you don't have a problem with that?' Maria noted that Luis' mother said nothing in reply, managing only the weak smile of a rebuked child. Maria longed to join in but as a rebuked child herself (she had the sore ankle to prove it), she resisted the urge.

Don Felipe jumped to his wife's defence. 'My, my, Luis. You're sounding like a socialist.'

'I'm a Nationalist, father,' Luis said. 'Proud of my country, proud of my people.' And with that he got up and walked out of the room. Maria looked at him, willing him to return her gaze. He did not.

She observed his parents' response. That her soldier should be the son of such hard-hearted landowners perplexed Maria. There were no obvious physical similarities that she could discern. And as for his character, it was clear that it was not cut from the same unforgiving cloth as that of his parents.

'He's got a good heart,' Dona Sofía said apologetically to the Captain. 'A soft heart,' added his father, as if it were an affliction.

A strangely sadistic smile darkened Captain Garcia's face. Maria's blood ran cold. 'Leave it to me,' she heard him say. 'I have a cure for that.'

On the other side of the door Cecilia had been pacing the corridor, waiting to push on with her plan. She knew she had to go in, but she was afraid to do so. Until she heard Luis. That boy. He'd always been a brave one.

'Dona Sofía, may I have a word?' she asked, her voice a tremble. Her mistress looked up to check for sleeves, and, though thankful for small mercies, she marched her housekeeper back out into the corridor. Sounds of subservience wafted in, punctuated by sharp, shrill reprimands. The guests waited for their hostess to return with tales of how the evening was going from bad to worse but when Dona Sofía came back in she wore a smile and announced that there would be 'a little break before dessert.'

'A splendid idea,' the Captain said.

'Indeed,' agreed Señora Gonzalez. 'Perhaps we can present the Captain with our lists.'

Doctor Alvaro stood up. 'Please excuse me, I've forgotten something,' he mumbled, then quickly went outside. 'See. He does have a list!' Señora Gonzalez purred. Maria slapped the woman about

117

the face with her eyes before chasing after her father who had already disappeared out of the door and past the window.

Outside, Maria was surprised to find that the guard posted at the front of the house was nowhere to be seen. As she went round towards the back, the guard on duty there had gone off too. Her father must have gone to check on Cecilia. As she approached the kitchen, she saw through the half-open door the missing guards, sitting at the kitchen table and tucking into plates loaded with the food that had been left over from the dinner. No sign of her father. He must be somewhere else. As she wandered off, perplexed, a hand brushed her arm. It was Luis.

She looked into the beautiful strangeness of his eyes. For a moment it was as if he looked into her soul with one eye and let her look into his soul with the other.

'It's not her fault,' he said, his voice tinged with sadness and affection. 'She's a good person deep down. Don't think ill of her. She's a product of her class.' Maria was moved by the compassion of his feelings but she couldn't help but notice the irony of his words. 'Like you?'

Luis smiled at her sharpness. 'Undoubtedly,' he said, 'but that doesn't mean that I can't see the good in *people like you*.' Maria laughed at this mocking of Señora Gonzalez's words. Feelings of attraction flooded her body. She lowered her eyes so that he couldn't tell.

'Help! Someone's taken the horse! Quick! Get the Captain! Call the guards!' Her father's cries, accompanied by the catching of hooves on stony ground galloping away, broke the spell and reminded her why she'd come outside to begin with.

Confusion followed.

Plates smashed on the kitchen floor, chairs clattered backwards, guards rushed out into the evening, arms outstretched, pistols cocked. Stray bullets shot through the air. Luis sheltered Maria.

The Captain made a brief appearance at the scene, shouted orders at the guards to go after the escaped animal, then, when satisfied that his guards were indeed running in the same direction, he returned inside to attend to Señora Gonzalez.

As the red sky changed to a deep purple, the light dimmed and a stray figure crept out of the larder, a weighty bag on his back. Cecilia hugged the figure then pushed him on. He squeezed Lola's arm for luck as he went outside praying for the mercy, and protection, of the fast-falling night. His shoulders hunched, he moved quickly, his eyes moving from side to side as he climbed onto the military motorcycle. He started it up. It roared into life.

'Manuel!' a voice shouted. Doctor Alvaro shuddered. Luis wasn't meant to be there.

Manuel's heart stopped for a moment as he looked into his childhood friend's face. The young men remained silent, not moving for what seemed like an age but as Luis' hand went down to his holster so Manuel's foot pressed down on the accelerator. Maria looked on, horrified. Luis pointed the gun at the boy he'd once thought of as a brother then lifted his gun in the air with both hands. He let off three shots into the sky.

The Captain ran out again. This time to see a renegade escape on a military motorbike.

Doctor Alvaro, who'd been watching from the shadows, put a hand to his chest. He watched the bike as it disappeared out of sight, looked at Luis as he replaced his pistol in the holster. He blinked, then blinked again. He could not believe what he'd just seen.

Back inside the farmhouse Señora Gonzalez was furious. The unexpected excitement of a runaway horse, a stolen motorcycle, and not one, not two, but three pistol shots, had made everyone leap out of their seats with wild abandon, arms flailing, legs spinning: an unpalatable sight for the woman whose hand, prior to the *distraction*, had been hovering above the piece of paper peeping out of her evening bag, poised to thrust it into the hand of the Captain. Yet though chaos surrounded her, she was determined to remain true to the cause. She would not lose her focus.

119

She coughed, tapped her glass as if it were a bell, clapped her hands, then raised her voice to a pitch so shrill that animals outside pricked up their ears. 'I hope you don't think me indelicate, but when would you like to take a look at the lists?' Though addressing the Captain, it was clear her words were intended as a prod to her fellow guests.

The mayor and his wife jumped to attention. He rifled through his pockets. 'What have I done with it?' he mumbled to himself. He blanched as he remembered putting it down on a table at home. His political opponents would be granted at least a reprieve whereas the shopkeeper who had inadvertently short-changed his wife would not. He was on the list that his wife had managed to locate at the bottom of her bag and that she was now clutching in a plump and clammy palm. Señor Suarez was on it too. He'd asked her once if she'd spare some of her time to help teach the labourers to read. She'd found the strength to say no but he'd put her in a very uncomfortable position.

As for the rest of the party, it looked as though they would soon be heading off. The doctor had already taken his daughter by the arm and was waiting inside by the front door. And the soldiers who'd been lured away by Cecilia with food in the kitchen were now standing near the car, shamefaced and terribly sweaty, heralding the imminent departure of the guest of honour, Captain Garcia.

The Captain was pacing, tempted to go out and give the boys a good kicking for not capturing the horse. As for Luis, Garcia boiled with a desire to smash the fool's witless brains in.

'Come, Captain!' Don Felipe said, slapping the disgruntled man on the back with exaggerated bonhomie in an attempt to breathe some life back into the flagging party. 'Let us retire to the drawing room and have ourselves a large brandy! And who knows, perhaps we'll find the name of the degenerate who stole away this evening on one of the lists we've drawn up for you. What do you say?' And with that Don Felipe steered the man back inside and into the drawing room. The other guests followed.

'Don't say a word,' Doctor Alvaro whispered into his daughter's ear as he led her reluctantly back into the lions' den. Maria looked at Lola as she topped up glasses and for a moment a look of understanding passed between the two girls. Then Lola moved swiftly on. 'Would you like a drink, Señor? Señora? Captain?' Glasses replenished, a semblance of order had been restored.

The Captain took a cursory look at the lists, lingering on Señora Gonzalez's, before thrusting them at Luis. He would have liked to be able to add that boy's name to the bottom of one of them at that very moment in time. He burped indecorously, unable to keep down his disgust at his hosts' son. Señora Gonzalez let out a soft giggle. As if to reward her, the Captain brought up the only name he could remember on her list.

'So, tell me about this Señor Suarez.'

The doctor inhaled deeply. His friend had escaped and he was glad of it. But Maria had no idea that her dear teacher was safe. Her head was still full of what she had witnessed in the courtyard and now this. Her nails pressed into the skin of her father's forearm. The priest came to life at the name of a virtuous man. He'd been conspicuously quiet during the brouhaha outside, the only sound coming from him being a strange rumbling every now and again. His head had been jerked back and forth in the air as a consequence of the armchair he'd managed to find which offered no support for it. And this in spite of the large ring of fat that went round his neck that looked so puffed up you would be forgiven for taking it to be a pillow. It was not. He shook his head, jowls swaying, in a bid to free himself from the warm, welcoming waters of sleep into which he had slipped in order to defend his friend, whose name had disturbed him and summoned him back to the world of the living.

'Señor Suarez? He's a charming man. A *good* man,' he said, wiping away dribble from his chin. 'A good Catholic, would you say?' the Captain asked, looking at Señora Gonzalez with a smile

121

on his face. The priest paused for a moment. 'He lives according to Christian principles,' he answered. 'He helps those in need, teaches the poor to read.' The mayor's wife fanned herself as words of self-justification flew from her mouth. 'I never did it. I was asked. I would never have done such a thing. I said no.' The priest looked around for someone to support his good friend. But not one adult came forward. Señora Gonzalez arched her eyebrows at the Captain.

Alvaro remained silent: he sensed the menace in the room. In a world where wrong was right and goodness came across as the ramblings of a stupid old man who wore a cassock, the doctor knew better than to waste his breath. Besides, he knew that the teacher was already safe. There was little need or point in throwing a punch when the fight for Suarez had already been won.

The priest's eyes darted round, searching. Was no one brave enough to stand up for Señor Suarez?

Maria looked at the people gathered together at the dinner. They had arrived this evening presenting themselves as an armoured flank of powerful citizens, a solid wall of smart suits and elegant evening dresses united together to protect the people of the village from the rough uniforms and over-shiny boots of interrogating officers. But Doctor Alvaro's daughter saw very clearly now the chinks in their facade, made by the corrosive effects of self-interest and village gossip. The word 'vipers' sprung to mind. Her father had advised her to stay quiet but her conscience would not let her.

'After all he's done for the village,' she piped up. 'Maria,' her father said, hoping to stop her from saying more. But he could not. She looked at him, disappointment in her eyes, rage in her heart. 'He's a good person,' she said, defiantly. 'A good teacher.'

'Never mind that. Who does he teach?' Señora Gonzalez spoke out, eyes narrowing, tongue flicking like the snake Maria now saw her as.

'Me. The children in the village,' Maria replied. 'And?' the older

122

woman pushed. 'Workers here. On the estate,' Maria answered, her hand gesturing outwards as if they were standing in the room beside her. 'They can read Marx and…'

Señora Gonzalez, one of the main witnesses for the prosecution, gave a victory laugh. 'Let me get this right, the man teaches them to read *communist* literature, is that what you're saying?' With the realisation that Maria herself had driven the last heavy nail into Señor Suarez's coffin, the blood rushed from the girl's face. She fell back. A glass smashed on the floor. It was her father's.

CHAPTER 21

The morning after the dinner party Maria had woken up to find that her father had already braved the patrolling soldiers in the streets to make a start on his rounds. He'd been awake all night, working out what to do, who to warn, and by the time Maria had stumbled down to the kitchen he had tipped off those most at risk, putting in place lines of communication and identifying hiding places. Lone dissenting voices were thus turned into one covert, but united resistance group as Doctor Alvaro shared his intelligence and welcomed these new members into the fold. 'Together we're stronger,' he'd told them.

But Maria knew nothing of this.

She poured herself a glass of water and rubbed her eyes, still tired after her own restless night. Distant gunfire had punctuated her sleep, and any dreams she'd managed to have fluctuated between Manuel triumphant (ascending up and away into the night sky to twinkle like a star, helped on his way by an angel) and Manuel defeated (lying in an ever-widening pool of his own blood, body riddled with bullets from the pistol of a devil, the wheel of his motorcycle spinning round and round). Unfortunately, she'd woken up with memories of the latter in the forefront of her consciousness and she didn't like it.

She let out a sound like a low growl. 'But he got away,' she told herself as she walked around touching familiar objects as if the physicality of the waking world could dispel her subconscious fears.

But the cloud created by her dreams only lifted to reveal the feeling of anger that she felt, that she could do nothing to shift. She was angry with the vipers for turning on Señor Suarez the evening before. She was angry with her father for not having told her that the teacher had escaped. How many other secrets was he keeping from her, she wondered. And she was angry with herself. Why? She pushed the answer away for the moment and directed her thoughts to her father. 'You are not to go out tomorrow. I forbid it, do you hear me Maria? Forbid it! Now go to your room. Get some sleep.' He had never spoken to her like that before and a brooding resentment wriggled inside her at the memory of it.

She clanked around the kitchen, thumping down the chopping board, tearing through bread, slamming down her cup, and pouring out water so that it sprayed over the sides. He'd had no right to be cross with her, she told herself as she devoured her breakfast without tasting it, when he'd been the one in the wrong.

She chewed herself to a state of calm so her breath became steady, her mind less troubled. Her guard down, the landowners' son crept into her consciousness. Anger flashed up within her once more only to be quelled by the immediate realisation that the greater part of her was happy he'd found his way in. The memory of looking into his eyes the evening before, all distance between them gone, caused her entire body to flush.

Ironic that the son of those bloodsuckers Don Felipe and Dona Sofía should be the only other person who dared speak out in the name of fairness last night. Unsettling that she should find a soldier in the Nationalist army so attractive.

Conflicting thoughts struggled for supremacy in her mind, about who he was, his family, his uniform, about what she'd seen him do, heard him say. He had been loud in both word and action and, it seemed to Maria, last night he'd brought about some kind of miracle.

Luis de los Rios. Everything about him perplexed her, though she did not find the experience unpleasant. His eyes, the strength, the calmness, the sense of right and wrong, they shone for her. The soldier with different-coloured eyes had inveigled his way into her imagination and aroused feelings that were complicated, that she couldn't explain. She'd experienced nothing like them before. They made her heart ache.

Unbidden, the image of Richard Johnson presented itself to her. Richard. She remembered telling herself when the English boy had first arrived in Fuentes that she would love him, and after only a few weeks that she did love him. But as she thought of him now, she accepted that she felt many fine feelings for him but not one of them was love. He roused none of the longing that the landowners' son made her feel. Luis. The very thought of him filled her with light; it made every part of her tingle.

Maria flushed with confusion and joy.

For Doctor Alvaro's daughter to experience such wondrous feelings and not to have a soul to talk about them with grieved her somewhat. She looked out of the window, watched the people milling round, saw pairs of patrolling soldiers. It appeared no different to how it had looked the day before when she had been allowed outside. She humphed as she pulled herself back in. She paced up and down, up and down, padding all around the room like a tiger in a cage. Lonely.

She went back to the window again, pulled up a chair and looked up and down the street, willing Luis de los Rios to appear. She waited and waited, her ankles changing colour in the heat of the sun. And then she saw him.

She withdrew hastily. From the shadows she watched him. He walked back and forth scouring the windows on her side of the street, looking for her.

126

Drawn into the light, Maria found herself pulled forward. Luis' eyes found hers and the moment they did she instantly pulled away. Caught. Her heart pounded, back against the wall, in the shadows from where she watched him as he walked on down the street.

He turned back to look up at her, his strange, imperfectly beautiful eyes straining to find her in the darkness of the room. When he reached the end of the street he lingered a while, looking for her one last time. He put a finger by his neck as though to loosen his collar, gave it a pull. Then he was gone.

Maria slid down to the floor, bending her knees as she went. He'd come to find her. Her entire being was overwhelmed by a myriad of feelings so strong and exultant that she could not resist them. She put both hands to her chest and looked up at the ceiling. Awash with joy she started to laugh.

The front door banged shut. It was her father.

'Can I go out now?' she shouted down the stairs, oblivious to the black mood he'd brought into the house. 'People are panicking!' he called back to her. 'Can I go out?' she asked again – she had not heard the word 'no'. 'MARIA!' he cried, blasting the myriad feelings that surrounded her to the four winds. She started. Her father's voice had broken the spell that Luis de los Rios had cast upon her as she clattered down the stairs. She rushed into the kitchen. There, standing in the middle of the room, a worn look upon his face, was her father. She stepped back for a moment. He looked grey.

Fury raged behind his drooping eyes and he slapped a dead weight wrapped in paper onto the kitchen table as if to prove it. He looked up and glowered at her. She would ask him if she could go out no more.

Maria blinked to bring herself back to the here and now. A shaft of sunlight struck the kitchen table, illuminating her father's offerings while making her momentarily conscious of the band of sun kissed skin across her ankles. They glowed with a warmth that brought a smile to her face as she bent down to touch them, a silent acknowledgement that her feelings for Luis glimmered within.

'The food queues are getting worse,' her father exclaimed, his head full of the complaints and worries that he'd been subjected to while waiting in them. There on the table was a loaf of bread and a rabbit wrapped in paper. Maria sniffed. The smell of meat left hanging too long in the heat invaded her nostrils, causing her nose to wrinkle in revolt. 'I know,' her father said. 'But the chickpeas will help,' he said, pointing to the sack of them next to the stove. She sniffed some more. This time with derision. If he thought she believed he'd done nothing but buy food and visit a few patients all the hours he'd been out he was very much mistaken.

'I popped in on old Lopez... then on Rodriguez. You'll be pleased to know Salva is on the mend. Pedro asked me to take a look at his mule. His mule! Incredible...'

Maria gave a snort as she arched her eyebrows. 'You've been busy,' she said, still not placated. He was keeping something from her, she told herself.

And she was right.

The teacher was safe. The Espinoza boys had gone, as arranged. And the doctor had witnessed with his own eyes Manuel's escape. But these small and not so small victories would have repercussions, and the tension in the atmosphere told him that it wouldn't be long in coming. He'd talked it through with Father Anselmo but neither man had much time left. After last night even the priest would be under suspicion.

'Many sick people in Fuentes,' Maria's father answered her vaguely. Yet all the while Doctor Alvaro burned with the knowledge that danger was fast approaching. He could almost taste its acrid tang at the back of his throat, and try as he might he could do nothing to stop it getting worse.

'Oh, I saw the Redondo boys again this morning,' he said,

128

trying to lighten his tone and knowing that his daughter had a soft spot for the village menaces. 'They were out?' Maria said. Her father gave a forced laugh and should have left it there if he'd wanted to persuade his daughter that everything was fine outside. Instead he answered, 'mucking about near the soldiers.' The words came out of his mouth like a torrent of despair and Maria sensed it. The brothers the doctor had stopped from getting trampled underfoot had, apart from a few mornings, been out trying to draw attention to themselves ever since. And they had succeeded. One or two of the soldiers had kicked a ball about with them, while others had ruffled the boys' hair and pushed them affectionately on their way when they'd ventured too close. For a while even Doctor Alvaro had seen this as a good sign, an indication that everything was going to be all right. But now, after last night, everything had changed. And to see the children throwing themselves at these men with rifles was for him like watching moths flapping around a deadly and all-consuming flame that threatened to flare up at any second. The panic that the doctor had accused his fellow villagers of was in truth his own, and it was increasing all the time. He had come in with the intention of not alarming his daughter, but he was finding it hard.

'The boys might love the soldiers, their father might support the army, but that fool shouldn't be as naïve as to believe that gives him and his children protection. After last night anyone might make it onto one of those lists.' And with that he cut himself some bread and sank his teeth into it hungrily. 'I didn't know Señor Redondo supported the army,' Maria said. The colour ran from her father's face. He'd said too much again.

Doctor Alvaro continued to gnaw away at the stale dry bread until his teeth ached and his gums bled. Señor Redondo. If not even a sympathiser like him could promise protection to his own children, how could someone like Doctor Alvaro? As Maria watched him she couldn't remain angry with him for long. The sight of her father moved her to pity. He was still keeping something from her, she knew it. But she had never seen her father so preoccupied, and it frightened her. She would not ask if she could go out again today. She placed her hand on his arm and it went rigid to the touch. Then he looked her in the eyes and embraced her. 'My girl. I've got you, my dear sweet girl,' he cried. And as she felt his tears on her shoulder then she cried too.

CHAPTER 22

Over the following days the atmosphere set. Or rather, congealed. Like fat. On the surface all was heavy, quiet, eerily calm, while below, unpredictably dark sulphurous waters swirled and spat in hellish lakes, bubbling away, getting ready to explode.

Maria felt it too, though thoughts of Luis created pockets of sunshine in her heart and put a smile on her face and colour in her cheeks, as well as her ankles, as she looked out for him at the window upstairs. Alvaro knew, had known ever since the night of the dinner. In normal circumstances he would have been glad of it. His daughter's singing drifted around each room of the house, lifted the mood. Love's hopeful melody lit up each sombre space with bursts of optimism. It would not have mattered a jot to him who the boy's parents were (Maria's father was the last person to condemn someone because of where they came from). The boy had shown himself to be courageous beyond words. But these were not normal circumstances.

The undeniable truth, the stumbling block, the forbidding mountain Maria's father couldn't get round, was the fact that this brave young man was a soldier in the Nationalist army. Put simply, Luis de los Rios was the enemy. And there wasn't a single thing anybody could do about it. There would be no future, no happy

131

ending. Any feelings Luis and Maria had for one another were doomed.

But for the moment, he was relieved to let the singing continue. Storm clouds were up ahead for them all and he could not begrudge his daughter her few moments of pleasure. Forces greater than the ones he had at his disposal would soon be marching their way to stamp out any flame that might have ignited in the heart of his daughter. And Luis de los Rios, no matter how heroic, no matter how strong the flame burning within his own soul, would have no choice but to march along with them.

Which was why Alvaro could not let his daughter out.

Doctor Alvaro's meetings with Father Anselmo since the outbreak of war had gone from weekly, to daily, to sometimes hourly, as the threat it posed became ever more urgent. An odd couple, their friendship had not gone unnoticed.

Doctor and priest got on well. Unusual for a self-proclaimed atheist and a man of God. However, on points of principle the two men agreed on much and on what to do to protect the villagers they agreed on everything. The priest had his contacts, Doctor Alvaro had his, and together they tightened their network. Ever since the start of the troubles they had done all that they could to help the most vulnerable citizens flee to parts of Spain that had yet to be 'pacified' by the Nationalist forces, parts of Spain that were still Republican. And they had taken great risks to do so.

'Better to die following your conscience than live without freedom, virtue and God.' So said Father Anselmo, and the doctor, for the most part, agreed. But as the idea of a glorious demise crept ever closer towards becoming a reality, a thought less edifying occurred to him, one that had been gestating ever since the dinner party and it was turning into a monster in his mind. If he were to be killed, what would happen to his daughter? They had no family. At least not in Fuentes.

And there was the glaring problem that his daughter had

created at the dinner. He let out a groan. In standing up for Señor Suarez, she had stood against Señora Gonzalez. The memory of Señora Gonzalez's twisted face loomed large in his mind, plots for revenge showing in a tic above the woman's left eye and the grinding of her teeth as they set in a grimace. Maria had put her own life in danger as well as his when she decided to make an enemy of that treacherous woman that night. Mad times, he acknowledged to himself with regret, when a father feels angry with a daughter for staying true, fighting for justice.

It was nearly four long days after the dinner and Doctor Alvaro had not let his daughter out. Not once. Not to help him out, not to get food, let alone to enjoy the warmth of companionship with a friend. A songbird in a cage.

'I don't know what I'm going to do, Father,' he said to his friend. 'I can't trust her not to get herself in more trouble with that loose tongue of hers. She can't keep her opinions to herself.'

'Oh to have a high-minded child,' Father Anselmo chuckled. 'Their path is never easy in our world. That's the nature of things. Rejoice Alvaro for God has given you a battling angel.'

The briefest of smiles flashed across the doctor's face before the look of fear returned. 'That's why I'm afraid to let her out. Especially now,' he said.

'Ah. So that's why I've not had the pleasure of encountering her while I've been out and about these last few days. Come now,' he said, patting Alvaro gently on the back. 'She's a spirited child. Ingenious. And she needs the water of human companionship to grow. If you don't let her out to see people she will find a way. It's in her nature and her will is strong. She won't be tethered. You, Alvaro, know that more than anyone.' The doctor nodded.

'Let her live. God will protect her and if He has His hands busy elsewhere then… *we* will.' With that the priest placed a large, hairy hand on the piece of paper on the pew next to him. 'Give her the names,' he urged as he picked it up and offered it to Maria's father. 'Trust her with them.'

*

The following day Maria clattered round the kitchen once more. Caged up, she was beginning to feel frustrated. She could read. She could write. But she wasn't going to do any of that. She threw herself down onto the chair and chewed away on cold cooked rabbit, furiously dipping stale chunks of bread into a cup of olive oil in an attempt to make them if not completely edible then at least soft enough to put in her mouth without feeling as though she was sucking on blades.

'*Vale*,' her father said.

'Papa?' Maria asked.

'*Vale*!' her father repeated as he turned a folded piece of paper round and round between his thumb and forefinger.

'*Vale*?' his daughter repeated, not daring to believe that this meant what she hoped it meant.

'Oh, *vale*! Yes. You can go out!' he answered, his words saying yes, his tone still expressing his reservations.

'Outside? In the village?' she checked.

He wished he could change his mind but it was no good. His words were out and they had made the childlike innocence of his daughter's shine with wondrous delight.

'Now?' she ventured, still cautious but still Maria. She was not going to let this opportunity pass her by.

'But only to buy food,' he cautioned, his head nodding sombrely. 'The queues are long, so you'll get to chat,' he said with a frightened laugh. 'But no hanging around. Just straight there and straight back.'

Maria nodded back with delight. Oh, how excited she was to have the chance to be outside again after days of incarceration. Queues. She couldn't wait to join them. The longer the better.

She bent down to sweep up her basket and went to go.

'But wait,' her father said. 'I want you to have this.' And with that he placed the piece of paper given to him by Father Anselmo into his daughter's hand. 'Guard it well as the names on this list will guard you.' And with that he gave his daughter the gentlest of kisses on the cheek. He had much to do.

CHAPTER 23

Strange how life goes on. That's what everyone says. Whether in the dirtiest war, after the most horrific accident, or the most heinous crime. Why is that? Probably because it does. For those still left alive. What they don't say is that it's never the same. Oh, people marvel that the sun still shines, the sky's blue, they still eat, drink, breathe, sleep. But it's what's beneath that's changed, what's inside that has been transformed forever. And it's what's hidden that you need to be on your guard against.

But sometimes, to try and find it and face it when you do, is far too hard a task.

Perhaps it's better to believe that life goes on as normal, to allow yourself to become blinded by the mesmerising effects of habit. Indeed, when the truth seems too onerous to bear, it might even be the only thing to do.

And so it was for Alvaro and his daughter. Five minutes after allowing Maria to go out to buy some food the good Doctor also took himself off into the streets. Inside, standing and staring at four walls worrying about Maria and how to protect her was making him feel anxious. Walls. They made an unwelcome blank slate against which to plot out his worst fears.

Outside, he could lose himself a little. He hooked a finger over his neckline and trailed it back and forth. He walked down the streets of Fuentes, saw shutters open, heard plates clatter. He felt lulled by the seeming normality of his existence, thanked whatever deity had created this illusion. Without it, he feared he might lose his mind. Oh, how to protect his daughter. As he walked past ordinary citizens going about their usual business he grew distracted, felt less uncomfortable. As he saw soldiers sitting in cafes and hanging around on street corners it seemed that they had been there forever. How long had these invaders been in Fuentes? Days? Weeks? Yet somehow even he was getting used to them.

Yet how to protect his daughter.

'Doctor Alvaro!' One of the soldiers posted on sentry duty at the landowners' the other evening stopped to greet him with a salute, though he did not look the older man in the eye. He had an embarrassed look on his face and something else, though Alvaro found it hard to place.

'*Buenos dias*,' Alvaro replied, returning the very slightest of bows back. He wanted to reach out his hand and put it on the boy's shoulders, so uneasy and strangely exhausted did he look. Here was somebody's son. 'Not sleeping?' the doctor asked. The boy looked up, his eyes red. Gratitude then fear flashed behind them. He turned and went on his way. *Who's going to protect you?* Alvaro sighed to himself.

Alvaro watched the poor boy who looked as if he'd had a bad night walk away. He looked as though he'd had the most terrifying of dreams. Coming in the opposite direction was the Captain. He gave his subordinate a supercilious leer.

'Doctor. Doctor Alvaro. Where are you off to on this gloriously sunny day?' he asked, a smile animating every part of his face. The sinister thread that traced itself through the fabric of the Captain's charming and self-satisfied façade was subtle. But undeniable. As the Captain placed his still smiling face close to his, the doctor could smell the danger. Alvaro's instinct told him to nod politely, walk on by. That way self-preservation lay. Yet the urge to protect others won the day once more.

Stubborn old fool, Alvaro thought to himself, as he recognised the weathered old man coming along the road, pulling his cart along behind him, slow, plodding. His head was down, like a bull, and he was heading straight for them, again like a bull, albeit a very old and decrepit one. Juan Rueda. No wonder his name and address were on one of the lists in the Captain's possession. Stubborn, determined, hungry for a confrontation, there was no way Juan Rueda was going to lead his cart round them. Alvaro studied the Captain's eyes. They betrayed not a flicker of recognition as the grey-haired peasant grew ever closer, had no idea he was looking for a fight.

Alvaro took a chance.

'Rueda!' he shouted as he threw his arms around the frail body of the man, stopping the would-be bull from attacking his unsuspecting quarry and turning his well-worn cart handles into fierce, attacking horns. 'Come Captain. This man here has the finest chickpeas in all of Spain. Look!' With that he pulled Garcia to one side, lifted his arm, then thrust it into one of the many baskets of produce in the back of the cart. Both Rueda and Garcia were so stunned by Alvaro's behaviour that they said nothing, simply watched him, as if he'd had a strange turn.

The doctor, heartened by their mutual silence, continued, slapping Rueda enthusiastically on the back. '*Adios! Adios*, my dear friend. I will come to see how you're getting on soon. Now look after yourself.' Then, turning to the Captain, he added, 'Fine chickpeas, the best in the country, the best in the world, Captain Garcia.'

Five long minutes later the doctor turned to see the old man disappear, step by painstakingly slow step, into the distance. The discomfort of making small talk with the devil had been worth it.

Meanwhile, two streets away, his daughter had been engaged in conversation with a person equally foul.

'Why, Maria! Maria! *Buenos Dias*!' The shrill voice of Señora

Gonzalez pierced the ears of the doctor's daughter. 'Such a wonderful dinner at the Cortijo del Bosque,' she exclaimed, overjoyed to be able to share anecdotes with someone who had been there too, even if it was someone she considered a child, and a treacherous one at that. 'You were no doubt overwhelmed by the setting... and the guests. But that's only to be expected. I would have felt the same at your age. Probably.'

'Yes, Señora Gonzalez,' Maria replied, her voice flat. She had no intention of playing the grateful, fawning guest, that much was evident.

'So what are you doing?' she asked the young woman, with a twitch of her nose, suspicion dripping from its tip. She looked radiant with clear eyes the colour of sherry, shiny brown hair shot through with strands of red and gold that dazzled in the sunlight, and skin so smooth and fresh as to make her look much younger than her thirty five years. Nature had endowed her with many gifts. Yet even though her skin smelled of almonds and peaches she couldn't hide the rot festering within from the villagers who knew her. And after the dinner Maria knew her. She knew her very well. Her hand tightened protectively around the note inside her pocket, given to her by her father, as Señora Gonzalez's hand reached out to take the girl by the arm. Solicitously.

'How is your poor, poor father?' she said, with such forced concern that Maria had to do all she could to stop herself from shuddering and answering flippantly. 'Well, thank you.' She nodded, attempting to break free from Señora Gonzalez's clutches.

'What are you doing? Where are you going? Who are you seeing? Didn't your parents ever tell you how rude it was to walk along the streets with your hands in your pockets?' she asked Maria, curtly.

Maria dutifully stopped doing so and with the rise and fall of her arm so she succeeded in freeing herself from the older woman's grasp. Yet she would not be shaken off. She walked alongside Maria. Bombarded her with questions and more questions. Señora Gonzalez. After what Maria had seen pass between her and the Captain last week, remembered how she'd waved around her list like a flag at him, Maria knew better than to see her as the harmless gossip she'd once taken her for. Though she greeted the woman most respectfully she would not be answering any of her questions. Maria knew that Señora Gonzalez could pick out the most punishable of intents within the most innocent of words.

'Your father...' She paused. '*Such* a caring man. Who is he looking after today I wonder?'

She turned to look at Maria and sighed with disappointment. 'Oh, you poor, poor girl,' she simpered. Maria's chest lifted with relief. She thought for one moment that Señora Gonzalez, insufferable leech of a woman that she was, had given up on her, no doubt in search of a victim with richer veins and looser lips than Maria's. But she couldn't bear to let the doctor's daughter off that easily. Señora Gonzalez was an important woman in this village, now that the soldiers were here. And she would have the last word.

She placed her soft fingertips on Maria's arm once more, this time to make sure the girl was listening, and manoeuvred her beautiful figure so that she blocked the younger woman's way. 'Oh, I think there are going to be a few changes around here after last week. Soon. Very soon,' she squealed, putting her delicate little fingers over her lovely little mouth. She smiled at Maria then looked into the distance with longing. 'Oh, but what am I babbling on about? Forget I ever mentioned anything. It's nothing. Nothing,' she added. She fluttered her eyelashes like weapons then closed them in faux-coyness as her hand reached into her bag and pulled out her little black book. Maria had heard and seen enough. This woman unnerved her, made her feel unsafe. She placed a hand firmly over the piece of paper her father had given her once more and clenched her fist around it for luck. She turned and walked away. 'Thank you and have a good day, Señora Gonzalez,' she called back as she went.

CHAPTER 24

Maria was growing accustomed to seeing Luis de los Rios walk past her window several times a day. Then one day he stopped. That was the day she came out of the shadows. That was the day when she knew something wasn't right. Her body leant out over the balcony, her eyes strained for a glimpse of him. But he was nowhere to be seen. Her young man with the unusual eyes seemed to have disappeared off the face of Fuentes. Gone in a puff of smoke.

It was the Captain who was to blame for that.

The evening of the dinner the landowners' son had not made a good impression on his military superior. He'd shown himself to be soft and privileged. Anyone other than Don Felipe's son would have got a savage beating for having let some red peasant make off with a military motorcycle. If the Captain had not been eating at his father's table Luis de los Rios would have been subjected to immediate justice. Instead, the Captain had to think of a more palatable punishment.

It hadn't taken him long to come up with one. He'd leant over to Don Felipe while still at the table and whispered in his generous host's ear, 'I'm going to make a soldier out of your boy. Trust me.'

Luis de los Rios needed toughening up, and the other two

141

useless guards too. The Captain had just the remedy for three such lily-livered milksops. New recruits. Boys from old families, not battle ready. Soft hands, soft ways. He would take them out with him on a 'hunt' the following week, a very special sort of hunt, where the prey would be bigger than any the spoilt brats had ever seen before. 'I'll sort him out.' At that very moment Maria had happened to look over at Captain Garcia. She'd seen the look of amused cruelty on the Captain's face. It had made her shudder.

'Thank you, Captain,' Don Felipe had said.

The 'hunt' was a staged killing. What Captain Garcia hadn't anticipated was that it would be the setting for a curse. Its location was about an hour out of the village. Captain Garcia had rounded up his three novices, and no more than eight men besides, and they all made their way in the dead of night along gravel roads, weaved their way up winding hills, thrown around in the back of a military truck.

'Out, men!' Captain Garcia shouted when they'd reached their destination. He shouted some orders to his more seasoned troops, who'd followed on in another truck, before returning to inspect his green recruits. He laughed as he did so. He did not expect them to laugh back.

His gnarled fingers wrapped tighter round the pistol he was holding at his side as he gestured to the young men to follow him. Still laughing, he led them to a disused quarry that opened up before them like a stage.

In the centre was a small bundle.

The Captain arranged his eleven young soldiers so that they formed an audience. He indicated to one of his old hands that he should come forward with a lit torch.

The small, dark bundle slowly unfurled. It was a young gypsy boy. Noise welled up at the back of the young boy's throat, its bile-tinged mucus gurgling, spitting, waiting to erupt; tears clouded the frightened child's already swollen eyes, slapping, breaking like waves, ready to sweep away the floodgates. They would come. But the boy still hoped. Prayed.

Luis de los Rios could not believe what he was witnessing. He'd expected to be punished in some way for his staged incompetence. But not like this.

'Watch this!' the Captain said, turning to the boys he'd brought with him. Though he'd seen it all before, it still gave Captain Garcia a cruel satisfaction to share the spectacle of fear and weakness with these would-be men. Young. From wealthy families. They needed toughening up. And what better way?

Peels of nervous laughter rang out in the dark as Garcia saw their faces. He cast his eye down the line, luxuriating in their discomfort. Each one avoided his gaze. All except one. Luis de los Rios. He stared at the Captain, unafraid.

Garcia stared back at him, but a distant gunshot reverberated in the warm, still night air reminding him to crack on with the matter in hand.

He swung round to face the snivelling gypsy boy, eyeing the wall of light-coloured stone behind the child's small dark frame with appreciation. A perfect backcloth for what the Captain had in mind for tonight. He raised his arm, pointed the pistol.

Pee ran down the child's leg, the torch and moonlight catching its glistening trajectory as it traced its way down bare skin, running like rivulets round trembling knees, trickling to pools that formed at his feet. The Captain yelped with delight , excited in the knowledge that the best was yet to come.

The boy cried. Tears drenched and stung his wretched face; mucus trailed from his nose, an excess of saliva-soaked bubbles. Anguish gushed from his mouth. The Captain snorted with delicious disgust at this vision of despair. He whooped at his stunned audience, inviting them to share in his delight.

But that was not it. No, that was still not it. It wasn't over yet.

'Listen to this,' the Captain shouted, knowing it wouldn't be long now. Because he'd seen it all before. Then it came.

Words rose up above the whimpering.

'Mother. Mother. I want my mother.'

The Captain never tired of hearing those heart-wrenching words. For in the moment the performance is at its peak. His actors have no more to give, nowhere else to go.

The Captain looked into the darkness of his young recruits before pointing the pistol at the child's stomach. He pulled the trigger. The gypsy boy jumped into the air then doubled over, just as Captain Garcia knew he would, the light wall behind him red with blood. But before he could say, 'he folds like a puppet,' a bellow filled the night air.

A bellow. Low. Powerful. The sound of the abyss. Every ear knew it. Every soul felt it.

'What's going on?' Garcia cried.

An older man was prodded quickly into view with the end of a soldier's rifle. Until now kept captive in the wings, waiting to take his turn to die, his animal cry catapulted him to the front of the queue. No more waiting. Plucked out of obscurity, he was thrust against the red splattered wall. He fell to his knees, cradled the dead child in his arms, shaking, sobbing, moaning.

It was his son.

'Stand up,' the Captain ordered. But the father carried on holding his poor child in his arms.

And then he cursed.

'Ha! Don't say you've put a gypsy curse on me, gypsy?' roared the Captain with mocking hatred. 'Gypsy!' Each time he found the word, the more it dripped with his distaste. 'Don't you hate them? Gypsies?' he turned to ask his troops, chewing the word over in his mouth like a piece of gristle.

The father started mumbling his curse once more.

'Speak up. It may as well give us something to laugh about as it's clearly of no use to you,' the Captain boomed loudly. 'Spit it out.'

He was about to give up on the old gypsy and pull the trigger when the man stood tall, the body of his dead son held up to the dark heavens above. He looked at the Captain. Disarmed him. 'My name is Diego Flores. May your own foul deeds turn themselves upon you.'

Silence followed. Then the curse once more. This time loud, deep, clear.

'May your own foul deeds turn themselves upon you, pull your flesh in pieces from your body. May your death be long and cruel.' It possessed the darkness all around.

There was a pause. A shuffling of feet. Then a single, forced, laugh.

This time the Captain did pull the trigger.

Diego Flores was no more. And gone with him was the hope and faith of the young men Garcia had brought along to watch. The Captain struck a match and in the flame Luis de los Rios saw the evil in his face. He was sickened. He looked at Captain Garcia with loathing. If he'd been in any doubt that he'd done the right thing in allowing Manuel to escape, all doubt had well and truly vanished now.

The young soldier next to Luis started to tremble. Luis nudged him but it was too late. He had already attracted the Captain's malign attention.

'Don't worry,' he whispered in the frightened young man's ear. 'Soon it will be your turn. To pull the trigger.'

The boy's breath became shallow, his teeth began to chatter. 'I'll make a man of you yet,' Garcia continued. 'Oh, the fun we'll have.' And with that the poor boy's knees buckled.

Captain Garcia stamped his foot, exasperated. With one quick movement he raised his pistol above his head, ready to bring it down with force across that of the soldier's.

'Leave him be.' The calm, strong voice of Luis de los Rios cut through the night air, holding the Captain's arm back. Surprised, he turned, his arm still raised, poised to attack now this new victim.

The small band of young soldiers looked on with dread.

Luis de los Rios looked at the Captain, unrepentant, unafraid.

Whack. Before he could stop himself, the Captain had brought the pistol down with force across the boy's flawless face, bruising the cheekbone, breaking the skin.

'Consider yourself lucky that I did not pull the trigger,' he hissed. Because if the boy who'd dared to speak out hadn't been the landowners' son, the Captain thought to himself, he certainly would have.

The second the Captain walked away, annoyed and nursing his knuckles, Luis de los Rios placed his hand on the trembling arm of the soldier, now distraught, standing next to him. 'Stay strong, Virgilio,' he said as he looked at the two dead bodies lying not so very far away.

146

CHAPTER 25

It was a Wednesday morning and Maria pulled herself up to sitting in bed. She pushed her dark, sleep-curled locks behind her ears. From the coolness of the still shaded bedroom she watched the searing shafts of bright light as they broke in through tiny slits in and around the shutters, illuminating the dust motes so that they resembled swirling sandstorms. She watched them from the coolness of her still shaded bed, fascinated, and commended herself on her skills of observation. She walked carefully over to the shutters and pushed them open just a little, bathing a slice of her room in sunlight and warmth. She squinted for a moment, put her hand to her forehead, shading her eyes. Then she saw it. The narrow rectangle of big blue sky. Still full of endless possibilities. She'd not seen Luis – looking up at her window from the street below, on patrol – for some days, but today she felt hopeful that she would.

She looked down through the narrow opening between the shutters and marvelled at the spectacle. The street below was full of women chatting and peasants leading their donkeys to market, their baskets heavily laden with fruit and vegetables, uniforms dotting the scene. Her eyes searched hopefully for Luis but made do with a pile of juicy red tomatoes when they failed to seek him

147

out. Cages of chickens paraded by below rattling round on the back of a cart and the strong smell of cheese made its way up, filling her nostrils. Maria felt hungry, for food and for life.

She washed, pulled her clothes on and went down to fetch her basket which she'd left on the kitchen table. As she picked it up she looked at a bowl beside it, full of burnt paper, black and light as a feather. She touched it with the tip of her finger: it dissolved into a million insubstantial pieces. If she could not remember all the names of those she could trust and to whose homes she could run to if needs be then it was too late now.

'I've a fancy for tomatoes,' she declared as she opened the door onto the world, and with that she launched herself towards the market. Today would not be a day to run and hide. Today was a good day. She could feel it as the sun caressed her skin and as the sky went on forever. She would buy food, cook her father a good meal; for a doctor the poor man didn't look after himself very well at all. And, if fate was on her side, she would find Luis. But before doing that she walked along the street and turned the corner. She was on her way to Paloma's. War. It would surely soon be over. Her head filled up with thoughts of Luis, her heart swelled with hope that she would see him soon.

Minutes can feel like hours, hours like minutes, and in the time it took Maria to get within striking distance of her friend's home so much had happened, so much had changed. The sounds and sights of children playing, women chatting, cartwheels crunching over dry ground, all of them had gone. Vanished into thin air. She looked around, saw a dark-haired man in uniform disappear down a side street. She had no space in her head to notice the emptiness, the heaviness that had fallen down like a cloak upon Fuentes. Her mind was fixed on getting to see Paloma and looking for Luis and all she could think at that particular moment was that the soldier she'd been watching wasn't him.

Yet that did not dismay her. Her heart was in such a mood as to wrestle every drop of joy out of even the most inauspicious of signs. To think that he was not there was still to think of him.

Maria skipped excitedly down the shady side of the street, rolling, splashing and carried high, delighting in her feelings for Luis de los Rios that sprang from her like a fountain. The sky was blue, the village peaceful, and Maria was happy. She started to sing.

A distant sound made her start. All skipping and singing ceased and for a second the list of names her father had urged her to memorise came abruptly to mind. She cursed her father: first for keeping her in, then for alarming her so. Her own fears buoyed to the surface of her consciousness, rapidly evaporating into the heat of the day as she raised her eyes to the cloudless sky. It reassured her, dismissed Maria's anxieties as a creeping contagion.

Next stop, Paloma's. She had to come out. Maria had so much to tell her.

CHAPTER 26

Knock, knock. 'What's that?' Doctor Alvaro asked.

'I can't hear anything,' Father Anselmo replied. 'If it's anything it's probably the birds again. They're forever getting trapped inside the nave.' The doctor's ears listened out for them. Their wings flapped furiously, they called out to each other.

Knock, knock, knock. The doctor jumped. 'It's not the birds. Outside. At the door. There's somebody there.' He'd bring some olive oil next time and take a good look in old Anselmo's ears. 'What are you doing?' he said as his friend went to the sacristy door.

'God opens his house up to all,' Father Anselmo said, pulling back the heavy, wooden door.

He fell back, a hand to his brow. There, standing before him was a young man, a soldier, his uniform shabby and tattered, caked with something dark. 'Help me, Father!' Anselmo led the terrified boy in. Fear was in his voice and his eyes.

The older men looked at one another. Even soiled, they recognised the uniform as Nationalist. Even injured, they knew the boy to be one of the guards posted up on Don Felipe's estate the week before. Both men recoiled, just for a moment, wary of the danger involved in taking this lad in. Yet the feeling quickly passed, swept away by the strength of their humanity. The doctor pulled the boy in, his gentle hands eager to heal the soldier's body, while the priest shone a light in his path with words to lift his spirit and nourish his soul. Alvaro bolted the door. Anselmo went to stop him but then saw the anguish in the young soldier's eyes. He had been drenched in evil, it would not do to welcome any more in.

The doctor and the priest set to doing what each of them did best while the soldier wept in silence, his chest heaving with pain and confusion.

'Hello! Is anybody here? Father? Father Anselmo? Doctor? You must be in here somewhere!' The click, click, click of tiny heels on the stone floor of the church reverberated all around, ricocheting off the sacristy door.

All three men froze. They waited for the banging. And it came.

'Father? Father Anselmo? I know you're in there! I have something to tell you. I have a message from the Captain, you know.' The priest held the soldier's arm firmly and kept his gaze. He shook his head. She did not know he was there. She could not know. His eyes told the soldier he had no reason to be afraid. The boy's heartbeat deafened him and drowned out the sound of the knocking and calling, his eyes revealed the struggle within. Doctor Alvaro smoothed the boy's matted hair to reassure him. 'Bother,' her thin, shrill voice said. 'Oh, how I hate those birds,' she muttered as they threw themselves against the ceiling, their frustration sounding out in their screams. 'Well, Father Anselmo can't say I didn't try to warn him. Ah well, I have to go now. I haven't come here to put myself at risk!' and with that, the click, click, click of tiny heels receded, Señora Gonzalez's voice said 'Ugh! Those disgusting birds!' as the heavy main door opened and closed. Then the click, click, click clicked on out and into the distance until it disappeared into thin air. All three men sat and listened, deafened by the silence.

They waited and waited, satisfied yet disturbed that they could hear nothing. Nothing at all. Señora Gonzalez had gone. Even the birds had gone, though it struck Anselmo as strange that this should be the case.

The priest was the first one to move, standing up to push to one side the heavy, wooden vesting table. He then pulled back the heavy curtain suspended against the wall behind it, revealing a hidden door, that looked more like the entrance to a cupboard.

'What's your name, boy?'

'Virgilio. Virgilio Lorenzana Macarro.'

'Well come, Virgilio Lorenzana Macarro,' Anselmo said to the boy, opening the door. 'We need to get you ready.' All three men crouched down to pass through the low doorway.

The doctor and the priest had listened to many wretched survivors telling their stories in this windowless room since the troubles had started. It was here that they, along with the teacher (before he'd needed to flee himself), had planned the escape of many to Madrid and other Republican held areas, and if some, like Manuel and the Espinozas, were fired up to join the guerrillas camped out in the countryside, forests and mountains, then so much the better. These were the only four walls in all of Fuentes that both men could trust not to have spying eyes and ears.

The priest lit some candles to provide light in the windowless room. Chairs lined two walls, a table with clean clothes and wash things sat up against another, and along the fourth, on the same wall as the tiny door, lay a bed with clean sheets and a Bible upon it. A statue of Mary looked down from above.

The doctor carried on cleaning the boy and checking him over. 'How old are you?' he asked.

'Seventeen,' the boy replied, his voice as broken as his identity. Seventeen. He looked more like seventy in the candlelight. The doctor sighed to himself, trying to keep at bay thoughts of his own daughter. He cleaned around the boy's bruised eyes as carefully as he could and picked out a mixture of what he knew to be blood, excrement and vomit from behind his split nails.

The boy started to sob. 'It is true about Baena... so many massacred there... and the killings... the Captain... death... I can't rid myself of the smell of it. And it's coming, it's coming,' he cried, the stench of war clinging to the insides of his nostrils, coating the back of his throat.

'We know, my son, we know. God knows, God forgives,' the priest said to him while looking up at Mary, wondering if He would.

'I have to go, we all have to go... before it's too late.' Though these words of a damaged human being disturbed Anselmo and Alvaro, they put them to one side. It was their duty to repair the damage. Besides, the soldier was too weak to stand let alone leave. The poor soul had no choice other than to sob himself to sleep.

Alvaro took out his pouch of tobacco and, sitting back in his chair, he rolled up two cigarettes. He threw one to Father Anselmo, putting the other between his own lips. Both men lit up, inhaling on the roll-up to draw the flame in. The two men sat without talking, the ends of their cigarettes glowing red with every inhalation. An unusual scene. Yet these were unusual times. Alvaro looked at the bottle of alcohol unopened on the table. It was intended for the people they were helping but today the doctor had need of it himself. Father Anselmo poured him a glass, then one for himself. He had need of it too.

'You'll be safe soon,' the doctor whispered to the sleeping soldier. 'Poor child,' he said as he looked at him. He was someone's child, someone's sweetheart, a fellow countryman, Spanish. His future, which must have looked so certain not so very long ago, now seemed completely lost. Alvaro thought of Maria again.

The candles flickered, went out. The doctor and the priest sat in the darkened room listening to the sleeping breath of the young boy, smoking and drinking. The church beyond was silent. And all around was too. The two men sat. Waited.

The doctor sat bolt upright. 'I heard somebody scream,' he said. 'No, it's just the birds again,' his holy friend assured him. 'They always scream when they're trapped.'

Though convinced it was the birds, Father Anselmo was also slightly perturbed. Both men left the wounded soldier to rest while they sought out the reassurance of the world of light.

Father Anselmo re-emerged into the sacristy. Something had changed, was making him feel unsettled. He leant behind the vestment table to straighten up the curtain that concealed the low doorway, thinking to himself that it had to be the meeting with the young rebel deserter that was disturbing him so. He and the doctor had helped many men to safety but none from the other side. But that wasn't it. There was something about the atmosphere. The silence. Eerie. Foreboding. He looked at Alvaro. He was standing nearer the main door, his neck slightly craned, a frown on his forehead. He too could hear nothing and it unnerved him.

Though the church was usually a place of quiet and calm the sounds of life still permeated the walls. Yet now, no sounds came in from the world outside, no buzzing of voices, no shouts from vendors making their way around the streets as children pawed the fruit. No occasional soldier stamping past in heavy boots making you feel jumpy. Nothing. It had all stopped. Like the calm before the storm, a pregnant sense of nothingness lay heavy in the air signalling the arrival of chaos.

And then it came. Both men heard it. At first it sounded like distant thunder, rumbling, getting louder, and louder. Doctor Alvaro looked at his watch. It was three o'clock. He had read the newspapers, heard de Llano's little radio chats, known about the lists where if villagers were on them they were at risk, heard the fear in the rebel soldier's voice... but that would all seem like a dress rehearsal compared to what he was about to experience. At three o'clock, on this very day, war – his war – was about to begin.

Tramp, tramp, tramp. At three o'clock on a Wednesday afternoon, soldiers' boots trailed their relentless way into the consciousness of the people of Fuentes, getting louder and louder.

154

Nearly everyone still foolish enough to be out ran home so that very soon the world outside was full of nothing but marching. And as the boots like drums beat their monolithic message of destruction, so the sound of blood flooded ears as if to drown all those who heard it, while their pulses throbbed as if to break the skin and burst the banks of vein and artery.

Doctor Alvaro and Father Anselmo opened the heavy church door and stood as if petrified. Both breathed in deeply, slowly, to quell the insurrection within. Alvaro's thoughts turned to his daughter. Father Anselmo's did too. The priest regretted having given his friend advice. His friend regretted having taken it. It seemed madness that either of them should have thought it was safe for Maria to go out. A poor decision, rashly taken. It was coming back to haunt both of them now. Doctor Alvaro's usually reasonable head was awash with conflicting emotions. He'd been caring for a deserter when he didn't know if his own flesh and blood was okay. He felt ashamed for resenting the young boy, but in that moment he didn't care. There, standing in the entrance to the church, the doctor turned around to look back inside. He begged Mary for mercy, prayed to a God in whom he didn't believe. 'Hurry home,' Father Anselmo said to him.

At three o'clock, when the storm started up, Maria was only a few streets away from her father. She was with Paloma. She'd had to see her. That had always been the plan and although her instincts had told her something didn't feel right as she'd got closer to her friend's home, she'd ignored them. She'd gone to buy some food but Paloma lived so close. Besides, what harm could it do?

When she'd got there, Paloma's mother had categorically refused to let her daughter outside. 'There's too many soldiers around!' Cecilia had mumbled, shooing Maria away. 'Now get yourself home!'

She was always going to be a hard nut to crack.

'Can I just speak to her for a minute?' Maria had pleaded.

'Paloma? A minute? No. Get yourself inside, for pity's sake.'

And with that Cecilia slammed the door shut. Maria walked off alone.

But the rock that was Paloma's mother had developed a fault line that had been getting bigger by the day. She'd succeeded in helping Manu, but where was he now? Then her Lola, usually so robust, had come over all weak, off her food, sick. Worry was pushing the usually strict Cecilia to new heights of strictness, new levels of unreason. And it was this that would push obedient Paloma to sedition.

Two minutes after her mother had said no, Paloma was breathless, at the end of the street.

'She changed her mind?' Maria asked.

Paloma shook her head, a look of relief on her face just to be out. And the last thing she wanted to do was to talk to Maria about her mother.

The two girls walked arm in arm along the eerie streets, their laughter filling the space, ricocheting between the vast expanses of whitewashed walls that lined the now cavernous walkways. A voice called down to them from an open upstairs window, heavy words raining down on them. 'Be quiet!' it said, low, warning. 'Get yourselves home, for pity's sake girls!' echoing the words of Cecilia, spoken only minutes before. The memory of it made the girls snigger.

They were untouchable. Maria was in high spirits. Happy. Blissfully so. And Maria's blissful happiness infected her friend, rampaging through her body like a disease, rendering her nearly as blind to her surroundings as Maria was herself.

It would prove to be fatal.

A sound of gunfire rang out in the distance. Both girls jumped out of their skins. They'd only heard it at night before. But though alarmed they still laughed, their giddiness at being together painting all around with an air of wonder. Maria scooped up gravel in the palms of her hands and threw it up into the air.

Fountain shapes sprayed in arcs down to the ground, dust falling like droplets. She didn't think that she'd heard a bomb before but she knew enough about them to pretend she had one in her hand.

Paloma laughed, but this time lower, flatter than before. Her capacity for mirth had developed a slow puncture that speeded up as another booming sound filled the empty streets. Paloma opened her eyes wide and looked around. She could see nothing, no one.

For the first time she noticed that they were the only two people walking along the street. It wasn't lunchtime. There was no reason for people's shutters to be closed. Nor their wooden front doors. Yet there was not a single one left open. There was not a tiled courtyard to be glimpsed anywhere.

Paloma's hand squeezed Maria's arm tightly. Maria laughed. Paloma laughed back half-heartedly. 'I want to go home,' she said in a whisper. 'Please not yet. I've got something to tell you,' Maria said. But as she walked on she didn't feel like it anymore.

Their high spirits disappeared into the blue sky above leaving not a trace below as the friends progressed on their journey. The air escaped from their deflating lungs and the sound of their supposed merriment, once fulsome, now dwindled to a tinny, tiny dot. It shrank as quickly as the silence all around them grew, a silence that threatened to overwhelm, engulf, and eventually obliterate them completely.

Silence. Even their own.

And then one-two, one-two. Louder and louder. The sound of heavy boots marched into the void. Hobnail boots – stamping, pounding, crushing, all vestiges of happiness squashed beneath relentless steps. Soldiers. Maria could hear soldiers. Getting louder. Closer. Her blood pumped violently. Her heart kept one-two time. Aggressively. If it could break out of its physical cage it surely would. Soldiers. That she had ever thought it acceptable to attract their attention when they first marched into town now appalled her. Soldiers. Interesting curiosities but a few days ago. She thought of Luis, her soldier. To think she was going to tell Paloma all about him. 'He is the enemy, Maria, remember that.' Her father's words tortured her. And the ineluctable, relentless beat of soles getting closer and closer told her that soon, very soon, those marching would all be her mortal enemies. She looked at Paloma. Fear was on her face with eyes full of liquid despair, nose running, bottom lip quivering. Maria was awash with guilt. It was she who had pulled Paloma into this.

She would do all that she could to save her friend.

'Mother's going to kill me,' Paloma said. Maria prayed that Cecilia would get the chance.

The soldiers were getting nearer. Boom, boom, boom, boom. Feet stamping. Drums drumming. Hearts pounding. Panic rising. Louder. Louder still. They were nearly upon the girls. It was time to run.

'Come Paloma! Come with me!' Maria called to her friend, her head turned back as she propelled herself forward as fast as she could, not watching, not seeing what, or who, was in front of her. Maria remembered the list of names given to her by her father, she searched for the nearest addresses. 'We can make it to Calle Rimono. My father says there's a house there we can...' As she turned a corner, running as fast as her young legs would carry her, Maria ran straight into a soldier. She looked up with terror into his face. The soldier with one blue eye and one brown. It was him. It was Luis. With recognition all terror and anger slipped away.

Her beating heart stopped. Time stood still. Events unfurled around them. They were locked together, in one eternal, golden moment. When she looked into his eyes she did not see an enemy. When he looked into hers he saw her tender heart.

'Paloma!' she said, bringing herself back to the world. 'You have to help Paloma.'

But Paloma was not to be helped. She gave a scream. All she

saw when she looked at Luis was the enemy. 'Stop!' Maria cried, reaching out for her. But it was too late. Her friend had gone and Maria had fallen to the ground. Luis helped her up. Her head swung back. She looked him in the face once more. It was the best of meetings at the worst of times. His eyes, warm and sympathetic, fixed on her, wishing her nothing but good.

'My friend,' she said, 'help her, please.' Luis went to the end of the road but something made him run back urgently. It was no use. Paloma had gone and there was nothing he could do for her now. He rushed down the road and grabbed Maria brusquely by the arm. She saw the look of horror in his face. He had seen something and Maria had to know what it was. 'I must look for Paloma,' she gasped as she wriggled away from him and ran towards the scene he'd run back from.

As Maria turned the corner Luis' hand reached out and caught her. He pulled her back into him and covered her mouth as she screamed at the sight that presented itself to her. The worst of nightmares.

Troops were herding women from the village onto trucks. Some were beaten, blood running down faces, arms and legs, clothes torn, faces bewildered, unable to move, a mind-forged rope having tied itself around their necks joining one to the other. The only one who dared to pull on it was Paloma. She bit and fought as two soldiers pushed her up onto the back of the truck.

Maria kicked to break free from Luis but he would not let her go. That he should let her see this vision of hell was something that he told himself he shouldn't do. But it was as much for himself that he couldn't move away. It appalled him but he had to see it. He would not pretend it didn't happen. Luis kissed Maria's head and soaked her hair with tears as he watched the Captain climb up next to Paloma and raise his hand above the head of the girl he hadn't been able to save.

Paloma stood up and fought fiercely, but she was savagely felled. Luis stared at the Captain. He'd seen him in glorious action before. It sickened him to the core to see a grown man get so much pleasure by inflicting pain on such an innocent young girl. The Captain held his hand poised before bringing it down violently and striking her violently across the face. With a hand to her cheek to stem the blood, Paloma sat back, dazed. The Captain pulled his fingers across her face, trailing them in the blood. He turned his hands round as if examining them. Then he laughed as he plunged red fingers in his mouth. 'I have a taste for this!' he cried. Those at their windows who watched fell back, deeper into the shadows. Those who sat on the truck trembled. And Paloma with the bleeding face felt the heat and wetness of fear burning between her thighs and running down her legs until it formed hot puddles around her feet.

Luis felt Maria go limp in his arms. 'I must take you home,' he whispered as he felt the lump in the back of his throat get bigger and the tears angrier. 'And I have to do it now.'

With his hand grasping hers, he dragged her round the streets, far, far away from the boots, and far, far away from a fate too savage to contemplate.

CHAPTER 27

Quiet streets, noisy rumours. Over the next few days there were fewer troops on the streets but the ones who were there patrolled their designated patches with menace. There were no more offers to carry women's baskets, no more kicking balls around with the village boys. The soldiers who were on duty were quiet, brooding, as dangerous and unpredictable as bulls.

Where the rest of them had gone was the source of much whispered speculation – perhaps they had gone on to pacify the next village, the Captain had even suggested that they'd gone on leave and were enjoying some much-needed rest and recuperation after the hardships of their campaign so far.

But it wasn't the soldiers that the good people of Fuentes were really interested in. It just felt less painful than discussing what was really gnawing away at them. A terror-drenched silence filled that particular void.

Though the stultifying summer heat lay heavy on every person in Fuentes, many shuddered with the chill that ran through them as Death's icy finger traced its broken, frozen nails over their bodies. Only the sounds of mourning, spewing and spluttering from behind closed shutters disturbed the eerie quiet, and added to its heavy load, giving the game away.

161

Sometimes a wail could be heard, sometimes a shriek, always the sound of anguish.

The war had begun and not just for Doctor Alvaro. A knife had been plunged into the very heart of Fuentes. No matter what the town's politicians had believed, the villagers were soon to learn that there was no such thing as a peaceful invasion. That they had opened their gates and welcomed their attackers in, would soon add an excruciating turn of the knife. Their spirit of conciliation would seem pathetic, love of country of no value to these invaders whose land, though it bore the same name, shared no other of its attributes.

Even the list makers would feel the pain.

The peaceful invasion had come to an end.

Women and girls as young as fourteen had gone missing that day. Paloma, she was only fourteen.

And while the inhabitants of Fuentes de Andalucía prayed for their safe return, the village was subjected to further indignities while it waited. Those on the lists handed in to the Captain on the evening of the landowners' dinner party were rounded up immediately. Local councillors and officials were put on trial. Executed. Some with apparent cause. Most without. Workers returning from the fields were taken in and taunted.

Fear spread throughout every home, fuelling horrific rumours and ghastly stories.

Yet the worst story of all was one that was so awful that no one could bear to pass it round at all. It was the one that everyone sensed. And so, in those holding days, between the day a truckload of soldiers left the village and the day that they returned, if any woman was harassed in the streets the fact that she had lived to tell the tale marked her out as one of the lucky ones. To make it home, shut the door and slide down to the floor, back pushed against it, that was something to be thankful for.

The unlucky ones were those who had been taken the day that

162

Maria went out for tomatoes and bread. And everyone knew it. They just didn't know how unlucky.

The rumour that some soldiers had gone off on leave to a large country estate was generally accepted to be true and passed on loudly. *El Aguaucho*, outside the town of La Campana, north of Fuentes de Andalucía, was identified as the estate in question. It had land, a well and plenty of space to accommodate a tired group of soldiers looking for some rest.

Passed on more reluctantly was the rumour of what happened to the missing women. This seeped round the back streets of Fuentes like malodorous gas. Some dared not inhale the noxious serpentine tale and those who did were left gasping for clean air. A truckful of women was what was required, on the Captain's orders, that day to boost the men after a punishing campaign to take the south, so the rumour unfurled. And when a truckful of women had been rounded up, eyewitnesses dared to whisper, they were herded together like livestock, all ready to be taken to slaughter. A truckful of women from the town – taken to experience some real men.

Disbelieving eyes observed trucks of soldiers drive away, their livestock for the weekend in tow. Some villagers watched from the shadows as scales of relief and guilt seesawed with confusion within their minds. Pleased it wasn't them, their mothers, their daughters, their sisters, who they could see being roughly thrown into the back of a truck by brutish hands. So sorry to see that it was the mothers, daughters, sisters of friends who, taken in their stead, had saved their own loved ones from this plight. Those poor women, they thought. Their lives will never be the same again.

CHAPTER 28

The moment Maria had closed the door of her house, the day Luis dragged her home, she leant with her back against its dark solid wood and slid to the floor. She crawled on all fours, pulling herself up the stairs, breaking down as she went. When she got to her room she lay herself prostrate on the floor, unable to find the strength to get herself onto the bed.

She lay there in a state of semi-consciousness, her mind falling between worlds. Luis had risked his own life to save hers. She wished he'd saved Paloma's instead. She flopped her head and knees to the side like a rag doll who'd had her stuffing heart ripped out. Nightmarish images came, unbidden, to her mind and she shook. She shook with the certain knowledge that Luis de los Rios had saved her from something dreadful, and with the no less certain knowledge – though she would have wished it otherwise – that it was she herself who had put her friend in harm's way. *Oh, Paloma.* She closed her eyes but the images played on the inside of her eyelids and wouldn't go away. She screamed inside.

'Maria?' Her father had gone round as many safe houses as he could possibly get to without getting caught but he hadn't found her. He'd heard the rumours and prayed to God for the second time that day. He gave a passing thought to the boy in the church. If Anselmo could get him to the Espinoza boys he would be better off than anyone still in the village. 'Maria?' he cried, his voice strained and vibrating with fear. But his daughter didn't answer. She had to be there, he told himself. He ground his teeth, tensed his face, clenched his fist. He punched the wall. It did not yield but the skin on the doctor's knuckles was split and bloody. The sound of his frustration rumbled up the stairs and seeped into his daughter's head. She moaned. Her father sensed her presence. He looked in all the rooms, ran up the stairs. 'Maria!'

He rushed to revive her, bathed her burning skin.

'Paloma. It's Paloma,' she said, delirious. That night Doctor Alvaro slept on the floor next to Maria. He cradled her in his arms.

When she awoke he tried to give his daughter something to calm her. Maria refused. She wanted nothing to make the suffering less. She would take nothing to make her forget.

Maria would fight. Stay strong. Face the truth. Accept responsibility. No matter what. No matter how seductive the promise of oblivion seemed in the shape of small pills at the bottom of an innocuous looking glass bottle.

Maria wasn't sure how long she'd been asleep.

The following days Maria stood sentry at the window, looking out for Paloma. For clues. Now, absolutely forbidden to leave the house by her father, all she could do was watch and wait at the upstairs window, wishing, hoping, praying for Paloma to appear in the street below. Fourteen years of age. Two years younger than herself. The sweetest, funniest, happiest friend. It crossed Maria's mind that she should try writing down what had been happening in the village these past days and weeks, but the memories of what she'd seen made her anxious.

She prayed that her friend had been dragged off the truck by vigilante villagers and was hiding in a safe house worrying about Maria as Maria was worrying about her now. But she knew better than to believe it. She'd seen Paloma pushed onto the back of a truck with her own eyes, witnessed the Captain strike her. If any brave soul had rescued her friend, word of it would be all around Fuentes by now. Instead everyone was whispering about the truckloads of soldiers that had driven away, whooping, jeering and taunting their female prey trapped in the vehicle ahead of them.

And that wasn't all they were saying. Some said the women were taken to cook and dance for the men. Others that they had been abducted to provide distraction of an altogether more sexual kind.

But it didn't really matter why they'd been taken, the most important thing was that they'd be brought back. And nobody thought for a moment that they wouldn't be.

Maria thought of Luis. He'd saved Maria, tried to save Paloma. If one good soldier existed, then surely others might exist. Hope glowed in the embers of her heart.

*

'Tell me what you know, Papa. What are people saying?' Maria asked. Paloma had been missing for two days. Doctor Alvaro looked at his daughter. Deep, dark shadows encircled eyes full of desperation. She'd not been able to keep food down, not been able to sleep at night. But he knew that she would feel better soon, that her appetite would return and that sleep would win out in the end.

Unlike the wretched relations of the missing girls. Doctor Alvaro had been called upon to care for them, although the rumours had got there first. 'They'll cook and dance then get brought back. We'll see them by the end of the week. I can feel it,' each father, husband, mother, brother and sister had insisted, clutching on to his arm so tightly that their nails very nearly broke the skin. But each one feared the worst. The doctor had been able to see it in their eyes, hear it in their

166

broken voices. Sedation had been the best that he'd been able to do for them.

He put his hand out to touch Maria's hair to make sure she was really there.

'It will be over soon,' he told her, unable to meet his daughter's searching eyes. 'They'll come back soon,' he told her as he sought solace in the floor. But just as his patients hadn't been able to fool him with their pretence at optimism, he couldn't deceive his daughter with his well-intentioned lies.

The throbbing heat still draped itself over the village. The air was still heavy with foreboding. Soldiers patrolled the streets with menace. Villagers found breaking the curfew were punished in the village square; others with republican connections were picked up in the early hours of the morning and taken no one knew where. Gunfire punctuated every hour of the day and night. Women kept themselves inside.

Villagers hid behind thick walls, wailing, waiting.

Doctor Alvaro went to his study. Planning. Preparing escape routes for those in line for a knock on the door in the middle of the night. He picked up the photo on his desk. It was of his wife, young, smiling, hopeful. He put it down. Maria. He couldn't protect her if the soldiers came for him. It was time to set his own escape plan in motion. Before it was too late.

167

CHAPTER 29

Knock, knock, knock. Doctor Alvaro jumped out of bed. His heart leapt with fear. It was the middle of the night. This was it. Maria appeared at his door, a metal rod in her hand. The sight of his fearless child amused him. Knock, knock, knock. But as he heard the knocking at the door for a second time all amusement disappeared. 'Go back to your room. And stay there.'

He went downstairs, his mind racing. The soldiers would have come for him, not his daughter, he reasoned. He thought of Anselmo. He would know what to do. Come for Maria.

He pulled the heavy wooden door open.

'Doctor,' a frightened voice gasped. A young man with messy hair and dirty face pushed past Alvaro, falling into the hallway. Alvaro arched his head and examined the darkness outside before quickly shutting the door, concern and relief etched on his forehead. 'Richard?'

The young man clattered around the dark house, Alvaro pushing him towards his study. 'Sit', he snapped. In the half light he could make out that the boy was wearing, underneath layers of grime, some sort of blue uniform, his dirty face streaked with dried tears.

'I came back to see if she was all right. Then she had so many things to tell me… I couldn't leave her… and now I can't get away. I need your help. Please.' Richard Johnson spilled his confused story out to Doctor Alvaro. Bit by bit, with the help of a why, who and what, the tired man slowly unpacked the chaotic words of this boy who'd been fool enough to get back into Fuentes without thinking of a safe way to get out.

He'd got word of what had happened in Fuentes as he was making his way back to England. And his mind was made up to return. Worthy sentiment. Stupid action.

'I've seen Father Anselmo,' Richard said. 'He will take care of the family. Once they've got Paloma back.' An uncomfortable silence followed the mention of her name. She was still missing and the minds of both men struggled to suppress thoughts of what might be happening to her.

Alvaro threw open the study door.

There, standing in the darkness of the doorframe was Maria, spectral white in her nightdress, the metal rod held above her head, ready to strike. And there, standing in front of her, was her father and a dishevelled man with pale, red-rimmed eyes and fair lashes.

'Richard.'

Her mouth fell open. She too had thought he'd gone back to England weeks ago. She didn't understand. She looked at her father for answers, but he shrugged his shoulders. It wasn't for him to give them to her.

She looked at Richard. He looked shabby, distracted, older somehow. And when he looked at her, she saw that he was searching for answers of his own. He knew, about Paloma. Guilt and shame dragged her eyes to the floor like lead weights.

Did he blame her?

Her father held out one hand to her and another to Richard and pulled them both in to his body. If only protecting them could be that easy. Maria dared to look at Richard Johnson from the safety of her father's chest. It seemed absurd that Richard should be here now. She noticed that he was trembling, his mind elsewhere. She reached out and placed a hand on his arm to calm him. It felt good to be able help someone.

'Come,' her father said to both of them. 'We have much to do.'

*

Doctor Alvaro slipped away before daybreak but not before cleaning the lost boy up and putting fresh clothes out for him. 'Sleep boy,' he said as he left. 'You need rest.' But though he slept no rest came. Visions of what had happened in the village haunted him, fear of what might happen to the girl he loved scorched him, and guilt that he might go back to England and never return shook him. By the time he woke up he felt exhausted.

'I know what they say has happened to Paloma,' Maria whispered as he entered the sitting room and went to sit next to her on the sofa. She too had had a disturbed night, and not only as a result of Richard's appearance in the middle of the night. Ugly words of violation had floated to the surface of her mind as she'd thrashed unhappily around in her bed after she'd returned to it. And they were continuing to do so here.

Yet ugly words of judgement now accompanied them. Her innocent friend had always assumed she'd get married. What if Fuentes, with its narrow customs and traditions, would no longer consider her fit for this? Damaged goods. Used. That's what she'd be.

Maria snorted. As if any of that mattered.

But the vile thoughts still came. She couldn't stop them.

She put out her hand and grabbed Richard's. It was comforting that he was here even if Maria couldn't fully comprehend why. He let her take it and he clasped his other hand over hers. That one movement made her feel protected, anchored, and she smiled up at Richard with gratitude.

The doctor returned to find Richard and Maria, asleep on the sofa, hands grasped tight like brother and sister. He went to wake them but changed his mind, instead hiding himself away in the study. There was much to do.

It was a dog barking in the street that eventually woke them. They looked at one another, bleary-eyed. The sadness was still there but a calmness had descended on them both. Neither one spoke. Words somehow seemed too trivial to be able to express how they were feeling at that moment in time. And, mysteriously, words weren't necessary, because both Maria and Richard knew – what each of them thought of Paloma, what each of them felt for the other, even that Richard had a secret love. The feelings were deep, painful, beautiful and no words were sufficient to express all of that.

Maria patted Richard on the back of his hand in thanks before moving to the window and beginning her silent vigil for her friend with the long dark hair, sparkly eyes and mischievous smile. She longed for her friend to return while bracing herself for the worst she could imagine.

Richard pulled up a chair to keep her company. He noticed her shiver, though the heat was now great. He responded with the gentlest of kisses on her cheek which caused ripples of warmth to lap the edges of the Paloma-shaped hole his friend had within so that, drop by drop, human kindness seeped in and gave her hope.

'Richard?' At the sound of Maria's father's voice, the boy stood up and made his way to the study, taking the warmth of human kindness with him. It seeped out of her little by little, allowing the cold to inhabit her Paloma-shaped hole once more and leaving Maria exposed to her own solitary thoughts. Still at the window. Still looking down into the street, looking for traces of her dear sweet friend. She would wait. For Paloma. For her lovely, lively friend, Paloma, to dance about in the street below and wave up at her, a broad smile of recognition on her face. And to retake her rightful place in Maria's heart.

CHAPTER 30

The hours passed and the doctor and the English boy did not appear from the study and Maria did not move from the window. A buzz of a fly filled the darkened room, loud and disgusting, asking to be squashed. It would be easy to swat it with a book, crush it with a shoe. It sounded slow, heavy, like everything else in this August heat. Maria's breath was quick and shallow. She willed Paloma back home, drawing up a pact with God, Jesus, Mary, and every saint she could remember, that she would be a good person for the rest of her days, be a good daughter, help the poor, go to confession... if she concentrated hard enough Paloma would appear. And now, to have the spinning of this spell broken by the monotonous intrusion of a fly, that living harbinger of death and decay, well, she was going to have to crush it.

The droning stopped. The fly, black and plump, landed on the small round wooden table next to Maria. A smile travelled across her face. One of the few she'd given since she'd last met up with Paloma. She lifted her arm up. Smack. Her hand came swiftly down. She must have hit the fly, though she thought it strange that she felt no ooze of guts spread across her palm. She lifted her hand slowly to see. No death was upon it.

Her eyes scanned the dimly lit room. She would not grant the fly a second chance.

Then it came. The buzzing. She turned her head in its direction. There it was, tracing circles on the windowpane. Though heavy in the heat, Maria jumped to her feet. This time she was armed. The instinct to kill was rapid. She peeled her notebook away from the glass. She thanked God. The blood smear upon it was deeply satisfying, certainly far more so than any mark she'd yet managed to make inside.

But her gratitude to the Almighty was to be short lived.

If the moment Maria took a deep breath in she was to feel elation at a foe defeated, the very instant she exhaled, all joy would melt away. On the turn of air in her body so sound trampled her entire being: the beating of drums pounded within her head, the one-two, one-two stamping of soldiers' boots pummelled her lungs, disturbing cheers of jubilation tore at her heart. She wrapped her arms around her ears. In self-defence. Denial.

Either way it was useless. It was too late.

She'd hoped to see Paloma. Now she knew she would not. The returning soldiers' cheers sent lightning through every fibre of her body, tracing its way to pierce her very soul. Needing but the merest of sparks to ignite, once lit the truth was unstoppable.

She looked at the squashed fly on the window in front of her.

Moving to the side, she took care to keep in the shadows, from where she watched, transfixed by the sight below. There they were, soldiers of the civil guard, defiling the streets of her beloved Fuentes.

Needles stabbed at her heart as she brought to mind the first time she'd seen them. These men. These fine Spanish men. Many young, attractive, neat haircuts, clean uniforms, polished boots. She cursed them, cursed herself.

Fuentes had surrendered to them peacefully 19th July. Was it really such a short time ago? So much had happened since then, though Maria recalled the day with excruciating clarity. And shame.

173

Alvaro was running through Richard Johnson's departure details for the second time. That he'd already gone through them in less pressing circumstances several weeks before irked him. The older man was about to ask why in God's name the fool had willingly returned into the devil's mouth when he heard it. A noise. Like thunder ripping the very sky asunder. The sound of boots crushing souls beneath them. Marching. Relentlessly. In time. An unstoppable war machine whipping up a storm of destruction. Getting closer. And closer.

Maria.

He rushed in to see her, leaning out of the window. She'd wanted to see Paloma for so long and now the soldiers were returning, the soldiers who had taken her. Paloma was coming home at last.

The marching grew louder and louder. It was Richard Johnson who pulled Maria away from the window, out of sight. Each one of them, Maria, Richard Johnson, Doctor Alvaro, waited in silence, their heads battling with images of women conjured up by stories they'd heard. Women with faces stained with tears; with shaven heads, torn clothes; made to drink castor oil, humiliated. Maria covered her eyes at the thought of what Paloma must surely have become. To look unscathed after such an ordeal, that would be impossible.

'Perhaps you shouldn't stay looking out of the window?' her father said to her, wanting to protect his daughter from the distress of seeing, as well as Paloma from the anguish of being seen. Paloma would be back with her family soon enough, what difference did it make that Maria would be able to say that she had witnessed her homecoming?

Doctor Alvaro went to close the shutters, but fear electrified his daughter's body, melting it into the slats and rendering it immobile. She had to stand and stare, even though she screamed inside with dread at the thought of what she might see. 'I owe it to Paloma,' she told her father as she freed herself from Richard's grasp and made herself ready.

Though no amount of preparation could have anticipated the grotesque carnival that would soon play out before her eyes in the streets below.

Boots clapped deafeningly. They were so close Maria could feel the dust stamped up in the air, feel it on her lips. And she could see rifles, parading rifles, their pointed tips erect, decorated with tattered flags. Shaken up and down, the flags fluttered, like damaged butterflies, their wings matted and torn. Maria looked on.

A tattered butterfly flag flew free from the tip of a soldier's rifle. It landed on the powder dry earth, its frayed edges now still. She looked at it, concerned. It took only the time needed for Maria to blink for her to understand what she was looking at. At first glance she saw only a tattered flag waving from a rifle, the next, lying still on the ground, she saw... She wouldn't, couldn't let herself believe it. Oh, the shame. The reaction was immediate. Vitriol stung the back of her throat. She fought to swallow it back but it bubbled up again as if to choke her. It pumped out of her mouth. Tears burst the banks of her eyes. While her nostrils secreted a mixture of both. She wiped a sleeve across her face, smearing tears, mucus and vomit across her cheek, matting her hair, clinging to her clothes. She blinked away the veil of tears and forced herself to see with knowing eyes. Her father tried to pull Maria to him. But she would not move away.

The true glory of war. There it was. She forced herself to contemplate it as it erupted outside. Regimented, organised, proud. The army marched below her window in time, torn, blood-stained undergarments attached to their rifles, the undergarments, Maria knew, of the very women they'd taken away only a few days ago. Were these the spoils of war?

The second she saw the bloodied rags she knew she was never going to see Paloma again. Instead she scoured the warrior faces of the returning troops for signs of guilt. She found none. Satisfaction. Hilarity. Pride. Scorn. They were all there. But guilt?

Not a sign of it. The closest she could pick out was indifference, there, on the face of the young boy on the other side, possibly shock.

Revulsion turned to anger, uncontrollable, strong. It seized her every sinew, wracked her body so that it shook. Her father reached out to calm her, but his hands were tired and no match for the strength of the violent convulsions that had taken over his daughter's body. 'Come away Maria! Please. Come away!' Richard pleaded with her, his own mind on fire with the anguish Paloma's family would soon be thrown into.

But Maria was deaf to all entreaties. She was in the grip of an overwhelming urge to propel herself forward, to fling herself over the balcony, to throw herself in the midst of the murderous monsters marching outside. She had to denounce them. She would surely be killed. And she didn't care.

As she went to lunge, Richard Johnson's hand grabbed her firmly by the arm and held her back, while her father's hand, stronger now, clamped itself effectively across her vomit coated mouth, stopping the scream. Maria would not be shining brightly with the flame of truth just yet.

Together they led her to the sofa on the other side of the room. She collapsed. Her father held her in his arms as she wept. This audacious Daniel would not be walking into the lion's den today.

'There are times when it's right to denounce evil,' her father said to her as he stroked his daughter's hair. 'There are other occasions when it is better to watch and wait,' he said calmly. 'The fires will always be waiting, burning, for these perpetrators of evil in their own special circle of hell,' he said, his hands now stroking his daughter's cheek with love.

'They should be punished!' Maria sobbed, pulling away from him. She reached out for her blood smeared notebook and flung it across the room. Writing! What use would that be now?

'And they will be,' her father said, 'but now is not the time and you are not in any position to do it,' Doctor Alvaro sighed. His daughter's life had been hard won. Her fragile mother had given everything, everything, to give birth to her. He wasn't going to let her throw it away so lightly. He resolved to dig deep. He looked at Richard Johnson. He heard the stamp of boots. He didn't have much time.

CHAPTER 31

'Poor Lola.' It was Richard Johnson who was the first person in the room to think of anyone in Paloma's family. 'Poor Cecilia,' Doctor Alvaro sighed, a close second, his voice heavy with sadness. 'First Manu, now this. I must go to them,' he said. Richard went to get up too. 'No,' the older man told him. 'I would be happier if you stayed here. For now.' And with that he was gone.

The parade of soldiers had long since passed but Maria's anguish had not. She still lay on the sofa, a molten mess bubbling away into the cushions, but her violent sobs had subsided into soft whimpers. Soon, Richard hoped, she would be falling, exhausted, into sleep. The light was fading, the incoming shade ushering a drop in temperature. Maria slipped slowly away. Richard Johnson watched her as she slept. Maria shook. The English boy went to fetch a cover.

His mind was in a mess. He wanted to be with Lola when Doctor Alvaro broke the news to her and her mother. She would need him. To think how devastated she would be made his heart ache. Yet to think of his Lola, the one with the cheeky smile and the way she said 'Richard Johnson', her voice so unapologetically Spanish as to not even try to pronounce her r's and j's in the English way, made that very same heart do somersaults of delight.

He shuffled awkwardly. Pure feelings tainted by images of barbarism. To feel desire with the memory of such brutality still fresh in his head made him disgusted with himself. Maria made a snuffling sound that distracted him from his thoughts. Poor Maria. He felt she sensed his feelings for Lola, but he had not yet spoken to her about them. He'd wanted to tell her, say the words, about Lola. But he wouldn't be able to tell her now.

The door opened then closed. Maria's father had returned. The man looked ill, shrunken. Compassion had drained him, truth had left weals on his soul and his body. He nodded at Richard.

'You're leaving tonight,' he said to Richard.

'But I…' He was about to say that he couldn't. He was thinking he had to see Lola, when Doctor Alvaro repeated, in a tone not to be argued with, 'Tonight.' The older man went into his study. There were things he needed to do.

CHAPTER 32

Cecilia wore black.

And, with the return of the soldiers, so grief scraped its indelible mark into the heart of the town. It scratched away at Fuentes leaving an open wound which its gnarled fingers and broken finger nails would not allow to scab over. The town screamed deep and low from the pit of its soul and the dust in the streets throbbed in the heat, the dry-flaky skin of a dying animal.

No one came and explained. Said sorry. Broke the news to the families of the missing wives, mothers, sisters and daughters. But they knew. Bloodied undergarments waved in barbaric victory were there for all to see. Even neighbours were afraid to be seen to console them. Only the brave, like Doctor Alvaro and Father Anselmo came to make sure they were surviving as to see if they were fine would be to ask the impossible: they would never be fine again.

The Captain put a curfew in place. Oh, there had been curfews before, but this one was to be strictly adhered to. If any disgruntled peasant was going to vent their spleen at being down a woman, better they do it during the hours of daylight when they could be seen and shot. They would be shot at night as well of course, but the cloak of darkness might allow them to wreak some havoc of their own first. They were so loyal to one another, some of these villagers. The Captain, after 'consulting' with Señora Gonzalez, agreed that soon it might be time to call on the help of some of the more observant citizens to keep an eye out for possible problems.

However, the imposition of any curfew was an unnecessary step, at least for the women. They had, understandably, issued a self-imposed curfew that extended to the daytime too. They stayed at home, only venturing out for matters of life and death.

'This village looks more like a prison with each passing day,' the Captain said, without the slightest trace of irony, as he followed Señora Gonzalez into her house the first day after the soldiers had returned. She was out and about for all to see. She felt no solidarity with the other women in the village.

Garcia gave a low growl, appreciating from behind the soft folds of the woman's pinned up hair and the delightful way she went so audaciously in at the waist and so fulsomely out at the hips which she accentuated with the swinging rhythm of her walk. He'd been looking forward to his meeting with Señora Gonzalez all week and it hadn't taken much to get her husband out of the way. Give him a horse and a band of Falangists to ride round the country with looking for communist scum for a day or two and Senor Gonzalez was more than happy. Senora Gonzalez affected a laugh by way of an *homage* to the Captain's wit which encouraged him to dig around in the limited word bank that was his mind for something to say that she might find wittier still.

'Where have all the women gone? Did my troops take that many of them away?' he guffawed as he followed her inside her house and sat himself down on a chair, slapping his thigh with self-congratulation as he did so. Señora Gonzalez blanched. *Why did he have to do that?* she asked herself. Not even she, in all consciousness, could carry on supporting the Captain if he openly boasted about what had happened. Well, at least he was inside, where only she could hear him. She swallowed hard, told herself repeatedly he was only joking, that none of it was true. She put it down to bad taste then clicked back into seductress mode. She feigned a tinkly laugh and placed her hand on Captain Garcia's shoulder. He placed his hand on top of hers. The weekly meeting had begun.

CHAPTER 33

Life was to carry on as normal. Shops would conduct their business as before, labourers would work on the farms, take in the crops, feed the animals, the school would stay open, villagers would go to church, people would get married, children would get confirmed, and the priest would preach that God's foot soldiers had arrived. There were several drawbacks to the Captain's plan – one in relation to the school was that the teacher had disappeared, and another was that most of the villagers didn't trust their self-appointed, self-anointed saviours. People moved quickly from home to work, work to home, never hanging round for fear of being apprehended by trigger-happy soldiers who had developed a taste for shooting people down at random whenever they'd wandered into the wrong place at the wrong time.

It had been Señora Gonzalez's idea to have soldiers shadow Doctor Alvaro. He'd not made it on to her original list but of late there was something about him that caused Señora Gonzalez's eyes to narrow. Whispering into the Captain's ear at one of their first meetings, it hadn't taken much for him to agree that the Alvaro man was worth keeping an eye on, doctor or no doctor. He was a man with a conscience and in the battle for Spain a conscience was an indulgence they could ill afford.

Luis was the soldier assigned to the task. Garcia's attempts to 'make a man' of Don Felipe's son had failed miserably. The boy had even dared to challenge his captain. That was why Luis was handpicked to stand and watch the doctor's house, then follow him whenever he went out. When the time came, and Garcia believed that it would be sooner rather than later, then it would fall to the landowners' boy to go and give the doctor his final call.

Garcia could tell the boy didn't like what he'd been asked to do, and this satisfied him no end. A reliable source had informed the Captain while in bed with him the other afternoon that the doctor had been instrumental in helping the Espinoza brothers escape. The spoilt Luis could have nothing in his arsenal to argue against that.

Alvaro had spotted the boy the moment his surveillance had started. He recognised him instantly as the soldier who'd dragged the three brothers out of harm's way; as the landowners' son; as the soldier who'd let Manu escape; and as the boy who had his daughter's heart. He hardened his own against him. This boy, no matter what he thought of him personally, was his enemy. And that he'd been posted outside to spy on him confirmed the fact. Alvaro could not afford to let his guard down in these exceptional, dangerous times.

CHAPTER 34

Cecilia would not take to her bed even though what was left of her family wished she would. Instead she would walk outside, the only one, apart from Señora Gonzalez, who still did. Soldiers looked at her as she passed them, a dishevelled, plump woman, her eyes distracted, as if looking for something or someone that was just out of reach. She never looked back at them. For her they did not exist. Her mind was so cluttered she had got lost in it and rarely surfaced to make contact with the world around. The only place that gave her peace was the church and so that was where she would take herself every day. She would open the door and stand there in the entrance, a small, round, black silhouette against the blinding sunlight. Then she would walk into the cool darkness and stagger to a seat where she would sit, sometimes for hours, crying and talking to Mary about losing a child. Possibly two. 'Oh Manu... oh, my Paloma. Are you there?' she would ask, looking into the shadows. Then she would ramble on unintelligibly, sometimes making cradling movements as though carrying a baby in her arms, sometimes crying, often both. 'Oh, an infant. I don't know anymore... Lola... my Lola...'

Father Anselmo would sit with her when he could and listen to the outpourings of a shattered mind and when she was ready to leave he would lead her home tenderly, a shepherd with a lost sheep, back to the fold where what was left of her broken family waited.

*

Lola had been waiting by the closed front door listening out for Richard, her hands ready to open the door as quickly as she could.

There it was, the knock. She pulled him in quickly, away from prying eyes, and covered his face with anxious kisses. He'd come back from Seville for her the day before the soldiers had returned, the ones who'd taken Paloma. He was risking his life again for her today. She'd known that he would.

This time it was to say goodbye. They both knew it. They both had played out what they wanted to say to each other many times over. 'I have something to tell you,' she said to him.

'I know.' But he didn't. She placed her arm protectively across herself.

'Don't cry,' he said, stroking her hair and cupping her face in his hands. Her eyes were red and her eyelids puffy. He placed his lips gently upon them. Lola went to speak.

'I am leaving tonight.' Richard cut across her, forcing his words out. They sounded more brutal than he'd planned.

Lola stiffened. 'How can you leave me now?'

This was not the sweet sorrow Richard had anticipated on his way to make his farewells this afternoon. Did she not realise that it was agony for him to tear himself away from her? That he was risking his life to even be here? 'Lola, my angel. You have made my life so very beautiful. I will never forget you.' His words were making things worse.

'I won't be able to forget you either,' she said, a hint of bitterness in her voice, 'even if I wanted to.' Her head drooped and her body withdrew from him, her arms folded. She wanted him to go, to save himself, but Lola could not find the words to release him, nor could she say things she needed to say without them now sounding desperate and needy.

She chose to say nothing. She'd already lost two of the people she'd loved most in the world. She was about to lose a third. She was heartbroken. Her sense of loss consumed her for a moment. She despised herself for her weakness as she grieved for herself. She tilted her face towards him, hoping to catch the light that shone from within his soul. Then she quickly looked away, afraid that her eyes might give away her secret.

'I love you,' Richard said to her. He had nothing else to say. He had to tell her because it was a feeling that was good and true, and he would be gone by tomorrow.

He held her hand. She looked down, her breath deep, her heart fluttering. 'I love you,' he whispered. She didn't know what to say, how to tell him. She imagined a child with red-blond hair, an image so vivid she gasped. She rubbed her eyes to make the vision go away. She had to tell him. There was no greater proof of love. She opened her mouth. 'I'm...' Richard placed a gentle kiss on her soft, smooth forehead. 'I will avenge Paloma. Those animals must pay.' Lola closed her mouth without finishing. She couldn't tell him now.

Within seconds he was gone. Lola watched him, a dark figure getting smaller and smaller until the distance swallowed him up completely.

She put her arms across herself once more and laughed in the face of the destiny that conspired against her. It would not defeat her. She was devastated at what had been taken away but in that moment she rejoiced at the life and hope that grew within her. She'd seen such wickedness in such a very short space of time. To create life out of love, how could that be so grave a sin? The image of the child with red-blond hair came to her once more. She smiled at the little piece of heaven that would soon replace what had been taken away. She was having Richard's baby.

Lola dropped to the floor, her head bent, hair flowing down towards her knees. If only she could have found the words to tell him.

CHAPTER 35

The next morning, at the crack of dawn, Maria got up to watch Richard Johnson as he made his escape. He was wearing the garb of a man accustomed to working the land, his incriminating hair tucked tightly away under a straw hat. He moved quickly and furtively along the shadows.

Her ears pulled her eyes to look up the street in the opposite direction. There she could make out two soldiers heading the same way as Richard, though they had clearly not seen him yet. And she had to make sure they never would. Before reason could stop her, Maria was already outside, basket in hand. It was vaguely ridiculous that she should look as if she was off to buy food at this time in the morning when the only people likely to be around were Rebel soldiers and those looking to evade them. But there was no time to ponder over fool proof plans. Now there was no choice but to think on her feet, act on instinct. A dangerous strategy.

She threw herself before them.

'You need to go back inside.' Her knees buckled. The voice was sharp and cold, but she recognised it immediately as that of Luis de los Rios. 'Although you don't have to,' his fellow soldier added, his voice deceptively soft. He made to relieve Maria of her basket with one hand, while going to squeeze her by the arm with the other.

'Stop!' Luis commanded as if to a wayward dog. The effect was immediate. Cowed, the soldier released his grip and lowered his eyes to the ground. 'Go!' Luis dispatched him to the end of the street with the point of a finger. The muscles in Maria's face set in a smile which she beamed at Luis without thinking. All thoughts of Richard were gone. Thankfully, so was he.

Maria felt Luis' arm wrap around her waist. It dragged her towards the open door of her house. Without saying a word, he pushed her inside, closing the door after her. She was safe once more.

*

Richard must have got away. Maria had watched him leave and Doctor Alvaro had heard no rumours to the contrary.

Life in the village went on. Even though its heart had been ripped out, it still pounded. Red, bleeding, its suffering on display for all to see. What had happened to it could never be undone, its loss could never be atoned for. But it was still alive. Its remaining inhabitants walked, talked, and breathed, even if some of them no longer wanted to.

Maria wished she'd been taken instead of Paloma that day. Her father thanked God that she hadn't, though he knew God had had nothing to do with it. He was only too aware that it was down to Luis de los Rios that his daughter was still alive. And the realisation that the man who'd saved her life was the same man sent to spy on him caused him much consternation. He himself would be taking Maria away soon enough. But until then he felt torn. It had not escaped his notice that Luis walked past their house numerous times every day, looking up for a sight of Maria on the balcony – a sight which, her father observed, she took great pains to grant him, all the while pretending not to. If these weren't times of war, Doctor Alvaro mused, how deliciously entertaining this behaviour would be. Instead, it took on a tragic hue.

Then there was the undeniable fact that this soldier who couldn't help but protect his daughter was duty bound to spy and catch out the doctor himself.

Nevertheless, his instinct told him that if anyone was going to look out for Maria it was this boy from the other side. The doctor was certain in the knowledge that he could let his daughter go about the village and Luis de los Rios would be there to look over her. He'd proved himself on numerous occasions. Yet Alvaro felt compromised. He would have wished it otherwise. But he had to put Luis off the scent. Lives depended on it. He had people to meet with, loose ends to tie up, and, until he could finalise the details of their escape it was something that he had to do, regardless of where it might lead the two young people.

'I won't be long.' The food stores were open when Maria next left the house with her basket. Doctor Alvaro watched his daughter as she walked down the street. Within seconds Luis de los Rios emerged from a side street, partner in tow. Alvaro nodded to himself, satisfied that his daughter would return. She would be some time, he knew, as food was growing scarce and the queues were getting worse, but the doctor breathed a sigh of relief that under the watchful eye of Luis de los Rios Maria would be safe. And that he would be able to carry on with the business of helping others, contacting the resistance, and making his own exit arrangements.

Maria no longer had any wish to sit in a small room and pour out her innermost thoughts onto a piece of paper. She couldn't face it. She was relieved to be out. And necessity had pushed other women to go about their daily tasks too. Standing in the bread queue with Lola, she enjoyed the silent companionship that she was coming to depend on. Both girls smiled at one another, Maria placing her basket on the ground while Lola clutched hers awkwardly, her arms threading under the handle, the body of the basket only accentuating what it was intended to conceal. Maria's eyes were drawn to the roundness of Lola's tummy when she heard raised voices coming from the butcher shop across the way. Both girls raised their eyebrows at one another in vague amusement. Who was it this time fighting over the last rabbit?

Lola lurched forward. Maria held her back.

'I'm going to kill you, you traitor! You whore of fascists! And I don't care what your vile friends do to me!' It was Cecilia. The poor woman had gone off like a volcano, spewing out angry words like liquid stones of molten lava.

'I thought she was at church! She's not come near the shops since Pa… for a while now,' Lola stuttered. 'I'm going to kill that bitch for upsetting her.'

As Maria heard the patronising, smug sound of Señora Gonzalez she felt an urge to kill her too.

'I only said that I thought General Franco was making a good job of cleaning up the country of reds and gypsies!' Captain Garcia's good friend was explaining to the rest of the queue. She omitted to reveal that she'd also added 'loose women' (with no trace of irony) to the list. It was this that had caused Cecilia to go off like Krakatoa.

As Lola ran to her mother's aid, the poor woman collapsed. Maria glowered at Señora Gonzalez. 'Shame on you! You disgust me.' The woman raised her neck like a swan. Her eyes flashed a warning at the doctor's daughter, but Maria looked straight back, unafraid. It was Señora Gonzalez who turned away first, unable to withstand the glare of the young girl's gaze as it scorched the surface of the woman's soul, revealing it in all its corrupt and spiteful ugliness.

Soldiers appeared from all directions. Maria's eyes scanned the length of the queue, eventually meeting the eyes of a shamefaced woman standing sheepishly by the meat counter, her hand outstretched towards the butcher. Caught. The disturbance had allowed her to secure the last rabbit for herself. She shrugged as she placed it quickly into her basket with a mumbled, 'I have many mouths to feed.'

What had the war reduced people to?

'At last!' Maria turned to look back at Señora Gonzalez of the incendiary tongue and hideous soul. The haughty woman was unashamedly upright once more. She seemed to turn her face towards Maria like a sunflower to the sun but their eyes did not meet. Instead they were directed at whoever it was standing behind Maria, a person who had the power to give this injured weed of a person the confidence to believe herself a magnificent bloom. Her eyes were all open, adoring. Maria followed to where they looked. She turned around, full of dread.

The relief she felt to see her own saviour, the soldier with the different-coloured eyes, was immense. It mattered little that he was the landowners' son. She looked straight at him. Señora Gonzalez had been in the wrong and, soldier or no soldier, Maria's instinct was to trust the actions of this guardian angel she saw before her completely. He did not prove her wrong.

He brushed past the woman, his judgement clear, and went to assist Cecilia with all the gentleness that he could muster.

'That's a disgrace. The Captain will hear of this!' Señora Gonzalez complained, as Luis helped a broken Cecilia out of the butcher's with the utmost care and respect.

Maria looked on. She could not deny that she was cheered by Luis' attentions and the moments that she saw him, spent time with him, were a blessed reprieve for her. Oh, she felt conflicted when she wasn't with him, felt guilt that she should experience such good fortune, but the fact remained that he had goodness within him, and it brought out the goodness within her too.

If she was playing with fire it didn't feel like it.

With her father's blessing and Luis' protection, she went out to see Paloma's mother the same time every day, to see if she needed anything. She helped with the chores, ran errands, prepared food… and sometimes even fed her. It broke her heart to see her friend's mother so but she did it without complaint, she did it to ease the burden on Lola's shoulders. And, perhaps most of all, she did it to alleviate her own guilt.

*

Piece by tiny piece, beauty was seeping back into Maria's life. And before either Maria or Luis could do anything about it, they had nurtured a love that was both rare and beautiful. It was also forbidden.

'I have to see you tonight,' Luis said as he walked with Maria to her front door. They'd returned from Cecilia's in silence, she lost in memories of Paloma, he thinking of a way to make the impossible possible.

'But the curfew,' she said, turning to look at him. 'I can see you tomorrow.'

'Maria. It's important. It has to be tonight. I'll be outside at nine.' Before she had time to say no, he turned and ran to catch up with a group of soldiers marching in the other direction. She ran upstairs to watch him. Another group of soldiers marched by with purpose. Then another. And another.

She slipped back out without telling her father to see what was happening.

A group of soldiers had stopped a boy up ahead and were pushing him around like a ball. Maria hid behind a bush and watched in horror. 'Hurry up lads!' a voice called to the soldiers. They marched on, forced to abandon their play thing now lying in a heap on the ground.

'Are you all right?' Maria saw that it was a friend of Manu's and she offered him her handkerchief to wipe away the blood streaming from his nose. He put his hand out and moved backwards. 'Oh no! Oh no, no, no! Get away from me whore. Dirty soldiers' whore. I know who you are. I've seen you, seen how you let them carry your basket, seen you laughing with them.'

Maria felt sick, her knees buckled. 'Please,' she said, 'just take this.' She tried to give him her handkerchief again.

'Oh no, no. Get away. They say you're the one they saved. They say Manu's little sister's dead because of you. Shame on you. Soldiers' whore!'

*

Nine o'clock and Maria looked out from her upstairs window. Her eyes were red but in the dark no one would ever know. The incident earlier on with Manu's friend had disturbed her. And now Luis was one, two… fifteen minutes late. He was never late. She wanted to see him so much that she felt sick. And she felt sick that this was so. She hated that she cared. But she did. Then she saw him, across the way, at the corner. She crept down the stairs.

Maria checked to make sure that no one was about in the street before pulling the door closed as quietly as she could. There in the shadows was Luis. She ran to him before following him down quiet alleys and ever darkening lanes.

A clandestine tryst. Out of character for Luis who upheld rules, did the right thing. And yet he'd suggested it. As for Maria, it was not the meeting up in secret that was the rub but the fact that Luis de los Rios was on the wrong side. She hated the Nationalists and the boy she loved was one of them. They should have been enemies.

Instead they were in love. She wanted what was best for him. He wanted what was best for her.

Unfortunately, Maria did not want what was best for herself.

She was still racked with guilt about Paloma and the incident with Manu's friend that day had been a blow to her soul. That was why, as she followed Luis to the shepherd's hut that night, she walked as if to her undoing. It was a wilful act. That she intended to ruin her life forever she had no doubt. And the thought dazzled her, shining blinding beams of light into every hidden crack and crevice in her mind. That she had found such joy with Luis made her feel guiltier than ever and so, with the destruction she craved, she hoped to leave no room for such feelings that threatened to overwhelm her. To be the author of her own downfall, what could be more just, more fitting. Her own life, ruined, to pay for the life of her friend. People would think she'd got her just desserts. And she exulted in it.

Walking through the darkness, an infernal beacon of moonlight illuminating their path, she gloried in what was to come. Disgrace? Hadn't she already fallen into a bubbling vat of it? Let Fate decide.

Her skin was hot as the angry pounding of her heart pushed her on. Hurry. Hurry. Her veins on fire as blood scorched through them. Thoughts of Señora Gonzalez pointing at her with a dirty fingernail, whispering, 'There she is. Shameless whore!' tap-danced about on the stage of her well-lit imagination with a click-click-clicking of the tongue. Maria appreciated the exaggerated eye roll that would accompany 'The one who got her friend killed.' Yes. The knife would go in. Repeatedly. Condemned to so many little deaths by heartless women stroking down the skirts of their own crease-free lives.

Maria was getting closer. Her breath shallower. The pounding of her heart pushed back the rising of her thoughts. She moved inexorably to her doom. She had no choice.

She looked at the back of Luis' head, allowed herself to be pulled along by the one she had chosen as her executioner, Maria his willing sacrifice. Tonight she would pay for her sins. This might be her last chance. He'd been late. He might never be able to meet up with her like this again.

When they fell into the shepherd's hut, Maria flung herself upon him, her moth to his flame, hoping for the end.

As she kissed him, she tasted guilt. She panted, eyes closed. That guilt could be so delicious made her weak at the knees. She trembled as she fluttered again and again towards him. Fumbling with his clothes, feeling the cool smoothness of his skin. Wanting more, embracing the danger, longing to find in ecstasy the key to her undoing. If the entire village condemned her as a whore, then she would not disappoint. Perhaps Luis thought her so too. Surely that was why he'd brought her here. With the zeal of the damned she thrust her hands around his buttocks, pulling him hungrily still closer to her. Flames of passion licked around him, threatening to sweep through every fibre of his being like a dry twig in a forest fire. For a moment he was powerless to resist.

The sound of cats screaming and screeching outside pierced the night air.

He froze. Pulled away. He took her face in his hands and saw the reflection of the stars in her eyes as she looked up at the sky through the roofless hut. She was love, life and hope to him. He sat back. His passion, on the verge of getting out of hand, had been brought back under control. He wanted her but not like this, furtive, guilty. Like animals tearing at each other down some back alley.

He loved Maria. He had felt it for some time but not as clearly as he did now. He had wanted to meet with her this evening. He had something to tell her. He put his hand in his pocket to make sure the letter he'd written to her was still there.

'Don't you want me?' she asked him, her body going limp with rejection. 'Yes. No,' he answered. 'Not like this.' He wanted to tell her he loved her but instead looked at her without saying another word. Her eyes were full of tears. He kissed them away. 'Please take me home,' she said.

By the time the couple had returned to the outskirts of the village Maria was silent with shame at what she saw as Luis' rejection of her and Luis was weighed down by the heavy burden of the news that he still had to tell her. He pulled her down a quiet alley. He was running out of time.

'We… I am being posted on tomorrow.' He broke it to her bluntly. It was the only way.

Her hand stiffened within his. She pulled her head back as his lips kissed her hair. She became deaf to his words as he whispered, 'I love you'. All she could think about was how he'd rejected her. She convinced herself that her actions had been motivated by love, not self-destruction, that he had turned her away. And now he was abandoning her.

'When this is over – and I pray that it's over soon – I will wait for you,' he said, a sad smile on his lips. 'One day, very soon, we will all be Spanish, no matter who wins.'

Maria did not reply. 'I will wait for you forever,' he said. And he meant it.

Maria shuddered with confusion, shook with unworthiness.

There was a call from another soldier somewhere in a nearby street. 'Quick, take this,' Luis whispered, thrusting a letter into her hand. 'I beg you to read it the second you get home. Remember, you're stronger than you know and one day you will prove it. Go now Maria! I'll be waiting for you. Remember that. I'll wait for you forever.' He kissed her tenderly on the lips. It tasted of forever. But then he was gone.

Maria stood there, a solitary figure in the moonlight. Was that it? Was it all over? Maria shuddered with confusion, shook with unworthiness. She loved Luis, hated herself. Hated Luis, loathed herself. When she had offered herself to him he had spurned her. Her fingers brushed over her lips. Had his lied? She started to cry and walked unsteadily home, no longer caring whose prying eyes saw her. She'd killed Paloma. Lost Luis. And she'd failed to be the soldiers' whore everyone thought she was. Maria despised herself at the very moment an arm draped itself firmly around her trembling shoulders. 'Hey, Maria!' She looked up to see the familiar face of the soldier Luis was regularly on patrol with. 'Luis sent me to make sure you got home safely. Come here love, let's get you back.'

She sank her head into his chest and he laughed. 'Here, come and sit down for a minute or two. You can't go in like that now, can you?'

The guardian sat down by her. He fondled her arm. Nuzzled the top of her head. She didn't stop him. He brushed the front of her dress. Within seconds he was kissing her neck, his body drawing ever closer, his lips working their way to her mouth. 'I'm off tomorrow,' he said, as if that explained the way things were going.

'Stop!' she said. He felt her go stiff. Her hand shot up. 'Not on the mouth.'

He hesitated, said, 'So let's get you home then.'

'Don't stop. No, don't stop,' she whispered. 'Just don't kiss me on the mouth.' The taste of Luis' lips were still upon hers.

'Are you sure?' he said. His concern very nearly brought her to her senses.

'*I want to have you give it to me like a real man,*' she said, reciting, as in a dream, words she'd heard on the radio. He winced for a moment but he did not need a second invitation. He slipped his hand up under her skirt. The soft warmth of her thighs made him shudder. The rough touch of his hands made her cringe. She closed her eyes until it was all over; when it was, she felt herself to be ridiculous.

She'd come out this evening with the intention of ruining herself. Well, she'd succeeded.

'My, you're a dark horse!' he whispered. 'Now you look after yourself, you hear me. Quick. Get yourself in,' he said, going to give her a kiss but, seeing the look she shot him, thinking better of it. Instead he gave her a gentle tap on the backside to show his appreciation. She despised him for being human. She despised herself more for being a fool.

'Oh, nearly forgot. Luis asked me to give you a message,' the soldier said as he turned and walked away. 'Read the letter.'

She slunk up the stairs. She pulled at her clothes, threw them on her bed. She washed herself. Over and over. To get rid of the smell. She brought her dress to her nose and sniffed it. She flung it down, ashamed, and as she did so she saw a folded piece of paper slip out of a pocket and onto the floor. The letter.

My darling Maria, it began.

She didn't read any more. 'It's too late,' she thought. 'Words. What power is left to them when actions make them weak? Worthless?' What was she to do?

She scrunched the letter up, threw it down on the floor; picked it back up, unscrunched it. By morning it was covered in ragged edged teardrops, the ink had run, the paper was crumpled, but still she couldn't bear to read it. Instead, she folded it as neatly as she could and placed it between the covers of *Don Quixote*. She'd never been able to finish reading that either. But it was as big and as heavy as a doorstop.

CHAPTER 36

'I need to go to Madrid,' Maria announced the next morning. 'You help everyone else to escape. I know. Why not me? And Madrid is where I can do something good. Meaningful. I have to…' Before she had finished speaking the certainty in her voice trailed off at the sight of her father, his head slumped upon the kitchen table, hands folded over his ears. He raised his head, eyes heavy, scorching tears tracing the rough, deep wrinkles of his face, finally soaking into tufts of hair. Dark grey clumps stuck out from behind his ears. His shoulders shook. Her father looked like Maria felt. He'd been working things out all night.

He too had made a decision, and as he looked up at his daughter, standing there, looking as wretched as he felt, her copy of *Don Quixote* held to her chest, he knew it was the right one.

All night he'd been grieving. He'd come to love life in the village. He'd lived here with his Maria for nearly seventeen years. He'd come here with her mother. They'd wanted to escape the noise and bustle of the capital, to start again in a village where nobody knew them. In Madrid he had just finished his medical training. He had met Ines, Maria's mother, and married her. But her family had never been happy with the match. He'd thought then that it was because they'd not believed him good enough for their daughter, but now that he had a daughter of his own he understood.

Life made things complicated.

Whenever he used to take Ines out her mother would urge caution. 'Be careful... not too late... don't tire her out...' while her father would say, 'Ines', as if in that one word and tone of voice he didn't need to say anything else. It was if they hadn't trusted him to do the right thing, even when he and Ines had got married.

Alvaro had thought that would all change when they knew about the baby. That they would be happy for Ines, for him, overjoyed to be expecting a grandchild.

They weren't.

But what had seemed bewildering then made some sort of sense now. Maturity, such a wonderful thing, a pity it had stripped the colour from his hair and gave him reason to loosen the belt around his belly.

Here, as he tried to work out what to do for the best for his own daughter, he felt closer to his wife's parents than ever before. Just as he, here in Fuentes, had been up all night going over how best to protect his daughter, so his wife's parents must have wrestled with conflicting thoughts and emotions when trying to work out how best to protect their Ines.

That she'd not been well hadn't been apparent to Alvaro when he'd first met his wife. That he'd not noticed how frail she was, how pale and slight, the vague discolouration around her eyes whenever she got the slightest bit tired, seemed strange to him now, particularly given that he was a doctor, but, at the time, all he saw was Ines, a vision of loveliness and youth. She'd suffered from polio as a child and, at times, as she grew into womanhood, her muscles would feel weak causing her great fatigue. She'd never told him.

The family doctor had advised against ever having a family. 'To have a child might put her life at risk,' he'd warned. But Ines hadn't listened. She hadn't told her husband either, even though, or perhaps *because*, he was a doctor.

She'd struggled with the pregnancy. She would never let him help. She didn't want him to know she had problems, though they were plain for everyone, apart from the young Doctor Alvaro, to see. His love was most certainly blind.

And Ines would never speak to him about the birth, though he'd heard the screams through the thick stone walls.

She was never the same after that.

When his wife stopped speaking to her parents he'd sided with her. When she wanted to move away, he'd agreed. Yet he realised now that everything they'd said, everything they'd done, was out of love for her and concern for her safety.

They had attempted to make contact repeatedly over the years. They'd even made a trip from Madrid to the village just so they could watch Maria as she walked along the road. Doctor Alvaro had told them to go. But now it was time to forgive. And be forgiven. They'd done nothing wrong. They'd loved their daughter. They would love their granddaughter too.

Maria looked at her father as he stood up and walked towards her.

'We will both be going to Madrid,' he said. 'Tonight. There's a battalion of Nationalist soldiers leaving today. There won't be many guards on patrol. The time is right for us.'

Maria's stomach jumped. She grimaced as she remembered the night before. 'I'll go and pack,' she said. Her father pulled on her arm. She looked back at him.

'No,' he said to her, sympathy in his eyes. 'We won't be taking anything with us. Say goodbye to it all now. Take one last look round.'

'No clothes?' Maria asked. He shook his head. 'Just the ones you're wearing. Nothing else.' *You, only you*, he thought. *You are my one jewel, my one precious thing.*

Maria hugged her father, felt the bones beneath the skin, and squeezed tight, dropped her head upon his shoulder to hear the life force within, loud and vigorous despite the gnarled facade.

Richard had gone, again. Luis would be leaving soon. Now it was their turn. 'I will go and see Paloma's family,' Maria said. Her father shook his head. 'See Cecilia?' she asked. 'To say goodbye, see if she has any news of Manu.'

But 'No' her father said again. 'You will see no one. No one at all.' Because to be seen to be visited by any one of them, he knew, would be not a touching farewell bid to the people they loved but a bullet in the back of the heads of those left behind. 'But they'll think me heartless and uncaring!' Maria complained. Her father said nothing. He moved to take his daughter's outstretched hand. 'Better to be thought heartless and uncaring,' he said, 'than to drape the ones left behind in suspicion.' He gave his daughter's fingers a squeeze. She squeezed his back. 'They'll be looked after, you know. Trust me.'

'So delighted you've decided we're going to Madrid,' he said to Maria, with a tired grin on his face. 'You'll be able to put your energy to good use there.' Doctor Alvaro smiled to himself as images played before his mind of Maria working in a workshop happily sewing uniforms; Maria smiled to herself as she imagined herself on top of a mountain waving a rifle in the air in victory shouting, 'For Paloma!'

In reality she would do neither.

Doctor Alvaro looked at his daughter, so robust with her round smooth cheeks and her strong dark hair that fell in waves around her face, her fingers so solid and strong. Her grandparents would adore her. He thought of his poor dead wife, so small and fine. A flower whose delicate petals dropped too soon. He felt sorrow that he wouldn't be bringing her back to Madrid with them.

203

CHAPTER 37

While Captain Garcia looked at Señora Gonzalez's latest addition to her list, Doctor Alvaro and his daughter were escaping under cover of night. The Captain had sent Señor Gonzalez out for yet another glorified horse-ride with a local group of Falangists, supposedly patrolling the area for enemies of the Spanish people. The Captain had also sent most of his men on and was now tying up loose ends before he could join them the following day. The dangliest of these ends concerned the clean-up operation to rid the village of the remaining left-leaning scum. The initiative would continue. Captain Garcia was here writing up the running order. A bottle of wine and a mountain of cigarettes were on hand to advise him.

'Well, my Señora Gonzalez! Who have you put down on here?' He sat back and smiled. Narrow-lipped. Cruel. He wondered, as he stroked himself, if he might come back and claim this magnificent woman one day. So the troublesome girl he'd met at the dinner at Cortijo del Bosque had crossed his hard-hearted woman one time too many, annoyed her enough to make her add her name to the top ('the top!' he laughed to himself) of her original list.

It would have to be the father that they went for first though, he said. Not that he had any qualms about picking up the daughter, it was simply that now wasn't the time to poke at the open wound. It might stir up fresh blood and, with the troop numbers down in the village, he didn't need that. But the girl's time would come. Sooner or later.

He considered if he should get together a band of men and go and pick up the doctor now. He puffed on the cigarette hanging out of the side of his mouth. He watched the smoke as it coiled its way to the ceiling, his face a crooked smile. It would be fun, he told himself. But there was no rush. The man was going nowhere. He had a daughter and patients to shackle him to the village, not to mention a conscience, the Captain thought derisively. Besides, the Captain had ordered Don Felipe's boy to keep father and daughter under surveillance and he'd reported nothing untoward from his hours of observation.

He confidently added Alvaro's name to his *non-urgent* list.

As Captain Garcia drained another bottle of wine (liquid gratitude from Don Felipe *for everything you've done for Luis*), so Alvaro and his daughter were waiting for a truck to pick them up and transport them to Madrid. That his daughter still clasped her copy of *Don Quixote* to her heart with one hand continued to puzzle the doctor. It also made his soul laugh. Of all the things to bring. That she used her other hand to stop her mother's rings jangling against the enamel sunflower pendant whose chain they now shared he understood completely. Little tokens of loved ones lost.

Doctor Alvaro had arranged for them to be picked up on the track that led towards a run-down hut used by goatherds before the war. Maria knew it well. They were to wait near the old olive tree, the one that had been uprooted years ago and now looked as if it had always been there. The two of them sat, their backs against the length of its wide, rough trunk and waited in silence as they listened to gunfire crackling in the distance and watched flashes like shooting stars lighting up the night sky. Far away.

Maria shivered, though the night was warm and heavy. Alvaro put his arms around her. Her teeth chattered with something like shock.

Then came the sound of a motor.

Doctor Alvaro peered over the top of the fallen tree trunk and watched as a truck appeared out of the darkness, its headlamps turned off though the glass still caught in the moonlight. He waited until he could make out the face of the driver. He recognised him. He tugged on his daughter's shawl. 'It's ours,' he said.

They climbed up into the back to find four goats and seven people already there, squashed together in a small space, sitting on the few belongings they'd managed to bring with them. They were no doubt from one of the surrounding villages but neither Doctor Alvaro nor his daughter thought to ask. They were all refugees together now, all headed for the capital. They wouldn't be returning to where they came from any time soon. Maria managed a weak smile, then sat, wedged in between her father and an old woman with a broken tooth, holding on to her book as if it were about to be prised away.

As the truck picked its way along secondary roads and stuttered down cart tracks, its human cargo within remained silent. Maria thought of Luis. She'd never met anyone with a soul as pure and beautiful as his. She drew her book into herself, closed her eyes and allowed her mind to revisit their moments together. Away from the complications of the outside world it didn't matter that they were on different sides because inside they were the same. The memories touched her soul and transported her to a place where everything was blissful. Last night he'd told her he'd loved her. She knew that she loved him too.

The truck hit a large stone. Maria shifted sideways. A pain brought back to her how she'd betrayed him. She wasn't the same as him after all. The rest of the journey she went over all the terrible things she had done. She struggled to make sense of them all. She'd thought herself so clever, so good, so much better than everyone else. But even the love she felt to be so pure was itself forbidden. Well, she was punished for it now. She looked around the truck hoping to find distraction. But no one looked back at her. No one made a sound. Even as the sun came up and birds broke into song only the goats replied.

The truck was slowing down, the brakes applied.

Outside there were voices. At last. They were getting louder, nearer. The canvas door was drawn back illuminating the gloom within.

'Welcome to the Republic,' a soldier's voice said. Nine sets of surprised eyes squinted into the sunlight (thirteen if you counted the goats).

'We've made it to the control post,' the driver shouted back at them, a trace of jubilation in his tired voice. 'We've made it. We've made it to Madrid.'

When Maria jumped off the back of the truck and into the morning sunshine she made a promise to herself – that she would do the right thing. That she might not be able to identify it when she saw it, she hadn't yet considered.

She looked at her father and held his hand like a little girl because the first thing she noticed in this strange city was people. Tens, hundreds of them. *So this is what it feels like to be a drop in the ocean*, she said to herself as they tumbled into the bobbing throng. But, if Maria was but a drop, she was a very fortunate one as others, too many for her father to even think of helping, drifted by, with heavy legs and even heavier hearts, caught up in the never-ending waves, bodies beaten, eyes sunken, on their faces a landslide of despair. They must have escaped from the surrounding villages. Some dragged their belongings behind them, others pulled tired children by the hand.

An old woman went by, slow, weak. She asked those who passed her either side for food. They all ignored her. The desperate sight tugged at the doctor's heart. He knew they hardly had the strength to turn their heads towards the hungry voice, let alone shake an answer. It made Maria angry. But sometimes those who don't help, can't help – a lesson she had yet to learn.

Before her father could stop her she had released his hand and was forcing her way through the relentless swarm of refugees to place a small package in the hungry woman's hands. Her fingers, unlike Maria's own, were frail, birdlike. 'It's not much but it's all I have,' she said. She thought she saw a look of gratitude flash across the old woman's face, but, if that was the case, it was not for long. All finer feelings were rapidly trampled underfoot by a terrible hunger. The starving woman crammed the food into her mouth. Maria looked away. By the time she looked back the woman had been swept away.

As Maria was helping out one person in need so her father was helping out another. The old woman with the tooth, who'd travelled on the truck with them, was stranded. Alvaro held her by the arm and lead through the crowd. Maria held her by the other.

One hour later and the three of them had not gone very far. Felicia was her name and she had a bad hip. Both knees were weak. Her back wasn't good. Maria was starting to feel restless. The newness of the city wasn't coming quickly enough to excite her about the future. The slowness of the journey was doing nothing to take her mind off her past: she could still smell it and it was starting to make her feel sick.

As she looked behind, she spotted a peasant with a donkey and a cart coming their way. Round-shouldered, pot-bellied, he rolled his eyes in derision as he moved through the shuffling tide of people. An unlikely specimen to restore one's faith in human nature. But, as the saying goes, you can't judge a book by its cover (even though most of us do). And this was never more apt than when applied to this gruff, rough, unprepossessing man: he had a heart of gold. He noticed the pained expressed on Felicia's face and took pity on her.

He wouldn't have stopped for the doctor nor his daughter –

they had the look of educated people who could take care of themselves; but his heart went out to the scrawny woman with the dodgy hip, defective knees and bad back. She didn't look long for this world and he couldn't have lived with himself if he'd not helped her. 'Hop in,' he'd barked, grudgingly accepting the other two as necessary baggage. Alvaro climbed up first. He pulled while Maria pushed and together they hoisted Felicia onto the back of the cart. While Alvaro went to express his thanks to the peasant Maria jumped aboard yanking up her clothes to do so. Felicia's eyes fluttered around the hem of the girl's petticoat as she flicked up her dress. There, deep red against the white cotton was the undeniable stain of blood. Maria released her dress immediately.

'Rodrigo,' the peasant said in reply to Alvaro's many questions. And that was it. For a while.

You couldn't force conversation. The doctor had learned that long ago.

Rodrigo's human cargo settled for watching the city as it rolled by, its houses getting denser, its trees thinner and fewer. A cart with a white coffin – it was for a child – rolled its way past them. Churches punctuated the way. But Maria took in none. The blood-stained petticoat brought back her crime. The embers of self-hatred glimmered within.

'Some's been gutted by fire,' Rodrigo said to Felicia. 'Some's been ransacked,' he added, pointing his head in the direction of a derelict church on the left. As they turned to look, a group of excited young men appeared at the damaged church doors dragging a monumental Jesus behind them. They pulled it to a clearing and set about beating it with metal bars, over and over. Soon it was nothing more than a heap of painted splinters on the ground. When done, they shook their weapons above their heads, victorious.

Sparks of excitement flared up off the embers of self-loathing as Maria watched the boys destroy the statue. Their anger. So unbridled. It called to her own. An energy so infinite. But it was

209

instantly quelled at the sight of Felicia as she rubbed her crucifix between her fingers. 'Here, let's hide that out of sight,' Maria said, removing the scarf from around her own neck and tying it round the frightened old woman. 'There', she said, patting it flat. 'No one can see it now.' Her father gave his daughter the slightest of nods in gratitude.

'God forgive them,' Rodrigo muttered. 'They know not what they do.' He turned around and gave his passengers a heavy-hearted smile. They'd never witnessed a scene like this before, he imagined. Well, it wouldn't be the last. 'You needs to be careful,' he said. 'In war evil reveals its ugly face. No matter where you are. Madrid has its dangers too.'

The three passengers fell back into their own thoughts for a while. Felicia's mind was full of horror, fear and confusion. She sat and shook her head. 'Animals,' she muttered.

Alvaro's was full of pity and sadness. He recognised the symptom, understood the cause. These were young men, frustrated, furious. The church had abandoned them, left them to rot, selling out their future to the highest, most powerful bidder. But to think they could cure themselves, rid themselves of this rot, by wanton destruction, no. This might relieve the pain for a while, but as a doctor, Alvaro knew this was no long-term solution.

Maria did no such thing. She looked back at the young men, now behind them, with something akin to envy, her own anger rekindled by the sight of theirs. The desire to destroy raged in her soul. To smash things up would not bring her friend back, not change what she'd done last night, but the instinct to do so was stronger than reason. She watched the boys until they became agitated dots in the distance, the flame of fury dimming with each turn of Rodrigo's large wooden cartwheels.

Rodrigo brought his cart to a juddering stop. By then the flame was dead.

'Get out now,' said Rodrigo, direct to the point of rudeness.

He shooed Alvaro and his daughter off his cart. He nodded to the right. 'I go this way with the old woman—' at this Felicia pulled a face '—and you needs to go that way.' He pointed straight on. 'That's all right. No need for thank yous. No need,' he said and then he set off, not caring to look behind him for fear of seeing two people still expressing their gratitude with waves and smiles. He never did like fancy ways.

'Are we nearly there?' Maria was tiring. Her conscience had not allowed her to sleep all night.

'Not far now,' her father said.

It was seventeen years since he'd walked along these streets but he knew the road up ahead as if he'd been walking towards it only yesterday. 'Come,' he said as he rushed on with excitement as if going to meet an old friend he'd never forgotten and couldn't wait to see again.

A convoy of army trucks rolled by, their heavy wheels like thunder on the now cobbled roads. Alvaro looked on with pride, Maria with admiration. These weren't Rebel soldiers but the ones who had remained loyal to the government, defending Madrid and fighting off its attackers. People filled the street, applauding the uniformed men as they rumbled past. 'They're off to the front,' a young girl said to Maria. 'No, must be Army HQ,' said another. 'This road ends up in the main square.'

Maria listened on in wonder.

CHAPTER 38

Maria's grandparents, her father said, lived in a spacious apartment in the Marques de Casa Argudin Palace, situated in the affluent district of Salamanca in Madrid. Planes had dropped leaflets on the capital stating that that particular area wouldn't be bombed (explaining why Alvaro found it to be far busier than he remembered). It also meant that it was safe. It wasn't far now. 'It's very beautiful. You'll see. And your grandfather... a good man. Caring. He'll love you. Your grandmother too. Kind.' That her father had never mentioned them before disinclined Maria to believe him.

They battled their way through the still growing throng. 'Many have turned their backs on the city... fled... but not your mother's family...' Her father's voice meandered like water down a stony hillside. He turned. Stopped. It was getting too busy. If they weren't careful they would get separated. He looked at Maria. Her shoulders were hunched, eyes shadowed. Her copy of Cervantes pulled on her arm like a dead weight.

'Here, let me carry that for you,' he said holding out his hand. She shook her head. Though she hadn't read it yet, a promise of hope was locked between its covers and she wasn't going to relinquish it to anyone. Luis. She brought the book into her body.

Her arm tensed. The thought that she'd betrayed him stabbed her in the heart. Her father only saw the pain of it in her face. He took it for fatigue. 'Then take my hand,' he said to her.

Their hands clasped, as strong as links, and so father and daughter forged a path ahead, over the cobbles, under the banners, past the soldiers speaking one language, and civilians speaking another. As hypnotising as the music from a snake charmer's pungi, the sounds and voices captivated them both, rendering them spellbound. Accents from all over Spain converged in the capital. There were the clipped sounds of English to the left. And that must have been an American accent the man with the cigar and the camera had to the right. 'It doesn't madder', he'd said to the mother of a child who'd run into him. Then, further along, came hissing shs and zhs and strings of long, round vowels.

'What language is that?' Maria called to her father.

'Russian,' he said. 'Not far now.' But she was no longer flagging. The shock of the new was beginning to ease the discomfort of her pierced heart and it was when she walked into the Puerta del Sol that she experienced its restorative powers to the full.

One moment in a dark, overcrowded channel, the next, spewed out into the light. The Puerta del Sol. It was as if she'd woken up to the city for the very first time. No amount of wandering around its outlying streets could have prepared her for this. She raised her eyes to gape at enormous posters displayed on high stone buildings. The paternal eyes of politicians looked down on livestock, people, cars, trucks and buses all moving round in the large open square below. There was a giant president Azaña, his face as if carved in the rock, watching her from on high as more truckloads of Madrileños rumbled by, all wearing dark blue boiler suits and cheerful red neckerchiefs. Crossing them were still more soldiers, leaning out of trucks and whooping with glee at her, their raised fists in salute at the magnified faces of Lenin and Stalin, whose eyes overlooked it all. She was dazzled and puzzled

213

by the scale and the strangeness of it all, her spirits lifting her aching limbs.

'Just down here.' Doctor Alvaro pointed down a side street festooned with flags. Banners proclaiming *'no pasaran'* ran from window to window. *They shall not pass.* Madrid was spirited and ready for the struggle ahead. Red Cross vans roared past. Maria's mind buzzed with the noise, glamour, excitement. She found the mood… festive. Her heart had been pierced but her head was still game enough to be turned.

'I feel a little dizzy,' she said, still holding her father's hand as he knocked at a big, wooden door. And then she fainted.

Juan Mendez had only ever seen his granddaughter when she was a baby and then once from the other side of a street in Fuentes when Maria was twelve years old. The years melted away as he looked at the child now collapsed in the doorway. Tears came to his eyes. *'Isabel!'* he shouted back inside before turning to his son-in-law. 'Let's get Maria…' He hesitated. Memories went off like fireworks at the mention of her name. 'Yes,' he tried again. 'Let's get her to a room… her mother's old bedroom. *Isabel! Isabel! You'll never believe it.* Yes, at once.'

He looked at the tired and dusty girl with the long, dark, untidy hair. Did she take after her mother? Or her father? Was she artistic? Musical? What did she like to do? Reading. The copy of *Don Quixote* clamped tightly across her chest told him that. What did she like to eat? Questions ran round his head, wild, impatient. 'Is that her?' his wife asked as she rushed into the hallway. 'Alvaro!' she said to the man holding her up. 'Is that our granddaughter? Bring her in!'

Arms touched, backs were patted, embraces were snatched but really there would be time for all that later. Isabel led Maria to a pretty room with a metal framed bed. Maria took a glass of water from her grandmother's outstretched hand and allowed her to remove her shoes. She'd forgotten all about her petticoat.

The apartment was a shrine. Photographs of Maria's mother

were everywhere recording every stage of her life. As a baby in her crib, as a child on a swing, in a restaurant, at a ball. Maria had never seen so many pictures of her mother. There she was with childish curls, here with beautifully coiffed dark hair. From a moon-faced baby she'd turned into a heart-shape faced young woman, fine-featured and delicate. Maria did not take after her. But she did, it struck her, look very like the woman holding her mother as a baby in an old photo on the console table in the hall.

And the resemblance, her father, knew, wasn't only superficial.

Maria's father was subdued. Now grown-up, he recoiled at the intransigence of his youthful self. It was time to make his peace with the authoritarian mother-in-law of the past and embrace the loving grandparent of the present. He hoped Isabel had mellowed as he went to join her in the sitting room.

'I—'

She put up her hand to stop him. 'Please. No words. Not about the past.'

'But I…' he started again.

'No. Really,' she insisted, tears in her eyes catching the light. 'It's over. You're here now. And that's more than I ever hoped for.' Mistakes had been made on both sides. There was no point trawling over them now.

Her daughter had been Alvaro's wife. He had no need to explain himself to Isabel. Neither had she to him. Although it had taken Alvaro years to realise it, experience had led him to understand, at last, that his wife had been Isabel's daughter.

Ines. Isabel's daughter. His wife. Maria's mother. She'd suffered twelve miscarriages before she'd become pregnant with Maria. He had no idea at the time. Some mercifully quick, barely noticeable, apart from to Ines herself. Increasingly obsessed with having a baby, she'd started to analyse every tiny change in her own body.

'What are you doing to yourself?' her mother would say to her.

215

'You have to stop this,' her father would add.

'Can't you remember what the doctor said might happen to you if you were to become pregnant?' Cruel words, Ines had thought at the time. Heartless. And it heralded the beginning of the end of the relationship between daughter and parents.

Alvaro said nothing at all. He didn't know about the pain, loss, misery. Ines had kept everything from him, hid the signs. That he, a doctor, had not seen them had been a source of constant self-reproach.

The thirteenth pregnancy, against all the odds, did not turn into a miscarriage. Ines had conceived a fighter. And she subjected her mother to the agonies of hellfire as she battled her way to survive. Awash with vomit, headaches to break you in two, a bladder that needed emptying every five minutes and skin so bad her face felt as if it was alive, so affected was it by the changes in her body, Ines struggled. But she was having a baby. And she was ecstatic.

Isabel was not.

Alvaro's heart ached as he remembered the arguments between his wife and her parents. The more Isabel and Juan told their daughter what to do, *for the good of the baby, for your own health, you silly girl*, the more dogged his wife became. And he was so blinded by her strength of will that he couldn't see how fragile the woman he loved was becoming.

It wasn't long after the baby was born that Ines turned her back on her parents forever. Alvaro had backed her up. He was sorry for it now.

216

CHAPTER 39

The good thing about returning to the fold of a rich and powerful family is that they can open doors for you, no matter how much you protest and say you want to get there on your own merit. And so it was for Maria's father.

His father-in-law Juan Mendez even had contacts at the Ministry of War.

'My old friend, Santiago Carrillo, can help us out I'm sure.'

Santiago Carrillo was made Councillor for Public Order when the government fled the city. Everyone knew his name. Juan Mendez and he had been friends for years. 'Never was I happier than when the left-wing government released him when they got into power in February 1936!' His voice had sunshine in it. Maria was drawn to wonder at him. And in that moment her mind made up a general truth: that any prisoner released from prison in Madrid by the government had deserved their freedom. It was experience that would show her this was not always the case.

'He knows all the war heroes: Lister, El Campesino,' Maria's grandfather continued, displaying the extent of his influence and enjoying doing so. 'But,' he added, realising he was following the wrong tack, 'you're a doctor, and if it's at the front you want to help out at, then leave it with me.'

217

A word in an ear was all it took for Juan Mendez to secure his son-in-law a position working with Bethune's blood transfusion service. The Canadian had made a huge difference in the makeshift hospitals set up near the battlefields around Madrid, saving lives. Another of Juan Mendez's many contacts, Norman Bethune was always on the lookout for doctors to assist him in his work. The war effort would always need doctors, especially on the frontline. Life, death and destruction. It was the nature of war. Yet it was the business of Bethune to patch up the injured as quickly as possible, and, wonder of wonders, to cheat death itself by bringing the wounded back to life. Blood. Miraculous stuff.

Doctor Alvaro would be a valuable asset. But placing Maria would not be so straightforward.

'I've a friend who runs a workshop… makes uniforms. I could get you in there tomorrow.' It wasn't that Isabel hadn't seen her granddaughter's fire and determination, sensed her eagerness to be active, guessed at her anger, but she'd also seen the blood. There on the girl's petticoat as she'd put the girl to bed on that very first day. The memory of it disturbed her. Her reason told her it was nothing; her instinct told her otherwise. She would talk to her granddaughter about it soon. But not yet. And so, for the moment, the workshop was where she wanted Maria to go.

But sewing didn't cut it with her granddaughter. Other options were proposed. Feeding the poor, helping the refugees, wireless operator, laundress, cleaner. 'You just say the word and I can fix you up with a job very soon.'

'No.'

That wasn't the word Isabel meant.

'Let me think,' said her grandfather, scratching his head. It was his turn to take on the mantle of responsibility to find his granddaughter worthwhile employment.

'There's a field hospital outside the city at Villa Paz. One of my friends…' Huge storm clouds moved over Alvaro's face. 'There's the *Servicio Canadiense de transfusion de sangre*,' Mendez said, moving swiftly on. 'Set up by the Canadians. Bethune and his mob. Linked to what your father will be doing. But you'd be working in Madrid.' The storm clouds lifted. 'Important work. Life-saving. And it's in a lovely part of the city. Not too far away from here and so less susceptible to bombing. So you might have no training, but you'll soon learn.' Not if she didn't want to do it in the first place though.

Her grandmother dug deep. She took Alvaro to one side. 'I can't believe I'm even suggesting this to you. But bombs are raining down on us. Turning living homes into skeletons. And the city is crying out for ambulance workers. So there is a job there for her if you think it suitable.' Maria's father closed his eyes for a moment. 'I know it has to be her choice,' he said. He imagined his daughter delving within the bare bones of once beautiful buildings, finding Madrileños with shattered limbs. Or worse.

'But no. Let me think,' Isabel said, sharing Alvaro's fears. 'I know a place where they need people to help out with making bombs for our side. It would be a safer option.'

Alvaro looked at the floor. War. Always a desperate state of affairs. But civil war, knowing that their own bombs might be used against old neighbours, family, friends. An impossible position to be placed in. And the doctor felt that his own particular circumstances had been made even more impossible: even the Republican government had left Madrid and fled to Valencia. Madrid was a sinking ship and he'd wilfully jumped on it, pulling his daughter up alongside him.

But it was far safer than staying in Fuentes. And they could make a positive contribution from within the city.

For him the noble course of action was to help the injured out in the field. As for Maria, she would work in the Bethune blood unit in the city if he had any choice in the matter.

He did not.

'What about *miliciana*?' Maria wanted to fight.

219

CHAPTER 40

Madrid, during those early months, was an exciting – distracting – place to be for Maria. At least, during waking hours. For every night her sleep would be peopled with loved ones betrayed. Paloma. Luis. And every morning she would wake up, her head bruised, as she remembered it was she who had betrayed them. She struggled between two worlds. She imagined the torment would never release her. Then there were the changes that were occurring within her body that she didn't acknowledge but couldn't ignore.

But as the sounds of life made their way up from the street below, and as the love of her grandparents and the kindness of her father enveloped her as she joined them around the breakfast table, so many of Maria's demons retreated to the shadows under her bed.

'I'm so pleased you decided to work at the laboratory.' She had been working for the Blood Transfusion Unit for over a month and her grandmother was relieved that all talk of becoming a *miliciana* had stopped. Maria had wanted to join the Women's Battalion of the 5th Regiment: fit young women dressed in khaki, often dishevelled after several nights in the trenches, she'd seen them marching up and down the Gran Via in twos and threes.

Loyal to the Republic. She'd not believed the rumours that they were only allowed to perform auxiliary duties, coerced into providing the three Cs, namely cooking, cleaning and caring, with a bit of special servicing of the male troops thrown in for good measure. She knew the already legendary feats of the likes of Lina Odena and Rosario Sanchez, both young girls like Maria herself; one who'd given her life, the other her right hand – quite literally – to fight for what they believed in. But the bombardment of photos in newspapers such as La Voz and ABC of women doing 'women's work' on the frontline (placed around the apartment most strategically by her grandmother) was enough to make her stop and think. She had no wish to die at the front with a dish cloth in her hand. Battles were being waged on the outskirts of the city, the fighting more ferocious than ever, but the truth of it was that it was fast approaching home time for the women there. The government was starting to call them back. Even Maria had to accept there was no point joining up now.

'Coffee, Maria?'

'Yes. Thank you *abuela*.'

'Listen to this, Juan.' Maria's father rattled the newspaper in his hand. 'Varela says that if he can't crush Madrid with four columns, then it will fall upon the shoulders of his fifth and most deadly unit to destroy the city. From the inside.' Everyone in Madrid knew the name of General Varela: a Rebel and Franco's dog. He'd failed to break Madrid with a powerful frontal attack from the west in November 1936. Street fighting and an entire city's will to resist had pushed him to the south of the city before stones, sticks and brooms had seen him off completely. His master had called him to heel. In February and March he'd been let loose to try again, this time to the east along the Jarama river, and the town of Guadalajara with a pack of Italians hungry for blood. He'd failed again. He had no choice but to try stirring things up from within.

'A fifth column. My, they're clever!' her grandfather exclaimed.

And it was true. He knew that Franco's general was well aware of the incendiary effects of his words on the people of Madrid. The very mention of a fifth column, Nationalist sympathisers working to crush the city from the inside, was enough to set the already anxious populace of the capital into overdrive. The idea of a secretive enemy force within would set citizen against citizen. But Maria understood nothing of this. Talk of manipulating the people bored her. The only detail that her hungry mind grasped was the undeniable truth that there were enemies walking amongst them, ready, at the given word, to strike Republican Madrid from within.

'Oranges!' The juice of the fruit trickled down Maria's chin. She wiped it with the back of her hand. Her grandmother handed her a napkin, an indulgent smile on her face. 'Propaganda,' her grandfather snorted. He blew his nose as if to rid himself of its taint. 'Designed to set us against one another. I'd like to take a look at that article when you've finished with it, Alvaro'. But propaganda or not, Maria found it was entirely believable that hundreds, thousands of enemy forces were operating within the city. Indeed, in this war that was theirs, where both sides spoke the same language, came from the same family, how could you tell who was for you and who against? The Germans and Italians on the battlefield, they were easy to identify, but here in Madrid… Maria noticed that her father had thrown a scrunched up piece of paper in the fireplace. She thought little of it as he struck a match and set it alight.

'We need to be on our guard against the increasing lawlessness that's masquerading as justice in these most dangerous of times,' Maria's grandfather said, a cloud across his face. His wife tried to silence him with her eyes but he would not be contained. 'Otherwise we will end up doing Varela's work for him.'

Maria had no idea what lay behind his words. That the government had freed thousands of criminals at the outbreak of the war meant nothing to her. She was oblivious to the fact that they walked free, reinventing themselves as political warriors, the physical embodiment of the will of the people. She knew nothing of the good people, friends of her grandparents, who were being arrested and imprisoned on baseless charges, accused of being Nationalist sympathisers or agents. Until recently Juan Mendez had been able to get them released. The rule of law still existed after all. But for how much longer would reason be able to withstand the surging panic unleashed by the idea of a fifth column, he wondered? He looked at Maria. She was gathering her things ready to go to work. He prayed he hadn't alarmed her.

By the time she was ready the dining room had cleared. Maria went over to the fireplace and, though she didn't know why, something compelled her to reach down and pick up the half burned pieced of paper her father had thrown in there earlier. She looked at it carefully. She could just about make out an address and the name of Father Anselmo, but nothing else. She felt hurt that her father hadn't shared the priest's news. She didn't know why but she scribbled down his address on a scrap of paper. She shoved it into her pocket, looked around to make sure her father hadn't seen her (he'd burnt the letter for a reason, after all), then set off.

She walked along the city's chaotic streets, snatches of her grandfather's conversation soon supplanting all thoughts of Father Anselmo's letter in her mind. Fifth columnists: the very idea of them excited her. She looked into the faces of passers by, trying to read them. Could he be a fifth columnist? Could she? But the morning was fresh and the sky was blue. And everybody out this morning seemed so purposeful. A fifth columnist, like her demons, would be better suited to lurking, if not under her bed, then definitely in the shadows. She gave her bag a little swing and allowed herself to be swept along by uplifting waves towards the blood transfusion unit. Towards her worthy job. Yet the stubborn need to do something more wouldn't go away. If not a *miliciana* then what? Her mind searched hungrily for an outlet.

A group of young women caught her eye. All dressed in blue jumpsuits and wearing *alpargatas*, the rope-soled shoes so familiar to her. They were sitting on sandbags, blocking a street while passing a fashion magazine round, closely followed by a red lipstick. The sight made Maria's heart race and her feet trip up. But she knew that wasn't it.

A slogan-plastered car beeped at her. She quickly jumped out of its way. 'I must watch where I'm walking', she said to herself. Impossible. Her eyes were pulled in all directions. Here a '*no pasaran*' banner, there a poster of a giant fist crushing a swastika'd plane. Promises of victory and the crushing of fascism were everywhere and they enthralled her. Now that was a cause she could warm to. She longed to be part of it.

Russians thundered past in armoured cars. Heroes, she thought, as she smiled at the sight of the numerous hammer and sickle symbols painted on the walls. 'The city's turning into a macabre stage for clashing ideologies.' She rolled her eyes as her father's words sprung to mind. Old people could be so cynical. It was true that Madrid was attracting some of communism's finest actors, hungry to snatch their moment in the limelight. And Maria liked to watch these, her matinee idols, as they threw themselves into their roles. But she too wanted her moment of glory. And it was for a good cause. She sighed as she saw the building that housed the blood transfusion unit up ahead. She was tired of having to wait in the wings.

Paloma. Maria pushed the memory down. But it was too late. Her heart pounded, breathing quickened. Her demons had come into the light. Faceless images of the enemy tormented her once more. She wanted glory but she also wanted revenge and the closer she got to her place of work the heavier the chains became that prevented her from getting it. Anger and hatred surged up out of nowhere and whirred round and round in her head. It revved up, like a car, unable to move forward, turning over and over on itself.

224

She stood outside the main entrance and paused, her hand on the door handle. She remembered some of her grandfather's words about the fifth column again. Forgot others. It seemed logical that there would be such a force. A shiny black car whose spokes dazzled in the sunlight sped past her, its tyres screeching over the cobbles. She turned to watch it. Heads protruded, hair swept back, black and yellow scarves billowing like sails, butts of rifles like masts. Voices yelped with excitement. *Death to all fascists!* In the passenger seat she caught sight of a boy with black hair, olive skin, and a scar on his cheek, waving a rifle and shouting out words of solidarity at people in the street. Her mind stuttered some more. 'Manu! Manuel!' Maria cried out. She was sure it was him. She watched the car as it sped away. In that moment she knew what she had to do. She released the door handle, stepped back and walked away.

CHAPTER 41

'Have you been to the Hotel Florida yet? It's full of foreign journalists!' Federica squealed with delight as she opened the beautiful wooden chest allowing its old lid to drop back hard, denting the parquet floor. But before Maria could answer, a deep voice boomed 'Careful!' from the far side of the room. Federica shrugged and said 'so what?' with a flicker of her eyelids. She didn't care much for being told what to do, nor how to do it. But as she recognised the man with the monstrous chin heading towards her, his smooth, black hair parted severely down the middle, she reeled in her defiance and cowered under a cloak of fear. The man with the monstrous chin had a monstrous body. He towered above her, eclipsing her completely. The girl held her breath. 'Sandoval.' A voice called him back. Federica rolled her eyes at her new friend. Still defiant – though she made sure her back was to him. And, Maria observed, a twitch now pulsed underneath the girl's left eye.

Maria was fixated on overcoming the fifth column in Madrid before her epiphany outside the blood transfusion unit: she was doubly so now. She attended meetings, joined groups, discussed enemy plots, imagined conspiracies. Speakers denounced 'bour-

226

geois policing'. So did she. They rejected 'old rules' accusing them of being inherently flawed for having been established by a 'bourgeois regime'. So did she. They argued for the need to 'cleanse our society'. So did she. She had found a new group of like-minded comrades. They went along to the same talks to listen to ideas they already shared.

It was at a talk about the importance of looking out for the enemy within that Maria had met Federica. Federica exuded physical confidence and belonged to a Communist group. 'Or possibly Socialist,' the girl had said. 'Either way we're definitely on the left.' This apparent ignorance Maria put down to self-consciousness and besides, any alarm she might have felt as a result evaporated when Federica invited her along to her group's headquarters. 'It's like a palace' she pronounced with a flourish of the hand. And that was because it was. The Condes de Rincon palace in calle Martinez de la Rosa.

When Federica had signed her new friend in, she led her into the building with pride and satisfaction towards the great hall. As Maria accompanied her, wings of excitement fluttering in her chest, so she imagined the acts of heroism she would soon be called upon to perform. 'There's a party tomorrow. You've got to come. You'll meet so many people there… What do you want us to do?' she asked a well-dressed young man sitting at a desk by the main door.

'Outfits.' He waggled his finger in the direction of some impressive old chests in the far corner. Maria's face flushed with disappointment. Federica's lit up with joy. She skipped past the walls decorated with standards and aristocratic coats of arms, pulling her new friend behind her. Maria cast an eye around the room. Suits of armour stood sentinel in the corners while an enormous fireplace dominated the vast space. A long dining table had been moved back against the far wall. 'A band will be on there tomorrow,' Federica said, squeezing on her friend's fingers. There were outlines on the walls where paintings had once hung.

As she looked around the room Maria noticed them carelessly propped up three deep near the main door.

'It's in the Plaza de Callao, the Hotel Florida, down the street from the Telefonica. You know. Not far from the Gran Via,' she said to Maria, continuing the conversation that Sandoval had interrupted. Maria's leg was feeling numb as if something was pressing down on a nerve. 'If you're interested I can take you along there some time. Full of Americans.' Federica gave a dirty laugh as if sharing a private joke with herself. 'Baths there too,' she added as an after-thought. Maria shifted position. Whatever it was that was causing her legs to tingle had stopped. But this alleviation of the physical pain she was feeling did nothing to assuage her gnawing frustration. She picked up a white feather boa and looked at it, incredulous. Maria had hoped to be doing more important things in her defence of the Republic than looking for fancy dress clothes in some old (albeit very beautiful), wooden chest. Federica pulled out a crumpled dress and held it up against her. It perturbed Maria that her stomach swelled ever so slightly beneath the folds of material. She pushed it away and told Federica she was here in Madrid to 'fight the fascists.'

'Aren't we all, comrade?' she giggled, continuing to share her knowledge of the best hotels, bars and restaurants in Madrid with Maria. 'And that's why you really have to go to Gaylord's. It's my favourite… hard to get in without an invitation. Sentries with bayonets stand outside the porte-cochere. They say General Lister and the military commander they call El Campesino drink there. When they're not giving it to them at the front, that is. What do you think? Fancy coming if I can get you in? It's *full* of Russians. They're like *bears*!'

'El Campesino?' Maria looked puzzled that any soldier should be called *the Peasant*.

'It's to accentuate his working-class origins,' Federica said, in a matter-of-fact way. 'He is communist after all. So,' she said, getting the conversation back on track. 'Fancy coming? To

Gaylord's?' She lit up a cigarette and proceeded to disappear behind a cloud of blue smoke. 'Cigarette? Maria? Maria? Fancy a cigarette?' Federica pulled on her sleeve. 'Cigarette? I asked.'

'No, no thank you,' Maria said, in a daze and feeling slightly nauseous.

Federica sat back on her heels and looked at Maria. Not bad looking, she supposed, but not exactly fun. She didn't even smoke.

'How about the cinema? The Marx Brothers are a hoot in *Night at the Opera*. I've seen it three times already and I've not finished with it yet… You will love it. I know you will,' Federica said. Maria forced a smile.

Workers carried in more chests. Camphor and dust wafted into the air as Federica threw them open. 'Sorry,' she shouted over to Sandoval. She put up her hand. 'So sorry. I forgot.'

'Well, remember!' he roared back.

'Who is that?' Maria asked. 'Says he was a political prisoner released at the start of the war but I've heard that…'

'Here! Now!' Sandoval stopped Federica mid flow. The girl scampered over to him and returned several minutes later head bowed.

'Such a beast,' she whispered to Maria. 'But not in a good way. You can sort through those, the one with the men's clothes in and I'll look through the evening gowns. Unless *you* want to, of course.' She didn't. Instead, she picked through frock coats, dress coats, uniforms and hats adorned with ostrich feathers. Federica held up a sparkling tiara and put it to one side. She'd forgotten all about Sandoval.

'Federica? Do you know many *milicianas*?' Maria did not want to give up on her dream.

'Oh yes, but most of them are pregnant now,' her friend answered in a tone of faux concern. Maria shuddered. She started to cough uncontrollably. Federica raised her eyebrows, whispered 'never mind' then she got up and moved over to a large wooden armoire. Opened it and rooted round like a pig at the trough.

229

'Look at these shoes!' she gasped, breathless with greed. All thought of *milicianas*, pregnant or otherwise, had disappeared from her mind.

'Do you have a boy?' Federica tried to squeeze her foot, ugly sister-style, into a delicate shoe made of pink kid. 'I do,' she said, flinging the ridiculously impractical footwear across the room. 'So bourgeois!' she hissed under her breath. 'He's been at the front,' she continued. 'Not now though. Injured. And has the most beautiful scar. Proved himself as a hero of the people. And still does, here in Madrid. Not afraid to do what's got to be done, if you get my meaning.' Maria did not. Federica threw another shoe onto the wooden floor. 'Why did those rich bitches have such tiny feet?'

Images of Luis burned within Maria's heart. They scorched themselves onto the pages of her memory. He would always be the better part of her. Perhaps she should read his letter. She closed her eyes to keep Federica from looking into them and seeing what was in her soul. She needn't have worried.

Federica, her nose back in the wardrobe, was snuffling round for larger shoes, her searchlight gaze intent on seeking out footwear to fit her proletarian feet. She had no interest in plumbing the depths of Maria's broken heart when she still had a magnificent shoe mountain to mine.

'What's he called, this boy of yours?'

'What?' Federica said, her voice muffled by velvet, leather and silk.

'What's his name?'

'Amaro. Amaro Pargo.'

'Like the pirate?'

Federica pulled her head out of the wardrobe, not amused. 'So what's yours called?'

Maria said nothing. Luis had taken over her mind and confused her. She glowed at the thought of his goodness, shivered with shame at her own treachery, prayed for his safety... and now

Amaro Pargo. Strange. That was what she and Paloma used to call Manuel when they were children. Paloma. Paloma, Paloma. *Whose side am I on?* Maria asked herself.

'Not have one? Never mind. Now I've got shoes to find.' Moments later Federica pulled her snout from the wardrobe and stood there, a third, hopeful pair of red velvet shoes hanging off her right hand.

'Want to know what my Amaro does?' Federica's heart swelled with the pride of a braggart as she leant over to whisper in Maria's ear. 'Well, he killed the enemy at the front, and...' She paused for dramatic effect, her voice growing even quieter. 'He pretty much does the same now.' With a finger pointed at the back of Maria's head, Federica went, 'Bang! Just like that.' She then stopped, looking round the room to make sure nobody was listening. 'And he goes out on special missions with Sandoval, looking for spies.' Her voice dropped to a melodramatic whisper. 'Says they're *everywhere*.'

231

CHAPTER 42

Though it struck Maria as ironic that the Communist Party whose HQ this grand palace had become should take such delight in the trappings of such lavish wealth, she still went along to the gathering the following evening where she hoped to meet Federica's boyfriend, the mysterious Amaro Pargo. What he did was meaningful. And what he did, she wanted – no, needed – to do. To avenge Paloma. To exorcise all thoughts of Luis and banish him to the other side once and for all.

The gathering would have been an elegant affair if it hadn't been so excessive. She and Federica had spent valuable hours looking for the most sumptuous and decadent costumes and it showed, their new comrades were dressed in the brightest satins and multiple strings of pearls. Federica had chosen the most extravagant outfit for herself. Trussed up in, and oozing out of, a deep red silk ballgown (feet weren't the only small thing those rich bitches had), she wore a tiara on her head, and so many ostrich feathers threaded down the back of her dress that they rose up and curled round her head like a canopy.

'Look!' Federica squealed, lifting up the skirt of her gown to reveal fine, red velvet shoes. She'd found a pair that fitted.

'Tasteful,' Maria said, with a hint of sarcasm so subtle that

Federica gave her a kiss. 'Oh, mustn't forget! *Salud comrade.*' She gave her little salute that looked particularly ridiculous given the clothes she was wearing. Maria, who hadn't dressed up for the occasion (not that Federica noticed), gave her a little salute back.

'Your boy not here?' Maria asked.

'Not until much later. Work!' Federica said as she tapped the side of her nose with her forefinger. A comrade dressed as a nineteenth-century dandy-cum-nobleman with an eighteenth-century wig and buckled shoes whisked the damsel in red silk away. Maria breathed a sigh of relief.

Perhaps she shouldn't have come, Maria told herself as she looked about the room. She had no time for frivolity and it was all around. *Hypocrites.* The thought came to the forefront of her consciousness like a lightning bolt. She wrestled with it, desperately pushing it back down to where it came from. People had a right to have fun in these sorry times. And who was she to judge, after all? But she had to get away before she said something she might live to regret. And she would if she didn't leave soon, she could tell, as the words queued up ready to springboard themselves off her tongue with great force. She'd come to meet Federica's boyfriend to see if he might be the contact she needed to get involved in something meaningful but he wasn't here. For a second, she thought she recognised someone. A young man. Early twenties. Possibly younger, dressed in a frockcoat embroidered in gold thread. His face was very familiar but try as she might, she couldn't place him. But the boy's face persisted in haunting her.

It was getting late. Federica's boyfriend hadn't shown up yet. It was time to go.

But as she turned towards the door a hand stretched out from inside an oversized gold sleeve and touched her arm.

'Maria. I'm Lope de Aguirre.'

Maria's eyebrows arched in mockery. Lope de Aguirre was the name of a Spanish pirate from the sixteenth century. Every girl and boy had heard of him. 'Wrath of God, Prince of Freedom, King of Tierra Firma? That Lope de Aguirre?' she said, amused. She had no idea who he was, but then again, there was something vaguely familiar about him. His eyes squinted, face crinkled, awkwardness exuded his every pore. She'd seen him before. 'Sorry. No,' he said. 'Forgive me. My real name is Virgilio. Virgilio Lorenzana Macarro.' He looked round, moved in towards her and whispered, 'a friend of Luis de los Rios and I recognise you from Fuentes de Andalucía.' She shuddered. Now she remembered him. But what was he doing here? The orchestra played. The good communists danced to waltz after waltz and Virgilio told Maria enough of his story for her to appreciate the parts her father and Luis had played in saving the life of this person before her. Federica saluted them from the other side of the ballroom. 'I can say no more,' he said. 'These are dangerous times for us all. There was a time when the difference between the sides in this war was clear. The Nationalists were brutes. I expected the other side to be the same. When your father and Father Anselmo entrusted me to people I considered criminals, I was afraid. I was their enemy. But they showed mercy, forgiveness, and they led by example not brutality. Your father was the one who told me that and for a while I saw it was true. But now,' he said, his eyes scanning the room suspiciously, 'I'm not so sure. The dividing lines are blurred in Madrid.'

Maria felt the floor shift beneath her feet. She saw Federica swaying towards them.

'Excuse me Virg... Lope,' Maria corrected herself. 'I need to get away. I have to sit down.' Her hand wrapped across herself.

'Down the corridor,' he whispered. 'There's a library, on the right.'

She rushed off for fear of being caught by Federica, but she needn't have worried. Federica was busy asking Lope about her boy.

She rushed towards the main entrance looking for the library

234

door. There it was, on her right, huge and as heavy as a tombstone. It pulled her inside.

A thousand books wrapped round the room from ceiling to floor. Maria quickly moved her head like a searchlight looking for life in the hallowed space. She found none. Satisfied that she was alone, she pushed the door to, took a deep breath and pushed her hair behind her ears. Her head raced, memories of Luis precious once more.

She went up close to the bookshelves, thinking of him. She dragged her finger gently along the volumes, reading the spines as she went. There was a copy of Cervantes, Garcia, Machado... Some she'd read, most she hadn't. She picked up a copy of Calderón. She remembered the quotation Luis had recited to her the last time they were together. She had to find it.

There were four high-backed leather chairs in the room. Two had their backs to her, flanking either side of the only window in the room. The other two were wedged in between three soft sofas that formed a U-shape in the centre. She allowed herself to sink into the nearest one. It wrapped itself around her. She flicked through the Calderón until she found the quotation. There it was.

'Even in dreams good works are not wasted.'

And in nightmares doubly so, she thought to herself. She closed her eyes. For a moment she was with Luis once more, in the shepherd's hut without a roof. She wanted to stay there with him, in her imagination, just the two of them, unblemished by the taint of war.

A sound intruded on her blessed communion. There it went again. It was a sniff. She opened her eyes to scour the room. She could see no one. Then came a cough from one of the high-backed leather chairs facing the window.

Maria went over and stood by the sniffing reader for quite some time before he realised she was there. Lost within the pages of his book, it was only when Maria coughed herself that he managed to find his way back to surface reality.

He slammed his own book shut, looked at Maria, leant forward, checked the door. Seeing that it was closed he sat back in his chair, visibly relieved.

'Antonio Rosario Jimenez.' Maria recognised the name. And this time it didn't have any piratical connection. A Madrileño born and bred, she'd heard about his family from her grandfather. 'Chose to stay. Defend the city. A forward-thinking family... Good people. Did much before the war to help those without the means to help themselves. Still do. But in this chaos we've fallen into that's not enough... They could be walking confidently along the boulevards of Paris or the streets of London now. Only the son goes about Madrid without fear. And that, I would say, is a mistake.'

Yet, Maria was about to discover, her grandfather was wrong in his belief that Antonio Rosario Jimenez was not afraid.

CHAPTER 43

Antonio Rosario Jimenez was well-read; that was how Maria had met him, perusing the beautiful book stacks, sitting in a tastefully upholstered chair. He had stuck out at the gathering, yet looked perfectly at home in the library. Unlike the rest of the party he hadn't dressed up as an aristocrat. No doubt because he was the only person there who really was one, and, in these dark times, he had no wish to draw attention to the fact – which was why he'd sought to absent himself from the main hall, leaving the hoots of delight at the palatial surroundings for others to make. He preferred to seek solace and safety in the protective pages of his favourite books. There, he could be as one with his comrades; there, he could truly enjoy solidarity, share ideals.

However, when Maria had first seen him at the window, sitting in the leather armchair, she couldn't help but feel a little suspicious of him. The gathering in the main hall had made her feel uncomfortable. Working girls wanted to be *infantas* while pretending to be communists; former Nationalist soldiers wanted to be heroes of the proletariat while pretending to be buccaneers. Luis had co-operated with her father to help people switch sides. Nothing was as she'd believed. Then she'd escaped to the quiet of the library, walking away from worker-as-aristocrat, only to find its negative sitting in the chair before her. Firecrackers of confusion went off within her head.

Antonio Rosario Jimenez. Aristocrat-as-worker.

Yet the book he was clutching in his hand called to her. 'What are you looking at?' she asked when the initial panic in his eyes at being caught reading had passed. He put his already closed copy of Calderón down and snatched a well-thumbed copy of Marx from the pocket of his tattered jacket. A pocket, Maria registered, that was hanging loose. No doubt pulled away at the seams, Maria thought to herself, to further distance him from his genuinely aristocratic background. A wave of music and raucous laughter thundered down the corridor and pushed its way under the door, crashing round the walls of the library. It licked their ears before fizzing away. Antonio placed long, elegant fingers uselessly over the closed volume on the table, his face tense.

'My favourite work by Calderón is *El pintor de su dishonra*,' she said, banishing the music and laughter and taking the seat next to him.

*

'It was ten o'clock before Maria thought to check the time. Her father would be waiting for her. She ran out of the room. 'Until tomorrow,' Antonio called after her.

Maria clattered to the end of the corridor. She turned to look at the main hall for one last time. There was Federica, in all her feathered finery, waltzing away with a man. Amaro? The one who put guns to people's heads? He looked vaguely familiar to her but in the half-light she couldn't really tell. She rubbed her eyes. She told herself she was imagining things. It was late. She was tired. And, besides, she no longer wanted to speak to Amaro Pargo. Whoever he was.

CHAPTER 44

The morning after the party Maria sat on her bed in her room preparing to read Luis' letter. She picked up her copy of *Don Quixote*, opened the cover, looked at the folded piece of paper. As she unfolded it, so her mind became scales, measuring the best of Luis, the worst of her. But her fingers did not falter and she would force her eyes to read the words upon the page. She took a deep breath then began.

My darling Maria,

As you read this I will be far away, or may as well be. Either way we cannot meet up again, not for a while. That's why I am writing you this letter, to tell you how much you mean to me. If someone had told me I would meet a girl in the way that I've met you I would not have believed them, not thought it possible. But I would have been wrong.

You have touched my soul with your goodness and loyalty. I pray our children take after you...

She covered herself with her arm. Her heart burned. She could read no more. His words were full of trust and tenderness and she deserved neither. She gave way to sobbing but as she looked at herself in the mirror she realised that she was enjoying this pain. 'You're not some tragic heroine in a novel!' she said to herself scornfully. She brushed her front down as if sweeping away the new life she feared was growing inside. 'You're just a...'

There was a gentle tap-tapping at the bedroom door. Maria quickly wiped her eyes. A smiling face peered around the door. 'Everything all right?'

Maria smiled back and nodded. It was her grandmother; she wouldn't let her down. In an instant Maria had decided that she would take her to the cinema to see the film recommended by Federica.

'I'm not sure I want to go. I'd hoped we might spend the evening together at home.' Isabel noticed the puffiness around her granddaughter's eyes. 'There's something I've been meaning to talk to you about.'

'Oh please, you must come,' Maria insisted. 'I think you'll love it. It's called *A Night at the Opera* featuring the Marx Brothers. I've heard it's funny.'

'Well...'

When it had been ascertained that the curfew didn't start until eleven and that bombs weren't going to stop Madrileños from going about their normal business and that yes, Maria did know where the nearest air raid shelters were, her grandmother eventually said yes.

*

It was early evening and Maria was waiting for her grandmother in the hall. Thoughts of Luis' letter had made her head ache and now she couldn't stop thinking about what she'd done to betray him. With the changes she could no longer deny were happening to her body, soon her shame would be visible for all to see. She started to pace.

Isabel was still in her bedroom, rummaging around the bottom

240

of her jewellery box. She anticipated a special night out with her granddaughter and it would turn out to be all the more so if only she could find the blasted ring.

There.

Isabel rushed down the stairs as quickly as her frail legs would allow. She dropped a small velvet box into her bag, the one decorated with fabric sunflowers. She threaded a fragile arm through her granddaughter's. Her heart sang with joy. She had resigned herself to never knowing Maria and now here she was, arm in arm with this beautiful, precious life. Tonight, she would prove herself to be the grandmother Maria needed.

The evening sky was bright and clear and there was not a hint of a breeze or a chill in the air. The streets were pleasantly busy and both Isabel and Maria floated along them, buoyed by their own thoughts. Isabel patted her granddaughter's hand. She knew Maria's secret. It would be all right. Everything would be all right. Isabel had come up with a plan. Maria could wear her ring (her hand moved instinctively over her bag to make sure it was still there). She could tell people that her husband was fighting at the front. Or had been killed. As she preferred. Isabel was going to find it difficult to bring the matter up but she was determined to do so, for her granddaughter's sake.

Maria's hand brushed over the front of her skirt instinctively. A voice in her grandmother's head shouted, 'Now!'.

She pulled Maria to a standstill. Her fingers fumbled around the infinite folds in her floral bag. Preoccupied, she didn't notice the searing noise crackling through the sky above.

Maria did. She looked around. No one was rushing, everyone was simply making their way slowly to the entrance of the underground station in the corner of the square. This was the well-heeled Salamanca district of Madrid. Franco had sworn never to bomb it. The planes were passing over on their way to causing havoc elsewhere. 'Es nada!' somebody cried. Nothing. Nothing at all.

The noise above grew louder. Drew closer. Maria looked up: German Heinkel 52 fighters. So low she could make out the swastikas on the wings. Then its metal jaws yawned open dropping its deadly contents on the people below. Panic, like wildfire, swept through the people. Mechanical screams pierced the air. Painful. Deafening.

'One of them's been hit. Come on!' a couple said, running past, beckoning the two women to join them. But Maria was transfixed. She watched as flames trailed from the injured plane that roared and screamed around in the sky like a wounded animal. It made a disturbing and dazzling spectacle as it fought to stay up. It started to spin out of control. Even as her grandmother pulled at her Maria couldn't tear herself away.

She remembered seeing Isabel fall against a wall as she herself was thrown to the ground by the strength of the blast. She put her hand out to break the fall but rubble fell away beneath sending her splayed out across the floor. 'I'm fine. Really. Quite fine,' she said, looking over at her grandmother but as she got to her feet she felt a pain in her lower back, then a dragging sensation in her abdomen. '*Abuela*?' she cried. As she stumbled towards her, Maria saw agony on the elderly woman's thin, dust-covered face. Maria held her hand, smoothed her hair. Creaking walls and beams, distant ambulance sirens, and her grandmother's shallow breathing, mingled to make one discordant din. 'Help is on its way. You'll be fine. I know you will.' Black smoke loomed like storm clouds in the air above. Ash settled down on them like snow.

'The baby?' her grandmother whispered, before breaking into a cough. 'The baby?' Her grandmother knew. For how along, Maria wanted to ask, but to see the fragile woman lying uncomfortably on a bed of rubble, such questions were unimportant. The dull ache in her back invaded her senses once more. She placed her hands over the pain as if to hide it. But Isabel read it in the girl's face. 'The baby's fine, *abuela*. The baby is going to be fine,' Maria said, the ache in her back seeping deeper into her abdomen, stretching its cruel fingers around her womb and drawing them in like a vice.

Isabel closed her eyes. Her head rolled gently on her pillow of stone. 'Stay with me! Look! Look into my eyes, *abuela*!' Maria screamed.

Her grandmother was drifting away.

The young woman let out a groan, primal, animal, as violent contractions wracked her body. The guttural sound roused Isabel. Ignited her terror. An electric current surged through her small, weak body. It twitched and crackled, fighting for life.

'The baby?' Isabel held out her birdlike hand to her only grandchild. Maria took it, enfolding it within her own. The sight of her ageing grandmother slumped on the ground, combined with her own pain, terrified her. Maria's fingers squeezed rhythmically in and out in time with her breath, as if pumping air into a blow-up doll, hoping to cheat the puncture. Her grandmother, likewise, willed the life force within to pass from her, to her granddaughter, to the baby she was carrying. Isabel swam in and out of consciousness, a watery world inhabited by her swirling hopes and prayers.

Isabel had known about the baby before Maria herself. The signs were obvious from the start. The nausea, the physical changes… She did not know the circumstances. But a life had started. All other considerations were as nothing. Her own child, Ines, had waited so long to have a child. So many miscarriages. And when she did carry a baby she did not bloom. The glow she had was a ghastly ghostly glimmer, a strange translucent green under the skin. Fertility did not plump up her flesh, no ripe peach was she. More a brittle, flimsy twig on which a growth had managed to stick and whose vigour and strength had caused her to bow and bend. The birth nearly broke her, threatened to snap her in two. Isabel had been distraught. Had wished it away. Until she saw it. Her. Maria. A vital, angry infant, hungry for life. All risks had been worth it.

Isabel lay on the stony ground looking up at her granddaughter. 'There's so much good in you,' she said, a sparkly eyed expression on her face. 'Always believe that.' Maria glimpsed the sparkle as it escaped down the side of her grandmother's dusty cheek, glinting as it caught in the light.

'Ines?' she whispered, her words weaker, speech slower.

'No. I'm her daughter, *abuela*. Your granddaughter, Maria.' The sound of the ambulance was getting louder. 'Hold on, *abuela*. Please.'

'Wear… the… ring…' Isabel fell back into the depths. Her body went limp. Her hand released the little velvet box.

Tears rolled down Maria's face. 'Don't go.'

'Quick. Two casualties. On the floor. Over here.' Stretcher bearers appeared. They ran to Isabel. Her eyes fluttered with the delicate life within. One took her pulse. The light went out in his eyes and Maria knew. Her grandmother was barely there. 'What's her name?' he asked, turning to face Maria. And then he saw it – blood, soaking into dust and debris, dark and red brown, in thick painful clots stretching out around the young woman like a moat.

Maria hadn't wanted to be separated from her grandmother but she'd had no choice. 'The young one's bleeding! Quick!' One hour later and she was no longer with child. 'An early miscarriage brought on by the impact of the bombing.' That was how it was explained to her as she lay in a makeshift hospital bed. There was nothing the doctors could have done about it. 'See it as a blessing,' one of the nurses on duty blurted out, her eyes quickly looking up from Maria's ringless fingers.

Maria was far away within herself. She'd heard the nurse's words. She'd recognised her look of judgement masked by sympathy. But she didn't care. She searched her memory to bring what she had lost to life. Her hand crossed protectively over her womb. She remembered the butterfly movements of yesterday and smiled. Thoughts of Paloma sitting next to her under the

244

olive tree flooded her mind with joy but Maria could not keep them alive for long. She couldn't keep many things alive. She flayed herself with scalding derision.

Another nurse came into the room. 'Your grandmother's—'

'No!' Maria cried. 'Don't say it.' But the sense of loss was immediate, debilitating, with or without the word. Dizzy, nauseous, thoughts of lost loved ones swam away from Maria. She looked at the nurse and blinked, seeing her properly for the first time. And the more this small woman in a uniform came into focus, with the beauty spot at the corner of her lips, her two front teeth that crossed over one another, and a look of fear in her eyes, the more distant Maria's loved ones became. She clutched on to them with every feeling nerve in her body. Until they snapped. Her womb went into spasm. She moved her arm across herself protectively but the pity in both nurses' eyes told her there was nothing to protect. She longed for Paloma, but now Maria's head hurt to remember her dear friend's face. She cried for her grandmother, but all that was left was a feeling of loss. This collision of being and nothingness was beyond all understanding and it took her breath away.

She looked at the nurse burdened with news about Isabel. 'Please don't say it,' Maria whispered. 'Not just yet.' And with that Maria buried her head in the nurse's shoulder. And sobbed silently and copiously. Hot tears rolled and rolled in waves, splashing over the rounds of her cheeks. By the time they'd formed rivers along the creases and folds of her neck they were cold.

In the minutes, hours, days and weeks that followed Maria was to shed an ocean of tears. She had lost so many loved ones. But in the loss of her grandmother she had also lost a form of herself.

'There's so much good in you, my darling.' She had no idea why, but these words, more than any others her grandmother had spoken, tormented her. They scorched the inside of her head. Maria found them incendiary because they were untrue. What had happened to Paloma had happened because of her, she had betrayed Richard with Luis, had found love with Luis only to betray him too, she had lured her grandmother to her death. And she had destroyed her own unborn child. Her guilt was incontestable.

Well, she would be willingly punished.

Her mind searched for ways to find the self she'd lost with the passing away of her grandmother. She dwelt on her crimes – this path led to self-loathing. She ruminated over those who'd made the crimes possible – this path led to revenge. Revenge. It seemed sweet, and she mistook it for salvation. She would pursue her accomplices – those who'd dealt the coups de grâce: the Nationalist soldiers who had abducted, raped and left her friend for dead, the pilots whose bombs had killed her grandmother, and the enemies within who somehow were responsible for all that was eating away at Madrid from within. Maria's rage was burning fast, turning into an uncontrollable fire. It was looking to engulf the enemy.

She was decided. If there was any good left within her, Maria felt sure that the only way she would find it was in destroying the bad without.

CHAPTER 45

She helped out any way she could, threw herself into anything and everything. Helping at the foodbanks, teaching soldiers to read in the nearby trenches in Casa de Campo on the outskirts of the city, putting up warning signs on unstable buildings bombed the night before within. She worked tirelessly for months. Yet whatever she did left her restless, dissatisfied. Her father looked on, helpless.

One morning she was out with Antonio Rosario Jimenez. The two of them had hit it off that evening in the library. Though she struggled to see the good in herself, she saw that it radiated from Antonio Rosario Jimenez's every pore. The pair of them had just finished putting up a keep out sign on a dangerous structure of what only the day before had been a solid town dwelling. Like a doll's house with the front removed, you could still make out the rooms. There a bedroom with a still intact bed, there a drawing room with the remains of a dresser. A tempting sight for the growing number of people in Madrid who had nothing. A goat jumped over the debris within. Loose plaster and masonry rained down upon it causing it to run out skittishly and escape with fright down the street.

Two comrades walking by stopped. One went straight past the

warning sign and stepped over some rubble. 'No!' Maria shouted. He went in anyway.

'Can't you read?' Antonio Rosario Jimenez asked.

'What's that you said, comrade?'

'He said, 'Can't you read?' Maria answered.

'Hey, Amaro. Over here. Quick. Come and have a listen to this, comrade.'

The man who'd stayed outside the derelict building bounded over.

Maria recognised him as Manu. Most of his face was now hidden behind a thick moustache and beard that covered the scar running up the side of his face but she would have known those eyes anywhere. Like his mother's. But he had not recognised her.

'Can't I *read*? Many of our comrades can't *read*. Good, honest peasants who fight for our freedom, protect our city, and you dare to ask, *can't you read*? Do you disrespect them, comrade?' It was not Manu who said this. He was studying Maria's face, trying to place her.

'Amaro! Amaro! What are you waiting for?'

With a sense of urgency, Manu put his hand on his comrade's arm to restrain him. To stop him offering to take the educated bourgeois that was Antonio for a little ride in the car. Now was not the time for that.

'Manu,' Maria said. 'Is it really you?' Here before her was the boy she'd seen speed past in the car all those months back. He was also Federica's boyfriend, the mysterious Amaro – there could only be one. Manu's confrontational friend glowered at Antonio Rosario Jimenez. 'Be sure to show more respect next time, comrade,' he snarled as Manu dragged him away.

'We need to meet,' Maria called after him.

248

CHAPTER 46

Manuel was in Madrid. After evading Nationalist capture in Fuentes de Andalucía, with the help of Maria's father and his mother, he had sought refuge with a guerrilla group, *Los Ninos de la Noche* (Boys of the Nights), in the high mountains behind the village of Frigiliana. There he carried out attacks on their Nationalist enemies before moving on to a guerrilla camp just outside Granada, and it was here that he'd first heard of Aleksandr Orlov. The Russian Orlov was a colonel in The People's Commissariat for Internal Affairs, and the man responsible for the training of all guerrilla units. He was based in Madrid, as was the guerrilla training school. Manuel had come to get trained up, to progress within the guerrilla ranks. But, it seemed, despite his experience, Orlov was not yet convinced of the boy's loyalty to the cause; Manuel would have to find other ways to prove his worth if he was going to win the great man over. That was what he was doing when he crossed paths with Maria: patrolling streets, righting wrongs, dishing out punishments.

'Be careful,' Antonio had warned her. He'd sensed Manuel's violent desperation: he'd nearly become one of its victims. But careful was the last thing Maria wanted to be. She was tired of feeling numb. She wanted to punish anyone who'd ever committed a crime and she'd seen and heard enough of 'Amaro' to know that he could help her deliver the justice that she, on her own, could not.

But she could never call him Amaro.

And now she knew who he was she had no problem in tracking him down, nor in getting him to agree to her involvement.

*

The first time Maria went out with Manu and his gang she was kept well from the action. She'd climbed into the back of the car next to a boy called Roco from Extremadura. In the passenger seat was Jordi from Asturias. The gruff one who couldn't read.

She'd hardly ever been in a car before. Manu drove fast sweeping her dark thoughts to the ends of her windblown hair. Exhilarated, she felt her past suppressed as Manu screeched towards an unknown, breathtaking future. Maria felt light and dizzy. Like a film star.

But as the gang ran out of the car to root out an enemy within, a large hand without pushed her head back inside the car. 'No, comrade. This is not for you.'

Maria waited. Anger and frustration gnawed away at her. And hatred, for the unknown fifth columnist her comrades had gone to deal with. She looked out of the back of the car willing them to reappear. Then they did, running as fast as they could. They piled into the car. Manu put his foot down on the accelerator. 'It's done, comrade,' they told her. 'It's over.' A thrill surged through her body. She told herself that it was because good had overcome evil. She saw the handle of a pistol sticking out of Jordi's trousers at the side of his waistband. Punishment had been meted out too. Her heart raced some more.

'There's a big one coming up,' Manu said to her as she got out of the car. 'The rat we're going to put on trial tomorrow locked many great men away in prison before the war. All wrongfully.

And we're privileged to have one of the greatest come with us to confront him. Are you in?'

'Yes, I'm in' came her steely reply, knowing that the second time she went with them she wouldn't be made to wait in the car. 'Meet you at five in the morning.' As the car got swallowed by the street so Maria looked up at the windows all around. Spies were everywhere, conspirators plotting away in darkened rooms. She felt a fluttering in her stomach to think that by this time tomorrow there would be at least one less of them. And she couldn't wait.

She went upstairs to her bedroom. Her fury was limitless. The guilty had to pay, they would always have to pay. And she was ready to do whatever it took to make them do so.

CHAPTER 47

Maria barely slept that night. She went over what she'd seen and heard in the car the day before. And in her fitful dreams she saw Manu and his gang of divine executioners meting out punishment with godlike wrath upon the guilty. She would support them in their mission.

She dressed in darkness and crept down the stairs. She had to be careful. After her grandmother's death she wasn't the only person at home unable to sleep peacefully.

She opened the door, closing it after her with the lightest of touches. There, at the end of the street, she could see Manu. He switched the blue painted headlamps on and off to signal her over.

They drove slowly towards their meeting place. Maria's heart thumped violently in her chest. Unsure, excited, giddy, she wanted revenge – although against who, she had no idea. Nor did she care. She could smell blood as her own coursed wildly through her veins, rushing and whirling round her head in torrents.

Manu pulled over. They had arrived. He and Maria got out of the car. He knocked on the door.

The sound shattered the silence. Maria winced. It was as if he had thrown a shell into the middle of the road. She waited for every resident in every apartment to come to their windows. They did not. Instead she saw a shadow at an upstairs window followed by the sound of movement from within. Someone was opening the door. It was Sandoval. So he was the great man. Maria had only ever seen him once before and that was talking to Federica.

He looked up and down the street then beckoned Manu and Maria in and up the staircase to the apartment on the first floor.

Manu greeted him like a hero.

'Window,' Sandoval instructed her while he whispered his plans in Manu's ear. Her eyes remained peeled on the street outside. Her ears pricked to the slightest sign of life. If any spy was on to them Maria would spot them.

Sandoval. She didn't like him but she didn't have to. It was sufficient that he had been wrongly imprisoned by the man they'd come to punish today. This had happened to too many good men before the war, like her grandfather's good friend, Santiago Carrillo, Councillor for Public Order. It occurred to her that Sandoval and Carrillo did not seem very similar but she told herself to stop being judgemental.

Instead, she observed the remaining gang members as they arrived one by one. A few walked boldly, swaggering as they made their way down the street, pushing their chests out, looking from side to side before nodding with self-appreciation. If they could have, they would have hammered on every door and demanded to be seen. But most skulked, eyes to the ground, praying to be invisible.

A strange assortment of people, Maria thought to herself. Instinctively she didn't trust them. From the way they looked at her when they entered the apartment it was clear that the feeling was mutual.

Each of the men lit up. They inhaled deeply, each exhalation an impressive cloud of smoke that filled the room. Red ash tips glimmered in the gloomy space. They slapped each other's backs.

Sandoval called them to order. 'We need to clean up this city.

Purge it of its rot.' Maria felt uncomfortable. She'd heard these words before. Images of Captain Garcia presented themselves to her unbidden. She pushed them aside and listened to what their leader had to say.

'The accused has family living in the Nationalist occupied areas, he has spread propaganda, he has religious icons in his home, he chose not to go to Portugal when he had the chance. I ask you why did he not go, comrades? What serpentine subterfuges did he have in mind? I'll tell you what. Members of his family infiltrated people's parties, he kept good, honest workers in servitude, he held onto the master-slave model of behaviour between the classes. I tell you he is an elite, an oppressor... and a fascist.'

Ripples of excitement swept and swirled around the room.

'What more evidence do you need of a man's guilt?' Manu said to her. Maria nodded in approval. Sandoval had restored her resolve. 'At last,' she said to herself, 'revenge. Today a fascist will be punished. And I will be part of it.'

Sandoval beckoned his band of avenging brothers to him for one last time, leaving Maria as lookout by the window once more. Though she could not make out what he was saying, his deep, gravelly voice left scratches on her conscience. He signalled that he'd finished with a laugh more wicked than joyful. The sound sent a shiver down her spine and as she shuddered Sandoval shot her a look so ugly that it reached into her heart, placed its fleshy palm around it, squeezed it, then released it.

She ran after Manu to the car, her legs heavy, her heart confused from being man-handled. But she couldn't turn back now.

It was still early – 5.30, possibly a bit later – as they drove through the empty streets, the car headlights off, in silence. Maria told herself she should be excited, jubilant that criminals would be made to pay. She should feel proud. But as the car pulled up outside a familiar apartment block in the grand district of Madrid that she knew so well she felt uneasy. Two more cars pulled up behind.

Knock, knock, knock. Sandoval rapped on the door with his rough bruised fists. The heavy sound disturbed the quiet morning air and must have awoken everybody in the street, but no one came to their windows to see what was happening. Perhaps because they knew. The clear clip-clip-clip of footsteps moved their way across the hard marble floor of the designated apartment. The person on the other side stopped. The pause engulfed Maria – she tasted his fear as she attempted to swallow her own. She'd been here before.

A servant opened the door. His eyes peered into the half-light to make out the faces of the unexpected visitors. His look of fearful resignation melted away at the sight of her. He beamed at her, his face for a moment full of hope, trust. It pulled at the paper concealing the cracks. It tore easily. She asked herself why she was here. What she was doing.

She knew him.

It was Ramon Figuera, the servant who had refused to stop serving the Jimenez family. Maria had heard the story from her grandfather. Ramon's wife had died in childbirth when having her third son and from that moment on the Jimenez's had treated his children as their own, paying for their education and helping them establish careers. One was a scientist while the other two had set up in business together. All three boys – Jorge, Tomas and Enrico – now lived in Suarezna. They'd asked their father to join them there. But he couldn't leave the Jimenez family, not after all they'd done for him.

'We've come to do a routine search,' Sandoval said, pushing past Ramon. The others, Maria included, followed behind him. Members of the group marvelled at the size of the room, gasped at the beauty of the mouldings and the highly polished parquet floor, felt giddy at the heights of the ceiling, looked with awe at the magnificent, sturdy door frames. It was clear that each one of them admired the proportions and elegance of this abode. Yet they nodded in envious agreement as Sandoval stood in the middle of the room and rolled out his arm as if unveiling the room and drawing it to the attention of his men for the first time. 'Such unnecessary spaciousness. Papers,' Sandoval barked at Ramon. The servant looked at Maria, an expression of concern for her safety in his eyes. She looked away.

'This is not your apartment?' Sandoval asked, knowing full well that it belonged to Señor Alonso Jimenez, one of the witnesses who had testified against him for theft before the start of the Civil War. Some people said Sandoval was a common criminal and yes, he had done things deemed illegal in the past. But he could always justify his so-called crimes to himself. Shame the courts hadn't seen things the same way.

He'd been working through those who'd got him imprisoned and this morning it was Jimenez's turn. Sandoval had planned a quick, efficient mission, with as few obstacles as possible. Jimenez's son was, thankfully, not here. Ramon, unfortunately, was. That he was here out of loyalty irritated Sandoval beyond reason. He was prepared to sacrifice himself. Well, so be it, thought Sandoval. *Your choice.*

'The Señor is trustworthy, I can assure you,' Ramon replied to Sandoval's question.

'Señor? Señor did you say? There are no Señors here, comrade,' Sandoval boomed, using the word *comrade* like a knife. Ramon breathed deeply. He knew who Sandoval was, understood how dangerous he could be, but he also had the measure of the man. As Sandoval cast his covetous eye around the precious objects around the room, Ramon knew that he liked what he saw. Once a thief, always a thief. He prayed the man's greed would distract him.

Sandoval strode into the living room. He picked up ornaments, went through drawers, didn't close them. Sandoval found a watch, inspected it closely – for a moment, Ramon imagined he might put it into his pocket. His watch-filled hand waivered as it hung down by his side as if not sure what to do with the valuable item in his grasp. This might only be a robbery after all, Ramon dared to believe.

But then Sandoval placed the watch very deliberately back where he had found it.

He pulled down on both lapels of his jacket and with his back to Ramon, Sandoval called back sharply, 'Now get him up, comrade.'

The manservant's chest tightened but he didn't move. 'Now,' Sandoval ordered.

Maria's eyes darted to the ornate crucifix still on the wall by the door. She'd remembered how Antonio had told her about it, how he'd begged his father to remove it but that his father had said no. His mother had been a very devout woman. His father too was a believer. *Faith isn't something you can switch off overnight,* he'd said to his son. *I'm not prepared to live a lie. Of course I support the Republic. That's why I'm still here in Madrid. But that doesn't mean that I'm going to deny all that was good in my life. Nearly everyone I know had some sort of faith not too long ago. A fact they've all conveniently forgotten.*

Maria looked over at the doorway. He was there. Señor Alonso, a shirt ill-buttoned for being done in haste, with black trousers over pyjamas. He combed his fingers through his hair as he entered the room, cards and papers clutched in his other hand. He looked at Sandoval carefully. Recognition followed by fear swept one after the other across his face. But soon he regained his composure. It made no difference. Sandoval was here to carry out what he'd wanted to do ever since he'd been released from prison at the start of the war, avenge himself on those who'd put him away in the first place.

'Search the place,' Sandoval ordered Manu, as he held out his hand for the documents.

'You will see that they are all in order,' Señor Alonso said, his voice not as assured as his words.

'You can buy anything these days, when you're rich,' Sandoval said to his gang, casting the papers aside. 'And corrupt.' He went and stood next to the crucifix and laughed. The rest of the band laughed with him. All apart from Maria.

'I think it's time we took Señor for a little walk,' Sandoval said, his voice cruel, his words barbed.

Maria's heart started to beat faster than ever. She wanted to stop what was going to happen but she did not know how. Ramon embraced Señor Alonso, a gesture of loyalty and love.

'Fawning moron,' snorted Sandoval as he pushed Ramon aside with one hand, thrusting a pistol into Señor Alonso's back with the other while nudging him out through the main door.

'He's a good man. An innocent man,' Ramon called out, as Sandoval's troupe followed their leader out. Manu looked down at the elderly man – he reminded him of a skinny version of his mother and it touched his heart. *Why*, he wondered to himself, *did the oppressed stay so loyal to the men who oppressed them*?

'How can he say such a thing?' Manu whispered in Maria's ear, irritated by the elderly servant's words. 'Because it's true,' came the barely audible reply.

What was happening? Maria had wanted to be a part of this so badly. How could she have got things so wrong? Shame was working its way up her body with its slimy touch. She wanted to cry for Luis. How he would hate her if he knew what she was doing. So would Paloma. So would her grandmother. 'You're stronger than you know and one day you will prove it.' Luis' words came back to her and pushed shame's blood-soaked cloak from off her shoulders. Well, Maria told herself, this was the day to prove it. Before it was too late.

'Wait! I've left my purse inside!' Maria patted her pockets in a show of looking for it. Not there, she raised her hands as if to say 'See'. 'I won't be a minute'. With a rapid turn she disappeared back inside the building. One long minute later she got back and climbed into the car. 'Looks like you've seen a ghost,' Sandoval quipped at her as he lit up a cigarette. Clouds of smoke billowed around the accused like incense. Maria panted like a thirsty pet, the huff, huff, huff making her more conscious than ever of the mounting tension in the car. The violin string was pulled taut. It might snap at any second.

Sandoval gave the order to drive on.

CHAPTER 48

Manu was at the wheel. He drove through the dead quiet streets of Madrid, heavy with silence. No one dared speak in the car. Only Sandoval.

'I told you I'd pay you back! Didn't think it would be so soon,' he said, his voice dark, his words darker. Señor Alonso said nothing. His reserve riled his persecutor. 'Think you're better than us, don't you?' Again, the polite, old man, with his buttons done up the wrong way, said nothing. Sandoval placed the point of his pistol up against his captive's forehead. 'I can do it here. I can do it now, you know.' Maria tried to steady her breath. *Choose your battles wisely,* she reminded herself, *wait for the right moment. You're stronger than you know.*

The band stopped at a checkpoint. There was a lot of saluting, and 'Hello, comrade' ricocheted back and forth. Papers were presented, another salute given. A finger pointed at Señor Alonso. 'Taking him to Casa de Campo,' came Sandoval's reply. A chill ran through Maria. The comrade nodded knowingly. They were allowed to pass.

At the checkpoint, benches had been dragged out of the university buildings and used as barriers. Manu drove around them and on through parkland full of vast oak trees. 'Pull over here,'

Sandoval ordered. Maria looked out at a wall that was riddled with bullets and stained the colour of death. It had once housed the Philosophy Department.

When Maria had rushed back into Señor Alonso's apartment she'd found herself genuflecting at the image of Mary, asking that she would keep and protect the innocent. She hoped now that the Virgin had heard her prayers. Casa de Campo. Maria was only too aware of what those three little words meant. Death by firing squad.

She'd thought this was a noble cause. Instead she saw that it was a grubby, petty, personal vendetta. Sandoval. Señora Gonzalez... Had Maria learnt nothing from the past?

She pushed her fingernails into her palms as she hoped Ramon had trusted her enough to do what she'd asked him to do – go to her grandfather's house, tell him what had happened. He would know who to call on, how to act, what to do.

She prayed Ramon had made it.

As Maria waited to get out of the car her heart was in her mouth. Manu got out first, Sandoval second. He leant in the back of the car and dragged Señor Alonso out, pulling on the back of his terror-drenched shirt collar.

'The trial won't take long,' Sandoval shouted back at his group. He pushed Señor Alonso against a wall, standing back as if to observe his prey. He then held up a light and shone it in the poor man's eyes. Blinded by the glare, Señor Alonso squinted ahead but could no longer make out anyone or anything. Not Manu and his expression of disdain, nor Maria and her look of surprise and horror – but Señor Alonso knew she was there. He prayed that the girl would not believe he was guilty.

Sandoval reeled off his supposed offences once more for the fun of it. Obtaining false papers, possessing religious icons, oppressing the workers and... spying for the enemy. 'What do you have to say?' he asked the man he was so going to enjoy killing. The surge of pleasure that he felt to know that this man

261

who had testified against him was truly afraid was unexpected. Who knew what untold joy he would experience when he got to put the gun up against his head and pull the trigger? His excitement was animal as he anticipated the taste of blood.

Maria looked towards the horizon. The sun was starting to burst forth, its orange light aglow across the sky. If she got away safely she would never get involved with the gang again. If Señor Alonso escaped unhurt she would only ever do good. Oh, please let her grandfather come. Please, please, she pleaded. Oh please don't let Señor Alonso die a martyr's death. She dug her fingernails into her palms still more.

'Where's the evidence against me?' Señor Alonso asked. Manu was shocked, Sandoval irritated. Maria in awe.

Sandoval held up a burnt out lantern. 'What's this?' Señor Alonso asked.

'Used to send signals to the enemy,' Sandoval pronounced. The old man laughed with disbelief.

'I almost, almost, pity you Sandoval,' he said. 'Why, every family in the city owns a lantern. You can do better than this.' Maria could hear the low growl coming from somewhere deep within Sandoval's body. It was getting bigger, louder. She looked around. Dawn was breaking and the sunlight was showing up all the cracks in the ground. There were haphazard piles of rubbish everywhere. She heard Sandoval cock the lever of the gun. In that moment thoughts of Luis came to her once more. How he'd saved her, how he'd loved her, loved her far more than she deserved. If she did nothing else in her pointless life she would do something to be worthy of him now. It was time to act. She stepped forward.

'Stop.'

Sandoval arched an eyebrow.

'I said *stop*,' she said. 'Now.'

A car had driven stealthily along the trenches. It pulled up behind them. No one noticed. All they heard was Sandoval as his low growl erupted into a volcanic laugh. 'You have some *cojones*, I'll say that for you. But put them away before I cut them off,' and with that he took aim at his victim once more. 'Keep the bitch under control,' he snapped at Manu.

'Time to die, Alonso!'

But then again perhaps not.

The time Maria had taken to distract Sandoval from his task was the time needed to save an innocent man's life.

'Gun down, Sandoval.' A broad Asturian accent boomed in the freshness of the morning air. Ramon had got word to Juan Mendez about this travesty of justice after all and it was the heroic military commander *El Campesino* (the Peasant) who had turned up to settle it. Sandoval kept his gun aimed at his quarry. His hand trembled, a sign of the turmoil provoked by the recent arrival. But he would not stop now. He was so close. Maria looked on, horrified. He was still going to do it.

Click. 'Gun down comrade. You know I won't tell you again.' In an instant everything changed. The familiar sound of a gun, the Peasant's gun, this time aimed at Sandoval's head, persuaded Sandoval that vengeance would not be his today. Maria heard the air escape from her lungs as her eyes watched Sandoval's arm drop to his side.

She collapsed, momentarily losing all feeling in her legs. Manu instinctively shot out his arms to support her. The Peasant shot her a look as if noticing her presence for the first time. Recognition and acknowledgement worked their way across his features. Strong girl, he said to himself. She'd done well, this granddaughter of Mendez's. 'Take the girl home.'

*

An innocent man had very nearly been murdered that morning. A friend's father, a family friend. Ironic that it was because she was friends with Antonio Jimenez that she was allowed to get involved with Sandoval and the group in the first place. Friends, enemies, all tangled together.

She clutched her chest as it contracted involuntarily with the horror of what might have been. That something so icy had been growing where her heart used to be she saw quite clearly now. But what if the man had been guilty? What then? Would that have made it any better? She'd thought so. But now… something had changed within her.

She lay back on her bed and let the tears coat her eyes. They welled up at the ducts, trickled over her temples, soaked into her hair. She had lost so much. Self-pity. It was an easy emotion to indulge. She turned on her side and curled herself up into a ball. So many ugly images, so many confused thoughts. She reached out to sleep to escape the torment.

'Maria?' She was awoken, what seemed to her, seconds later – it was six hours. She put one hand to her matted hair. She cradled the back of her skull. She had a pounding headache. She squinted towards the voice. It was her father's. He was due to return to the front the following day. She blinked, forced her eyes to look at him, to see what she'd been putting him through. Everything about him seemed smaller to Maria somehow. It was as if sorrow had slowly eaten away at him from the inside leaving a stretched and sagging carapace. He was doing the only thing he could do – saving lives. It was draining him. But so was she. She tasted the bitterness that comes before tears lining up in preparation at the back of her throat as she realised that she always had. She swallowed it back down. Crying wasn't going to make his sorrow go away. It wouldn't erase all the hurt she'd caused him.

She'd been part of something hideous that morning. That was undeniable. But she'd also stopped something far uglier still from occurring. Paloma wasn't coming back. Her grandmother was gone. They were dead and she could do nothing to make it otherwise. But she could, like her father, help the living. She had much to think about.

Over the next few days she spent time with her grandfather, remembering her mother, her grandmother. They read to one another. Looked through the pile of newspaper cuttings she had kept ever since her arrival in the city. Most were of pictures of *milicianas* posing for photos with rifles thrown across their shoulders, smiling broadly. But one was an article from Mundo Obrero that dated back to 5th October 1936. She read it out loud:

'... The law of war is a brutal one, but we must adopt it without sentimentality, with neither aggressiveness nor weakness. We cannot sink to the sadism of the fascists.' Maria winced with the memory of how close she'd come to this. 'We will never torture prisoners' She winced again. 'Nor will we humiliate the wives of traitors, nor murder their children. But we will inflict lawful retribution rapidly and impressively so as to tear out the very roots of treachery.'

'*La Pasionara*,' her grandfather said. Maria nodded. Dolores Ibarruri, also known as *La Pasionara*. Guiding light, heroine. 'Fine words,' he said. 'Inspiration for a whole city.' But fine words didn't always lead to fine deeds. Words, so easily twisted in a corrupt mind. And that mind had been hers. She remembered Señor Alonso standing there at the Casa de Campo, genuinely perplexed, the father of her friend Antonio, the man whose goodness, generosity and courage her own father and grandfather admired. She'd left her home on that morning convinced that she would soon be meting out divine retribution to the vile and the wicked. She would be the scourge of the gods, the righter of wrongs. But now, as she read *La Pasionara*'s words, she realised that she was not. Her grandfather put his arm around her. She closed her eyes with relief. 'You saved him. Alonso's alive because of you,' he told her. 'Yes,' Maria said. *And he's also alive because of Luis*, she thought.

As she lay in her bed that night, she thanked the heavens that she hadn't joined the ranks of the vile and the wicked.

She rolled back on her bed, filled with a sudden lightness of spirit. Goodness made her mouth smile and her eyes beam. And thoughts of Luis made her soul sing.

CHAPTER 49

It is often said that in order to right wrongs even more crimes have to be perpetrated before the balance between the two is reset. A pendulum swings too far one way; it then must swing too far the other. The laws of physics dictate that it is so, dragging an unstoppable train of events in its wake. Extreme action begets extreme reaction. Only when this has been achieved can any sort of equilibrium be re-established.

Maria shuddered. She'd been part of that reactive swing. A ghastly mirror image of the ghastly crimes that she had witnessed. She'd believed herself to be on the side of truth and justice. She now knew that that had never been the case. Señor Alonso had been innocent, the unwitting target of Sandoval's vicious vendetta.

Yet while he'd been saved, Maria saw that decay and destruction were getting a firm grip of the increasingly diseased capital. Barely visible men, hats pulled down, coat lapels raised, waited and watched from the shadows. They'd always been there. She hadn't seen them until now. Drive-by shootings in the street were becoming a regular occurrence, carried out on the say-so of dubious spies with axes to grind. Not so long ago she'd wanted to be part of this angry, violent world.

Not anymore.

The government might have long gone, abandoning the capital to set itself up in Valencia; the politicians might have been replaced by journalists and photographers from all over the world greedy to witness, record and photograph the last glorious embers of a dying kingdom; the Germans and Italians might be reducing the city to ashes with a relentless, cruel bombing campaign, but Maria no longer wanted to kill indiscriminately. The terrifying phoenix that was her rage, even that directed inwards, was melting away, leaving nothing but a profound sadness. And a will to do good. For over a year she worked at the food banks, volunteered as an ambulance worker, helped care for orphaned children, assisted at the hospital units... she did anything and everything.

Then one day there was a knock on the door. 'Are you Maria Alvaro? Daughter of Doctor Alvaro?'

'I am.'

'Then this is for you.' And a middle-aged woman embraced a surprised Maria. She handed her a letter.

Hospital General de Catalunya, August 1938
Dear Maria,

If this letter reaches you it is testament to the will and determination of the woman who has delivered it as well as the generosity and faith of her son, the doctor who's been treating me ever since I turned up at the hospital.

I remember very little of the first days here but when I regained consciousness Doctor Fuertes knew all about the time I spent in your small village in Andalucía. He said I should write to you all, no doubt to lift my spirits, give me a reason to live, and when all I knew was that you had family in the Salamanca region of Madrid, he even managed to turn that into the most fortuitous of coincidences: that is where his family live too. Life and hope are all, he tells me, and as I write this I dare to imagine that you will read this letter.

I'm lying in a hospital bed in Suarezna, shot for the second

267

time. I say that not for any sympathy as in truth I am well on the path to recovery, but because it takes me back to the first time it happened.

I intended to write then, to let you know I was fine, to say the goodbye that I never got round to, and to thank you. Instead I wrote and phoned and wrote some more to newspapers, politicians in my own country, to get the truth out there about the plight of yours. It got me nowhere. Ugly facts don't make it to the front page, when a nation can be seduced by the impossible glamour of a royal marriage and a scandalous one at that. King Edward VIII abdicates British throne to marry American divorcee Mrs Wallis Simpson. The way the press is, it wouldn't surprise me if such frivolous headlines made it to the front pages of your papers too.

I felt too ashamed to write to you after that.

So I joined the International Brigade and threw myself into combat. If my government wouldn't commit, I would. I needed to do something glorious, you see, after what happened to Paloma, and to do all I could to protect you, Lola, your families…

But killing a boy in a different uniform is never glorious. I should have learnt that lesson the first time I got shot. It was at the Battle of Jarama. One of Franco's boys hit me in the leg. He raised his gun to take my face off but then thought better of it. I know it sounds mad but I felt I knew him. He seemed familiar somehow, but perhaps it was simply his humanity that I recognised. It was only after months of freezing days and nights shooting at boys barely big enough to fill out a uniform that I have found any fellow feeling of my own.

I don't know who the enemy is anymore. A life for a life, that's what I wanted when I first started out here, but I've seen too many men bleeding to death in cold ditches to believe that is the answer. A man may be on the opposing side but sometimes he's no more or less of a monster than me.

Forgive me if I speak too plainly but now is not the time

to hide behind sugar-tipped lies. Truth is what is needed and as I lie here in my hospital bed I am thankful to be alive.

I can't bring back the dead and to think that I could by killing frightened young boys and so adding to their number now seems absurd.

The war seems to be coming to an end here and though I can never tell truth from fiction, such is the power of the wordsmiths who spin our propaganda today, it seems the war is drawing to a close all over Spain. That's why I wanted to thank you for your friendship, the memory of which has helped me through my darkest hours. The day we went on the picnic, you, me, Paloma and Lola, was the happiest day of my life. It was the day I fell in love with her, with Lola. I love her still. It seems strange to be confessing this to you now but, as the sister I never had, I always thought you knew as you were closer to me than anyone.

I don't know where she is. All I know is that Father Anselmo made arrangements to get her to safety. I pray that he did.

There. That's what I can do. Write, write and write some more to and about the people I love. Tell the truth, and tell you all exactly what you mean to me. Although I don't know where Lola is, I plan to come and find her when this war is done. It could take some time as not even Doctor Fuertes's mother will be able to trawl the whole of Spain for her! Stay brave and strong and good, my darling sister Maria. You matter so much to me. I meet you often in my dreams and I long for the day when we meet up again in life.

I pray that this letter reaches you and if it does, send me your news. I am to be sent home to England soon to convalesce and Doctor Fuertes tells me post can get through, though every word is read. I write my address on the back of this letter in case you have forgotten it.

Your loving brother,
Richard

'Well, brother! Thank God for my compassionate soldier and for the Doctor Fuertes of this world.' Maria said to herself. She sat back and closed her eyes to enjoy the letter a moment longer. It was as if her English friend had looked into her very soul. She smiled.

Richard was wrong; she hadn't known about Lola, but now it all made sense. And now Maria knew where Lola was. Or at least knew the whereabouts of someone who could tell her. She went over to her copy of *Don Quixote*. Hidden within its pages was Luis' letter and the scrap of paper that she'd used to write down the address that she'd found burnt in the fireplace: Father Anselmo's. She laughed. She now knew what she had to do. She went over to the bureau in her grandfather's study and picked up a sheet of paper and a pen. She started to write her first letter.

'Dear Lola...' she began. The thread of communication had begun.

CHAPTER 50

Olvera, October, 1938

Dear Maria,

I hope this letter finds its way to you as yours did to me. You sound different but I still see you between the lines and all that I once found annoying in you I would give anything to be able to throw my arms around now. So much has happened. When I think about it I feel such sadness. But to weary you with my tales of woe and sorrow when you must have so many of your own is not why I'm writing.

Instead I want to thank you for letting me know Manu is alive. I can't wait to see him and I can't wait for this war to be over so that I can introduce him to his niece.

Yes, I have a daughter and she makes my life a joy. Everyone in the village adores her, not least because she looks so unlike the other children. She doesn't even look like me. People are curious about her father as a result, but that he's not around does not arouse suspicion. That's one good thing about the war – probably the only one when I think about it. People have too many other concerns to spread gossip about whether

I'm married or not. Besides, I wear a ring – that was Mother's idea. She's changed too.

That so many men have been wasted makes me weep, not only for myself. You see, I'm different too.

I've told you I have a daughter. I've even hinted at what she looks like. Have you guessed her father's name yet? I hope so as I really cannot bear to say or write it for fear of breaking down. All I will say is that I loved him. I always will and if I never see him again I am so happy to have his child in my life. She reminds me of him every second of every day. She has pink cheeks, lots of freckles and fine red blond curls. There. If you hadn't guessed already, you're bound to have worked it out by now, you were always so clever.

But it's Paloma she takes after in character. She has the same kind way about her that I used to find so annoying in my sister but which now makes me want to take her by the arms and swing her round. I would love you to see her when the bad times have passed. I would love you to see me. I miss my sister. I miss you.

Father Anselmo is here too. A Republican priest. Can you imagine such a thing? Yet here a priest is just a priest. He is perfect for this village and this village is perfect for him. He's the one who helped us escape. All those hours he and Mother spent together yielded some earthly benefit after all. He's planning our next move, possibly to Malaga, for when the troubles have ended, and he believes that will be soon.

Tell Manu I miss him. We all do.

Paloma sends kisses – yes, that's what I've called her. How could I not? I send kisses too.

Lola

It was the second letter that Maria had received in two months and it was the second time she had been floored. 'Well!' she gasped again.

CHAPTER 51

That Lola had been in love with Richard made sense to Maria. She knew that Richard had been in love with Lola too no matter what the rest of the village had believed. And now to discover there was a child. Nothing could bring Maria's friend back – what Richard had said in his letter was true, no amount of killing would ever resurrect her – but to be able to celebrate a life, that was worth something.

She re-read the letters she'd received from Lola and Richard and placed them on her desk together. She had one more letter to read, a very important letter that someone had written to her before she'd ever come to Madrid. She turned her sunflower pendant round and round between her fingers then she leant over to pick up her copy of *Don Quixote*. It did make a damned fine door stop she thought to herself as she picked the sturdy tome up from the floor. She placed it on her desk and let it fall open to reveal a folded piece of paper nestling safely in amongst its many hundreds of pages. She took the paper out, unfolded it, smoothed it the best she could. She played with her pendant once more as she looked at the handwriting distorted by tears and wrinkles from being scrunched up and thrown on the floor years before. It was the letter she'd promised to read. Luis' letter. And now she was ready to read all of it.

My darling Maria,

As you read this I will be far away, or may as well be. Either way we cannot meet up again, not for a while. That's why I am writing you this letter, to tell you how much you mean to me. If someone had told me I would meet a girl in the way that I've met you I would not have believed them, not thought it possible. But I would have been wrong.

You have touched my soul with your goodness and loyalty. I pray our children take after you.

There. I've written it and I am proud to have done so.

I love you. That you must surely know. And still I have put you in danger time and time again. Please forgive me. Well, now I cannot, and though the thought of not seeing you every day distresses me more than I can express, knowing that I will not be putting you at risk makes the absence bearable. Yet we will be together again very soon my love. This war that divides our country will come to an end in the next few weeks and when it does I will be by your side once more.

As I write this letter I realise I know you so well, yet know so little about your life, a deficiency I plan to address in the lifetime that will be ours.

There. My plan unravels once more. War, an ugly business, yet its hideousness emboldens me to reach out for beauty and not let it slip away.

Maria stopped reading the letter for a moment and clutched it to her heart. She let her head fall back though she was a fool to think that would stop the tears. The moment she looked at the letter again down they splashed. Words already distorted by tears became more distorted still. She went over to find a handkerchief in her dressing table drawer to catch them as they fell. She read on.

274

To leave you is to leave the greater part of myself behind but I hope that I too take the greater part of you with me.

The poor girl howled.

All my love,
Luis

She turned the letter over. There, hastily scrawled, was the part she'd seen many times.

Meeting place: the Parque de Malaga (by the monument to Antonio Muñoz Degrain)
Time: 10–11am
Day: Friday
I'll wait for you.

CHAPTER 52

Manu had attempted to contact Maria eighteen times after that fateful trip to the Casa de Campo. The first ten times it was either her father or her grandfather who fended him off, aware, without caring, that this might bump their own names up on a list. They could equally have had Manu's name added to some other list if they'd wanted, such was the dog eat dog atmosphere that had set in, but they resisted all offers. Manu was only a boy after all, albeit a potentially dangerous one. And he was trapped, along with everyone else in the city. The following seventeen times he called, Maria had the strength to turn him away herself.

But then two things happened to make her think again.

The first was bread raining from the sky. It was the last months of the war, though Maria didn't know it at the time, and planes were dropping loaves over the capital. Each was wrapped in the Spanish flag with the words *'In national Spain, united, great, and free, there is no home without a hearth or a family without bread,'* written on it. People were hungry in Madrid. Worse than that, they were starving. Rumours that the bread was poisoned went round. But it mattered little. They were so hungry they ate it anyway. It was clear the people had had enough. It made Maria realise that so had she.

The second thing that caused her to think again was the letter she received from Manu's sister, Lola. It piqued her conscience, stirred her memory, and made her realise that, no matter what, Maria was bound to Manu. He'd dragged on the ties of loyalty between the two of them but Lola's letter reminded Maria that she knew his family as well as she knew her own. Paloma had been his sister, Cecilia his mother, and, after her own father, she knew them more than anyone else in the world.

And so, on the eighteenth time of his calling, Maria agreed to see him. She owed it to his family. And she'd had enough of the war. Besides, there was something she needed to ask him.

It was spring 1938 and even though the sky looked like it had been painted by El Greco, heavy with black, white and grey with only the smallest of blue patches peeping through, Maria agreed to walk around the Retiro Park with him, armed with an umbrella and a heavy coat. The chestnut trees were always so beautiful there, even in the rain, and she loved the peace she experienced sitting under their broad-leaved bowers no matter what the weather.

As luck would have it, it was dry. She sat on a bench, Manu next to her and she breathed in the cold air. It was refreshing, clean, and as she looked around at all the trees and flowers in blossom and bud she too felt the first flush of something beautiful take root within her heart, and it warmed her. A memory of Luis fluttered around her, as pretty and delicate as a butterfly. It landed on her shoulder. She did not flick it away. He would love it here, she thought.

She smiled at Manu with the promise of new beginnings. He smiled at her in between blowing on his hands then rubbing them together.

She shared Lola's letter with him, reading it out to him sentence by sentence. He stopped her when it came to news about a child. This information did nothing to warm him up. A cloud of shame hovered over his features, followed by a look of concern for Maria.

'Oh no,' she exclaimed, shaking her head. 'We were never close in that way, Richard and I.' She laughed. Manu didn't.

'I wish I'd killed the bastard,' he said.

'A walk around the lake?' Maria said, tilting her head in the direction of the expanse where a lake had been before the war. In a blacked out city a reflected moon would be all the information an enemy pilot would need to locate his next target. The water had to go.

Maria and Manu walked along the path in silence. Maria had to make him see the good in what she was telling him. Lola was alive, and Cecilia. A cause for celebration in itself. And the baby. The very thought of her lifted Maria's heart and gave colour to the world. It would lift Manu's too if he would only let it.

'So why did you want to speak with me?' Maria asked.

Manu did not answer straightaway, instead he coughed as if to clear his throat, and even then, the words that followed did not come out smoothly.

'To say sorry… about what happened. At the Casa de Campo.'

Maria said nothing in return. She had nothing to say. She did not blame Manu for what had occurred. She was ashamed of the part she'd played in it, ashamed that she'd sought it out, ashamed that she'd wanted to shed blood that night. She had gazed into the abyss willingly that morning and it had stared right back. She had known at once that she had to tear herself away. Perhaps Manu did too. She nudged into him, hoping a playful push could convey more than any words how very sorry she was too.

'Hey!' he said. Images of Lola flashed before him. Lola, his annoying sister who used to nudge into him all the time when she was little. He moved his neck from side to side as he recovered his balance but the words Maria had hoped to dislodge still didn't flow. She didn't know what else she could say; he didn't know how to say it. Maria looked into the waterless lake. The sight struck her as absurd.

278

'Is she well? Lola?' Manu said at last, the frosty edge to his voice slowly thawing.

'Oh yes, she is so very well Manu. And happy,' Maria answered, hoping to melt it completely with the warmth of her words.

'And the baby? A girl, you say?' Manu asked, his words both hopeful and hesitant. Maria nodded. Manu was nearly there and she was overjoyed. She took his hand in hers. For her sake as much as for his. They would both need to hold on to each other when Maria told Manu the baby's name.

'She's called her…' Maria paused to stem the flow of tears that were queuing up to be shed behind her smiling eyes. 'She's called her… Paloma.'

Manu cried. It had been a long time. They hugged one another like cubs and raised their arms in the air while they both shouted 'Paloma!'

'Look,' Maria said, pointing up at the sky. 'The clouds have all gone. Let's walk some more.' And they did. While they reminisced. 'And Manu,' she said, remembering to put her question to him before she forgot. 'About that night at Cortijo del Bosque, the night of the dinner, when you escaped, I saw you come from the direction of the kitchen. I thought there was a soldier on guard.' Manu nodded his head in response. 'What happened?' she said.

279

CHAPTER 53

When she got home the first thing she did was go to her room and unfold the much loved though very dog-eared piece of paper. She extracted it from the depths of Cervantes for the second time that day. She looked at its deep folds, ran her finger around the soft and tattered edges and looked at the beautiful shapes of tear stained ink letters on greying paper. And as she read the words they formed so she conjured up an image of the person who had taken the care and time to write them. His eyes were before her, one brown, one blue, and she felt that he was with her. She turned the letter over and read the words she already knew: *Malaga, midday, Friday*. In themselves there was nothing inherently beautiful in these words. They were informative, nothing more. But if she went to the place at the time specified oh how life would open itself up to her like a rare, exotic flower.

She had thought herself unworthy of such happiness, thought Luis undeserving of her love, for oh so many reasons. But she had endured and survived the suffering. She had been taken to the edge of bitterness and found it to be a lonely, cruel place, as for revenge, she found it harsh and unforgiving. Bitterness, revenge, punishment – they were all prey to corruption. She'd been guilty of them all. But as she held Luis' note in her hand all guilt melted away and understanding and forgiveness came in its place.

Today was a day for righting wrongs, shedding light on confusion. Manu had revealed to her that Luis had been the person who had allowed him to escape the night of the dinner while Maria had a strong suspicion that Luis had saved Richard too. Her hand glided over the letters she'd received from Richard and Lola. She still had one letter to write to Richard; she would see that she asked him about the soldier who saved him then.

She re-read a section of Richard's letter: '... remembering our days together in Fuentes, that picnic, the bike ride, I realise now that I would like very much to know how she is...' It seemed so clear to Maria now. She would write to him, tell him about Lola's baby that was so obviously his.

*

By the time Richard Johnson received the news from Maria he'd been home for three months. He was convalescing at home in Chelsea but wasn't proving to be the easiest of patients for his parents, Margaret and Peter. He'd meant it when he told himself that war was a futile exercise and that the only useful thing he could do was to treat his loved ones well, but it was still driving him insane to read the misleading headlines in the newspapers, and as for his parents, they were driving him round the bend. He wanted to beat the pudgy faced Franco to a pulp and dispatch his mother and father off to the Outer Hebrides for a while. He consoled himself with the knowledge that they liked it there. But still. Human nature. One minute contemplating the meaning of life in all its beauty, the next wanting to smash it to smithereens. He blanched at the very thought of it in all its paradoxical contrariness.

'Cup of tea, dear?' his mother asked, her voice wavering with a recently developed tremor, as she popped her head round the door.

'You're so English, Mother! A cup of tea isn't the answer to all the world's problems.' She withdrew almost scraping the floor apologetically. The poor woman was thrilled to have him home, safe, but frustrated that she didn't seem to be able to say a thing right in his eyes.

His father rushed in, a letter in his hand which he slid behind his back as he saw his wife slide out. 'Yes please, darling,' he said, following her.

Richard was vaguely aware and irritated by excitable whispers coming from the hall.

'Oh, but I nearly forgot,' her mother said as she fell back in the room, nigh on hopping with delight. She looked back into the hall where her husband was waiting in the wings, willing her on. Her son expressed his impatience with a kick of his footstool. His mother looked back into the hall again. Then said it. 'You'll be looking forward to reading this,' she splurged, allowing her tiny wrist to spring gently before she threw a letter into the air. It landed in Richard's lap. She left the room, jubilant, hoping the letter was what he'd been so obviously waiting for.

The moment he saw it he flushed with pleasure. He looked down at the letter in front of him. It made him smile to recognise the unmistakably Spanish handwriting and wonder at the miracle that such a thing should exist – nationality expressed in the writing of a word. And a wonder still greater, that he should know the very identity of the writer. Maria.

She had written four pages, eight sides, to him.

The first half page of the letter Maria had written in English. It was faultless – she'd produced eight grammatically perfect sentences. Verb endings were sound, tenses appropriate. Yet they communicated so very little of importance that by sentence six Richard was starting to lose the glow of excitement that had preceded the careful opening of the envelope.

That she gave up on the English was a blessing all round. A liberation for her because at last she could truly communicate

282

and a relief for Richard who bathed in the feelings she set free
in the words on the page that danced and played and ran and
jumped all around him.

His eyes now raced over the words. He found the one he was
looking for – 'Lola' – followed by some that he wasn't expecting
at all. He threw the letter in the air and shouted 'Paloma!' His
parents came rushing in. Richard got up and kissed his mother.
He kissed his father too.

He looked up and out through the window at the all-too-
typical English sky. Uniformly grey, with only one shaft of yellow
light breaking through quite low in the sky, he marvelled at its
beauty and how he could ever persuade Lola to love it too.

Maria's work was done. She had written the letters she'd had
to write, now it was time to read the one she'd been given for
the third and last time.

CHAPTER 54

War was over. Maria was out in the streets with her father and grandfather the day the nationalist forces celebrated. 19th May 1939. All of Madrid was there to cheer. Neighbours, servants and concierges would have been forced to denounce them if not.

Maria looked up at the planes overhead spelling the victor's name; they almost made her laugh. Almost. F R A N C O. Crass. In the way dictators so often are. It was absurd that her country should be ruled by a madman of limited intelligence. Yet it was a reality.

A young woman, about Maria's age, with cheeks so sunken you could use them as shelves, pushed past her. 'Peace is here at last!' she said as she made her way through the gathering crowds. Maria started. It was true, the war was over. Surely that was a cause for celebration.

But this peace, she asked herself, would it be any different?

She looked at the soldiers as they paraded by, rifles erect, and she shuddered. The old hatred bubbled up to the surface of her consciousness once more. She stood there, glowering. Yet as she searched their faces for answers Maria slowly felt the anger slip away. These soldiers were more than the uniforms they wore. All human, all flawed. If she had learned anything during this vile war it was that the capacity for people to commit good and evil was the same on both sides. Not that this excused it: it did not.

She continued watching the procession. Soldiers – young boys, gnarled war veterans, mercenaries – paraded by before her. On horseback, motorcycles, in trucks, on foot. Wave after wave of them. The crowds applauded, saluted. Then it was the turn of decorated generals to come by. They saluted back to the crowd, their arms strong and proud, standing upright and firm in the front of chauffeur driven cars. All except one.

Maria stared at him. There, sitting in the back of an open top car was a man she thought she knew. Slumped and shrunken, only his uniform kept him upright. And even from a distance Maria could see that the man's skin was a patchwork of open sores across his cheeks with a disease eaten nose. Who was he? She studied him. A shiver of recognition passed through her entire body at the memory of the man's coldness. It was him. Captain Garcia. And he knew her too. His cruel eyes had picked her face out from thousands in the crowd. Maria felt pity for the surrounding soldiers; they'd had compassion squashed out of them, been used as a brutalising force. Even the Africanistas who had been pulled from Morocco to punish the Spanish people, they were victims too in their own way. But Garcia. He'd been a sadist of the worst sort. Maria stared back at him. There were some things she could never forgive.

Killing in war was inevitable. Yet even war must have its rules. When these rules are broken, that's when the most heinous of crimes are committed. And Garcia, Maria remembered, had broken all the rules. She played with the sunflower pendant around her neck with one hand, and patted her hard-backed companion, Cervantes, with the other.

She still felt the guilt when she thought of Paloma. She'd made a mistake that day in calling for her. But she saw now that it was an innocent one. She'd been an unwitting pawn in a very ugly game. She had been a child herself, taken the wrong turning at the wrong time. A mistake – and she would always regret it. But it was not she who had committed the crimes against her dear, sweet friend. She stared back at Garcia; she felt no sympathy for him.

As she watched the victory parade go by tears rolled silently down her cheeks. The crowd swayed, causing her to lose her footing slightly. Her father, still by her side, caught her. She looked in his eyes. She saw her sorrow reflected there.

CHAPTER 55

The war had been over for almost a year now and Maria and her father were living in Malaga. By day Doctor Alvaro was working at the Sanatorio de San Jose in Malaga, treating patients with nervous conditions. By night he was attending the sick in the poor areas of the city; the Civil War might have ended but division between the haves and have nots was still stark. He was also working with an underground group smuggling people to safety. The good doctor was the same as he ever was, helping the persecuted and oppressed, of which there were many in the aftermath of the war; he just had to be careful that he didn't get caught and add to their number.

Maria too had found work, helping the sick; on her father's advice, she said nothing of the past. If Doctor Alvaro was concerned for his own safety in these deceptively peaceful times, he was doubly so when it came to his daughter. She'd lived in Republican Spain during the war; he knew that women were being thrown into prison for less. And now the Nationalists had won, it was time for them to fashion the people in their own image. There was no more *right to choose*, no more *liberty*. Men had to be strong, hard-working, virile; women caring, obedient, virtuous. The true masculine; the eternal feminine. Both would be patriotic. Both would adhere to the Catholic Church.

His daughter had a free spirit and a strong will that she'd already exercised negotiating time off every Friday. She would need to disguise it.

Yet, after nearly four years of being trapped in Madrid, both Alvaro and his daughter knew they were the lucky ones, alive, and with the same hopes and beliefs that they'd always had. And every day the sight of the sea and the vast, blue sky reminded Maria of the dreams she'd had for her future as a young girl. She might laugh at her younger self, but she could not deny that here, in Malaga, she was living one of those dreams.

Today was Friday, the day Maria went to wait by the monument of Antonio Muñoz Degrain in the botanical gardens. Often she'd been late to it. Sometimes she'd not been able to get to it at all. But today there was nothing to stop her. She pushed open the shutters and breathed in the fresh, sweet air. 'Malaga!' she said. And although it struck her that by the time the sun had set later that day she would not have found Luis, she exalted in the hope that she might. She looked up at the sky above, so blue, so infinite, just as she'd done as a child. Her heart swelled as it filled with the purity of her dreams, thankful that war had at last released its blood-soaked talons sufficiently for her to be able to go after them. She'd left Madrid, turned down the opportunity to leave the country. She prayed that fate would do the rest.

Maria picked up the sunflower pendant lying on top of her carved wooden jewellery box. As she put it on, she missed a breath as her mind took her back to Paloma and the hopes and dreams she'd had for her future. She gave a whimper at the loss but stopped herself from remaining in the past. If war had taught her anything it was that neither self-pity, self-destruction, nor blaming herself or others could bring Paloma back to life. The futures they'd longed for would never be. Maria no longer looked to be happy. She knew she could never be that. But what she could do, what she had a duty to pursue, was a future with a purpose, a life with meaning, with people she loved and who loved her in return. And that Friday morning she would run to embrace it.

She started by picking up the book whose pages had protected Luis' letter for so long and placed it in her basket. Then she wrapped the chocolate she'd bought the day before, along with some almond biscuits that she'd made, in some paper and put that in too. Oh, and she'd nearly forgotten. It was Lola's birthday tomorrow. She picked up the red polka dot scarf she'd chosen for her friend. Maria wondered about wrapping it up but then looked at her watch. 'Too late!' she exclaimed, hopping around while she attempted to guide her toes into her shoes.

Malaga buzzed and crackled beneath her feet as her heels mutely clicked along its wounded streets. The body of Malaga had received a savage beating during the war, yet it still managed to dazzle Maria with its tattered beauty. It had a voluptuous sensuality to it that not even the bombings had been able to obliterate, nor the victorious troops had succeeded in suppressing; the music of tragedy and ecstasy cried out from upstairs windows around the narrow streets of the old town, voices plaintive, guitars rousing, hands clapping, more beautiful than she could ever have imagined.

As she walked along the Calle Carreteria she came across a tram stop. As the tram was in, it caused a temporary hold-up as people fell in and out, one after the other. Men dressed in smart suits, polished shoes, dark hair brilliantined and combed back; one or two in overalls. Women in fitted cotton dresses, hair pulled back with a ribbon or tied up in a chignon, small heels. Maria watched them all, fascinated, moving again as they moved. All were smoking, many chatting, the throng dwindling as a couple tumbled into a bar here, a café there. Pairs of nuns punctuated the chaos. Maria loved to observe it in all its infinite variety.

When the mass of people had finally dispersed all that was left was a little boy: a skinny strip of nothing. He walked down the side of the road trying to disappear down the cracks. Maria looked in her basket. She went over to him and gave him the chocolate. She could give chocolate to Paloma another time.

*

'*Tia*!' Ten minutes later and Maria was standing at Lola's door. It was Malaga that Father Anselmo had succeeded in moving them to after all. The moment the door opened a girl's little legs skipped their way past her. 'Why are you always late?' her sing-song voice asked as she placed her small, pudgy, pale hand in Maria's soft, brown one. Maria made saucers of her eyes then led the girl's to the contents in the basket. Stubby fingers picked up the scarf, their owner's eyes confused.

'No, silly,' Maria said. 'That's for Mama. For tomorrow. It's this I think you might be more interested in.' And with that, Maria gave the wrapped package that contained the almond biscuits a shake.

'Aaah!' the child said appreciatively, her free hand reaching out to take it.

'Oh no. They're not for now. They're for later. We have to go to the gardens first!'

'Quick then *Tia*. Let's go,' she cried, pulling on Maria's hand.

'Bye, my sweet girl,' Lola called out. 'Thank you for the scarf. It's lovely Maria. Be a good girl for your *Tia*!' she reminded Paloma.

'I will, Mama. I promise.'

When Lola had closed the door Maria picked her best friend's namesake and niece up in her arms and gave her a kiss. 'Oh, my little white dove. How dear you are to me!'

By the time Maria arrived with Lola's daughter at the botanical gardens the little girl had biscuit crumbs around her lips and down the front of her clothes on her lips and the birds had been screeching happily above for hours. People were milling about, passing the time of day, and children were playing. 'Don't run off now!' her proud guardian called out just as the little girl proceeded to do precisely that.

Not far from them stood a man. Handsome, strong build, with strange and beautiful eyes. Maria did not notice him. He was no longer standing at the monument and she only had eyes for it and the child. He had noticed her, however, and he could not move. It started with the words, the voice that caused a hot-cold feeling to run through him like an electric current. Then, as sound became form, he remained transfixed. He saw it was her. Maria.

She was dressed in black, like most people these days, though a touch of yellow escaped over the buttoned up jacket, lighting up her face. There she was, with her flicked-up nose, brown, almond shaped eyes, her full lips a deep pink. And she was smiling.

She was alive. She looked happy.

He'd been waiting for this moment for so long.

When the life returned to his limbs he went towards her. But as the little girl flung herself into Maria's arms he stepped back. He watched in wonder as Maria's dark hair, as unruly as he remembered it, waved lawlessly around her head, getting in her eyes so that she could see no further than the noisy round limbed child that she was swinging round in her arms. Something about the scene caused the rhythm of his heart to change from a frantic beating to a low, dull, heavy thump that hammered him ever more forcibly to the spot.

This child, with red-blond curls and bright pink cheeks, could be no older than three, four at the oldest, Luis calculated as he looked on. His instinct told him to walk away. That it was over. That his purpose in coming here now had no sense, would only bring heartbreak, spread confusion. Yet he made himself watch. He had to make sure, make sure she was happy.

He studied Maria carefully, in spite of the pain it caused him. He had to know. She beamed with delight at the child, a beatific smile on her beautiful face. He would not have expected anything less. To see the tender way she kissed the small girl's pale forehead while drawing loose tendrils of golden hair away from her eyes with the lightest of touches was an exquisite torture.

He had come to claim her. He saw that it was too late. Maria's eyes shone with hope at the wondrous child who now danced around in the dappled sunlight, unburdened by the cares of the adult world. Waving her arms around like a windmill she orbited Maria as a planet does the moon.

A gypsy woman looked on and was saying something to him. He was deaf to her; he only had eyes and ears for the young woman with the long, dark hair.

'My darling Paloma!' The second Luis heard Maria call the child's name he knew. It was time for him to tear himself away. He looked at Maria for one last time. She'd closed her eyes and turned her face heavenwards to feel the warmth of the sun on her cheeks. He recognised the enamel sunflower pendant around her neck as she twiddled it between her thumb and forefinger. 'Do you still do that for luck?' he whispered. As if she'd heard him, she looked up along the path in his direction, scouring the benches and groups of people with her eyes. But she didn't spot him. 'You've already left the past behind, my love/' Luis sighed.

Maria. The love of his life who was no longer his future. He watched her, his angelic eyes stubbornly cloudy. But he'd seen enough. She'd had a child and she'd called her Paloma. That had always been her wish. They'd talked about it together in the ruined hut outside Fuentes. Despair stabbed at his heart but it was right that she was happy and he would do nothing to spoil that. It was time for him to walk away from his sun, stars and moon.

As he made his way back to the university he wondered what would have happened if he'd not turned her away when she'd offered herself to him that last night. A lump came to his throat. Too late, he thought. He thanked God that the woman he loved would live a happier life than the one destiny now had in store for him.

A woman wearing a bright red polka dot scarf passed Luis as

he headed back to work and for a moment she paused as though she recognised him. '*Buenos dias, Señor,*' she said, convinced that she did. Her face broke into a broad smile to prove it. But Luis didn't smile back. He neither heard nor saw her, despite seeming to look straight at her, so locked were his thoughts on the woman he would always love and might never see again.

By the time the bright red scarf had permeated his conscience Luis was nearly at the university and the woman wearing it had moved on. Her sights were now set on someone else she knew, and who most certainly knew her, causing her to quickly forget the man with the faraway eyes.

'Paloma!' she said. The girl ran to be picked up. 'Mama!' she cried.

'Well, I never!' the gypsy woman said to no one in particular.

CHAPTER 56

That night, lying on top of his sheets, Luis told himself once more that he was happy for Maria. He stared at the ceiling fan whirring round and round. He ought now to go and lead his own life, he thought. It would be a half-life to begin with, he had no doubt, but while he still had a life to live, he owed it to those who had died, he owed it to his parents, to live it as best he could.

The next two Fridays he stayed away from the park. He started to accept invitations to dinner from well-meaning matchmakers intent on introducing him to some very lovely young ladies from good families. Reports wafted their way back to his mother. Her boy, once he'd found one of their own to marry, might even consider returning to the fold. But her hopes were to be short-lived. Luis attended such dinners four, possibly five times. It was no use. His heart wasn't in it. He wasn't fooling anyone, especially not himself.

And so, on the third Friday, Luis went back to the park. He turned up at nine – ridiculously early – and waited, sitting far enough away from the monument not to be seen, but near enough to know if Maria had turned up or not. The madness of love had taken hold of him.

Nine-thirty came and went. Ten. Ten-thirty. Eleven. She was late. But Luis had been early and he was going nowhere. His gypsy friend waddled over to keep him company. '

She will be here,' she said to him. 'She comes here most Fridays. I know because I see her.'

'Who does?' Luis asked, not wanting to open up his heart to a relative stranger, little realising that he'd done so already in every move he made.

'It's written all over you,' the kind-hearted woman replied. 'The One. She's your fate, she is.' Luis did not reply, but her words rang true. It was Maria. It would always be Maria. She was his future and he would not run away from it if that was what was best for her.

Dirty fingers with even dirtier fingernails grabbed Luis' arm. 'The One's just arrived.' She chuckled. 'You've gone all hard,' she cackled as she felt every sinew in his body tense up.

Heavy chains wrapped themselves around Luis' heart. 'She loves that child like it was her own, doesn't she?' she added, mischievously, hoping to rattle them a little. But Luis didn't notice.

Instead his eyes were drawn to a woman that looked like a dark-haired version of the little girl. He'd seen her before some-where and it perturbed him that he couldn't place her. He watched her as she walked up to Maria and kissed her on the cheek, going over in his mind where he'd come across her. And she reminded him of somebody.

Both women sat down on a bench.

'What you wouldn't give, eh, to hear what they're talking about?' Luis' companion whispered in his ear.

'Mama! Mama!' The fair-haired little girl ran towards the two women.

'Now you can't fail to hear that.' Luis' friend snorted. 'My, she's got a fine pair of lungs on her! Watch this!'

The curly haired child hurled herself at Maria's friend and smothered the woman with kisses. Luis watched as Maria put out a hand to stroke the little girl's hair and kiss her goodbye. He watched as the familiar-looking woman walked away with the child. Luis missed a breath. 'Oh, if you was a fiddle your strings would snap, you're pulled so tight,' the gypsy joked with him again. 'No child. And *no husband* if I'm reading the signs right. I knows these things.' She nudged him in the ribs again. 'I can see them,' she added, mysteriously. He moved along the bench, giving her a puzzled look. 'Her hand! Can't you see?' she whispered loudly now that he'd moved away from her a little. 'And I thought it was my eyes that were misty!' The clairvoyant one wiggled the fingers of one hand then pointed to where a ring should be with the other.

Maria wasn't married.

'Well? What are you waiting for?'

Luis watched as Maria picked up the large tome she'd just taken out of her basket. He laughed as he guessed what it was. 'Go on!' his companion urged him. 'She's staying for something, and to see her eyes swivel round like beacons in a lighthouse it's certainly not for that doorstop she's holding in her lap!' As if on cue Maria craned her neck from side to side to check the path. 'There! See! She's doing it again!' Luis' gypsy friend leant over to nudge him meaningfully in the ribs yet again and drew her index fingers like guns and pointed them in the young woman's direction. 'She's on the lookout for someone. And I swear on the Blessed Virgin, she's on the lookout for *you*.'

Maria sat there, looking far away, before plunging her head back into her weighty tome.

'Get over there!' Luis stood up but his legs wouldn't move. 'Go on!' Luis' friend hissed at him. 'Life doesn't wait. And love can haunt you for the rest of your days if you turn your back on it. Ignore the call of the destiny at your peril.'

But what if she's happy? Luis looked at Maria as she let the weighty tome lie heavy in her hands. She didn't seem so very happy. As he saw her beautiful eyes full of sadness, her shoulders dropped as though carrying an unimaginable burden, his heart lurched towards her. But his feet still refused to move.

'Put the girl out of her misery,' the gypsy shouted. 'Take that blasted book out of her hands!'

As Luis walked towards her his soul swam through the memories of his past. He revisited the first time he saw her in Fuentes de Andalucía, recalled her courage at his parents' dinner, her spirit when they found themselves alone. His Maria. Fiery, outspoken, good. How the memory of her had made him determined to make wise choices when surrounded by all the wickedness of the last four years. Because of her he had striven to be stronger, better, kinder. Her goodness and beauty had helped him withstand the ugliness of war.

One step: *What am I doing?* Two steps: *My heart's beating faster.* Three steps: *I'm nearly there.* Four steps: *I feel light-headed.* Five steps: *'Maria!'*

As her name came out of his mouth so the joy and light of the world entered his soul. Maria looked up, her eyes full of love. 'At last, Luis,' she said. 'It's you.'

CHAPTER 57

Three months later and Luis was eating with the Alvaros again. 'I'm home!' the doctor called out. 'Is Luis here?' Maria jumped up, smoothing the creases out of her dress.

'We're coming, Papa. We're just cooking.'

Doctor Alvaro smiled to himself. His daughter radiated joy. Happiness lit her up from within, causing her eyes to twinkle and her lips to dance, while her whole body cried out that she was alive. As Luis de los Rios appeared behind her, no less glowing, Doctor Alvaro fought the urge to shield his eyes. He too seemed vibrantly alive. The older man felt sure that he could even see the young man's heart pounding within his chest. It was strangely glorious.

Still, he was the girl's father, after all, and no matter how transcendent the feelings between her and Luis, he'd rather not see them, nor bear witness to their intimacy.

'Let's eat,' Maria said.

This was the thirty-seventh time the three of them had sat down to have dinner together. Neither one had asked about the war experiences of the other; perhaps they never would.

Instead they focused on the everyday. *'I met the kindest woman today,' 'I bought a novel,' 'I queued for bread.'*

Ten minutes later and the meal was done, finished by everyone. *Even faster than the last time*, Doctor Alvaro noted as he surreptitiously glanced at his watch before furtively peeping at his daughter and the man that she undoubtedly loved. Doctor Alvaro's joy to know that his daughter was blessed enough to have tender feelings for Luis de los Rios fooled him into letting his eyes linger longer than usual on the lovestruck pair. Long enough to understand the meaning behind their meaningful glances. This was something else Doctor Alvaro would have preferred not to have seen. Fingers brushed, feet flirted. He was beginning to find it all quite unbearable. He pulled at his collar; the atmosphere in the room was getting stifling, despite the fan spinning round on the ceiling above. He stood up and cleared his throat.

'I won't be back until much later. Out for the rest of the evening, I'm sorry to say. Please excuse me Luis, Maria.'

'Oh, not at all, Doctor.'

'Please, be careful Papa.'

There was no resistance, only gratitude in the young couple's eyes.

It was still light when the doctor stepped outside into the street. The air was warm and heavy but he inhaled deeply at any rate. An unstoppable force had filled the apartment and he knew that it was only going to suffocate him if he got in its way. Relief to be away from it steadied his breathing. He stood with his back against the old, wooden door and laughed.

He'd left his daughter and Luis de los Rios alone. He didn't know if they would end up with one another forever, that was up to them, but he could see that they were right together. Always had been. Even when they were in Fuentes de Andalucía. And if they belonged together he wanted to make the path, that had in truth been spectacularly perilous to this point, as smooth as possible. War, geography, family, circumstances – gargantuan obstacles – had all failed to block their way. And he, for one, would do so no more.

He wanted to give them some time, to talk, and say, and do, all the things that needed to be said, and done. And if they still wanted to be together after that, well then, he would give them his blessing. As he walked off, into the sunset, he laughed some more.

CHAPTER 57

Malaga, 1943

Dear reader,

I've written many letters in the course of this novel and so I thought it only fair I write one more to you.

The first thing is that yes, Luis and I did get married, with my father's blessing.

The second thing is that no, we don't have any babies, though not for lack of trying. We'd like some, but to like and to have inhabit completely different worlds.

As for Lola and Richard, let's just say the Second World War has complicated their plans.

Life's like that – uncontrollable, or at least, beyond the control of man and woman. Yes, if there's one thing I've learnt about life, it's that it's as haphazard as a game of cards where you have no say in the cards you're dealt only in the way you play them.

I've written over three hundred pages and as I look at the pile of sheets on the desk before me, I feel quite giddy. It's as if I've performed some magic trick with the cards in my hand; with a shuffle here and a sleight of hand there, I've given it order and meaning. What was random now has sense. I say again, we cannot choose what life throws at us, but we can choose how we shape it, what we do with it, and that's what I've done here.

Not that any of this reads like the work of a Calderón or a Cervantes. Though I wouldn't know as I've still not managed to finish a single thing by either. Nor is it likely to appear on any highbrow reading list, with all the romance that's in it. Still, I hope you don't think any the less of it, or me, for that. Rather I hope you see it for what it is: a story written by an ordinary person of, I confess, unexceptional qualities, who makes many mistakes, loses loved ones, but who is destined, for whatever reason, to live through and survive extraordinarily desperate times.

So many people died between 1936–1939, so many women, so many girls… brutal, meaningless deaths. It's not for the likes of me to express the horror of murderous acts I cannot comprehend and do not wish to visit. But it is my duty to tell a tale that I do know, of a simple friendship with a fourteen-year-old girl, and to shout about the shocking truth of what happened to her. The crime perpetrated against Paloma has to be acknowledged, as well as the joy and love she brought into the world. I am ordinary in so many ways, yet extraordinary in one particular: I am alive, and as such destiny has assigned me a very special role – to dedicate my novel to Paloma and the thousands of nameless girls who were killed during the Civil War. Loved and lost but not forgotten.

I have tried to be truthful, to show myself as the ridiculous, vain girl I used to be, and sometimes still am. That I have spent too many pages on myself proves that. Perhaps you haven't liked me very much. Neither did I for many of the years I was writing about. But that's not what's important. I now see that I'm no better than other people, but I have also learnt that I'm certainly no worse. My only crime, if you can call it that, *was that I called for a friend when I was sixteen; sheer wilfulness, I admit. But I did not kill her. My behaviour was thoughtless and selfish; it was not a murderous act. I was a girl at risk myself that day, but, by some coincidence, my life was saved. Paloma's wasn't. That I still had a life seemed like a sin to me for so many years. But then you know all that.*

Now I see that war is the real culprit and all those who commit crimes in its name.

Perhaps that's why my story has a happy ending: not to exonerate myself (although it does that), but to show that war cannot crush the human spirit completely. It's a celebration of the power of love and hope after all, and I don't apologise for it. When all the cards were stacked against me it was love that endured.

That's not to say there'll be a happy ever after. That's not to say there won't. Life still has some cards to play and our daily lives in Malaga are hard. Food is scarce. My favourite street cat has disappeared, no doubt in someone's pot. Father tells me there are camps where the authorities take people suspected of left-wing sympathies. There's a rumour that Manu has been taken, along with thousands of others, to work on a new monument outside Madrid. Spain has a long, treacherous road ahead. That Father only tells me these things when Luis is not around should tell you how fragile our lives together still are.

But as I look out through my window and see the oranges on the trees, hear the children play their games, catch guitars break young girls' hearts, watch the birds soar in the limitless blue of the sky above... I can't help but rejoice in all the infinite, precious things in life. They'll always be there no matter what happens. And so, dear reader, remember, it's not the hand you're dealt that counts, it's how you play it. And on that note I'll end.

Maria

ACKNOWLEDGEMENTS

I thank Simon, Joe, Tom and Harry for their unwavering support and for not minding when they recognise themselves in my work. I hope to make you as proud of me one day as I am of you.

My heartfelt thanks also go to Charlotte Mursell and Dushi Horti for their contributions to this novel set in the Spanish Civil War. The Spanish Civil War started with a coup in July 1936 which heralded the death of democracy in the country as Nationalist forces fought to take back power for Church, army and the landowning classes. Societal divisions were wide, politics polarized, and this led to the cruellest of wars, often pitting neighbour against neighbour, father against son. That's why I chose to introduce Cecilia and her family and present them in relation to Luis and his. The Alvaros I placed in the middle, as intermediaries between the two.

The civil war also turned Spain into a theatre where the competing ideologies of fascism and communism struggled for supremacy. Hitler and Mussolini put their weight behind Franco's Nationalists while Stalin bolstered the dying Republic. Many lives were lost in battle.

Yet a politics of fear pursued by the Nationalists in newly occupied areas meant that many civilian lives were lost too.

Punishment of Spanish citizens in general was legitimized by the officers in control, and the punishment of women in particular was meted out with ferocious zeal. Republican women suffered greatly. The catalogue of crimes committed against them makes for a horrifying read. Many had their heads shaved, others were given castor oil to make them soil themselves, while torture, rape and beatings were commonplace. Then there were the killings.

It was a specific incident that occurred in Andalucia during the Spanish Civil War that was the trigger for this novel. A truckful of girls, some as young as fourteen, were taken away by Nationalist troops from the village of Fuentes de Andalucia and driven to a nearby finca. There it is said they were raped, killed and thrown down a well. The troops then returned to the village, waving their victims' under garments from the tips of rifles like victory flags. I wanted to acknowledge this horrific crime. But I also wanted to celebrate the life that was lost, Paloma's life and the lives of all the girls like her, while through the character of Maria I wanted to apportion blame where it was due.

With Maria I imagine that I have created a character that very few people other than myself will much like, but even in her immature, self-centred view of the world, she is not responsible for the outrages that are committed in the novel. War and those who control it are.

I'm indebted to the following works for informing my work. All errors are entirely my own.

The Spanish Holocaust, Inquisition and Extermination in Twentieth Century Spain (pp 158-159 in particular which refers to the abduction of the girls and women from Fuentes de Andalucia), Paul Preston

Hell and Good Company: The Spanish Civil War and the World it Made, Richard Rhodes

No Pasaran! Writings from the Spanish Civil War, Pete Ayrton

Don Quixote, Cervantes. The butt of my jokes for so many years. One day I may even get round to reading it.

Dear Reader,

Thank you so much for taking the time to read this book – we hope you enjoyed it! If you did, we'd be so appreciative if you left a review.

Here at HQ Digital we are dedicated to publishing fiction that will keep you turning the pages into the early hours. We publish a variety of genres, from heartwarming romance, to thrilling crime and sweeping historical fiction.

To find out more about our books, enter competitions and discover exclusive content, please join our community of readers by following us at:

🐦 *@HQDigitalUK*

f *facebook.com/HQDigitalUK*

Are you a budding writer? We're also looking for authors to join the HQ Digital family! Please submit your manuscript to:

HQDigital@harpercollins.co.uk.

Hope to hear from you soon!

Turn the page for an exclusive extract from
The Artist's Muse...

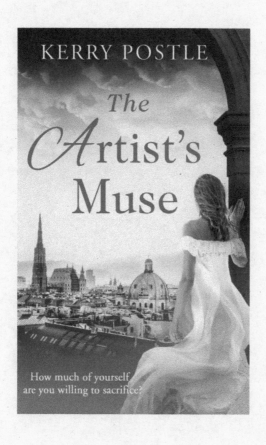

'woman is soulless and possesses neither ego nor individuality, personality nor freedom, character nor will.'

Otto Weininger, *Sex and Character*
Vienna, 1903

PROLOGUE: VIENNA

Modelling. The first time I did it, I didn't like it. But Hilde told me to look as if I did. Or, failing that, to do as I was bid. I was only a child yet the future of my family – now living in Vienna, due to circumstances that I will reveal to you in due course – would depend on how well I got on in Gustav Klimt's studio one gloomy Tuesday afternoon in November 1907. And Hilde, already successfully established as one of Klimt's favourites, knew how much I needed – my family needed – this job.

Monday 4th February 1907

We had arrived in Vienna, city of hope, some nine months before that fateful afternoon in the studio, yet I remember it vividly even now. It was a brutally beautiful February day when we made the journey into the big city. As we set off, we must have made a strange sight. Katya was ten, Frieda eight, and Olga only seven, while I – the oldest and biggest of us – was twelve.

I, and even Katya, looked like giants, our young girls' bodies bursting out of what we had on, exposing uncovered skin at wrist and ankle to the harsh cold of an Austrian winter's day, while Frieda and Olga, wearing big-sister cast-offs, swept the floor with their hems. Our shoes, squashed-toe small or hand-me-down loose. But we dared not complain for fear of upsetting our mother whose life had now become a veil of tears, the tangible evidence of which she wore with the pride of the recently bereaved. It was hard to lift it up to see what she'd been like before.

Yet I for one was pleased to be going on this adventure. I had never been on a train before and the second the doors slammed shut, the whistle blew, and the engine started to hiss and puff its way out of the station, I was hypnotized. As I looked through the frost-framed windows, so the train took me on a mesmerizing trip past ice swords hanging from snow-tipped trees, single magpies frozen on walls, field upon field of virgin-white snow increasingly disturbed by man the closer we got to the city – and then there was bustle.

We had arrived in another world. We stumbled out of the carriage, our belongings slapping down on the stone platform like dead dogs behind us, our eyes taken this way and that by the coming, going, dashing, crashing, and hurtling in every direction of the bodies now swarming around us. Overwhelmed and in the way, we shuffled, dodged, and collided our way out of the station, the mist of the new gradually lifting to reveal, to my delight, a world of possibilities.

Velvet bows and fur trims whispered to me of riches. Well-soled, perfect boots tapped out the rhythms of success. Education and employment would be ours in this twinkling land of plenty.

I failed to notice my mother's face, grief-grey, her brow furrowed by the yoke of responsibility, as she led us out into the cold Vienna air.

Like ducklings, we followed her, single file, climbing onto a busy tram, which drove us round the Ringstrasse. Grand and wide, it encompasses Vienna's heart, and it shone that day, like a band of gold encrusted with monumental jewels shimmering against a heavy sky. Transfixed, I dropped my head against the window, the plump whiteness of my cheek squashed flat against its glass like a suction cup while my mind conjured up a waltzing world of sparkling interiors and sweeping staircases as dazzling façades danced before my eyes.

And I let myself dream of an opulent world, full of luxury, laughter, and ease, of all the magic I would find within this golden ring, encircling as it did this capital of empire. For a little girl like me, with her imagination full of grand balls and princes (who weren't going to die in the night), the Ringstrasse was an ideal place to be.

The tram juddered. It veered to the right, crossed over connecting lines. But my cheek, momentarily squelched out of position, soon settled back into place while I now marvelled, dribble trickling down my chin, at the mannequins in ballgowns in the glittering window displays of a shopping street. Back in my innocent dream world once more I wondered which dress I would wear to the ball in the house with the sweeping staircase.

Yet in a second, with the blast of a klaxon and the scream of a horse, the spell was broken. Followed closely by the impact.

Your world, the way you see it, can change in an instant.

With the dull thud of metal and wood on flesh I was violently shaken out of my reverie. Something terrible had happened. Within seconds, hordes of people, shouting out excitedly in unrecognizable languages, appeared out of nowhere. It was as if they had pulled themselves up through the cracks in the cobblestones, their sewer-drenched poverty tainting the golden streets of the city of my dreams. Replacing fur-trimmed coats with filth-edged jackets; taffeta ballgowns with worn, ripped clothes.

What did they want? Why were they shouting? The travellers on the tram stood up to find out, blocking my way, though sounds of ugliness pushed their way through. It was only when the tram pulled away that I saw the encircling crowd: baying hounds around their weak and injured quarry. I heard a voice say, "E'll not get as far as the knacker's yard,' but I had no real grasp of what it was that I saw that day, even though I sensed its menace. I dream about it still.

However, if the accident had disturbed me, it was clear, from her trembling fingers, that it had disturbed my fragile mother more. She placed a shaking hand on my shoulder. It was time to get off.

She stood up; we followed, watching her exhausted frame nearly collapse as she struggled to lift her bag off the tram. I rushed to help her though she pointed me to little Olga who'd been lifted off the tram by a foreign-looking young man with a thick moustache and a wavy mop of dark hair, a book in a foreign language peeping out of his coat pocket. I said thank you and he nodded. I suspect that he wasn't a true Austrian.

'I'm so proud of you, Wally; you're such a good girl.' My mother sighed heavily when we'd all made it to the pavement. She gently pushed the hair away from my eyes, before kissing me on the head with a barely audible, 'I can manage now. Please don't worry.' But she couldn't. And I did.

As we stood there, an old, well-dressed man approached us. Cupping his hand over his mouth, he spoke quietly into my mother's ear, his eyes roaming furtively over Katya, Olga, Frieda, and me. She found the strength to turn down his kind offer of help that afternoon but as I watched her I wondered how long it would be before she buckled.

It was clear that she was – we all were – going to find it hard to survive in this place of extremes. My poor, sweet, weak mother, her light frame resuming her heavy walk, tears rolling silently down her face, leading us to our new lives with all the enthusiasm of the condemned to the gallows. We knocked on the door of number 12 Favoritenstrasse. We waited for Frau Wittger to open the door with the chipped black paintwork. We had arrived in Vienna.

says, 'that's me.' And then, with hushed embarrassment, she leans closer to Mama and whispers, 'You won't be seeing him again.'

At this I notice my mother sway a little. I put out my arm to steady her. I fear she's growing weaker and I have visions of my sisters floating away untethered for want of a mother to hold them in place. Twelve and 12. It's my time. I can do this. I push them in front of me, Katya included, as I am the eldest, extending my arms around the shoulders of the two younger ones to give strength to their sapling limbs.

Katya copies me, which I don't begrudge on a day like this. Together we cross and link limbs in an intricate, delicate way. We will be strong together, my sisters and I.

A broad smile stretches out the wrinkles of Frau Wittger's face, which softens at the sight of us. 'Oh, such little ones. Such lovely, lovely little ones. Come in, my dears. Look at you all. Oh, my dear girls. Come in. Come in.'

She nods a welcome to me, then Katya, before bending down and taking Olga and Frieda by the hand. I first think her overly clucky, like a broody hen, but as I see my little sisters relax, catch the relief sweeping across Mama's face, I am soon grateful for the gentleness this stranger brings, and for the excess of warmth with which she tries to thaw us. 'Oh, you poor dear mites, you're frozen,' she cries, as she beckons us inside.

She leads us to our room at the top of the house. We follow in silence, pulling on heavy bags while I clutch tired hands. 'If you need anything …'; 'if you get any trouble …' She bombards us with kindness and offers of help we'll never remember.

And as we make our way up creaking stairs, and along dark corridors lined with closed doors, she lights up this new and shadowy world with the exuberance of her voice, wraps us in the warmth of her words so that we feel protected from the harsh shouts and coarse laughter that come from the rooms along the way. Though Mother asks, 'Are we your only guests?'

'A key, look here, you've got a key,' she pants when she gets to our room at the top of the house. There is a lock, and with a rattle and twist of the key we are in. A sharp blast of icy air hits us. I look at Mama.

Frau Wittger looks to heaven. 'Oh, it'll soon be warm, once you makes yourselves all comfortable up here!' she wheezes, more in hope than belief, and with that she abandons us, taking her optimism with her.

The room is miserable, with a bare wooden floor, its discoloured curtains drawn, drawn to conceal a broken windowpane I discover when I go to open them. Cold air comes in through the cracked glass, causing the curtains to flap around.

Katya tells Mama what she should do: leave, move, go back, say to Frau Wittger … But I know that's the wrong thing to do. I know that Mama has no choice. Not one of us has any choice other than to stay here, and we're lucky Frau Wittger's such a good, kind soul.

I look at the bed and I'm about to suggest to Mama that she go and have a rest in it when there's a knock on the door. It's Frau Wittger, now quite flushed, perspiration around her nose and across her forehead. She's made her way back up the stairs. It hasn't been easy for her. And there, tucked under one arm, she has the prettiest white bedcover, embroidered with the daintiest of pink rosebuds. Dangling from the other arm is a basket so heavy she puts it down the minute I open the door.

'For you and your mam,' she says, offering the bedcover to me. As soon as I take it, she holds her side, clearly in physical discomfort, before bending down to pick up the basket. Once inside, she closes the door and sets the basket down. She hugs Mama before leading her to the bed and helping her to remove her boots.

'Lie down and rest, dear,' she says soothingly, though Mama casts a look of anguish over her daughters in protest. 'That's why I'm here,' she assures her softly. 'Now cover your dear mam up with that cover, why don't you, girl,' she tells me. 'Then you little ones can bring that basket over and we can see what's inside.' By the time Olga lifts the cake out, Mama is asleep.

CHAPTER 2

The first nine months are tough. To set the tone, Mama does not get out of bed for three weeks, and when she does she looks as though a noose has been placed around her neck. Exhausted, that's what Frau Wittger tells us is the matter with her, but Mama's not done a day's work yet.

The elderly woman we've only just met cooks, cleans, and cares for us as if we're her own.

Her rooms are on the same floor as ours and she opens them up to us with a joy that doesn't blind us to Mama's suffering but helps us see there's something more. That Olga and Frieda play 'searching' in her drawers full of broken costume jewellery is a rare and unexpected pleasure for this woman with no children, as it is a welcome escape for the little ones from the groans our mother makes as she grapples with her own demons. She's not a kind stranger for long.

The rent on the room's been paid in full for the first three months by my father's sister, Aunt Klara, and Mama's grateful to Frau Wittger for, well, just about everything else. Having four daughters is not for the financially challenged, ironic considering that's what Mama is. Even Frau Wittger, no matter how lovely she thinks we are, will soon be struggling to maintain the support she so wants to give us and which she's under no obligation to provide.

Mama needs to get a job and so do I. I'm twelve, I live at number 12 Favoritenstrasse and I can do this. When I announce I won't be going to school no one argues – not even Mama. Especially not Mama, when it turns out that the first job she herself gets is the wrong one. She takes it because it's in a pretty building – all exotic. She thinks she's crushing flowers when what she's really doing is making insecticide. As she's as delicate as a butterfly she was never going to last there for very long.

As Mama leaves I start, but I may as well have kept going round the revolving door as two weeks later I'm out. I'm underage. Someone reported me. Children must receive eight years of school. It's the law. Who knew? From the number of children in the factory, not many. Mother's been sentenced to eighteen hours' imprisonment. That's certainly tightened the rope around her neck. We're all worried about her. I've just got to get another job. These are fast-changing times.

I go to school with the others for a month. Then I get another job, this time in a bronze factory where I work with the soldering irons. But they are powered by gas. Which makes me pale. Giddy. Ill. I have to see a doctor who tells my mother who's weaker than me that I need a nourishing diet and plenty of fresh air (which is all that we have to live on).

Mama has lost one job. I have lost two. We're wasting time, not earning money. Frau Wittger whispers to Mama about the workhouse, the very mention of which is as effective as a dose of smelling salts on her.

And that's how Mama's ended up in the glasspaper factory. It's an unpleasant dirty job, but she does it without complaint. She gets me a job there as a counter, putting glasspaper sheets into packs ready for the salesman to take around the country.

At home things are better for a month or two. We have money for food, bills, even ribbons.

His name is Herr Bergman, the travelling salesman. He doesn't come in that often. But when he does the other women and girls go into a flutter. Flapping, flirting. He has his favourites who giggle as he whispers in their ears, their dirty-fingernailed glass-dusty hands pressed against their oh-you-saucy-devil-you mouths.

Herr Bergman, the popular travelling salesman.

He's so busy tending to his admiring flock that he doesn't notice me at first. I'm quiet, conscientious, don't even talk to the other girls, as what they like to discuss in hushed tones punctuated by ribald laughter does not interest me at all. But one day – it is the day when I tie my hair with the new shiny black satin ribbons I bought with some of the money Mother allowed me to spend from my wages – he demands a counter, 'the one with the red hair and the black ribbons', for the stock he has come in to collect.

And he watches me while I re-count the pile of glasspaper that I set aside for him earlier in the day.

'… forty-eight, forty-nine, fifty.'

'Beautiful hands.' No sooner has he said these words than jealous eyes pierce me. Eyes of women who know exactly what he means.

I am even more silent than usual as I do my work that after-noon, and after a few sarcastic 'nice hands' remarks, by the time I go to find my mother to go home, the tense atmosphere has lifted.

But, as I walk along the corridor towards my mother's work-room, a man's hand grabs me and pulls me into the stockroom. It's Herr Bergman. He knows all about me. Feels so concerned for me. Wants to give me a fatherly kiss, because – sad creature that I am – he feels so sorry that I don't have a father to look after me. I freeze. Can't move as he gives me his fatherly kiss. Then he releases me. What should I do? What if I lose my job? Should I tell Mama?

For the next few weeks I keep it to myself. Avoiding Herr

Bergman. Until I can't. He comes in one day, leans over to whisper in my ear the way I've seen him do to other girls before. But, unlike them, I do not giggle. I do not put my hand to my mouth in an oh-you-saucy-devil sort of way. And as he pushes himself hard against my shoulder I do not move.

'I'll see you later, Beautiful Hands! I've got a little something for you that I think you're going to like.'

For the rest of the day I don't hear the other girls call me names. All I can think about is Herr Bergman.

It's late but I can't delay any longer: it's time to walk along the corridor. Within seconds he's pulled me into the stockroom, so eager to shower me with paternal affection and give me my surprise that he doesn't get round to closing the door.

My mother screams. And screams. Her small hands pull at him. With a back sweep of his hand he knocks her to the ground, stepping over her while sneering, 'I was doing you a favour, you silly cow.'

See now why my voice is getting angrier, my words more knowing? Because I am angry. Shocked. Doing things I shouldn't be doing, seeing things I shouldn't be seeing. Forced to grow up quickly. I'd thought of painting my life better than it is, as I'd wished it to be – Lord knows it doesn't make me feel good to read over what has happened – but I can't. No. I'll not give this story a sugar coating, lay claim to an innocence that experience has already tarnished with its guilt-stained hands

Bitterness. That's its true taste. And if you have a daughter who'd never think or say what I commit to paper, pray she never has to endure what I have had to endure. Because if she does you'll soon hear a change in her voice.

We are out of work again.

That night in bed, as I cuddle the sleeping Olga on one side and Frieda on the other, the atmosphere is dead calm. Katya is still awake, pretending to read in the corner because she doesn't know what to say to me. Nor I to her. And so there we are, silently listening. No rain, nor wind to disguise the hysterical sounds of our mother falling apart in the other room.

'So what am I to do, Frau Wittger? I have no strength left. I don't know how much longer I'll be able to protect them. Stupid, stupid, stupid, stupid girls. And after what I've done I might never get decent work again. She'll end up on the streets. They all will. Oh my lovely stupid girls, what will become of them?'

Katya and I, scorched souls silently screaming in the next room, cry tears that run over the molten lava of our mother's love.

As I listen to Frau Wittger console my mother while she sobs, I wish I'd been strong enough to let Herr Bergman give me what he thought I'd like. If my mother's to be believed, somebody's going to give it to me anyway.

'There, there, dear. There, there. You need to sleep. Believe me, things won't look so bad in the morning. Your Wally's a good girl. None of this is her fault. Nor yours either. I'm not promising anything yet but I think I know how we can get over this. Your Wally's a good girl, and a pretty one. But I think I've got a way to make that work for her. Again not promising anything but fingers crossed this could work out well for all of you. Now off you go to bed.'

Mother sleeps on the floor that night, the noose so tight around her neck the next morning her eyes are bulging.

Shot to bits by grief, pain, misfortune, and the challenge of bringing up girls in a city full of predators, Mama's on the brink of giving up. And who could blame her for that? Not I. But I won't. I won't give up. Not ever. I will be strong and do whatever it is Frau Wittger has in mind.

**If you enjoyed *A Forbidden Love*, then why not try another
exquisite novel from HQ Digital?**

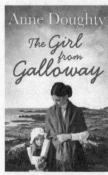